LOVE OR BARBARISM

A NOVEL

CHARLES THOMAS

First published by Charles Thomas in 2025 in South Africa.

ISBN: 978-1-0370-7512-4 (print)
ISBN: 978-1-0370-7513-1 (e-book)

The author acknowledges the affection and supportiveness of his
wife, Sandra, and their children, Robin, Sharon and Michael.

Layout by Boutique Books

For Andrew, who inspired it

". . . and I mused on what an absurd thing love is after all, that a person's entire frail life is founded on such absurdities."
—Imre Kertész: *Liquidation*

". . . love is a kind of craving . . . to love is indeed nothing else than to crave something for its own sake. [But] craving, as the will to have and to hold, gives rise to a fear of losing."
—Hannah Arendt: *Love and Saint Augustine*

"Life is what happens to you while you're busy making other plans"
—Allen Saunders (1957)
—John Lennon (1980)

LOVE OR BARBARISM

PART ONE

CHAPTER ONE

First the tremulous *pirriwit-pirriwit-pirriwit*, followed by the rapid *bok-bok-bok-bok*, overlapping and impatient. Then a drawn-out *pirripeee, pirripeee, pirripeee*, and again the *bok-bok-bok-bok*— unmistakable!

Bokmakieries!

Rosa froze. When had she last heard bokmakieries? Their love song right there outside the cottage window could hardly be chance. She drew fiercely on her cigarette. When she was a toddler her father had told her that bokmakierie pairs were inseparable and that their effortless harmony expressed unwavering fidelity.

On the bed alongside her lay Nikki, tangled in the sheets, snoring lightly. Nikki's face was pale and egg-shaped, her hair a great reddish bush. On the pillow it made a gorse-like nest for the sleeping face. Rosa resisted the impulse to blow smoke at the face, but smiled at the thought. She also resisted sliding her hand along Nikki's arched, slender back, there so invitingly poised . . . but she stared with intensity at the right shoulder blade, at the finely-detailed tattoo of a lizard, there— tiny, twisting, in an upside-down, ready-to-pounce position.

The bokmakieries fell silent. Rosa waited for them to start up again. She sat still, allowing her cigarette smoke to drift. She became aware of the distant thrash of the sea, and tried in her mind to anticipate its ebb and flow.

Her mobile camera-phone lay on the dressing table across the room. I want to get a shot of you guys. She eased her naked self out of the bed, trying not to disturb Nikki, and was halfway across the room when the singing started up again. She struggled into her jeans, and grabbed her phone. At the window, she caught sight of one of the birds, perched high in an oak; its bright yellow underside contrasted vividly with the green of the oaken foliage. Rosa got the shot, and smiled as the camera shutter clicked. Where was its mate?

Outside the window, a clear blue day, shrubs, the oak and potted plants, but no bokmakierie mate to be seen.

Rosa finished her cigarette, stubbed it out in an ashtray on the windowsill, and checked the picture she had taken. She smiled. The image was near-perfect.

By the time Nikki woke up, Rosa had showered, brushed her hair, repainted her fingernails, made a fresh jug of coffee, finalised the draft presentation they had been working on all morning, and replaced the picture of her husband, Tubs, with the bokmakierie shot as her mobile phone's wallpaper. She had checked and replied to all her queued phone messages and scanned through all twenty-seven unread e-mails on her laptop computer, and was passing the time checking through a project feasibility report needing sign-off by month-end. Simultaneously, an inventory of all the things the cottage needed was taking shape in her mind: a mat for the bathroom floor—she had seen a great design at the Rondebosch craft market last Sunday (a rickshaw man and his rickshaw wagon that Tubs had dismissed as kitsch, but that she must nevertheless see if she could get, it was a mistake not to have bought it when she'd had the chance.)—coasters, place mats, something for the wall of the second bedroom to replace the Tretchikoff print (talk about kitsch!) and a new saucer to replace the one Nikki'd chipped this morning.

She turned her attention to the document she had been reading through most of the morning. Frustratingly, it was riddled with inaccuracies and flawed assumptions, slowing her down, keeping her on high alert, forcing her to make copious margin notes and to highlight the more outrageous assertions; clearly the author was concerned less about feasibility than persuasion. But it was her job to block bogus proposals, and she prided herself on how meticulously she had always been at it.

For Nikki, too often waking up was like recovering consciousness after crashing to earth from the sky—a battered-and-bruised feeling. It was no different now. Her first thought was, oh boy, I really must change my habits. She sat up in the bed, gradually recalling where she was and how she had gotten there. Her temples were mildly throbbing, and her mouth felt like oh boy, a dead mouse lies rotting on my tongue. It had to be the beer she had had at lunch. No question, she would have to go for a milder brand, and maybe not have so much of it at a time. Her cigarettes were close by. She reached out and lit up, and lay flat on her back, sending the smoke in streams towards the ceiling. Rosa, she thought, Rosa. It occurred to her that the throbbing in her head was partly the sound of the sea, so much a part of her, in her heart, in her blood. The sea. It caused her as much joy as pain. A beer would do right now, she thought. Its rushing tingle would wash away the current harshness on her palate. The cigarette was great, like nourishment— bread to the hungry, wine to the thirsty. In no time, she had clouded up the room. This moment, this lying here in this bed and this puffing away at this cigarette . . . the sea outside and Rosa in the next room, just the two of us in this silent house alone, and with brilliant daylight all around, this was a moment to die for. It occurred to Nikki, that this right now was maybe the finest instant in her whole life. Had she been happier, ever? Could she be happier, ever?

In the lounge, Rosa was seated at the large wooden dining-table, engrossed in work on her laptop. During the morning, numerous files and documents had been strewn all over, now they were neatly stacked, ready for packing away. Nikki came out of the bedroom, naked except for her necklace. She went and stood behind Rosa, and put her hands on Rosa's shoulders. Rosa stopped working and sat motionless for a moment. The fingers on her shoulders were gentle, like the pitter-patter of a pet bird. She tipped her head back slowly, till it gently lay against Nikki's breast. Nikki bent forward and lightly touched her lips to Rosa's forehead. The sun was streaming into the room; within three hours, it would be setting behind the mountain peaks along the western skyline. The slightest of tremors passed through Rosa's body. Savour the moment, she said to herself. Tonight, tomorrow, sometime soon there's going to be the mother of all prices to pay.

For a while, neither spoke. For a while, both listened to the sea, the birdcalls, the occasional voice of someone far below on the beach. Time stood still, but the heart of each in her own body moved rapidly—ka-doof, ka-doof, ka-doof.

Like a bird, light and fleet-footed, Nikki went dashing down the first dozen-or-so steps of the cracked, uneven footpath which linked the cottages on the mountainside with the beach road below. She swung around, and, arms akimbo, stood looking up at Rosa, who hadn't even taken the first step. She smiled up at her. Rosa held onto the handrail. Her steps were firm and deliberate; she descended slowly, with a dignified air. "You're a really classy chick," said Nikki. "I'm convinced you've got royal blood."

Rosa tried to conceal her delight at the compliment by rapidly explaining that she was not the sporty type, and that she envied Nikki her agility. "I wish I could move like you," she said. "So athletic. But don't let me slow you down. I'll catch up with you down below."

"Nope. I must learn to slow down. I'm like this—half animal—because I spent so much of my childhood in the company of a dog on the beach," said Nikki. She laughed.

"With *Dingus!*" said Rosa, laughing, too. "Who names their dog *Dingus?*"

"Hell, I miss that dog. He was without a doubt my best childhood friend."

The stepped footway was steep, and in places gave way to just a rough concrete ramp, overtaken here and there by stiff mountain brush weed. Most of the cottages on either side of the pathway were surrounded by high walls. Behind one such wall, a dog began to bark. Nikki paused and spoke to it. She mimicked its barking, and in an imploring tone urged it to join them for their walk on the beach. The barking stopped and was replaced by an urgent panting and yelping. Rosa smiled as they continued down the pathway. "That's not the first wild beast you've tamed today, girl."

"Ah," said Nikki, taking Rosa's hand and squeezing it gently. "'Those petty wrongs that liberty commits'—are you familiar with Shakespeare?"

For a brief instant, Tubs's image flashed through Rosa's mind. She thought about the presentation that she had to have ready for work tomorrow—the preparation of which provided the pretext to be here at the holiday cottage today, just she and Nikki. From the footpath, she looked out over the wide blue bay. The sea was calm. Rosa breathed deeply. She took a clump of Nikki's hair in her hand and yanked Nikki's face towards her own. She planted a smacking kiss into Nikki's pliant lips, and said, "Honey, you are the prettiest wrong *I've* ever had the pleasure of committing liberties with."

Now both of them were dashing down the steps. They made it to the road below, with Nikki hardly panting, but with perspiration beginning to bead out all around Rosa's hairline. They hurried along the beach road.

"I love the sea," said Nikki. I'm sure I've got gills somewhere inside me." She hopped, she skipped, and Rosa expected her to do a somersault.

"The sea's not all it's cracked up to be," said Rosa. She had an immense smile on her face. "Sharks, blue-bottles, drownings, and—ugh—seaweed!"

"Let's see how literate you are, Rosa. Who said this?" And Nikki chanted

I must down to the seas again, for the call of the running tide
Is a wild call and a clear call that may not be denied

"Some crazy poet describing *you*."

"Masefield, you illiterate geek." Nikki skipped into the road and back onto the pavement.

"OK! You're so literate, who said, " *'Women have the right to decide what they want to do with their bodies?'* ""

For a split second Nikki stood motionless. Then she started forward again. "Ha! Nobody said that. You just made it up."

"Mandela, of course."

"That's so trite, anybody could have said it."

A railway line separated road from beach. There was a subway, dark and draughty. As they passed through it a train roared by overhead, drowning out their laughter.

The beach sand was soft underfoot.

"I feel the breeze in my hair," shouted Nikki, pulling off shoes and socks as she ran towards the water.

At the southern end of the bay surfers in wet-skin suits were paddling about on surfboards. Children were playing in the shallows, jumping and screeching each time a wave splashed their faces. Overheard, seagulls went careening at high speed.

Rosa sat on the sand, feeling the sun and breeze on her face. In the distance, Nikki was frolicking around as the tide washed up against her legs. The beach was everything the tourist brochures said it was: beautiful, white, sandy, situated in a valley between the Kalk Bay and Fish Hoek mountains. To complete the picture, there even were the famous trek-fishers doing their thing not far away towards the Kalk Bay side. From Rosa's distance, they were all blurry colour-and-motion.

Am I dreaming all this? Rosa wondered.

Unbidden, the image of her husband, Tubs, entered her thoughts. She tried to suppress it.

From where she sat, Seal Island was plainly visible some four or five kilometres into the bay, a mere strip of rock, seeming ever-so-slightly to float out there on the waves. Maybe that floating illusion—if illusion it was—was caused by the scuttling about of the Island's tens of thousands of seal residents, all cooped up on that tiny postage stamp-of-a-space—all no doubt eager to avoid becoming shark fodder. Rosa drew a sharp breath at the thought. It was well known to her, from so many recent press reports that the waters around Seal Island were swarming with Great Whites who terrorised the seal community pretty much like a gang of thugs could terrorise a quiet neighbourhood. But the scary thing was that these Great Whites were increasingly encroaching shorewards. Something like a week ago, the local papers carried a report of sightings of a good six or seven of them drifting in the breakers less than a hundred metres from the beach. If it took a sprinter less than ten seconds to run a hundred metres, how long would it take a Great White to swim, say, sixty metres? Rosa's gaze settled on Nikki cavorting in the surf. She had been joined by three small children, who were as wild and energetic as she, and whose shrieks Rosa had no doubt would be audible all the way up the mountainside. Let's say a shark is able to dash through the water at what—seven seconds per hundred metres? Simple arithmetic means it would reach Nikki within two seconds of sighting her.

Why do I think these thoughts?

Rosa stood up and walked briskly towards the water's edge. Nikki's jeans was completely soaked. Rosa looked her in the eye and soundlessly mouthed the words, Honeybunch, I am seriously wild about you.

"Huh?" said Nikki, pausing momentarily and cupping her hands behind both ears.

"I said, 'how about a walk along the beach?'"

"Oh, right, of course that's what you said." Nikki laughed and mouthed back, *And a plague on your house too.* "What'd I say back?"

"Probably something obscene, you mangy bitch," said Rosa, gushing with laughter as she turned away.

Nikki laughed out loud. "Hey! Not in front of the children. Just call me *Kakkelak*." She left the children playing in the surf and dashed after Rosa.

They walked in the direction of the trek fishermen, their bodies so close that with each stride they felt a pleasant bumping at the hips.

4 am. Am I awake? How do I know it's 4am? I feel my body stiffen, and as it stiffens, the body against it stiffens, too . . . but only momentarily—the stiffening of two bodies, one after the other, effect following cause, just as common logic says it should . . . who moved first, me or Nikki? Who was the prime mover, she or me? Ah, Nikki, Nikki . . . it is 4 am . . . all around, nothing but darkness. At first, I think it's the darkness behind my eyelids, but as I continue to wonder how I know it's 4 am, I begin to realise it's the darkness of night all around me . . . all around us. I have to think about it before I am sure it's Tubs, my husband, tight up against me . . . in our bed, our marital bed . . . and a deep, satisfying, warmth, a delicious, all-enveloping, vacuum-sealing warmth . . . this warmth is caused by Tubs against me, and I think of Nikki . . . I will be alone with Nikki later today!

Rosa realised that she had been awake for a while, maybe not awake, but in and out of sleep, and that the possibilities of the day ahead had been endlessly rummaging through her mind. Sudden sight of the clock, its fluorescent hands, had interrupted her floating thoughts. 4 a.m. Another two hours before she needed to get up. No sign of light yet. The birds outside—silent, still asleep. Dogs, cats, mice, rats, fleas, lice, flies, bats—everything, all God's creatures, all silent, all still sleeping. But, a car—yes, a car already, on Forest Drive, not far away.

The smooth greased zoom of it through the night. Soon, soon it will be day, and I'll also be smoothly zooming away down Forest Drive, off to Fish Hoek with Nikki! Just me and Nikki . . . Fish Hoek!

Again, Rosa's body jerked involuntarily, causing Tubs's body to start. His breathing stopped for a moment, then continued evenly. He tightened his body around hers. *The sea is high again today, with a thrilling flush of wind.* She had chanced upon these simple lines in a book by Lawrence Durrell, and almost every time she thought of Fish Hoek, the lines came to her, bringing a flush of emotion, *they so perfectly describe Fish Hoek.* Now she was completely awake, and impatient for the sun. But she didn't want the warmth of Tubs's embrace to end. She would have to lie absolutely still . . . if Tubs woke up, the spell would be broken . . .

. . . Tubs woke up . . . He shuffled out of bed, and in the darkness, scrambled across the carpet to the bathroom. Rosa curled herself up, not wanting to lose the precious warmth. She lay listening to him in the bathroom. Soon he was back in the bed alongside her. She could tell that he knew she was awake. He wrapped his body around hers, and after some initial moving about, settled into complete stillness. But she could feel his alertness, the electricity of it coursing through his blood, the fine tension in his sinews, the spring in his muscles. What was he thinking? She might have drifted off to sleep again . . . she had not picked the actual moment his body changed from being motionless alongside hers . . . now he was on top of her, and she knew that the first light of dawn was up, she could see his silhouette quite clearly . . . Her response was eager, coordinated . . . they were practiced lovers . . . Whenever she saw ballroom dancers or ice skaters on TV, and marvelled at their coordination, she told herself that she and Tubs achieved just as much coordination at *their* sport, lovemaking, were capable of winning prizes for it, if prizes were to be won for it. Certainly, ten out of ten every time!

This morning, when it ended, she was on top of him, sprawled across him like a fishnet. Now, the birds in the garden were chirping noisily. Several motor vehicles were to be heard on Forest Drive. The room was sufficiently lightened by the rising sun to make all the objects in it stand out clearly. Tubs's lips and tongue were gently toying with her left earlobe. His hands were on the concave of her back. She liked the hardness of his body. A car passed in front of their house. She quickly disengaged from him, and hurried to the bathroom.

My girlfriend went to London and all she got me was this lousy T-shirt was emblazoned across the front of the fish trekker's T-shirt. Rosa marvelled at the hugeness of the man's arms and legs. He had a section of the net firmly in his grasp, and was heaving against the tide with a slow, remorseless rhythm. Nikki ran over to him, found a place on the net to grasp, and began pulling with him. He seemed only mildly curious, maybe even amused, but took no special interest in her.

It occurred to Rosa that maybe half the trekkers were in fact not trekkers at all but merely visitors to the beach, who, like, Nikki, probably thought, oh, what fun, let's go help bring in the catch. Rosa was tempted to join them, but held back at the thought of getting all wet. She found a place on the sand a safe distance back, and sat down to watch.

Waves converged from all sides, twisting and folding around the trekkers' feet. Bits of water jumped free and slapped people against their thighs and shoulders, and smaller children in their faces. The backwash constantly gathered and dashed into the oncoming waves, dragging people's feet in multiple directions. What a party, thought Rosa, her eyes never leaving Nikki, who was soaked from head to foot.

It was easy for Rosa to tell the real trekkers from the amateurs. Like with everything else, the guys who did it for a living were so much more economical with their movements. You could tell from their eyes that this was a chore, a necessary evil, something in the best of all possible lives they would never be doing. But there was also a practiced competence, almost undefinable; it was to be seen in the order which emerged from the chaos. When the first of the netted fishes suddenly became visible to everyone, glinting and thrashing, everyone gasped, everyone except the real fishers; they simply relaxed the anticipation which Rosa realised with hindsight had shown on their faces a minute-or-so before sight of the first fish appeared.

And then the whole netful was visible. It was as if the sea had consciously sunk back to reveal the loaded net, a teeming mass of silvery motion.

Yellowtail!

Rosa's interest was suddenly gone. She rose from the sand and moved slowly away. A smiling, panting Nikki ran up and joined her.

"My sentiments are with the fish," said Rosa. "Pure, helpless victims, if you think about it. Born losers."

"Well," said Nikki, "I suppose if *we* didn't get them, the sharks would've. Life's a bastard and then you die."

The trek back to the cottage was a long, slow one. Rosa thought of Tubs, and she thought of Nikki. Far out over the bay, a fine mist was coming across towards them. Seal Island was already lost in it. The sun was set to set. It lay behind a bank of clouds on the western skyline. Soon, a day that Rosa was sure would alter the course of her life would be done and she would have to contend with the fall-out. Kiddie voices, embellished by the constant background roar of the sea, followed them up the stepped mountain path back to their cottage.

"You are one incredible chick," Nikki had said when they got back from the beach. Up at the cottage, Rosa had produced a full change of clothing for both of them. "Incredible. You think of everything." Nikki was overjoyed, she would not have to travel back in her damp, sea-hardened jeans. Hurriedly, clumsily they stripped, tearing off everything. In the shower cubicle, they shrieked as the first blast of water came arcing over their bodies. They giggled and chatted non-stop. Their bodies were slippery in the warming water, and slid and nudged and jostled against each other. Nikki's lizard tattoo also seemed to be slipping and sliding about. Rosa shrieked with laughter at the thought of it jumping onto *her* shoulder. The water formed a canopy over them. Their bodies gleamed in the steamy light. We're like the seals on Seal Island, said Rosa. Like the yellowtail on Fish Hoek Beach, said Nikki. The air was thick with the smell of lavender. The plastic bottle of lavender-scented soap gel slid out of Nikki's hand and rolled about on the shower floor. (*She slipped on a bar of soap and hit her head and died.*) When they turned off the water, their bodies cooled rapidly. Ee-ow-ee. They sprang out of the cubicle, rushed for their towels, and at high speed, wiped themselves hot and dry. Within minutes, they were dressed, breathless, and ready to leave. Separately, both sighed as they turned out the lights of the cottage, shut the door and headed for their waiting vehicle.

The ride was like a transition between dreamscapes, a tunnel through reality. It was this morning's ride repeated, but in reverse. This time the sea was on their right—on Rosa's side of the car—and the mountainside on their left. The streetlights flashed by with the same measured drift as this morning, accompanied by the same languid jazz music from the car's CD player, and illuminating their cab at intervals which Nikki timed at one-two-three-four, one-two-three-four. Outside, everything was a mix of dark and light; whole patches of sea were simply smears of black, but closer to shore, the waves' foam crests were white and vivid. When Nikki looked at the mountain, she saw a blur of scrub running away on her left. Every now and then she thought she saw what looked like smatterings of campfire against the black density. *Bergies*, no doubt— Cape Town's ubiquitous homeless mountain tramps. Nikki longed for a cigarette. The car was smooth and light, whisking effortlessly through the seaside suburbs of Clovelly, Kalk Bay, Muizenberg, as it carried them homeward. Although it was only early evening, the road was almost deserted; what other cars they saw were mostly going in the opposite direction. Lights were on in buildings lining their route, but there were few people to be seen. Nikki was half asleep. She longed for a cigarette, but knew *you don't smoke in other peoples' car*. A general ticklishness was ruffling her skin all over, especially her scalp and neck. It was a crawling kind of sensation, as if her lizard-tattoo had sprung free and was scooting about like a playful puppy. She tugged lightly at her necklace, and dabbed with her fingertips along its fringe, trying to still the agitation that was happening there, an agitation not much different from an inflamed clitoris. She sighed heavily, determined not to smoke. In her head, carnival lights were flashing brightly, mimicking the streetlights. She was simultaneously running on the wide-open beaches of Langebaan with her dog Dingus running arcs around her, and in the cooped-up shower with Rosa, scrabbling and wrestling, breathless, half-smothered by the smell of lavender. Happiness had a way of evoking sadness. Nikki felt its imminence, and forestalled it by speaking. "So, are you happy with what we achieved, today, Rosa?"

Rosa did not answer immediately. She, too, might have been in a reverie, lulled by the encroachment of night around their speeding car, and by the events of the day. Eventually she said, "Yep. I think we're ready for what tomorrow might bring. If that's what you're referring to."

"Boy, am I *ever* so tired—hi, honey, I'm home, what's for dinner?" She spoke in a mock-flat tone, her eyes half-drooping, half-grinning. She let out a chuckle.

At the sight of her on the threshold, Tubs's breath was momentarily arrested—ah! She was so incredibly beautiful! Despite himself, he rushed up to embrace her, whispering playful terms of endearment into her face. He stroked her hair and kissed her on the lips and eyes. A moment earlier, when he'd heard her vehicle pull into the driveway, he stiffened in anticipation of reprimanding her for arriving home on her own after dark—*you know how dangerous this town can be*. Now, his heart raced with the thought of how precious she was to him, and his strongest impulse was just to stand there and hold her tight.

"Such passion," she said, stroking his arms and shoulders, and returning his kisses. "Why don't we just do it in the road?"

"Let's, lets!" He laughed. "John and Yoko would be proud of us."

"Well, all *you* might need is love, but first, I must have a bath." She disengaged from his embrace. "What a day I've had! I am *vrek* exhausted."

He watched her charge off up the stairs to the bedroom. "I anticipated something of the sort," he shouted after her, "so you might be pleased to know I prepared your favourite dish."

"No!" she shouted back from upstairs. "Nobody can love me that much. Grilled kingklip? Tubs Lethlabe, I don't deserve you."

Tubs smiled effusively. "And a chilled bottle of Chardonnay to go with it. I'll set the table. Hurry, now."

Rosa ran a bath. She needed to *deep-immerse*, to penetrate to a realm where purity reigned. Nothing like a warm bath to steam-clean the soul. She poured in liberal amounts of lavender salts, and watched as the substance spread, turning the steaming water a pale blue. She sank in down to her chin, so that her earrings floated level with the surface. The last time she had suffered life-altering guilt was a good twenty-odd years ago. At the time, her most closely guarded secret was that she was plain bad—rotten, actually, to the core. The thoughts that ran through her mind, then—unbidden! They were dirty, ugly, wicked. She was a sinful person. Her main sins were jealousy, envy, malice, vengefulness … and *lust*. Nobody knew where the little girls hands strayed at night, what they did when the lights went out, how of their own accord they would know what to seek and where to find. *Such a lovely kid*, people were always saying. Pretty. Cute. Bright. "What a sweet child, what lovely eyes; what a pretty smile." Oh, sure! What people didn't know was that she was wicked and corrupt. In thought at least, and, of course, with her own body. But *she* knew, and God knew, and it had to happen, sooner or later—that God would run out of patience. Not a day went by that she didn't ask His forgiveness, but sooner or later—it was inevitable— He would as He did, run out of patience. Finally, it happened: the punishment, swift and furious: her mother's death, early one morning, the instant the sun clipped the horizon. *In police custody. Slipped on a bar of soap. In the shower. Hit her head on the tiled floor.* Everybody blamed the police, but she knew better: for her part, having killed her mom, she had paid her dues. She now owed nobody, including God— *especially* God—anything. From the moment of her mother's death, she had lost her fear of God. For a number of years yet, He continued to exist for her, but not as an awesome, all-powerful tyrant—instead, as a spiteful, vindictive old bag, beneath contempt. Having done His worst, He had exposed himself as nothing more than a pitiful sham. She was liberated. Her mother had died for the daughter's sins.

The air was suffused with the fragrance of lavender. Rosa put her head back against the rim of the bath. The steam was slowly seeping in beneath the surface of her skin. Her eyelids closed of their own volition. Dimly, her mother's image appeared and disappeared, then reappeared.

When she was a child, she had suffered a child's guilt. In time, she was able to outgrow it, to rationalise that actually, the underlying problem, the real cause of all her woes, was that she had been the victim of child abuse—child abuse of a special kind, for, what was it but child abuse to raise a child in terror of God? Her psyche had been seriously screwed-up with such rubbish as, if you are a bad girl you will burn in everlasting hell—in Joyce's *boundless, shoreless, bottomless lake of fire*. Pure child molestation: a guy in the sky with an all-seeing eye. Laughable to an adult, yes, but to a child? She had been burdened with a monstrous conscience, and for what? If He didn't want her to enjoy it, why equip her with a clitoris in the first place? Mistaken guilt: like serving a prison sentence for a crime you didn't commit. Wasted time, wasted guilt. Rosa remembered hating her parents for a long time, once she had decided that it was all their fault. *That* was during her leftwing hate-phase, the time in her life when she hated almost everything in existence. In time, she got over it, as one gets over most things, but theism . . . she would remain theism's sworn enemy for life.

The water exerted a gentle upward pressure on her legs. Faraway, in the dining room down below, she could hear the sounds of Tubs preparing the dinner. The warm water against the back of her neck had a soothing feel, one that she wished to prolong. But, mustn't keep Tubs waiting. She ripped herself from the water-cocoon, and vigorously towelled her body down, every inch of it, while she watched the bath water swirl and bounce and eventually ease into an enervated stillness.

This afternoon, the yellowtail fish had thrashed about in the shallows. Nikki's teeth had glistened in the sun. A giant in a London T-shirt had just effortlessly dragged in a net-pile of fish.

With her gown loosely round her, Rosa trotted out on bare feet to the bedroom to find something suitable to wear.

The candle in the centre of the table was an imposing cylinder, the length and thickness of a man's forearm. It resembled a piece of carved wood, grainy brown in colour, with figures of gyrating stick-people etched all round. Around its base ran a white band of wax with a pattern of symmetrical triangles deep-etched into it. Just knowing she would love it, Tubs had bought the candle for his wife from an upmarket store in the Waterfront—*that specialises in exotic, tasteful African art*, he'd explained. Rosa genuinely admired the candle's simple craftsmanship. She wondered whether it had been hand-crafted in a remote village or machine-made in an urban factory. When lit, its flame was always calm but intensely bright. It was a candle that exuded character, she thought. Not for the first time, it was the centrepiece of a carefully constructed ode to beauty, as Tubs would have it—he couldn't construct a lasting monument (such as a cathedral) to his dearly belovéd, so he did the next best thing—concentrated the power of his brand of meticulous creativity for an ephemeral burst of adoration, the point being glorification of that glorious creature, his wife.

The candle was the dining room's single light source, but Tubs had artfully arranged it so that it reflected off a number of surfaces—the plates, the cutlery, the dishes, the glass top of the dining table—to create a self-reinforcing blend of light and shadow that moved with the flame's movement. The effect was to concentrate the attention, to gently draw husband and wife into an embrace within the narrowness of that light-island, so that they hesitantly at first, then passionately, kissed and sighed. Then they dropped each into their own chair, neither speaking, not making eye contact. Tubs felt the moistness of her mouth linger on his lips, the lusciousness of her fragrance in his nostrils, the rustle of her dress on his ear. They ate.

"The wine's intoxicating, the food superb." Her smile, her teeth, her eyes were radiant. "And the company's—"

"—The company's bewitching," he said.

"I'll drink to that."

She found it difficult to speak, the right words wouldn't come. Every time she looked up, he was smiling in her direction. It was an effort not to make it seem an effort to return the smile, to make sure it didn't seem forced, exaggerated. He seemed to be expecting—hoping for—her compliments on the food, but how many times and in how many different ways do you say, *the fish is sublime?*

He asked her, how was Fish Hoek?

"Great, great. We managed to find some time to walk on the beach."

"That must have been good."

"Yes, fantastic. They were trek-fishing—yellowtail."

"Ah, yellowtail. I know kingklip's your favourite, but next time we have seafood, it has to be yellowtail."

"Yes, sounds good."

Tubs poured coffee into two identical handcrafted mugs. "And Nikki? How's Nikki?"

"Oh, fine. We worked like Trojans to ensure we'd have time left to walk on the beach. You know how crazy she is about the beach."

"Yes. Grew up in some Third World seaside dorpie, didn't she? Which was it, Langebaan or Strandsonderwater?" He laughed, expecting her to laugh, too.

She smiled, feeling suddenly very tired. She looked at her watch. "Is that the time, already?" She looked at the coffee steaming in her cup, and wondered if coffee was such a good idea at this time of night.

After a moment's silence, Tubs said, "I'm concerned about you, Honey. I've said it before, and I'll say it again: I think you work far too hard."

Somewhat taken aback, she hastened to respond. "Not at all. Today everyone works hard—in the private sector, anyway."

"Yes. It's scary. A sixteen hour day's become pretty fashionable in this day and age, especially among black yuppies. We seem inadvertently to have exchanged masters. In the bad old days, it was apartheid that ruled our lives, today it's work. Somewhere along the line we blacks got duped."

She sipped on her coffee. "Well, if I look at how positively work has impacted *my* life, then I should earnestly pray for it to impact every other South African's life as well."

"Be careful what you pray for, Honey. The reality of work for most people the world over is a return to barbarism, a soul-destroying and degrading necessity—something to which almost anything else would be preferable."

"Whoa. You're missing the point." Suddenly, she was annoyed. Was it his feeble attempt at humour at Nikki's expense—*grew up in some Third World seaside dorpie, didn't she?* Or maybe his reference to 'we blacks?' Probably just his whole smug self-assurance. "The trouble's not with work, work's fine. People will do almost anything if they want to do it or if it benefits them. The problem's with exploitation and unfairness." She was almost choking.

He knew the spell had been broken. He knew it had happened somewhere between when he'd poured the coffee and when he'd said be careful what you pray for. What a clumsy idiot he was. She works too hard, she's tired, I shouldn't hassle her. He looked at his coffee. "I guess you're right," he said, trying to sound gentle rather than contrite. "I'm just worried that you drive yourself too hard, my dear." He ventured to make eye contact.

"Yes, I know." Her voice was gentle.

She got up and positioned herself behind his chair. She put her hands on his shoulders, and bent down and kissed his forehead.

Relief, like a mountain stream . . .

Somewhere in the neighbourhood a dog was barking. The sound grated. At irregular intervals, cars flashed by on Forest Drive, out of nowhere into nowhere. The wind was up, and, as was always the case, she kept thinking she heard human voices being carried on it—sad human voices, lamentations, curses, cries for help. Whenever that happened, her thoughts turned to the townships. *They're murdering one another again, tonight.* Sad exploited humanity. She lay in bed with her book open, but it was no use. *I knew I shouldn't have had coffee.* Tubs's body was hard up against hers. He lay completely still, but she knew he was not asleep. No doubt, he would make his move as soon as she put out her light. Like the voices on the wind, Nikki's image kept appearing and disappearing. Now a gate began banging in the distance. *Oh, boy. It's going to be that kind of night. Why did my mother choose The Struggle over her family? That's got to be why I'm so screwed up.*

Tubs's hand lay resting on her hip. At irregular intervals, it twitched ever so slightly. She became aware that it had found its way under her nightshirt. Flesh against flesh. Before long, it started a slow, uncertain caressing action, stealthy, like a nighttime border crossing. *Right. Let the games begin.* She laced her fingers into his. His arm tightened around her. She put out her light and swung herself round to face him. Their lips met. The day ended pretty much as it had started.

CHAPTER TWO

Cold leftover pizza in the fridge was all there was, it would have to do. In the microwave, it blistered and smoked; Nikki's impulse was to throw it away, but it would have to do. She sat with her elbows on the kitchen table, and reflected on how hard everything in this flat was—the table, the chairs, the bed, everything, hard and sparse.

Why does emotion always have to intrude? The pizza in her mouth was dry and bitter. Why can I never enjoy simple happiness without feeling—what? I feel happy and sad and guilty all at the same time, when all I want is to feel just plain happy. I know I'm "just plain happy" when unwanted thoughts of my childhood days intrude.

She went and sat cross-legged on her bed and smoked two cigarettes in quick succession. She sat directly under the ceiling light, and her shadow formed a throne beneath her. Between her knees was the shadow of her hair, a frizzy crown of twigs and squiggles. The air was thick with blue-grey. Her mind kept going back to Fish Hoek, Rosa in the flesh. Rosa was not the first, nor the first black person, nor the first woman, but certainly the first black-woman. The first time with someone from the same workplace, too, *nogal*. And she's my boss! Nikki drew deeply on her cigarette. Her lips made a smacking noise. When she was a child in Langebaan, that was the noise her father's lips made when he sucked on his crayfish bones, the effort to reach an inaccessible essence. But not only her father. All of them—she, her two brothers, and even her mother, who always tried to be so ladylike. Nothing like crayfish to strip the veneer. What would her mother have said? Rosa? A nice name, yes. But a woman, my child? A *black* woman?

My mother said I never should

31

Play with the gypsies in the wood.
If I did, she would say
Naughty little girl to disobey

But what would be her worry—that it was with a woman? A *black* woman—the sheer profligacy of it all? All of the above—Yes? No? Maybe? Probably.

Nikki went and opened the window, and cool evening air carrying the slightest hint of sea-salt streamed into the little flat. It felt to her as if the flat was the back-end of a long narrow tunnel, and she, the furthest-removed speck of humanity. She stood a moment at the window imbibing the freshness of the night, then went back to the bed and lit another cigarette.

She looked at her watch. 20:43. The entire night still ahead.

She imagined her mother and Rosa in the same room—what a joke! Hi, Mom, this is Rosa, Rosa this is my mom. So, what do you say, Mom? Have you ever in your life seen anything so impressive? No, I thought not, coming from Langebaan, and all. Well, welcome to the new South Africa. She's my boss, Mom, and I sleep with her. Oh, yes, she's married . . . the point of your question being?

Mothers can be such fascists. She should be proud of me, but she's mortified, another cross for her to bear. Her husband never did want a third child, and girls are always trouble, etcetera.

But, Mom, did you even know that she's a high-net-worth Black Diamond yuppie? Even in your warped value-system, surely that makes a difference?

Nikki attacked her cigarette, and soon, smoke resembling storm clouds filled the room.

Why does emotion always have to intrude?

I'm actually a slut. Sluts sleep around, with anybody and all-comers. There's no emotion, only the pleasure of lust. Yep, that's me. Rosa's a thing of beauty; she doesn't deserve a slut in her life.

But she's bewitching, an enchantress, irresistible … married. This is not going to end well.

I could so use a beer right now.

She felt an impulse to call someone on WhatsApp and invite them to come share her bed with her. When last had she done so? She could picture the last person—a once-off guy—she couldn't even remember his name. That was a good three or four weeks ago, and it had been good with him, but she'd never seen or heard from him again.

You wouldn't like people to refer to you as white trash, *would you, Nikki?* No, Mom. *Then learn to keep your room clean, child. For crying out loud. How can you live in such filth and disorder?* What's changed since Langebaan? No nagging Mom . . . actually, no Mom . . . and no Dad, no brother Chris, no dog Dingus, no nothing. Her one living family member—that is, if he were still living—was her older brother, Victor, who one fine day just fucked off to Australia, and was never heard from again. *Stoksielalleen,* all on my ownsome lonesome in this great big world . . . But I've got Rosa—yeah, right . . . me and Tubs . . . we've got Rosa.

CHAPTER THREE

The traffic lights at the corner of St Stephen's Road and Forest Drive turned red. Rosa put her vehicle into neutral and set the handbrake. She turned on the radio. Music came at them from all of eight fitted speakers. She tapped her fingers and hummed along. When the lights changed, she turned the car left and accelerated into Forest Drive. The sun was rising. It was visible through the foliage of the pine trees lining Forest Drive. "Like a jewel in the hair," said Bill.

"Are you referring to the sun, Dad?" asked Rosa.

"How'd you guess?"

"It's how I've thought of it, too, on occasion."

"Incredible. Great minds think alike."

After a brief silence, he said, "you were off and away pretty early yesterday morning . . ."

"Yes. I was at the Fish Hoek cottage for the day—had lots of work to do finishing a presentation needed for work, today . . ."

". . . And got back pretty late last night."

"Eight o'clock? Eight o'clock's not late."

"It was after dark, and you were alone."

"That doesn't make eight o'clock late."

"It was after dark, and you were alone."

"Dad, sometimes I don't know the difference between you and Tubs. I suspect it has something to do with the Xhosa male's deep-seated need to dominate his women."

"Please don't patronise me, Rosa. You know it's about concern for your safety. If I didn't know you better, I'd say you're being defensive."

"Defensive? Defensive about what?"

34

"You tell me. How normal is it for a female employee to spend from sunrise to sunset at her private holiday cottage doing office work when she's got an office—and office hours—in which to do it?"

"It's completely normal in this day and age, Dad. You've obviously never heard of the sixty-hour workweek, right? And by the way, I'm not actually an employee. I partly own the business and might very well be its next CEO."

"Workaholism is like alcoholism; it's a dread disease. Don't destroy your life on work, Rosa. It's not worth it."

"Don't worry, Dad. My work ebbs and flows. Right now it's flowing, but with a bit of luck, it'll slow to a trickle in a few weeks. Then I'll be seriously loafing around."

Logic told him there wasn't a god—small g or big G—but then, it wasn't logical that he should have a daughter like this. *I mean, come on!* It was like hitting a cosmic jackpot or something—one chance in how many millions that someone like me would have fathered a being as incredible as she? He thought of his late wife, Zoliswa, and felt a sudden—what?—sadness, maybe? The trouble with caring so much for someone is that you never stop worrying about them. And the more you worry the more morbid your thoughts become, and, so, the more you worry. It was a miserable business. His daughter was like a delicate hothouse plant, incredibly dazzling, but so, so vulnerable. He sometimes wished she were just an ordinary village girl, locked away in the African midlands somewhere, barely literate. "Harvesting mealies," he muttered.

"What was that, Dad?"

"Nothing. I was just thinking how different you'd have been had I let you grow up with your grandmother in rural Transkei after your mother's death, instead of raising you here in the city, myself."

"It would certainly have done wonders for my spoken-isiXhosa."

She continued tapping her fingers in time to the radio.

35

Her father would always be number one in her life. When she had rejected God she had pretty much replaced Him with her father, and—unlike God—*he* delivered. He's getting old, she thought. He's had a tough life. Wifeless all these years, now . . . I don't believe in ancestral worship, but I worship my mother, and I know he does, too. I'm sure in some ways I came to fill for him the void created by her death . . . which means he worships me, too. She sighed. I am not worthy.

"Were you on your own up there?"

"Pardon?"

"At the cottage, yesterday?"

"A colleague was there with me. We worked together . . . you might remember her, Nikki Addo . . . she visited me at home once or twice."

"You mean that young white girl with the loud voice and wild red hair?"

"Ha! Yes, that's Nikki. She's a delightful person."

"She smokes, doesn't she?"

"Yes, I think so. Not much, though. More for the fun of it."

A right-turn, and they emerged from pine-lined Forest Drive into wide open Jan Smuts Drive. The traffic was sparse, and Rosa could put her foot down. On their left was the Cape Flats railway line, linking the outlying townships and suburbs with central Cape Town. Bill listened to the whine of the vehicle intensify as they picked up speed. Jan Smuts curved alongside the railway line till some three-and-a-half kilometres away, a bridge over the line took them onto the N2.

"Is Nikki your personal secretary, then?"

"Oh, no, Dad, I don't have a personal secretary. Nikki's a business analyst." She continued to tap her fingers and started to hum along to the music.

"A business analyst? Sounds important. What does a business analyst do?"

She looked at her dad and chuckled. "It's not adding up, is it, Dad? Why would your topflight executive-manager-daughter need a ragamuffin white girl with her at her exclusive seaside retreat?"

"Oh, rubbish, Rosa. Can't I ask a simple question?"

"Ha, sorry, Dad. I couldn't resist it." She increased speed, merging into the N2 traffic. "Nikki's job is to unravel all the complexities and obfuscations to be found in corporate reports and financial statements. It's a highly specialised role . . ."

"Makes sense . . ."

She knew it made no sense to him, but she had got him off her back. She resented being treated like a child, but how do you tell your father that? She sensed that he was sulking, and she wished she could somehow mollify him before dropping him off at his comrades' place in Langa. That's where he and the remnants of the little revolutionaries' club—led by Zoliswa until her death in the nineteen eighties—spent every Monday, Tuesday and Thursday, moldering together. Now, in his old age, living in a cramped gardeners' cottage on Rosa and Tubs's residential property, he had little in his life but endless hours of reading, of maintaining the garden and swimming pool—and of visiting his comrades in Langa.

They turned into Bhunga Avenue, and Rosa reduced speed, her vehicle purring like a pampered kitten. The beauty of this baby, thought Rosa, is that it can almost anticipate what I want it to do, and then it goes and does it, and so elegantly, too. Boy, do I love my car!

Bhunga Avenue was narrow and pot-holed. It was the single road into and out of Langa via the N2, and at this time of the morning was crowded with minibus taxis and with pedestrians rushing hither and thither. On the pavement just ahead, a lively group of schoolchildren began to peel off the side of the road into the path of Rosa's oncoming vehicle. She had anticipated this, and braked without abruptness. The children's eyes were a mix of triumph, gratitude and merriment. Rosa sighed. She looked at her watch. Suddenly, she was impatient to be free of her father. She needed to be out of this place, and alone with her thoughts. She had an important presentation later in the morning, and, besides, she also pretty badly wanted to see Nikki. It was a matter of drudgery for her and Tubs to have to be ferrying him to his comrades here in Langa three or four times a week, so that they could heaven-knows-what—reminisce on how the anti-apartheid war was lost? But, he's getting old; we must continue to humour him.

The meeting room was still dark when Rosa entered. The smell of Oakwood greeted her, and quickened her pulse-rate.

The door she had left open admitted no more light than a single candle, clouding all colour in the room, and dulling the gloss of smooth surfaces. She raised the blinds on all the windows, startling a pair of blackbirds on one of the ledges outside. They hurtled off into the Cape Town morning.

Mechanically, she unsleeved her portable computer from its nylon casing. The screen prompted for a password. She keyed it in, and watched as the lights and icons came up. With her right hand, she activated the start-up routine.

How did it happen? How did I end up in bed with her? How shall I start my letter of remorse? *Dearest, dearest Tubs, I am so, so, sorry . . . I have done a terrible thing . . .* No. The terrible thing is not the problem. It's what made me do the terrible thing that's the problem . . . *I have fallen in love with another person . . . a woman . . . a white girl. . . an employee . . . And I am so, so sorry, because*—and this is the truly devastating part—*I am actually not sorry at all . . .*

The control panel for the room's presentation equipment was wall-mounted, at a level Rosa would have described as breast-high. It resembled the keypad of a handheld computer. Rosa went over to it, and lightly touched one of its buttons. Immediately, on the adjacent wall, a silver screen unfurled itself from a metal cylinder horizontally set against the ceiling, and slid down the wall in the smooth, grudging way that thick syrup would, if spilt down the leg of a table.

In present-day South Africa not too many months ago, a young woman in some village was almost lynched for wearing trousers. What fate awaits the likes of me? Am I terrified? Should I be? The company's name appeared on the wall-screen: *Lumina*. In a cottage in a village in a forest on a mountain overlooking the sea, yesterday, a terrible and wonderful thing happened to me. Fish Hoek will forever be the most idyllic place in the world for me. Rosa closed her eyes, bowed her head, and with all ten fingers, raised her necklace to her lips and pressed them there for a slow instant.

Quarter to ten. Soon the room will be crowded. Soon I begin my presentation.

Coffee was brought in—*black as the night is black, black like the depths of my Africa*. Now, where on earth does that come from? Rosa smiled to herself. To live the *geared* life, that is my religion. What does *gearing* mean, Rosa? Nikki had asked when they were sipping coffee up in the Fish Hoek cottage yesterday, when Rosa put the word into the presentation they were preparing for today. Gearing: to borrow against what you've got, certain you'll be able to repay what you've borrowed, backing yourself to invest the borrowings at a profit or super-profit— which is the whole point. Gearing means borrowing. Borrowing means doubling your capacity. Doubling your capacity means heaven on earth—which is the whole point.

My dearest, dearest Tubs . . .

Ten-to-ten. Soon the room will be crowded. Soon I begin my presentation. Soon the course of history changes.

Nikki came into the meeting-room, and there was Rosa—all the sheer, pure beauty of her. The sight stopped Nikki in her tracks, stopped her breath and then made it race. It drained the blood from her cheeks, made her knees go limp, moistened her under-arms . . . Her head felt itchy, she scratched it. Ah, damn, she thought, elation rising within her.

The room was filling rapidly. There was chatter-and-laughter, a restrained joviality. Much coffee was being consumed, as was usual at meetings of the Lumina executive team—someone had once joked that Lumina's annual coffee bill was probably high enough to fund the country's deficit, and Rob Ferrie, the company CEO had replied, in all seriousness, that it wasn't a joke, it was a fact. He stood there, now, mug in hand, speaking earnestly to Rosa. They were a little distance off from the others, and although he leaned close to Rosa, he did not obscure her face from Nikki's view—in Nikki's view, the face of a goddess. God's finest creation by far, thought Nikki. And to think, yesterday I fucked her. Head reeling, Nikki poured herself some coffee and joined a close-by group and fell in with their chatter-and-laughter.

At ten o'clock, everybody sat down.

It occurred to Nikki that everything in this room—*with the definite exception of me, myself*—was an improvement on God's work. For starters, the sheer perfection of the air-conditioning system, the way it purified God's natural air, and maintained it at temperature-levels that constantly recalled the calmest, most mystical of beaches at dawn—that was something that surely even God should be in awe of. Mankind, take a bow. When you sat in a room like this and the air-conditioning was on, how could Heaven possibly be a nicer place? God aced. If He had any kind of decency, He would cede His throne to Man—now, already.

Rosa had no doubt that, after all was said and done, the Lumina management team would have the courage to go into a deal with the Chinese. Sure, there'd be a thousand questions, there'd be anxiety, there'd be angst, there'd be questions about the risk of treading untrodden paths, about losing control—and that, moreover, to a foreign company, and not just foreign, but Chinese into the bargain (communists, are they, the Chinese?). Questions about what will our customers say, about would the government even approve the deal, questions about setting a maybe dangerous precedent . . . And then, of course, the prescription that perhaps we should think about it some more, about let's not rush or be rushed . . .

But thankfully, thought Rosa, Rob Ferrie was still at the helm, and he would persuade the nigglers to come on board, to buy in, to follow his lead—*her* lead, actually . . . to sign on the dotted line . . . When would her turn come to run this company? She had done so much to build it, she was in fact already doing so much to run it. Rob was already into his sixties, and for a while now, had been dropping hints his retirement was imminent.

Soon I run this company, thought Rosa. Soon I be Rosa Lethlabe, CEO. Delusions of grandeur? I think everyone in this room maybe not likes it but expects it, the moment Rob retires. A deal with the Chinese will give his retirement package the mother-of-all boosts, the perfect send-off. Then, the appointment of his successor—or should that be successoress? The dawn of the era of Rosa. Oh, wow.

Rosa started off her presentation by emphasising how much money Lumina would make from this deal, how much cash would flow into the pockets of the individual company directors, all of whom were present in the room, all of whom were listening to her presentation, all with arched avidity. She reminded the group of the many projects, the expansion plans, the various upgrades that had had to be put on hold for lack of funds. Now comes along this once-in-a-lifetime windfall. "Jintao wants to buy 40 percent of our company," said Rosa. For this, she thought, but did not say, they are prepared to pay a shitload of US dollars. "There will be a massive injection of cash into Lumina," she said, "and by massive, I mean humungous." She showed a figure in US dollars on the screen. It covered the full breadth of the screen. "*That* humungous," she said. "And that amount you're looking at is nett of costs—conversions, deductions, transfers, commissions and the myriad other fees involved," she said. "I'm sure you will agree, this will be great for our future growth, for our company's image in the marketplace, and of course, for our shareholders."

"This company—" said Mickey Swanepoel, who sat closest to where Rosa stood—close enough for her to see the threads of dog-hair entangled in his jersey (he kept two thoroughbred German Shepherds at home), the finger-smudges on his spectacles and the blue in his temple-veins. He sluggishly, noisily (and, Nikki thought, from where she sat, hippopotamustically) moved around in his chair to alter his sitting position, settling his shoulders against the chair's back-rest, and calmly crossing his hands and resting them over his paunch. "This *Chinese* company," he said, "what's it called—*Jentoe* or something?"

Damn, thought Rosa. I should have foreseen it—Jintao-Jentoe, the perfect play on words. *Jentoe*: Afrikaans for prostitute. For slut.

Clyde Petersen, who was sitting next to Mickey Swanepoel, burst out laughing—a hoarse, whinnying sound that brought a smile to other faces in the room. "Jin-*tao*, Mickey!" he shouted, "Jin-*tao!*" and continued laughing, upwards into the air. He had huge shoulders ("If you think this is big, you should have seen them when I was still swimming competitively," was his usual comment when anybody remarked on their size); they quivered when he laughed.

"Ah, Mickey, you devil," said Rosa, forcing a smile. "I'm sure you've caused Clyde to wet his pants, there. But, we don't all understand Afrikaans, Mickey. Tell the rest of us—in English—what a *jentoe* is."

"Ha, ha, let's just say it's a *very* bad woman," said Mickey, winking at Clyde. "Not the type a decent fellow wants to go near—right, Clyde?"

"But, seriously," he continued, "has this Jintao got any kind of profile outside of mainland China? How do we know they're even for real? I mean, maybe they're the Italian Mafia in disguise." This triggered a fresh burst of laughter from Clyde.

Rosa chuckled briefly. She was unamused by Mickey's flippancy, but welcomed it as an opportunity for her to show some equanimity. Clearly, she thought, it was going to take more than dollar signs to wow this lot. As self-appointed salesperson-in-chief for this deal, she believed it was important that she appear to cope effortlessly—even disdainfully—with any sign of resistance or hostility from anyone. She felt the eyes of the room on her, Rob Ferrie's in particular, Nikki's in particular.

"Yep, Mickey," she said, "we'd certainly not want to get into bed with the Mafia, now, that's for sure." She smiled, and could see from the reciprocating smiles of others in the room—Rob Ferrie's, Nikki's—that her smile was perceived to be emitting nonchalance—splendid. "For this very reason," she said, "Nikki and I did some pretty extensive homework around who and what this Jintao is."

Yesterday, up at the Fish Hoek cottage, she and Nikki had prepared a total of twenty seven slides on *The Jintao Investment Company of China, Ltd.* Facts and figures gleaned from the 'Net, from business magazines, from reports and other documents obtained from the (very helpful) Chinese Embassy in Pretoria, from overseas contacts—especially US- and UK-based friends of Rosa and her husband, Tubs. Rosa had been as anxious as Mickey or anybody else to determine the credentials of this company—short of personally visiting China.

Everybody listened in (what Rosa took for rapt) silence, as she presented the facts on Jintao—pen-pictures of their directors (all, as it happened, members of the Chinese Communist Party, and all senior Chinese government officials, as well); the company's financials going back ten years; their product-and-service range; their mission, vision, values and strategic goals; their national and off-shore operations (it transpired that they had branches or subsidiaries or associate companies in a number of Asian, European, Australasian and American countries. Africa was the one continent where as yet they had not established any presence); who their auditors were (a Paris-based accounting firm); their contribution to a sustainable environment; and their commitment to policies for the promotion of employee growth and development.

Jintao, according to Rosa's analysis, was flush with cash, and was keen to open up Africa. Why had they chosen Lumina as their vehicle? "Well," said Rosa, "I think we can feel very proud of our lovable little Lumina. It seems we're more than just some obscure, little Global South outfit—we must have done something right to have attracted the attention—nay, the interest!—of an international company like Jintao. So, take a bow, folks."

Throughout, Nikki's fingers were poised over her keyboard like ten sprinters in their starting blocks. The signal she awaited was Rosa's call for back-up information on Jintao, The slides they had prepared for the presentation contained mostly summaries, extracts, abridgements, quotations, inferences—that is, crystallizations—made from the voluminous source-material that they had gathered, and which they had stored in electronic format on their laptop computers. "We must blind them with science," Rosa had said. "They must have the sense that every fact we utter is supported by a mountain of research."

Issie Yacoob signalled to speak, and a smile came to Nikki's face. Yesterday, at the Fish Hoek cottage, she had thought of him while drinking a beer straight from the bottle—like the bottle, Issie Yacoob was hard, smooth and fragile . . . At one-forty centimetres tall and weighing little more than a standard household pack of sugar, Issie Yacoob was not a commanding physical presence. However, he was noted for his brains—"the closest thing to pure thought on the planet," was how Rob Ferrie had once referred to him. "Yon-Issie," was what Rosa and Nikki jokingly called him in secret, because in a meeting, once, Nikki had sent a cellphone text message to Rosa which read, *"Yon Issie has a lean and hungry look."* So, Yon-Issie he became for them from then onwards.

"Something we need to check out," said Issie, "is what Jintao is doing in Bermuda."

"As far as we could ascertain," said Rosa, "their presence there is strictly legit. Bermuda of course, is one of the foremost tax havens in the world, enabling firms to maximize tax avoidance opportunities."

Issie smiled. "C'mon, Rosa," he said, "let's not be naïve about this. You know as well as I do, that the line between tax avoidance and tax evasion is less real than imaginary."

"Oh, yes, I know that, Issie." answered Rosa. "But, let's be fair. After all, our very own Lumina—and I daresay, every single individual in this room as well—is committed to using every legal means available to keep their taxes down to the minimum—as we say in our *Policy Statement on Tax Compliance*, we have a *duty* to do so . . . So why should there be any suspicion on any other firm that espouses a similar philosophy?"

"Is that what they're doing in Bermuda, then—legally avoiding tax?"

Rosa tried to fathom his smile. He was so slight he hardly cast a shadow. His expression behind his thick specs was all but inscrutable. If she had to hazard a guess, she'd say he was simply amusing himself. It was unlikely he knew something incriminating about Jintao and their corporate ethics; it wasn't his style to expose it this way—he'd have run to her or Rob Ferrie immediately had he heard anything. So, this was just Yon-Issie enjoying his fifteen seconds of fame. But for her, it was an opportunity once again to impress with how meticulous was her research-work.

"Well, Issie," she said, smiling back at him, "if you know something that we don't, you'll need to speak now, or forever hold your peace." (She said "peace" but thought "piece," and thought of Issie's wife, who, like Issie, took up little more space than a playing card. The smile she saw appearing on Nikki's face suggested to her that Nikki probably had the same image, too—of Yon-Issie holding his piece.) "We managed to get hold of Jintao's *Policy Statement on Ethical Business Practice,* and waded through all fifty or sixty pages of it, Nikki and I."

"Fifty-seven pages to be exact," piped in Nikki, "at least in the English version. I've just called it up onto my screen, here. It covers everything—compliance with anti-trust legislation, guidelines to employees on receiving gifts and favours from customers or suppliers, disclosure of confidential information to unauthorized third parties as well as non-disclosure of material information to authorized parties such as the auditors, abuse of company property, payment or receipt of bribes, conflict of interest, and of course, compliance with tax legislation." She paused for breath. "We also obtained stats on all the internal disciplinary hearings they've held at every single location, worldwide, whenever any employee was suspected of breaching the policy. According to a written confirmation we obtained from Jintao's corporate auditors, neither Jintao nor any of its subsidiaries has ever been indicted for any reason. In addition, we wrote to Jintao's bankers in Bermuda—"

"—Whoa! Enough," said Rob Ferrie, putting his pen down with a clunk, and whipping off his specs. He narrowed his eyes at Issie and said, "Issie, surely you don't need further convincing."

Issie smiled and said, "Not long ago, the leader of China—Deng something-or-other—"

"—Deng Xiaoping," said Nikki.

"Deng Xiaoping—thanks, Nikki—this Deng Xiaoping-guy said, *'As long as it makes money it is good for China.'* I don't think he added anything about ethics, so I worry that some of his followers might decide that any which way will do."

"Folks," said Rob Ferrie, turning away from Issie and glancing at his wristwatch, "we've been at it for more than two hours, already; I think we need to start drawing matters to a conclusion, now. Are there any last questions or comments before we sum up?"

"There's one more issue that merits scrutiny," said Leigh Irving-Moore, inclining her head to the right and allowing her hair to slide down over her ear. Leigh was senior director for the Inland Region, and after Rob Ferrie, was the longest serving member of Lumina's executive team.

"It's the question of culture-fit," she said, taking her hair in her thumb and forefinger, and looking at it briefly before tucking it back behind her ear. "I know that the Chinese have been in Africa for decades, and should by now have adapted to African realities—but Africa's not *South* Africa. I foresee serious compatibility problems between us and them—unless they're willing to change, big-time."

"We've got *culture* down as a project risk," said Rosa. "But I should say, whatever difficulties of a cultural sort we've identified so far, none of them is a show-stopper. Our first priority is to approve the deal with Jintao—*in principle.* Only then will it be appropriate to address project-risk."

"Gotcha, bitch," thought Nikki, unable to suppress a smile. Leigh had also been thought of at the cottage yesterday. Idiot that she was, they were expecting her to raise some non-issue at the meeting—*she always does!* "I notice a pattern with Leigh, Nikki had remarked. "She's always trying to disguise her lack of brainpower, but almost always ends up looking the clot she really is."

Rob Ferrie thanked Rosa and Nikki for all the effort they'd put into their presentation, and "for providing *"such wonderful"* structure and guidance to the meeting. "You ladies are the ultimate professionals." He ended by getting the meeting's agreement that Jintao's offer was acceptable in principle, but that before signing anything, a visit to Jintao's Beijing headquarters was necessary. "I'd like to go and spend maybe three or four days there."

CHAPTER FOUR

At the supper table that evening, Rosa tried to keep her voice nonchalant as she told Tubs and Bill her boss would be travelling to China, and that he'd need ammunition for his negotiations, adding: "I've got to go back to Fish Hoek tomorrow, Nikki and I, to work out some more details ahead of his trip."

"It puzzles me why you have to be working off-site, when you've got an office," said Bill.

Tubs had prepared a tandoori beef casserole, which simmered audibly in its see-through glass dish. "Wow, Tubs," said Rosa. "Looks like your finest work, yet." He came up alongside her and burrowed his nose and lips into the tender flesh below her earlobe, and whispered: "Honey, you ain't seen nothin' yet." The sensation of his lips and moustache against her necklace made her utter a short, sharp chuckle, and jerk in her chair.

Opposite them, Bill was thinking to himself, I like the way he likes her. He looked at the wine in his glass and smiled at it, and it seemed to him that the wine smiled back. He looked at Tubs again, and continued smiling. Yep, he thought, that's pure adoration I'm seeing on that boy's face, his wife's his world. As a father, I find it pleasing that my little girl's husband feels that way about her. Did I feel the same tenderness towards my wife? And she, towards me?

"This Chinese firm—Jintao—they're flush with dollars, and trawling the world for investment opportunities," said Rosa. "I must say, it's a sign that we've come of age in South Africa—our industry I mean . . . as far as I know, this is the first time such an offer has been made to an S A company, so it's rather flattering . . . And, Dad, to address your question, it's helter-skelter at the office. We need a quiet environment to do our thinking-work."

"Be careful this Jintao doesn't rebound on you," said Bill. "Everything in capitalism's about self-interest. Even if these Chinese investment guys spend their dollars on your projects, it will be to benefit themselves, not you, ultimately."

"Sounds like win-win to me," said Rosa. "I can live with that."

Next morning, the traffic lights into Main Road, Muizenberg showed red as they approached, but they were delayed there only briefly, before being able to speed on again. The beach road passed between the technical college campus on their left and a sheer green hill-rise on their right. Dew covered the cars parked on both sides of the road, and glistened on the walls of all the brick-faced buildings they passed.

With the sun rising over it, the sea had a shifting green lustre from horizon to shoreline. A lone surfer was to be seen cutting through the waves. Some four or five kilometres in the distance, the village of Fish Hoek lay huddled all vague and blue in its mountain cove. Rosa felt a rush inside her chest that brought an involuntary moistness to her eyes. Her instinct was to accelerate—break through the sound barrier!—but she curbed the impulse, preferring, instead, a calm, moderate speed as the perfect foil to this suddenly-charged emotion taking a grip of her. These were days she knew she would remember, would cherish— maybe, would regret—no, never regret!—for the rest of her life. This was a kind of pinnacle, a kind of perfection. She must prolong it. If there was a heaven, she was living there, now.

Alongside her Nikki lolled in her seat, humming tunelessly, and lightly tapping her toes against the floorboard. Rosa stretched over and lay her hand, open-fingered, on Nikki's thigh. Nikki went still, momentarily. Then, without looking at Rosa, took her hand in hers and began fondling the knuckles and fingers, unavoidably brushing the jewel that sat like a hump in Rosa's wedding-ring. The car leaned through a bend as Nikki raised the hand and pressed it to her lips. She held it there for a drawn-out moment, leaving on it a moist imprint in the shape of a wreath. She put the hand back against her thigh, and continued to stroke the fingers, the knuckles, the wedding ring; and the hand stroked back, gently-gently.

You gave me the response I wanted, not the one I needed.

And what was the response you needed?

Rejection.

Rejection?

Rejection.

And what would you have done with rejection?

I would have retired, with grace and dignity.

And forgotten about me?

Entirely.

Entirely?

Entirely.

Give me a kiss.

A kiss?

A kiss.

A right-turn took them onto the tarred mountain road which sloped between rows of sleepy cottages and overhanging trees. In places, roots below the road's surface created bulges resembling legs under a blanket.

"Soon, soon," said Rosa, struggling to contain her excitement. As if of its own accord, the car turned off the road and drifted into the paved cottage driveway. Rosa turned off the ignition; the motor died so abruptly that the sound of the sea seemed to rush into and bounce about inside the car. She and Nikki sighed simultaneously, their eyes beaming.

Inside the cottage, they didn't stop to open the curtains or windows; they just dropped their things on the front-room table, and made straight for the bedroom; their footsteps were slow but resolute; their hands and shoulders touched, brushed, scraped. In the bedroom they turned to face each other, smiling, not speaking. Slowly, ritualistically, they stripped the clothes from each other's body, releasing what felt to Rosa like a preternatural heat into the room. There was total coordination in their movements, a kind of free-form jazz improvisation, thought Rosa—not rehearsed but perfectly attuned. Their breathing merged in dissonant moans.

Rosa lay on her stomach, her chin on the cross of her forearms. She drew on her cigarette, taking care to direct the smoke-stream away from Nikki who lay beside her, fast asleep, left thigh, supple and smooth against Rosa's buttock. Am I dreaming this? If I could have one thing different in my life, thought Rosa, it would be that my mother were still alive . . . With the passing of time, Rosa had come to see her late mother more and more as a late sister, who, had she been there, would have been the companion in childhood and adolescence that Rosa had never had—would now be filling this sudden, undefinable void that *I don't understand but know exists . . . exists inside me as a deep hole-within-a-hole.* She drew on her cigarette, and looked at Nikki through the drifting smoke. Nikki's hair was a brazen, tumbling thicket—dark as the night is dark, thought Rosa . . . dark as the depths of my conscience. A thread of vein was barely visible on Nikki's left eyelid. It seemed to come and go with Nikki's breathing. I could lick it off, thought Rosa. I could lick it off without waking her up, I could be so gentle. Could she be the sister I never had? But then I wouldn't be here in bed with her, I wouldn't be aching so to devour her body. I wouldn't be here on this irreversible road with her . . . If I had had a sister, as kids in our parents' home we'd have shared a bed, we'd have shared secrets. In the middle of the night in bed in the dark together we would have been as one, and would have been able to hug each other and share our guilt. You can't share your guilt with your mother. I needed then as I need now, a sister more than a mother . . .

Rosa closed her eyes, and listened to the ocean. She became aware that her pulse-rate had risen, and she tried to will it to slow. Behind her eyelids, jagged fibrils of static shot about in the dark. She made an effort to see her mother's face, but all she saw was the face of a wooden sculpture—brown, shiny, lifeless. Her fingers began to feel the heat of the dying cigarette, and she thought she'd take one more puff, but, no . . . there was a bitterness on her palate that repeated swallowings wouldn't relieve. She stubbed the cigarette out, rubbing it around in the ashtray for longer than she needed. Then she rose, careful not to disturb Nikki, and made her way to the bathroom. Anytime, now, she thought, anytime now, I'm bound to hear my bokmakieries sing.

There was a strong smell of coffee in the room. And the sea, the sea. The sea seemed to be crashing off the walls and flopping about as if in an echo chamber, slapping up against the furniture, roiling about under the bed, forcing itself on Nikki's attentions. Her ears could distinguish the nonstop now-distant, now-close-by roar of the sea from the rushed gurgling it made—or perhaps the gurgling was coming from the coffee, not the sea? Or perhaps she was smelling the sea and hearing the coffee? She opened her eyes, and realized that she'd been dreaming—a non-specific rush-about of images and sensations. But the coffee-smell was real, and the thirst she felt for it was real, too.

A cigarette, a cigarette, my kingdom for a cigarette. She sat up in the bed, and the covers slid off her like sea water. She was naked except for her bead necklace. She lit a cigarette, and exhaled a shaft of smoke, rod-straight, into the air above her. Had this thing with Rosa gone too far?

The smoke-rod diffused itself around her. Smoking the cigarette had intensified her need for coffee. She got up quickly and found her clothes, neatly piled on a chair at the side of the bed. She dressed, swiftly—bra, panties, T-shirt, jeans: all on in two ticks—and went into the next room, where Rosa sat bent over her computer.

On the wall beyond where Rosa sat was mounted a large bronze analogue clock which showed eleven fifteen. Nikki checked her wristwatch: eleven fifteen, too. Damn. The last thing she had wanted was to oversleep. She slid into a chair opposite Rosa. Through the large plate glass window in the room, she saw that the sea and the sky were two different shades of blue.

"Wow, you seem to have moved along pretty briskly, here," she said, awed by the brilliance of Rosa's smile—a smile I feel to the roots of my hair, thought Nikki, a smile that makes my lizard-tattoo want to sprint about with joy. The documents which they had brought along with them had all been sorted into neat piles on the table. Between them on the table stood a steaming jug of coffee, a bowl piled low with sugar, and two large mugs.

"The last thing I wanted to do was to oversleep," said Nikki in a mock-plaintive voice, ". . . and, like last time, leave you with all the work." She poured herself some coffee.

"You're a beast," said Rosa, "but, did anybody tell you how cute you look when you sleep?" She looked up at Nikki, and delighted in the wild profusion of her hair—red as my heart is red, she thought, ". . . especially with the way your tongue hangs out," she said, chuckling, "like a great pink landing strip for flies and other yucky bugs." She mimicked the look by crossing her eyes and swivelling her head and tongue in opposite directions.

Nikki shrieked with laughter. "You lie, you lie" she shouted, drumming the table with her fingers. She affected a high-pitched, whinging tone, and said, "Oh, please don't tell my mommy, please don't!"—and clasped her hands together against her chin, in the image of Dürer's *Praying Hands*.

"Don't tell your mommy what?" said Rosa. "Don't tell her that she's got the world's most fabulous daughter?" The laughter drained from Nikki's eyes. "Don't tell her that her daughter's on my mind day and night, night and day?" They stared into each other's eyes without blinking, and tears began to form in Nikki's. "Don't tell her that her daughter's got me on the very verge of . . ." Rosa's voice was hoarse. She tried to continue speaking but couldn't. She abruptly dropped her head and stared at her hands, which lay limp and palm-up in her lap. After a moment, and still staring at her hands, she continued. "When we got to the cottage here this morning—in fact, *before* we got to the cottage here this morning—you gave me the response I *wanted*," said Rosa, barely audibly ". . . not the one I *needed*."

Nikki raised her coffee mug to her lips, and felt the converging heat of it against her cheeks and nostrils. Her tears and the steam from the mug gave the sea and the sky, visible from where she sat, a congealed, soupy look. There was a brief silence before Nikki spoke. "And what was the response you needed?" Nikki's voice, too, was hoarse, barely audible. Her eyes glistened.

"Rejection."

"Rejection?"

"Rejection."

Nikki had lost her virginity at the age of sixteen, but she did not experience it as loss—on the contrary, it was far more like buying a ticket to Disney and eagerly jostling to get through the entrance gate. From the very beginning, sex was everything it was trumped up to be. That first day it had been in her bedroom in a hurry with all her clothes on with a school friend with all his clothes on, with her dog Dingus on the floor mat looking on, and with her mother in the kitchen cooking supper. Then and ever since, *ecstasy* was her preferred word for it; in the twenty-odd years since that first day, she must surely have done it a thousand times or more. But the big but was: she had never done it with anybody because she was *in love* with them—this was going to be a first with Rosa . . . if it could be said that she was *in love with* Rosa.

Rejection. Rejection? Rejection. She would have been able to reject Rosa in the way that a starving dog would have been able to reject cooked ham—right now, girl, I'm ready to pounce all over you. She paused for an instant in her breathing, then got up and walked round the table to where Rosa sat, sensing how Rosa went tense and expectant, sensing how the sea outside in the distance went tense and expectant. She sank to her knees at Rosa's side, and put her arms around her waist. She put her lips to Rosa's ear, and whispered, "And what would you have done with rejection?"

She saw Rosa's eyelids flutter, once, twice, and how, with her right thumb and forefinger, she twirled her wedding ring in her lap. "I would have retired," she heard Rosa say, with the hint of a smile in her tone. ". . . With grace and dignity."

Nikki loaded her reaction to this with mock-shock: "And forgotten about me?"

"Entirely," was Rosa's gently emphatic reply, while she squirmed from the itching which Nikki's breath made in her ear.

"Entirely?"

"Entirely."

Then they grinned at each other, and Nikki, tightening her embrace on Rosa's waist, said, "Give me a kiss."

"A kiss?" It sounded muffled—Rosa was speaking with her mouth pressed up against Nikki's necklace. . .

"Yes, yes, yes, a kiss."

Yesterday there was no cloud to be seen, but today a coldish wind coming in over the south-western mountain peaks brought with it a low-slung cloud-mass which spread in the sky like spilt ink. Night will be coming early to Fish Hoek, thought Rosa. Maybe there'll even be rain . . .

She sat on a quilt on the sea sand, her back against the wind. Her jacket was zipped all the way up to her chin, and her beanie covered her ears and eyebrows. Fine spatterings of sand occasionally flicked her cheeks causing her to hunch her shoulders and clench her fists. She made a mental note to bring along a beach umbrella next time. Yet, there were people on the beach who needed no protection from the wind—children especially, and very old women, who strolled about in nothing but their bathers, and who dived into the sea without any apparent forethought—with the kind of spontaneity that Rosa knew (and was sometimes glad that) she herself lacked.

Nikki was one of those people. From where Rosa sat, she could see Nikki in the water in her bikini, a one-woman riot, cavorting there in the waves, clearly impervious to the weather. Rosa smiled. She could not look at Nikki without feeling a muted elation, a sense of being on the verge of something keenly anticipated. It was not a strange feeling, but a rare one. At some distant time in the past, this was how it had been with Tubs, especially in the days leading up to their marriage.

Rosa watched as a small crowd of children quickly grew around Nikki, each child joining her in her high-energy antics—hurling themselves like chucked furniture into the swirling foam, and looking for the waves to break over their bodies and bowl them over; then they would fight off the pull and suck of the water and hurry to their feet not to miss the next wave. Rosa noticed how passersby slowed to look and to smile their approval—and she smiled, too, for what, after all, was the purpose of childhood but to have a whale of a time?

After about thirty minutes, Nikki abruptly ran out of the sea, disengaging from it in splintering sheets of water. She ran up the beach to where Rosa sat, shedding water-shards in her wake, and flopped down, all reedy and breathless, onto a beach towel that Rosa had spread out on the sand for her.

"I could *so* use a cigarette, now," she said, propping herself up on her elbows.

"Let me light one for you," said Rosa. "You're all wet and briny, like a beached eel."

They laughed.

Nikki smoked her cigarette with the ardour of a flat tyre being pumped, her chest visibly expanding with each inhalation. Rosa watched with some wonderment how rapidly Nikki's back and legs dried in the wind, and how large and erect her goose pimples were. A drop of water, like a live thing, found its way loose from the hair overhanging Nikki's brow, and plopped down onto the towel in front of her. She swept the hair back with her left hand, but tufts of it almost immediately sprang forward, again.

Rosa unzipped the cooler bag that she'd brought along. She took out a can of beer and passed it to Nikki.

"Incredible." said Nikki. "How'd you guess?" She snapped the can, and a wisp of steam escaped. She drank. "Aren't you going to have one, too?"

"Nope," said Rosa. "I'll skip this round—I'm driving, remember."

"Of course. I admire your discipline."

Rosa noticed that the sky over Seal Island was still cloudless, but that it was growing less and less blue, more and more ash. She had the impression that the horizon had stolen closer to shore. She smiled at the thought as if it was a joke, but the impression persisted. Throughout her life, she'd been receiving praise for a whole miscellany of things— her beauty, her intelligence, her sophistication, her discipline, her work ethic, her achievements, her coolness under pressure . . . But nobody had ever praised her for being free-spirited, rebellious, uninhibited, sensuous, spontaneous . . . She looked at Nikki: a beer in one hand, a cigarette in the other, lying in the wind half naked on a public beach—and that during working hours, too, as if it were the most natural thing in the world.

"Have you ever dreamed of living somewhere really, really far away?" Rosa asked, "like in the Amazon Jungle or in Timbuktu, or anywhere else like that—Siberia, perhaps?" She half expected a wisecrack-reply, but noticed that Nikki reflected for a moment before answering.

"I've thought about it—often," said Nikki. "Often, I've tried to picture myself as a Mother Teresa-type nun in a convent somewhere in the Indian boondocks, succouring to the poorest and most downtrodden of the earth, but no matter how hard I try, I find I can never really get serious about such an idea, it just seems so improbable. Chances are, if it did happen, I'd be dead in a matter of hours, like a fish out of water. Nope, for me it's a modern city like Cape Town or bust."

"And yet," said Rosa, "I'd expect that if anyone could make such a leap, it would be you, Nikki Addo—from a one-horse town like Langebaan."

"No," said Nikki. "I don't travel well, it was difficult enough making the leap from Langebaan to Cape Town . . . Hell, I remember what a green country bumpkin I was when I first arrived in the big city. I was terribly self-conscious, and thought everyone who looked at me could tell I was this *boere-nooientjie* from the countryside."

"I could so easily have ended up a country girl, myself," said Rosa, "after the death of my mother. When I was a kid, eight or nine, I think, my father often took me to his people in a peasant village in the old Transkei. When my mother died, he briefly considered leaving me there to be brought up by his mother, but decided against it, as he couldn't bear the thought of being separated from his daughter, having just lost his wife. Well, thank God. I would probably have ended up being sold off as some male chauvinist pig's bare-breasted fourteen year-old bride. And the scary part is, I'd probably have been happy about it."

"Yep, that's the kind of fate I'd have suffered had I stayed on in Langebaan—some village idiot's breeding machine-cum housekeeper." A glint came to her eyes. "Instead, I've got you, Babe." She grinned broadly.

Rosa tensed her muscles against a fresh gust of wind that hit her like a sudden rush of emotion. At the far, northern end of the beach, she could see the trek fishers hauling in their nets, and thought she could distinguish the one with the my-girlfriend-went-to-London T-shirt. "I know this sounds crazy," she said, avoiding eye contact with Nikki, "but that's the best thing anyone's ever said to me."

Over her left shoulder, she saw that a train was just rounding the bend from the Kalk Bay side of the mountain. She became aware of its rhythmic clatter, first as an impulse so slight that it felt merged in with her heartbeat, then as a growing noise seeming to come from the mountain rather than the train. For a wild second, she wanted to throw off her cap and jacket, and rush screaming about in the wind. The thought was amusing. She smiled at Nikki and said, "Maybe someday, we two should just up, and run away to London, Paris or Rome." She rose to her feet. "In the meantime, there's work to be done—let's go."

Back at the cottage, Rosa did not join Nikki in the shower, but immediately set about finding her starting point in the document-under-construction, as well as summoning the mindset needed for a plus-minus two hour spell of intense labour. She was soon deep-immersed in the work, and experienced Nikki's entrance into the lounge, some ten minutes later, as something purely sensuous.

The document was writing itself, and Rosa's instinct was to let it.

Nikki had little trouble tapping into Rosa's mental zone. She opened her laptop, and within seconds her fingers were skipping over the keyboard, causing a multitude of vying images to burst onto the screen. Around her on the table were various lever arch files and

Manilla folders, all marked *Jintao*. She dragged three of the files closer, and opened them to sections which she expected would be relevant to the task at hand.

"We've got to produce a document that persuades both our Lumina management team *and* the Chinese."

"Yep. And there's every likelihood the Chinese will be an easier sell."

"We have to produce a *business* case for community housing and other social infrastructure—an investment proposal, something that they'll find sufficiently attractive to risk their money."

"The profit potential must make their eyes bulge."

"Yep, with greed. Isn't that what capitalism is all about? Capitalism will solve any problem, as long as there's money to be made."

At six o'clock, Rosa flicked a glance at her wristwatch.

"Enough," she said. "I need a break."

She went to stand at the window.

"The sea, the sea. The loud and turbulent sea."

Nikki went and joined her at the window. For a moment, they simply stood there looking at the sea as it slowly darkened.

Each could detect the static from the other's body—see the individual strands of hair in the other's eyebrows. Without forethought they found their mouths touch, brush, moisten. Their breathing came warm and quick.

Silently, they made their way to the couch, where Nikki lay with her head in Rosa's lap.

"You're an amazing person, Rosa." Nikki's lips barely moved. Her eyes were shut. A bolt ran through her as she felt Rosa's hands move in her hair. Her heart beat faster, she tried to keep her body motionless. Rosa's fingertips now were lightly roaming over her lips, her eyebrows, ultra-lightly tickling her ear. She heard Rosa's deep rapid breaths, and was unable to restrain a barely-audible moan.

They packed up and left as dusk was settling. Outside, the air was crisp against their cheeks. Rosa pulled her jacket collar closer round her neck. She noticed that Nikki wore a thin short-sleeved T-shirt, but seemed impervious to the falling temperature.

No person in sight, but lights in the windows of several of the cottages suggested that they were indeed occupied. No doubt, there were hidden human eyes watching them as they got into their car, noting their cheerfulness, maybe wondering at their unity-yet-diversity.

Rosa allowed the car slowly to drift downhill towards the beach road.

"You're an amazing person, Rosa."

"Love means not—"

"—having to say "you're an amazing person, Rosa.""

Nikki smiled. "When I was a kid," she said, "I used to chant along with everybody else in church the words, "I am not worthy Lord, to touch the hem of your garments." And I really meant it. I really believed I was a foul wretch unworthy of His love. And although I've long ago renounced Christianity and all religion, there are certain beliefs and attitudes that Christianity's drilled permanently into my bones."

"It's not only religion that does that," said Rosa. "Lately, every time I try to understand myself—make sense of my own beliefs and attitudes and behaviour, my mother surfaces. I was a nine or ten-year-old kid when she died, but her influence, her shadow over my life ..."

"... disproportionate, yeah. I'm guessing *you'll* have a similar influence on the lives of many people, yourself, Rosa ... but it will be positive, you're an amazing person."

"If you keep saying that I'll start to believe it. It makes me think of the tight-knit group that my parents were a part of—the comrades. They used to call one another "comrade" all the time. It would be "How's it going, Comrade Simeon?" "Oh, I'm fine, Comrade Zoli.""

61

"What's for supper, Comrade Hazy?" "Fresh fruit and veg, Comrade X, Y or fucking Z.""

Nikki laughed. "Where I come from it used to be "Brother This" and "Sister That.""

"I think they all just took themselves too seriously."

A reflective look came to Rosa's eyes. "Anyway, the point I want to make is that I loved that those comrades all loved me. Whenever they arrived at our place for a meeting or something, they would greet me with so much delight in their eyes and their voices. And my dad would often try to impress them with how bright I was. He'd get me to name the letters of the alphabet, and to spell my name, to count up to a hundred … name the days of the week, the months of the year. But, young as I was—I was still in nappies—I could tell that my mother didn't like that kind of—what?—exhibitionism … she never sang my praises, not even to me."

The beach road was near-deserted, and despite the strong wind keeping a constant pressure on the left-side of their vehicle, they were able to speed through Fish Hoek Main Road, then onto the strip of road that took them past Clovelly, Kalk Bay, St James and Muizenberg.

"You talk about struggling to be worthy of the mercy of God—you don't know nuttin'" said Rosa, with a sudden chuckle. "The struggle to be worthy of the mighty Zoliswa's attention—that's what I spent my early childhood on, and for the most part, failed at."

There was a brief silence in the car, during which they both became aware of the quiet purring of the motor. Involuntarily, their eyes followed the streetlamps rushing backwards on either side.

""*Just like your mother,*" the comrades used to say. It was always meant to be a compliment. My mother, after all, was a leading light in the Movement—a Lenin, a Trotsky. Who could dominate the floor at meetings like Zoli? Who could produce pamphlets of greater inspiration with less effort than Zoli? Whose intellectual prowess was just plain

62

simply dazzling? And whose speeches produced more thunderous applause than Zoli's? She was a genius, they said; she might have been president of the Movement had she been a man … had she lived …"

"Yep, I can see why they'd say "just like your mother,"" said Nikki.

"But then," continued Rosa, "she went and got herself arrested; she went and got a five-year banning order slapped on her vainglorious arse. Those were choices she made. She could have chosen to be a good wife and a good mother. Instead, she chose to be a good left wing socialist comrade. She made me hate The Cause … Was she devoted to The Cause or to the adulation it brought her? Jail-time was a badge of honour … a banning order earned the highest respect in Movement circles … But did she want to die for The Cause? She surely knew it was a possibility, yet, she was unfailing in her commitment. She worshipped The Cause and it worshipped her right back."

Again, there was a brief silence in the car.

"Boy! That was some monologue!" Rosa tried to laugh. "Apologies! I sometimes get carried away."

CHAPTER FIVE

She was lying on the beach at Langebaan, her head resting on the dog's rump. She could feel his moist panting against her forehead, and wished he would turn his mouth away. She tried to get up, tried to open her eyes, to call his name, Dingus . . . but was unable to. The sound of the sea, of voices, of speedboats—yes, somewhere in the background—or was it in the foreground? Maybe caught up, entangled in her hair? Mixed in with salt and sea and sand? There was a smell, too, a small but insistent smell, one that made her feel all vomity—her own sweat? Dog's breath? Seaweed? It reached down all the way from her throat to her lungs, making them burn, making her nipples burn, making the entire length of her windpipe seethe like a propane torch.

She couldn't shake the feeling that death was close by, maybe a live being in the room right there with her now, ready to jump her, to wrestle, to rape her.

If she could just stay conscious.

She heard the sound of rush-hour traffic on Kenilworth Road. Her heart beat a little faster. She realized that she was emerging from lost consciousness. She managed a weak smile. Morning breaks and I'm alive, oh happy day. But her eyes wouldn't open; she remembered how her eyes had run when she went to bed last night, how she had given up trying to wipe them dry. *Now they've turned to stone.* Mother! What if they never opened again? She worked them open with the sides of her forefingers, and recognized her room in the semi-light of a new morning. A terror that was slowly mounting in her breast subsided, and she closed her eyes again.

She wished her mother were there to massage her aching body with magic childhood lotion, and to calm her mind with sweet talk . . . there, there, relax Mommy's Babba . . . *alles gaan regkom* . . . don't worry, Mommy loves you . . . no school for you tomorrow and no running about on the beach either, till you're well again, Mommy's little sweetie . . .

She wished her mother were there; she wished Rosa were there; she wished her body didn't feel so broken. What would Rosa say if I should die? And my father? He'd be all stiff-faced at the funeral, all full of blame and self-hate. But he's dead already . . . like Chris . . . Her fingers clutched at the bedding, ruffled like a sea-stiffened jeans, and she felt a sobbing wanting to start up, wanting to flood through her burning throat and lungs, through the nausea and through the disgust she felt at wanting to cry.

She found her phone. "Going to be late today," she keyed in. "Feeling a bit under the weather."

Rosa's reply was immediate. "Oh, shame. Will stop there on my way to the office."

To splash water on my face and drench my hair—nothing like water to revive oneself. Curtains need to be opened, too, to light up this room. Wash my face, brush my teeth, open a window for air—a mug of coffee, switch on the TV, smoke a cigarette. No, not smoke a cigarette.

Rosa arrived within ten minutes, and, in the doorway, clasped Nikki in a prolonged hug. "You're not looking well, Honeybunch."

She ushered Nikki to the bedroom and settled her under the blankets. "Look how red and swollen your face is—and your voice! You must have had a dreadful night. Is there no medication in the flat? Maybe we should call in a doctor to come look you over and prescribe something."

She made two calls, one to her doctor and one to her boss Rob Ferrie at Lumina. "Clive's a great GP. Says he'll stop here on his way to surgery. And Ferrie has no problem if I skip office today. Fortunately I've no appointments in my diary. Besides, there's always video-conferencing . . ."

Nikki lay motionless in her bed, wondering if she were dreaming.

"I'll stay with you today," said Rosa, taking off her jacket. She tossed it onto the chair where she had put down her laptop. "Have you had anything to eat, yet? Can I get you something—a glass of milk, maybe? I'll warm it in the microwave. What do you normally eat for breakfast—toast?" She went and sat on the bed alongside Nikki. She smiled. "Am I fussing too much?" She laid her head down on the pillow beside Nikki's. Her lips rubbed against Nikki's fevered cheek as she sang. "You are my sunshine, my only sunshine."

Nikki felt Rosa's lips and teeth and breath against her cheek. Something inside her went whoopee.

Rosa laid an arm and a thigh lightly across Nikki's body.

Together, in whispered tones, they sang, "You make me happy when skies are blue."

Nikki wondered, what if it's more than flu? What if it's AIDS? Or Covid? A tremor ran through her, and she felt Rosa's hand gently squeeze her shoulder.

I wouldn't be offended if she referred to me as white trash, said Nikki to herself. I'm nothing compared to her, I'm mostly disgusting, while she's all class. For me, love is screwing your head off, for her it's caring about someone. "It's an aberration," she thought, and felt a sense of mirth. "It's God having a laugh."

Clive arrived shortly after nine. He was short of stature, mustachioed, and wore his golf-shirt tucked into his chinos. He and Rosa were on first name terms; they greeted each other with an embrace and a peck on the lips. "Enter the family doctor," she said with a smile as she led him to Nikki's bed.

Nikki was surprised at how youthful-looking he was—a *kapok-hoender*, bantom fowl—was what her mother would have called him. Her instinct told her that he could not be a doctor, but the competent manner in which he probed with his words and his stethoscope reassured her.

"Bad case of flu," he said.

Nikki thought, like his hands, his eyes are gentle. His whole manner is gentle. I'm not livestock, she thought, I'm a human being, and clearly, he cares.

She submitted a buttock to be injected, and wondered if Rosa had ever had to appear naked in front of this GP.

He called Rosa into the room. "She'll sleep," he said. "But she'll still need some stuff from the pharmacy." He found a gold-plated pen in his leather bag, and wrote out a prescription and a certificate putting Nikki off work for three days.

"Thanks so much, Dr Clive," said Nikki, feeling much better than a minute ago, cheered that she could speak without feeling pain in her throat.

The doctor left, and Rosa said she would go down to the pharmacy right away. She put on her jacket, and wished to know if there was anything else she needed to get while she was at it. Before departing, she planted a lingering kiss on Nikki's forehead.

Rosa was hardly out the door when Nikki's pain and discomfort returned. She felt crumpled under the blankets, and hoped the injection would work soon. At the spot where it had been administered, she felt a light throbbing, and was sure a blue mound would form there; she hoped it wasn't bleeding—imagine Rosa comes back and finds me in a sea of blood.

She started coughing, and held a tissue to her mouth, hoping that when she inspected it, as she certainly would, she'd see no blood on it. Her temples ached. The skin on her cheekbones felt stretched. Her vision was all blurred. And her mind was in confusion about Rosa. How did Rosa love her? she wondered. How and why? Did Rosa love her like a pet, like she herself used to love Dingus? "Pet-love is a pure, up-lifting kind of love," she told herself, trying to believe it. "But it's a love between *un*-equals." Does she love me like I'm a pet puppy? And me, what about me? Do I return her love like I'm a pet puppy? Nikki lay staring at the ceiling through narrowed eyes. Why would she prefer me to Tubs? Why would she risk her marriage, her career, her entire life on someone like me? For my sake or for hers? If she loves me like a pet, there'll be no broken hearts, I should be glad. Pets and masters love for life, lucky me.

Rosa returned not only with the prescribed medication, but also with a bottle of massage oil, a bunch of red roses, and a bulging bag of groceries.

She brought yoghurt to Nikki in a small glass bowl, and laughed when Nikki said "yoghurt's for geriatrics."

She arranged the roses in a vase which she placed on the pedestal at Nikki's bedside. "Ah, beautiful," said Nikki. "Buds as shy and tight as virgins. Please photograph them while they're still so fresh and unspoiled—before they discover Original Sin."

"Wow," said Nikki when she saw the photograph. "I see detail in this picture that I didn't see in the real thing."

Rosa uncapped the bottle of massage oil, releasing scent of eucalyptus into the atmosphere.

For some reason, that smell depresses me, thought Nikki.

Crossing her arms, she took hold of the sides of her nightshirt, then pulled it off over her head. She gasped at the suddenness with which the naked air made her flesh shrink; she sank down hurriedly onto the flat of her stomach, clenching her arms to her breasts.

Rosa applied the oil to Nikki's neck and shoulder blades in generous amounts; Nikki felt the effects immediately.

"I feel like I'm being re-booted," she said, smiling. "I can feel the lights popping on inside me. I can feel them changing from red to green."

She turned onto her back, and thanked Rosa in a voice half-hoarsened by flu and emotion. "For being the most incredible . . ."

Rosa's lips—moist, pouting—were poised above hers, close enough for her to feel Rosa's breath on her cheeks.

She allowed her eyes to close, waited for the touch of mouth on mouth, braced herself against the lightning bolt that would shoot through her body when—as—their lips met; the merest of whimpers seeped out through her parted mouth, overflowed into the silence of the room like an excess trail of bodily fluid.

"You need to sleep," said Rosa, speaking into Nikki's mouth, so that Nikki felt rather than heard her words. "I'll be here when you wake up."

On waking up, Nikki found herself thinking, my body's a moulded casing, custom-made to fit around me. But she knew this was an illusion, and not an unfamiliar one, either. At times it seemed to her as if her consciousness and her body were separate beings, with she her consciousness, and her body just a loose wraparound. At other times, she was all-and-only body—raw, live flesh. She smiled and avidly clung to the blankets around her, thinking, if there's life after death, this would be what a corpse would feel like inside its coffin.

The flat was quiet. Apart from now-a-car-then-a-car on Kenilworth Road and the random barking of a dog some way off, nothing was audible to Nikki under her blankets. She strained her ears for clues to

Rosa's presence in the flat, but there were none. I can't hear she's here but I can feel she's here, she said to herself with rising elation.

She rose and put on her gown, and, humming the tune of "You are my sunshine," drifted out of the bedroom on unsteady feet.

"You slept for nine hours," said Rosa, who was seated in front of her laptop at the table in the lounge.

"My god! What is the time, now?"

"You're looking like the proverbial million dollars," said Rosa.

"I'm feeling a lot better. What time is it?"

"Time for your medication, Li'l Babba," said Rosa, rising from her seat and heading for the kitchen. She came back with Nikki's pills in one hand and a glass of water in the other.

"Is that supper I'm smelling?" said Nikki.

"I hope you like lamb cutlets," said Rosa.

"Ah," said Nikki, her eyes lighting up. "They're to die for!"

"With roast potatoes and boiled veggies."

"You're killing me softly with your love!"

When Rosa departed, the moon was high and bright. Nikki lingered in the doorway for a moment, half-expecting the moonlight to warm her face. "Love and madness," she said out loud, and smiled. She gently closed the door, and trotted off to bed knowing she had seldom felt happier in her life. I could of course just enjoy it while it lasts, she thought. It seemed unreal to her that it had happened at all—she and her boss, chalk and cheese. She'd had some weird relationships and encounters in her sex life, but this was something else entirely—never before with a married woman, and she's my boss, too.

Back in bed, she sat upright. I need to smoke, but my throat's raw.

The secret is to keep this casual, too, but how? Her mind conjured the image of the youthful-looking doctor Clive this morning, administering the injection to her buttock, his gentle hands so soft, so close to the vicinity of my . . . a mild shudder ran through her. Did he detect the sudden hunger which his close presence aroused? The difference between me and Rosa; she would never dream of going to bed with him, but me—nymphomaniac that I am—I want to devour anything that walks.

She snatched up the pack of cigarettes lying alongside her medication on the bedside table, and scrabbled a cigarette from it, causing bits of tobacco to float onto her lap; she lit the cigarette, and drew deeply, watching how the tip glowed like an active USB drive.

Blake was the last. Like the yummy Dr Clive, Blake, too, had a moustache, one that tickled, especially across the navel. He had smiled so emphatically when he saw her stroll into *Monsters* that his moustache seemed to smile, too.

At *Monsters*, the usual crowd—Maury in his resplendent leather jacket, Avril whose miniskirt was perhaps a touch too mini, attorney Angie van der Poel, and good old sexy Blake. Hell, if I weren't all full of flu right now, I'd get dressed and head straight for *Monsters*.

How long ago was it? Three weeks, maybe? She recalled with a smile how she had wondered, "so, who's it going to be tonight—Bryan? Avril? Probably Blake."

She recalled how she and Blake had left the joint at midnight; how they had strewn their clothes all over the bedroom floor; how loudly he snored afterwards, how his footsteps faded into the night when he left, how many empty beer cans needed to be cleared away next morning.

She put on a gown and made herself a mug of coffee, and sat sipping it in bed. She recalled a remark she had overheard her mother making to her father about an old whore in Langebaan all those years ago: "Sy's vrot genaai." Screwed rotten.

Shortly after 7 a.m. next morning, a text message came through. *How'd you sleep? How're you feeling this morning?*

71

Great, was Nikki's reply. *Might get up and get dressed today.*
Don't you dare. Will be there shortly. With breakfast.

Her knee-joints made a light snapping sound when she swivelled out of bed. There was a stiffness in her neck, but nothing serious, she thought—no doubt a lingering effect of the medication. In the bathroom, she stared hard into the mirror, and was surprised at how much she was beginning to resemble her mother.

She splashed cold water over her face and hair, and towelled vigorously.

How long ago it seems when she was just a young student in Cape Town, and her parents had arrived at her door, all the way from Langebaan, unannounced. She could smile about it now. "To come see how our little girl is faring," had said her mother—my goodness, what have you done to your hair? Both parents were wide-eyed at the sight of her blazing scarlet bush. They were also wide-eyed at "how squalid this flat is, my child—and this neighbourhood, is it safe?" Her mother thought she had lost too much weight in too short a time—was she smoking? Drinking? Getting enough sleep? Breakfast was very important, it was always easy to see (especially in the eyes and the complexion) when someone was neglecting breakfast. Her mother hoped that she was managing her finances well, that she wasn't throwing her money about on whims and fancies, and making spur-of-the-moment decisions. "When last have you looked at yourself in the mirror, Nikki—have you seen what you look like? Your clothes are really shabby my child. I don't want to come here and do nothing but criticize, but clearly, you've gone one way since leaving home."

As she dressed and tidied the room, Nikki recalled how, throughout, her father had maintained this grim, angry silence, nodding along while his wife spoke, and studiously avoiding eye-contact with his daughter. All he'd said was, "And I don't suppose you've been to church at all since you're living here, right?" It was a massive rebuke, filled with self-loathing, Nikki had thought. He blames himself for everything.

Rosa arrived with two steaming omelettes in Styrofoam packs.

"Good to see you're looking good," she said, putting the food down. She placed her hands on Nikki's shoulders, and gently squeezed. They embraced. Their lips touched, the touch lingered. Each felt the other's breath on her face, in light warm uneven spurts. In the moment, only the rustling of their clothes was audible to their ears, a rustling as fervent as their trapped ardour. They sighed then giggled.

"Let's not let the food get cold," said Rosa in a whisper. They sat huddled at the little kitchen table, not speaking, but exchanging glances and giggling, and searching out each other's knees under the table. Sunlight streamed in through the window, glinting off their faces and cutlery. And Rosa found herself marvelling at how much joy there can be in simple pleasures.

Nikki put her knife and fork down. "I don't know, but suddenly I feel funny . . . my head's started spinning . . . maybe I should lie down for a moment . . ." She rose unsteadily. "Maybe the mushrooms? Maybe I didn't chew them enough." She tried to smile. "Be right back . . . just going to the bathroom."

Rosa watched the frail body as it warily crossed the floor . . . how bony the body was, how caved-in the buttocks looked. She's definitely not fully recovered, yet.

She heard the lock of the bathroom-door click into place, and stiffened. Now why would she lock the door?

For Nikki, vomiting was a commonplace—"It goes with the territory," she'd often joked, "an occupational hazard for one with my lifestyle." And yet, horrendous as every bout of vomiting was, she'd never thought of changing her lifestyle. Now, as she hung over the lavatory bowl in the cold cramped bathroom she made a solemn promise to herself: never to binge again, to discover what moderation was, and to programme that into her DNA. Her knees should have felt comfortable on the toilet-mat, yet they felt bony and hard and painful. Her whole body felt bony and hard and painful. She shivered. Her bum was at a higher level than her face, which was streaming from eyes and nose and mouth into the insensate lavatory bowl. And roiling about in there, just centimetres below her nose, was the reeking, multicoloured mush that her spasms and lurchings had hauled up out of her. All she could do was to hang-in-there-kiddo, and wait for the next bout, and to prayer for an end to it all. And the next bout—and the next and the next and the next—came in uninterrupted avalanches that left her panting and close to losing consciousness.

At the door, Rosa was frantic. "Nikki, are you alright in there?"

Breathe slow, breath deep, breathe slow, breathe deep . . . Ah, Christ—the throbbing in her temples, the weight on her cranium and eyebrows. Once, someone had said to her, try not to think of a pink elephant. Now she was telling herself, don't think about vomit, don't think about stink fish, don't think about decaying flesh, don't think, don't think, don't think.

"Nikki . . . Unlock the door . . . Are you OK? What's happening in there?"

"I'm OK," said Nikki, and was astonished at how feeble her voice sounded. She tried again. "Don't worry 'bout me, Rosa . . . I'm OK . . . I'll be out soon."

"Nikki, please let me in. If you don't, I'm going to break the fucking door down. I'm going to call the doctor, you don't sound good."

"I'm OK, Rosa . . . Really I am . . . Just a bit of queasiness . . . I'll be alright . . . Really." Incredible. One minute you're happy, having fun, doing your thing . . . the next, you're virtually at death's door. What could account for such abrupt swings?

Nikki recognised the symptoms of recovery—the receding headache, the clearing vision, the calmed-down stomach. Ah . . . She rose to her feet. "I'm fine, Rosa," she shouted, and was pleased that the strength had returned to her voice. "I'll be out soon . . . just as soon as I've cleaned up this mess."

When the bathroom door opened, Rosa was relieved to see the smile on Nikki's face. "Witch," she said. "You had me *damn*-worried."

"Battered but victorious," Nikki chuckled. She had a large white towel draped over her upper body, that Rosa said made her look like a mobile polling booth. She laughed as she strolled back towards the breakfast table. Her hair had been brushed straight back off her face, and she smelled of toothpaste. "I need a smoke," she said. "Sorry about all the drama."

Ten minutes later, she was back in the bathroom, back on her knees, back over the lavatory bowl.

Rosa called Clive, who arrived within half an hour, wearing a baggy blue jeans—faded at the rump and knees—and Adidas running shoes. His mobile phone was in a black leather pouch clipped to his belt. Surprisingly for Nikki, he smelled of cigarette smoke. His arrival brought an immediate sense of calm to her, and she was relieved to have avoided another vomiting attack while awaiting his arrival.

He perched himself at the edge of the bed where Nikki lay, and felt for his stethoscope which dangled and swayed like a referee's whistle. He spoke non-stop as he examined her, questioning her about her symptoms, her past health problems, her family history, her habits, what she had had for breakfast, and interspersing his questions with comments about how the weather was changing. He measured Nikki's temperature, her pulse rate and her blood pressure. He checked her throat, her tongue, her teeth. He tested a urine sample and a blood sample, and checked for scars and bruises on her body. He estimated her height and weight and checked his estimate with her. He checked her eyes, her nose, her ears. Lastly, he checked for organ enlargements.

When he was done, he sat back and looked her in the eye and said, "Congratulations, young lady. You're pregnant."

On the table at Nikki's bedside stood a cold, empty teacup, having been drained of its contents one sip at a time by a recalcitrant Nikki some ten minutes ago. After Clive's departure, Rosa and Nikki had embraced standing on the lounge floor, and had wept silently onto each other's shoulder, not knowing why, just feeling the need to. Then, still silently, but with smiling eyes, they had stripped down to their necklaces and gotten into bed, where they lay on their backs, each immersed in her own thoughts.

Once, Rosa leaned over to Nikki, her shadow preceding her. Nikki's lips instinctively parted, and Rosa snappily kissed her on the mouth, then sank back into her pillow. They lay listening to the barely-perceptible noises in the flat—the fridge, the clock, a fly buzzing. Nikki allowed most of her cigarette to waste away in the ashtray. She felt a welcome lassitude pervade her body, and hoped it could be prolonged—thoughts of Dingus always helped. Her mind easily conjured the well-worn image of herself as a six- year-old beach waif running circles on the Langebaan sea-sand, with Dingus—shaggy and clumsy—loping alongside her, always coming close to bumping her over, always somehow just missing, always churning up the sand around them, always trying to outsprint her and succeeding. The day Dingus died . . . the day Dingus died. Nikki felt the faintest prickling of teardrops behind her closed eyelids, and tried to wish them away but knowing the spell was broken. She took a deep breath that caused her ribcage to expand, and that caused the bedding beneath her to rustle. The lassitude began to return, and she tried to clear her mind of all thought, to suspend herself between nothing and nothing. At some point, she felt, settling over her navel, the flat of Rosa's hand, and a special warmness permeated her body. She lay her own hand over Rosa's and pressed with the gentleness of forming-dew. It occurred to her that the sweetness that was lingering in her mouth was the saliva from Rosa's brief kiss. She felt a fleeting tingle on her teeth, and thought about her vomiting episode that morning. It was as if the little something that had begun to form inside her had attempted a breakout. Why won't it try again? Pregnant was never a word she would have thought to use in relation to herself.

She spoke, aiming her words at the ceiling. "So that's what this vomiting was all about." Her voice was low, a sweet whisper. "This high drama," she said. "Nothing more than morning sickness, would you believe it." She turned and faced Rosa, who was still lying on her back, her eyes closed but fluttering just perceptibly. "Given the angst I put us both through" said Nikki, "I would rather have hoped the cause would have been something worthier—cancer, maybe, or heart failure. Bilharzia, perhaps. But no, it turns out to be mere morning sickness. Which means, yes, a stupid thing happened to me a month or so back. I must have been totally sozzled to have allowed it to happen; A hundred times I've told myself I'm in control, it will never happen, and then the hundred-and-first time . . ."

A smile appeared on Rosa's face, and for a moment her eyelids fluttered more rapidly. Nikki smiled. She rolled onto her stomach, and held her face close to Rosa's. "How pregnant am I?" she asked. "Certainly not *half*-pregnant. Ten percent? If morning sickness starts a month-or-so after conception, then I'm one-ninth pregnant—which *is* just about ten percent." A giggle escaped Rosa's lips.

"So, what's inside me?" said Nikki. "How much of the little scamp already exists? How *formed* is he or she? Maybe he's nothing more than a teaspoonful of blood as yet, or the tiniest bit of skin-and-bone. Perhaps I even vomited him up this morning. He's probably no more than a few stray atoms circling each other. I'm sure if I sneezed he'd go flying. He or she, or for that matter, *they*—after all, why shouldn't I be carrying twins, or even triplets. Multiples of myself."

Rosa burst into laughter. "Three little jumjills," she said.

"Yep," said Nikki, laughing, too. "All with blinding red hair."

"A whole veld-fire of red hair. Three burning bushes."

"We'll set the world on fire."

Rosa sat up abruptly, and with a huge beaming smile said to Nikki, "Can you believe it, you're going to be a mother. A mother! If you're going to be the mother, then I'm going to be the father! You are carrying *our* child. Congratulations and jubilations!

"For some crazy, dumb reason," said Nikki, as if to herself, "I feel— you'll never guess it—*proud!*" She looked at Rosa with mock incredulity. "Can you believe it? Proud! I have this impulse to want to phone my mother and father, as if they were still alive and living in Langebaan." She sank back onto her back among the pillows. "Hullo, Mom? It's me, Nikki. Of course, it's you, Nikki, do you think I don't know my own daughter's voice? Mom, you'll never guess. I'm going to have a baby . . . Mom? Are you there? Yes, Mom, I'm pregnant. Hold on . . . *Ohmygod, James, guess what? Nikki's pregnant . . . she's going to*—Nikki, are you sure? When did it happen? How? Are you OK, did you see a doctor? I'm fine, Mom, I'm fine. And Mom, I'm coming home soon, to see you and Dad, soon-soon—bye, bye."

"Whenever I'm happy," said Nikki, a tremulousness in her voice, "I think of sad things, and want to cry, and the saddest thing for me is Chris, the way he died . . . and then my other brother, Victor, just upping-and-leaving to go'n live in Perth and never making contact with us ever again . . . I always see both as really vicious acts—*acts of wanton violence* as the newspapers would've put it—aimed against us—my parents and me, and I wonder why anyone would hate us so much to want to be that vicious towards us . . . Really scary."

There was a brief silence. Then Rosa spoke. "Their first grandchild, too, *nogal!*" she said, a smile in her voice. And they both said together, "*They would have been so proud*," and laughed together.

"I could never have dreamed any of this," she said out loud. "It's as if a wave from out of nowhere has come and knocked me off my feet, and dragged me out to sea." For an instant, she saw Chris's wet, lifeless body, the jeans all stiff and salty. "And it's like I still haven't recovered my balance. And now this baby. Oh, my mother would have been so proud, Rosa! I'm sure of it."

Nikki restrained a whoop. One of the many small aches in her heart was one that she reserved for her parents. Things could have been so different, so easily otherwise, and the Addos could have been so much happier as a family. Why did Chris suicide himself? Why did Victor take flight? Now Nikki felt the need to restrain the tears that she felt welling up. "Hell, I could use a cigarette," she said, "but I won't, I mustn't, not now that I'm pregnant." She gently massaged her belly, and half expected to feel a kick whispering back against her hand. The idea made her smile. She wondered at what age the kicking would start. She wondered again how her mother would really have reacted to the news—she was sure Dingus would have loved the kid. Perhaps she should take one of the pills Dr Clive had prescribed, and just go into a deep sleep—sign out for a while, it was all too much for her.

Next Saturday morning, Rosa arrived at Nikki's place before seven, in cold, drizzly weather, and they drove through to the Waterfront, where the breeze was heavy with salt. The restaurant they chose for breakfast had large windows overlooking the sea. Inside, it felt warm—"like there's a log fire burning," said Rosa, as they took their seats. Outside, the sea was covered in an anaemic mist, through which the rising sun looked like a rusty coin.

A smiley-faced waiter appeared at their table. He had bushy eyebrows and a gold stud in his left ear. His moustache was so thin it might have been penciled on. He offered each of them a copy of the menu, printed out on large tablet-like posters.

The place was filling up quickly. Rosa found the familiar restaurant noises most agreeable—chattering voices, tinkling glass- and silverware, shuffling feet, chairs scraping—there was something *warm* about the gentle bustle.

"Rosa, I need to tell you this," said Nikki. "I lay awake for a long time, last night. Thinking." A dreaminess had suddenly come to Nikki's eyes, and Rosa wondered if a mood-swing was imminent. "I need to turn over a new leaf," said Nikki. "Now that I'm going to be a mother I need to behave like a mother." She twisted in her seat. "And I need you to help me, Rosa. I need you to make me a solemn promise." She placed both elbows on the table, and held the fist of her right hand in the clench of her left. Her eyes blazed. "I need you to promise me that you will never leave Tubs, Rosa, no matter what."

"Ooh," said Rosa. "You don't beat about the bush, do you?" She tried to force a chuckle.

"I'm dead-serious, Rosa. You must promise me."

"Wow, the girl sure does sound serious," said Rosa, managing a genuine chuckle. "So! What brings this on?"

"Oh, I knew it, I knew it," said Nikki. "I was rehearsing all night how I'd start off this conversation, and guess what?—yes! it comes out all wrong!" She mock-slapped her cheeks.

Rosa laughed. "So, d'you want to start again, then?"

People were coming and going. There was an ebb and flow to the buzz. At times the sound from the TV sets which were mounted in each corner of the room was audible, and automatically attracted people's eyes to the screens. Conversations adjusted themselves to the general noise-level, always pulling back to a pitch at which, beyond their own tables, individual conversations were lost in the buzz.

The waiter returned with their order—blueberry muffins, a fresh glass of orange juice for Nikki, and for Rosa, a steaming latté.

"I demand that you promise me, Rosa. I'm serious. You have to promise me."

Rosa felt a sudden surge of annoyance. Her eyes dilated. She stared hard at Nikki. "You know that's not a promise I can make." She surprised herself by the harshness of her tone.

"Then we've got a problem," came the counter from Nikki, who felt a slow stiffening of her neck muscles.

"Let's say it's a promise I can make but might not be able to keep," said Rosa, attempting a smile. "There are forces bigger than me . . . and that is not meant facetiously."

"You do realise then that I am left with no option but to . . . Now I'm beginning to sound melodramatic. But how else to say it? It's going to be impossible for me to carry on if I'm going to be the cause of—"

"It might already be too late."

"Please don't say that."

Rosa's eyes turned to the windows, through which the sluggish sea was barely visible.

"You say you spent hours rehearsing your speech, Nikki . . . yet the best you can come up with is, *don't leave Tubs, Rosa.*"

"I'd be keen to hear a better solution, if there's one."

"There's no win-win in the kind of game we're playing here. Someone wins, someone loses. If I decide to stay with Tubs, then you and I—the both of us—we lose. It's as simple as that, and, moreover, I'm not sure that Tubs wins. Just think, if I gave you up and stayed with him, he'd have an unbearable witch for a wife. The marriage would sooner or later crack up. On the other hand, if I stayed with him but continued with you, do you suppose the marriage would then survive—I think in the circumstances, both relationships would suffer. It would actually be a worse solution. Nope . . . there's only one way with this."

"As much as I want to spend my life with you, Rosa, as much as I'd like you to be my baby's co-parent with me, there's no way it can be at the expense of your marriage. No way."

"Impasse," said Rosa. "That's what we've got, here. An impasse." She saw a defiance in Nikki's eyes that looked like a last stand.

"Maybe we should try polyamory," said Nikki, blinking rapidly.

"Poly-what?"

"Polyamory—a polyamorous relationship is one where there are more than just two partners—and it's fully consensual."

"You mean one where there are three or more spouses in the same marriage?"

"Yep, that's it, pretty much."

"Polyamory. That's a joke, right? You can't seriously think that you, me and Tubs in a three-way marriage would work."

"Who knows? Maybe it could . . ."

"Snakes alive. You're not joking."

"We wouldn't be the first. I don't know if it's legal anywhere, or if it is, what the specifics are, but in places like the UK and the US it's openly practiced by consenting threesomes and even in some cases, foursomes."

"Not only would Tubs be scandalised at the thought of sharing me with anyone, let alone with a young white chick!—besides, there is no way I'd want to share you—my young white chick—with him or with anyone else. So that pretty much settles that."

"Well, I suppose even if somehow we were able to make it work, it would be impossible in a place like Cape Town or anywhere else in South Africa for that matter. We'd have to go and practice our polyamory elsewhere on the planet." She attempted a smile, but her eyes refused to light up.

"We'd never be able to make it work, period. It's an outrageous notion. I myself wouldn't tolerate it, never mind the rest of South Africa. End-of-story."

"So, where does that leave us? We're back to square-one, then, aren't we?"

"Oh, yes you bet—we're back to square one with a vengeance."

They were silent for a moment. Nikki was mildly alarmed at Rosa's reaction—wow. First time I see her actually show some anger; she looks genuinely the *moer*-in, thought Nikki, feeling faintly flattered. She loves me, yeah, yeah, yeah.

"It's a bizarre thought," said Rosa. "I can see two people and a dog working out, or two people and their child, or two people and an aging parent . . . Always two people and a tag-on of any number of others . . . I can even see three or four people in a very close relationship with one another, but not in a marriage-relationship. Not if one of them is me, anyway. Any marriage that I'm in is a marriage of two people."

Although she spoke with emphasis, she didn't raise her voice above the general hubbub. The waiter returned. Rosa ordered another latté, and Nikki said, "Latté for me, as well, please."

Nikki sat back. She placed both hands over her belly and tried to imagine she was feeling a fully-formed foetus; she thought she heard a gurgling-sound coming from the region of her navel; it induced a brief elation. In a few short months, my baby will be borne. What else matters? Her impulse was to say to Rosa, *Not as open-minded as we thought we were, are we?* but her instinct told her it would come out wrong. Instead, she said as gently as she could, "Perhaps it's a mistake for us to reduce the problem to a choice between alternatives. I'd be more than happy with the following scenario: You stay married to Tubs and live a normal life with him—including having kids with him, and on the side you have a secret thing going with me. I'll be your mistress."

"My tag-on? In other words, nothing changes?"

"Yes, but the difference is we'd be reconciled to it . . . we'd have accept it and we would make it work."

"You're proposing that I or we go on cheating Tubs for life . . . that I continue to play the good wife . . . continue conning him into believing I'm the good wife and even become the mother of his children—all while sleeping with you on the side. My relationship with you is thus forever to be a nefarious, shadowy affair, always hidden from the eyes of the world . . . something shameful, disgusting. Forever we're obliged to be seeking creative and fail-proof ways to avoid detection by a disapproving world, to live like creatures of the night, slithering and sliding from under one rock to under another . . . "

"Well! I wouldn't put it quite like that . . . "

"It won't work, Nikki. It won't work."

Outside a cruise ship glided by, its lights soggy-looking in the morning mist. From where they sat, they could make out the shapes of people on the bridge and decks, and noticed how deeply the bow dipped in its forward thrust. They were also able to discern the odd bleak flash coming from the decks, which they guessed were from the cameras of tourists taking pictures.

Their drinks arrived, and they sipped in silence. When they spoke, they restricted themselves to small-talk and jokes. From time to time there was eye-contact with other patrons, and each time they made sure to brighten their smiles and to offer or return a friendly greeting.

Out in the open, on their way to their car, the weather kept them bent over; it muffled their voices and nagged away at their ears; the coldness pressed into their cheeks and eyes; within minutes they were soaked and shivering. They walked arm-in-arm, moving slowly, unsteadily, taking care not to impede the passage of other pedestrians. They kept their faces close, and snatched peeps into each other's eyes. This would make them laugh and want to kiss, but it was awkward, and their clumsy attempts made them laugh more.

Back at Nikki's flat they rushed to the bedroom where they stripped down to their necklaces. In the shower, their breathing came in short rapid bursts, eliciting animal noises from their throats. Under the impetus of the shower's conical veil, mouth sought mouth; water and saliva intermingled, and their bodies were slippery and elusive to the touch. They passed back and forth a bottle of lavender-smelling shower gel and squeezed its contents over breasts and shoulders, and watched the profusion of suds and steam wash-and-swirl. The intensity of the lavender-scent in their nostrils had a smothering effect, lacing their ecstasy with panic. Rosa tried to talk, tried to utter known words into the space beyond herself, and half-laughed when the words wouldn't form. She reached out and clutched Nikki's wet red head and drew it to her left breast, where she held it for Nikki's eager lips and tongue. In her head, bokmakieries were singing.

PART TWO

Chapter Six

The forecast was for a low of 13 degrees and a high of 22. Outside, the wind was gusting, at times creating noise, at times creating music. Rosa listened to what sounded like a loose roof tile clattering in time to the rattling of a window frame. It would be a cold morning, she told herself. She would have to wear a coat to work today.

Her collar was up around her ears when she drove out her driveway into the dark, her headlamps keeping a yellow zone of daylight in her sights. Five thirty, but the sky over Pinelands was still far more black than blue. Along Forest Drive the streetlights were bright points that illuminated only their own bases. The odd car whisked by, each time bringing to her a sense of community. Up ahead, the dark bulk of the mountain was visible on the city's western fringe. Covering the top of the mountain was a dense cloud mass that seemed to be clinging to it as a tissue-paper would cling to an inhaling nostril. Rosa smiled. In Cape Town, everything resists the wind. Cape Town felt fresh to her—so different from maybe London or Beijing, say. What a contrast. Despite there being thousands of Capetonians in London on any given day, she could live there freely—uninhibitedly—she and Nikki, without any serious risk of being recognised on the streets. But in Cape Town? Not a chance. In Cape Town everything had to be furtive. Yet, Cape Town was home, a more natural setting for her to live her life—that is, for her and Nikki to live their lives together as—yes, lovers.

At a red streetlight, she hastily tapped out a text message to Nikki. *Luv you.* Before the lights changed, a text came back, *luv u2.* How do I not elope with her? thought Rosa, her eyes moistening.

The lights changed to green, and she set the vehicle gliding forward. Her thoughts turned to Tubs as they so often did when they were preoccupied with Nikki. She imagined she could still feel the warmth of his flesh against hers—hard, hairy, horny and constantly rhythmic. Last night had been a night to remember. She couldn't recall when sex with him had felt that good. At your worst, she had said to him, you're world-class. "You obviously have your national colours in this sport," she had added, and he had chuckled with delighted. She wished she were back in bed with him right now.

As she took the curved off ramp to the N2 heading west, a hint of sunrise glinted briefly off her rearview mirror. She merged into the sparse N2 traffic and settled back for the last twenty minutes of her trip, her thoughts turning to work, as they usually did when she got to this stretch of the road.

I need you to promise me that you will never leave Tubs, Rosa, no matter what.

It's a promise I can make but cannot guarantee I'd keep.

Well then, how about polyamory?

Indeed! Since the first mention of the word, Rosa had thought non-stop about polyamory as a serious option but just couldn't see it working. She wondered: when Nikki raised the idea of polyamory, she had Tubs in mind as one of the threesome, but was her notion restricted to a threesome? Even after she and I started getting serious, she continued to bed-it down with other partners . . . has this changed, I wonder? Rosa felt a sudden coldness. She hunched her shoulders so that her coat collar curved more closely around her ears. Ahead of her, the hard face of the mountain was growing larger and clearer. She could see the strength of the wind in how much the firs on the slope of the mountain bent, and could feel it in the trembling of her hands on the steering wheel.

It was close to 6 a.m. when she came off the highway and cruised into Adderley Street, approaching the city centre from the Foreshore-end. Abruptly, as it always did, the city centre closed in on her, obscuring her view of the mountain and reducing the amount of sky still visible to her. It was much brighter here than on the open road, what with the still-illuminated streetlights and the lights from the office buildings all around. The wind was tearing into the few pedestrians out there, but inside her tightly-sealed cab, she felt it as no more than a vague sense of foreboding.

A few months ago I jumped into bed with a girl for the sheer hell of it—playful naughtiness, nothing worse than watching a porn movie in secret with a pal. How did it morph into this life-transforming dilemma?

She pulled into Lumina's deserted parking garage where the sense of night still clung with medieval insistence.

Did she love Tubs? Certainly not the way she loved Nikki. As she made her way to the lift, she Googled the word love on her cellphone. *A profoundly tender, passionate affection for another person; a feeling of warm personal attachment or deep affection, as for a parent, child or friend; sexual passion or desire.*

Unhelpful.

The lift was warm and bright. I love Tubs enormously and value my marriage to him. It would be devastating to suddenly lose him. I love my job. If I were to suddenly lose it, it would certainly destabilise my life and cause me enormous trauma, at least in the short term. I love my house and can't imagine having to move . . . I love my car like a pet and would be very unhappy to lose it, too . . . In fact, my whole bourgeois lifestyle, I've got to admit it, I love it . . .

But my father. The mere thought of losing my father saddens me as if I had actually already just lost him. I would be inconsolable. And

Nikki. If I were to lose Nikki my own life would cease to have any meaning. My mother, my father, my Nikki, my all.

She exited the lift with a purposeful stride, her footsteps beating a rapid, even rhythm on the laminated floor. She forced herself to focus on work. Must not let personal issues crowd out work and career issues. The metal nameplate on her office door shone brightly. Just a matter of time, she thought, and the title on my nameplate changes to CEO.

Life stabilised in a glorious cycle—Nikki, Tubs, Dad, work. Nikki, Tubs, Dad, work. Nikki, Tubs, Dad, work. All her priorities in place. Nikki was now no longer just Nikki. Nikki was now Nikki the mother who would soon be birthing *our* child. Constant fussing needed, a mental checklist for the great day when it comes. Tubs continued to be Tubs, the caring, obeisant husband who couldn't believe his luck to be married to a goddess. Dad, my dad, my link to my pre-life. As always, brooding, anxious, worried that I was too delicate, but constantly amazed at how I was making my way in this late-capitalist world. And work, Lumina! The site of the blossoming career of Rosa Lethlabe, soon-to-be CEO.

But I'm not so naïve as to expect that it could simply continue like this, on and on without interruption.

The interruption came some four months later.

Chapter Seven

My dear, dear Rosa

Once upon a time, there were two young chicks who were madly in love with each other. Chick One was a rich, bright and pretty chick, and had a very important job, while Chick Two was just your ordinary everyday working-class chick. Nevertheless, they loved each other very much (sigh) and dreamed of a future together (sigh) . . . but the gods conspired against them (alas), and their fairytale came to an abrupt halt.

Moral of the story: when an irresistible force (e.g. a marriage) meets an immovable object (e.g. a pregnancy) you have two losers: the married chick and the pregnant chick.

My dear, dear Rosa

We've been over this ground so many times before, what can I say that's new? I keep repeating the same things over and over again in the hope that some magical solution will pop up out of nowhere.

I'm trying to understand why I would rather die than be responsible for wrecking your marriage, and why this was not the case till I discovered I was pregnant—that there were now two hearts beating inside my single body. (Of course, it might already be too late—I pray-and-pray-and-pray that this is not so.)

Perhaps it's for the better that we call it quits and do so now . . . they say you can't change the past, that even God Almighty in all His glory can't change the past . . . but maybe we can . . . if the past is something that exists in our memories, then perhaps we can change the way we remember things.

So, let's just remember out thing as a brief episode—a moment of heavenly bliss.

As you'll no doubt have noticed, I've decided to disappear off the scene completely. (You will admire the meticulousness of my planning—I do believe I've made myself totally untraceable.) My apologies for the suddenness of it; I know it will cause you a degree of inconvenience, Boss, since you'll now be minus an analyst for a while. But this was the only way I could do it.

One way of looking at this is, "the bitch dumped me." Another way is, "this is the only way to ensure long-term happiness for both of us—(bitch knows what she's doing.)."

Hard to say where-to from here, except that much time needs to elapse. I'd like to believe that we'll meet up again in the (distant) future and live happily ever after, but no, I've got a whole lot of doubt. There are just too many variables. I once stopped smoking for three years, then foolishly took a puff again, and that one puff was my undoing, I was back to smoking, and with a vengeance, making up for lost time—a dumb analogy, I know, but appropriate nonetheless. Which is why my departure has to be (near-) permanent.

My best and earnest good wishes to you in your marriage, your career, your whole future. Crazy thing for me to say, but I'll say it: "I hope we never meet again"—you will understand perfectly!

Yours truly forever
Nikki

It's the flippant tone in so much of the letter that I find hurtful, thought Rosa, after reading the email through twice. More hurtful than the humiliation of being dumped. Chick One and Chick Two—good grief. That has to be the unkindest cut of all . . . so totally out of place; it trivialises the whole relationship from start to finish.

It was late Friday afternoon. Because her windows were on the east side of the building, Rosa could not see the setting sun. But she could imagine it. She knew it was windy out, so she guessed that Table Mountain in the west would be covering over with fast-rushing cloud into which the sun would be descending, perhaps *plunging,* as if on a suicide mission. Outside her window, she could see the shadows of buildings on other buildings stretching away toward the sea. She could hear that the traffic in the streets below had picked up—it was Friday afternoon, everybody wanted to get home. Since three o'clock already, there'd been a steady flow of staff members at her door to say cheerio, enjoy your weekend.

So, is this really *The End,* then—the big inevitable break-up, the part where the heroine's supposed to cry inconsolably? No baby, forgeddit. I aint dat kinda heroine.

Rosa's eyes narrowed. She had read the letter through with a sense of incredulity. This flippancy . . . was it mere childishness, or was it Nikki's way of covering—maybe denying—the real pain she was feeling? I'd so like to believe *that,* thought Rosa, but I can't chuck this gnawing damn certainty that she's simply been stringing me along all this time. What an idiot I've been. Damn. You don't often do that to Rosa Lethlabe.

Rosa pictured the sun flashing through the clouds—*like a bullet through the church.* Now where did I hear that dumb saying before? Like a bullet through the church. She clenched her fists till they hurt. I am so fucking mad, she said to herself. So fucking, fucking mad.

She grabbed her phone, and speed-dialled Nikki's number, and held her breath. Five rings, then: *The subscriber you have dialled is not available. Please try again later.* Rosa wasn't sure if she was angry or relieved. Outside her window darkness had fallen. The few lights that had gone on in various buildings looked watery through her window.

She's left me with the speed of a bullet through the church. It occurred to Rosa that she'd heard the saying from Nikki when they were up at the Fish Hoek cottage—their relationship had taken off "like a bullet through the church," except that Nikki had used the Afrikaans, *die koeël is deur die kerk*—the deed is done, it cannot be undone.

She returned to the spreadsheet that she'd been working on before Nikki's email came through, but struggled to regain the focus needed to continue working on it. A slow, faint throbbing had begun in her left temple, and she tried to brush it away with her fingernails. She re-opened Nikki's email and read it through slowly, refusing to believe it was real. She picked up her cellphone and began to scroll through the images of Nikki on it, but discontinued abruptly when she felt the imminence of tears. She made another attempt to get into her spreadsheet, but when the effort proved ineffectual she turned off her computer in a huff, and began to tidy her desk.

Nikki had been absent from work since Wednesday. *Not feeling well today*, had read her text message to Rosa on Wednesday morning. *Going to stay home in bed today. Apologies. See you tomorrow.*

Thursday came—same story: *Sorry, Rosa. Still not good. One more day should do it. See you tomorrow.*

Of course, I should stop at her flat on the way home, thought Rosa as she left the building. But she'll not be home, or she'll not open up, or she'll already have changed addresses. Or there's a chance she's sitting there anxiously waiting for me to call in person—*knowing* I would, expecting me to. No, bad idea. The next move should be hers—and the next and the next.

Traffic flows out of the CBD were smooth and fast, and Rosa was out onto the highway within minutes. She put her foot down and watched the mountain recede in her rearview mirror. She flashed past other vehicles on the highway—zip, zip, zip, and was tempted to accelerate to the car's full potential. Hospital Bend came up. Without slowing, Rosa tightened her grip on the steering wheel and marvelled at the ease with which the car seemed to guide itself through—without wavering, without deviation. She approached the fork that would take her to Nikki's flat or, if she preferred, all the way to Fish Hoek. Furrowing her brow, she chose the Pinelands turn-off instead, and willed her mind to turn to thoughts of braaivleis, red wine and Tubs.

Opposite Rosa's house in Pinelands stood a small pine grove which swayed in rhythm to the wind; it acted as a barrier against the raw fury of the south-easter, which it caught in its web of foliage and reduced to a mere whimper on the surface of the swimming pool in Rosa's backyard. Rosa was reclining at the poolside, and could hear the clash of branches in the grove beyond; she stared vacantly at the even shuddering of the water in the pool, and contrasted this in her mind with the comparative wildness of the open sea at Fish Hoek. From where she lay, the wind in the pines was audible as a great alternation between howling and sobbing, but against her naked arms, it was nothing more than a gentle, almost-sensual stroking.

Tubs's body glistened like a showroom Mercedes Benz. He had swum four lengths of the pool before unsleeving himself from the water and bounding over to the grill where the chops were braai'ing.

"Remember, I like mine underdone," said Rosa. "Red, like my wine, but tender like my . . ." She chuckled and thought, *tender like my Nikki's heartbeat.* So many times had she lain with her ear against Nikki's heartbeat!

"Tender as my wife's sweet kiss," said Tubs, flashing a shy glance at Rosa. He took up a pair of steel tongs and turned the chops over one by one, eliciting mini-shrieks from the coals as they were spattered by the red juice of the meat.

Rosa pictured Nikki at the poolside with her and Tubs—a fleeting image of pale-skinned Nikki cavorting in a loose-fitting bikini. Not polyamory, thought Rosa. It couldn't work, but *polygamy* could—that is, if I were the one with the two spouses.

Tubs stood at the grill with his back to Rosa. He had a towel draped round his midsection. Legs of a Greek god, thought Rosa as she observed the bulging contours of his calves below the towel. His upper body was equally sculpted.

Share him with Nikki? *No way José.*

They spoke little during supper, and what they did say was half-whispered. Rosa was particularly attuned to the little sounds that his presence made—the scraping of his chair on the veranda tiles, his cutlery against his plate, his biting and chewing and slurping . . . she thought she could even hear his perspiration evaporating into the night. He exudes a magic undiminished by my agitated state, she thought. It seems ages ago since I was with Nikki . . . Where is she now?

Where is she now?

"Dad, where is she now?" The child had asked so very many times.

"She's in heaven, Darling," or "Don't worry, Honey, she's in a good place," or "She's thinking of us all the time, Honey," or "I miss her, too, Darling—very much," the father would say. And always a look of sorrow would come into his eyes and always he'd want to (and often did) embrace the child and, maybe, sob along quietly with her.

A sorrow too deep for recovery, a pain which had had to be borne. The pain was all in the timing of that death, and its suddenness. *Why rob a child of its mother? What kind of God are you?*

Now his love for his child changed; now he loved her with a desperate, intense hunger, like madness; and she felt it, felt the anxiety, the insecurity, the craziness of a father who was terrified he might, in the absence-through-death of his better half, screw up this kid's future—and the kid knew it and felt it in every interaction with her father, and at numerous times wished her mother's death had not imposed on her this burden, this irritation of a fussing, worrying, over-protective father. At the end of the day we have so little control over what really matters in this life.

Tubs had taken a chop cutlet between thumb and forefinger. He raised it to his month, unsheathed his splendid rows of sheen-white teeth and bit . . . She could feel the ecstasy of the juices squirting over his tongue and palate. He chewed; his eyes glowed and his lips glistened. She chuckled, and he chuckled too, happy that she was happy. It occurred to her that he was as precious to her as some of the ornaments in her lounge—those stone sculptures she had brought back from a trip to Zimbabwe, the ones that came with their own certificates of authentication. But this wasn't something she could say out loud unless she could get away with making it sound like a joke.

"Is my dad staying in Langa tonight?" she wanted to know.

"Yep," said Tubs. "He's getting involved with some issue that the community is mobilizing around. He'll be speaking at a meeting tonight."

"Why does that make me worry?" she said.

"I know what you mean," said Tubs, systematically running his teeth along the bone and ripping it clean. "I actually asked him if it'd be safe."

She picked up her cellphone and typed out a message to her father. *How's it going? Hope it's OK. Let me know.* She followed this up immediately with a message to Nikki's number. *How's it going Honeybunch? Missing you already. Please come back, all's forgiven. How about we go to Fish Hoek 2morrow? Love u, Love u, Love u.* She pressed the send button before she could have second thoughts.

A message came back from her father. *Fine thanks see you tomorrow.*

OK, one down, one to go.

I need a drink, she thought to herself, feeling suddenly—what? *"melancholic's the word"* she decided. She refilled her glass. The wine had a dull wooden taste. She made it flood her mouth, and it flooded her senses and awakened a mild throbbing in her temples. She waited for the phone to signal a new message, but the phone remained lifeless on the table alongside her plate and wineglass. There came to her the fleeting image of her mother with herself and Nikki in a London coffee shop overlooking the Thames—but the image was as dull as a London winter's day. Inside the imaginary coffee shop a roaring fire and them delighted and gay, a close trio with elbows on the table . . . in the image her mother dressed in black, laughing loud and melodically into the air—so much teeth and energy! And Nikki? Nikki matching my mother's laughter for sheer joy, Nikki, in the image, dull as it was, encapsulated in a mad pink polo neck jersey that resembled a flood of wine in the mouth, and loving both mother and daughter with equal passion.

If I should walk out on this guy, thought Rosa, would he experience the loss as a death? She looked up from her eating, and noticed the strong look of appeal in his eyes. Like her father, he wanted so much of her—she, who in her turn, had wanted so much of her mother. This guy absolutely worships me, she told herself, and I'm not deluded, I feel the power of his adoration as I felt the power of my father's caring—burdensome and intrusive, something it makes me feel I don't deserve but constantly have to be justifying. An imposition. Was this what Nikki felt—an imposition so intolerable the only way out was flight?

"I'm not on my A-game, today, Tubs. You might have picked that up."

Immediately he was out of his seat and at her side, for she had begun to cry.

She relaxed into the stone-hard embrace that his muscles created for her, and felt like a bird on a ledge. This is what I would have given up for Nikki, she thought, as she tried to find comfort against his welcoming chest . . . Just as my mother had given me up—forsaken me—in favour of her own death . . . just as Nikki had given me up—forsaken me—in favour of my own marriage.

Tubs made no attempt to speak. He kept his body submissive and still, only stroking her hair with the tips of his lips, gently-gently, so that she experienced it as the merest of shiftings beneath her scalp. She touched her tongue to his nipple, and got a taste of the lingering pool-water there. Ugh.

"I think I need an early night tonight," she said, rising to her feet. She wished her phone would sound but knew it wouldn't. She kissed Tubs on the forehead. "Thanks," she said, and walked off.

Chapter Eight

When enlarged to fit a 50-inch TV screen, Nikki's face was almost the size of the Mona Lisa. Her eyes and teeth—vivid as gemstones—were what stood out in the picture that started off Rosa's collection. All round the edges of the picture, as if physically stuffed into the frame, were copious tufts of wild red hair, setting off the uniform paleness of Nikki's complexion. Rosa couldn't look at this picture without feeling a twinge of something inside her. She always prolonged her gaze at this one before setting the programme to run automatically, to scroll through all forty-seven pictures that she had stored on what she referred to as her Nikki-flash.

A picture of Nikki shaking the seawater off herself at Fish Hoek beach appeared on the TV screen, her lean, pale body in nothing but a loose-fitting bikini, flashing in the sunlight. Ah, another of my favourites, thought Rosa with a smile. Every time I see that picture it's as if I can feel the water splashing onto my face.

She checked to make sure her cellphone was set on silent, then dropped it down on the couch beside her. The pictures of Nikki had been set to slide-show mode, so at regular five second intervals the next shot would pop up. Rosa smiled a different smile with each picture that appeared, as each one triggered a different happy memory. God, that girl was so good for me, thought Rosa. It's depressing how easily I can lose what matters to me. First my mother, now Nikki . . .

"I saw Kubheka today," said Bill. "We were in the supermarket in Langa, me and the guys, when I spotted him. Yes, Kubheka! Back in the nineteen-

eighties, he was the kingpin responsible for getting us safely in and out of the country."

Kubheka, *Rosa repeated to herself, picturing a hulk in dark glasses.*

"We made fleeting eye contact," Bill continued. "It was hard to know if he recognised us or not, as he gave no indication."

"Why didn't you go up to him, and say hello?" said Rosa.

"I'd heard he was still in the game," said Bill, "so I was worried I might inadvertently compromise him, though I wasn't sure how."

"Are there still revolutionaries needing to be ghosted out of the country?" asked Rosa.

"If so, far fewer than in my day." Bill chuckled. "There's never a shortage of people wishing to escape the law, so I'm guessing he'll never be short of work."

"Did anyone ever get caught?" Rosa wished to know.

"Never. Kubheka was superb."

Chapter Nine

For Rosa, the beach at Langebaan Lagoon was flawless as a pretty face—the kind that, despite yourself, you wanted to gawk at, to kiss.

In a single motion, she unbuckled her seatbelt, slid from the cab and hopped from the gravelled surface of the parking lot onto the undisturbed sea-sand, taking a few steps forward before stripping off her sandals and pressing her bare feet into the sand, still hard from the overnight tide.

There was a light breeze, delicious on her flesh, coming at her in short wafts that made her shirt billow. She arched her back and raised her face to the sky, inhaling deeply.

Tubs left a trail of knotty holes in the sand when he sprinted from the edge of the car park straight into the water; immediately his shorts got all soaked as he splashed about in the shallows. He looked back at Rosa, and his smiling teeth were visible even from that distance. She giggled at the sight of this crazy husband of hers, whose sheer instinctive delight, she noted, was attracting approving grins from several casual onlookers on *this fabulous beach this fabulous morning*. Ah, Nikki. Your hometown, your birthplace. My pilgrimage.

Rosa rolled her jeans up over her knees, and tiptoed across the expanse of sand to the expanse of water to join Tubs where he stood; the thrill of cold sea rushing over her feet induced a muted yelp. *Eina!*

"Oh why didn't I bring my bathing shorts along," said Tubs in a mock-whine tone. He slid to his knees and watched in wide-eyed joy as the water bounced up round his waist. His splashing caused tiny pinpricks of water to pellet into Rosa's arms and face, and she stepped back rapidly, half-dreading half-hoping that in his playful zest he might wet her completely.

"The shops should be opening soon," she said. "You can go'n buy yourself a bather– and be sure to get a towel, too."

She looked back in the direction of the car park. Beyond it could be seen the narrow access road flanked on both sides by an assortment of cafés, restaurants and tiny clothing stores. Her gaze drifted to the flat stretch of beach on her right, where a group of kids and their dog were playing with a large inflated beach-ball. Her heart-rate quickened. Twenty- or thirty-years ago Nikki was a kid running wild on this same beach—Nikki and her dog, Dingus. Rosa stifled a laugh—who names their dog *Dingus*!

They had left Pinelands a little after five this morning, so that they could be on the beach by seven—to witness and be part of daybreak over Langebaan Lagoon. It had not been for nothing, Rosa thought. The sheer freshness of the place was exhilarating. She had had little trouble persuading Tubs to come to Langebaan today, even to get up before sunrise "to avoid the traffic," as she had put it to him. She wasn't surprised that he'd jumped at the idea. It meant filling his Saturday, taking his car "for a decent long spin," and spending the day (with his wife) on some faraway village beach that he'd heard enough about but never before visited. For some weeks now, Rosa'd been relishing the thought of coming to the beach at Langebaan—to *trace Nikki's footsteps in the sand*. It was going to be a fun thing, nothing grave and sombre. She was quite sure she was over her Nikki-addiction, but loved it that she cherished the memories, and hoped it was the same with Nikki, wherever she might be. Initially, Rosa had wanted to drive out on her own—something to which Tubs would probably have assented—but was glad she'd brought him along, for his ever-cheerful demeanour: his company would ensure no risk of her getting all brooding and introspective.

A spurt of laughter escaped from her mouth.

"Huh?" said Tubs, smiling and frowning, which induced more laughter from her.

"How can you name a dog *Dingus*!" she said. "Nikki . . . she's from this place. As a kid she used to run around on this beach with her dog whose name was *Dingus*, of all things.

"Yep, pretty bizarre," said Tubs, "but I've heard worse—like really coarse, obscene words for dogs' names . . ."

"Ooh, I don't want to know, but I can just imagine!"

Out several hundred metres into the Lagoon was a small, deserted-looking island covered in low stout foliage. If there was a bridge to it, thought Rosa, the first thing local young couples would have done would have been to cross it to go'n have a good cuddle in the bushes, there—had Nikki ever done it? For a brief instant the image of herself and Nikki totally naked on that island, and wrapped giggling together in a single blanket flashed through her mind, sending a cold-sea shudder through her chest, making her want to sing and dance, making her tug at her necklace; she was conscious of a low cooing in her throat, soundless—more imagined than real.

The car park was filling up; people were arriving with beach umbrellas, folding chairs, cooler boxes, kite surfers. A little beyond the kids who were playing with their dog and beach ball, a teenage boy was getting set to fly his kite. Made of a supermarket's plastic shopping bags, and shaped like an ice cream cone, it was as tall as he was. The sky was of a uniform blue found usually in computer simulations. Where Tubs and Rosa stood, the water was bubbly and clear, you could see your feet in it. For a time they stood with the sun on their backs, keeping their minds and muscles braced to the pull and push of the tide. They watched, fascinated, as two fishermen, kneeling in the sand close by assembled fishing rods from numerous loose parts which they took from a gunny sack.

After a while, they went on a drifting walk along the waterline, he holding her hand, she submitting to the spirit of his tenderness. "Just like a honeymoon couple," she thought, and positioned her shoulder under his armpit. He put his arm around her shoulder and kissed her lightly on the forehead. Her ear was close to his heartbeat, and she could feel a pulsing sensation in her temple. They walked in silence, aware of the fragile magic of the moment, wanting at all costs to prolong it.

But a group of kids and their dog came galloping up behind them, startling Rosa with the suddenness of their rough laughter, sweeping past with surprising speed and chaos.

"Damn kids," said Tubs indulgently, but Rosa was shaken; she stopped in her tracks for a moment to regain her composure. Her immediate impulse was to scan the group to see if any of those kids looked like she fantasized Nikki might have. There was a girl, maybe six or seven years old—a blondie—who was particularly uproarious, but she was heavy-boned and clumsy, and in the way she laughed and pounded the sand with her heels, seemed less graceful and civilized than even her dog. No, that would not have been Nikki.

They walked on, her hand in his. But now, to Rosa, it felt foolish, somehow.

On their left, abutting the length of that section of beach were rows of suburban houses separated at intervals by tarred streets which ended abruptly against the beach sand. A number of the houses were displaying for-sale signs.

"Perhaps we can take a closer look on our way back," said Rosa.

The beach narrowed to a point beyond which walking was not possible. The point was marked by a line of wooden stakes planted at intervals several metres into the sea. Here the briny scent of the sea was strongest and the colour of the water seemed more vivid; there was a to-ing and fro-ing of seagulls skimming rapid and low. With outstretched wings, one of them settled onto the rim of a municipal notice board and just stood there motionless, allowing the wind to blow symmetrical furrows through its breast feathers. Small heaps of shells and other sea debris lay drying in the crevices between small rocks in the sand; a thin film of insects hovered over them.

Before starting their walk back, Rosa and Tubs sat for a few minutes on a clump of rocks, lolling their feet in the water and idly watched the growing number of kayaks, kite surfers and yachts skimming the narrow channel between the beach and the shrubbed rock island out in the lagoon. It occurred to Rosa that, except for a small number of converted properties, these were all residential rather than holiday cottages along this section of beachfront.

On their stroll back, their eyes were on the cottages that they passed; they noticed that in almost all cases, front doors and windows were wide open and people, all lightly clad, had come out onto their stoeps and front gardens.

"If we want to buy a holiday place out here," said Tubs, "we're probably looking in the wrong part of Langebaan. This here looks like a pretty settled community—it'd feel like an infiltration to move in amongst them."

"Agreed," said Rosa. "I wouldn't want a place in the middle of a residential area, even if that place is right on the beach, as these cottages are. Although, I must say that a number of these places have a quaint old-world charm about them."

"Yep, pretty in a turn-of-the-century sort of way."

"Here's a good example," said Rosa, as they approached a low grey house constructed of raw masonry blocks. "I can just picture the builders—guys with sweaty black backs toiling away in the unrelenting midday sun to erect this place, brick by onerous brick." Rosa was feeling a funny kind of buoyancy, and her remarks were reminding her of Nikki—the flippancy, the giggling, the irrational joy.

"Slave labour without a doubt," said Tubs, trying to stay with her tone. "The same labour that had built the whole of civilization as we know it."

A steep corrugated iron roof overlapped the walls of the house. At evenly-spaced intervals in the walls were three large-paned sash windows, each curtained with a different fabric. There was a covered porch, with an ornate black steel handrail round it. On the porch, on a pew-like bench, sat a woman wearing a floppy white hat, the brim of which was folded up off her forehead. She appeared to be staring at them. Rosa smiled in her direction and was delighted when the woman raised her hand in a greeting and shouted, "Hullo, nice day, isn't it?"

"Oh, we're loving it," said Rosa. "Langebaan is pure magic."

The woman smiled as if she were being personally complimented.

"Are you from Cape Town?" she wanted to know, rising to her feet. "Is this your first visit to our little town?"

A patch of yellowing buffalo lawn separated the house from the waist-high boundary wall where Rosa and Tubs stopped. The woman tiptoed off the shaded stoep into the morning sunlight and slowly approached them at the wall. Her face, for Rosa was reminiscent of the moon—lines, blotches, craters, aged but ageless, majestic, mysterious.

"That's right," said Rosa, "We're from Cape Town, and this is our first visit—can you believe it? A mere hundred-'n-odd kilometres away, and we've never driven out here before."

"It's a shame," said Tubs.

"Well, better late than never," said the woman, smiling. She was clearly of advanced age; it showed in the dryness of her wrinkled face and in her bent, yellow teeth. But her eyes were animated, they sparkled with the same energy of the sea beyond. "I hope you'll be staying a few days," she said.

"Regrettably not," said Rosa. "We just drove out this morning to have a look at the place. We've been meaning to since a friend of ours—Nikki Addo, who used to live here—told us about it."

"Nikki who?" asked the old woman, her eyeballs suddenly shifting to their inner corners so that they appeared to stare down the sides of her nose.

"Nikki Addo."

"Addo?" The old woman cast her gaze upwards. "Yes, I remember the Addos who lived here, but that was some years ago."

Rosa's heart started pounding.

". . . James and Marie. They had some children. One of them was a cute little redheaded girl."

"That's right!" said Rosa, almost shouting. She resisted the impulse to jump up and down on the spot.

"They used to belong to our church," said the old woman, now a faraway look in her eyes. "But they're dead a good many years, now."

"You wouldn't by any chance know what their address was, would you, ma'am?"

"Yes," said the old lady," they used to live here on the beachfront, too. But that was years ago."

Rosa's heart beat so fast it made her eyesight hazy.

"A little further up," the woman said. She leaned over the wall and looked in the direction of the car park. "You have to walk on past the car park . . . you'll see a row of houses on the other side of it, also facing the lagoon, although set further back . . ."

"Oh, thank you, ma'am, thank you," said Rosa, aware that she needed to rein in her excitement to avoid Tubs's questioning looks. "Much appreciated."

"Nice people the Addos were. Did I say they belonged to the same church? Unfortunately, they died many years ago . . ."

"Of course, ma'am," said Rosa, "but we're keen to see the place. We're friends of their daughter, Nikki, as I said—the adorable redhead." Tubs smiled and cast a quick, quizzical glance at Rosa.

The old lady described the Addo house as a white one. "Like many others on that strip of beach," she said. "But the only one with a chimney, I think." She seemed to have become totally self-absorbed. "But whether it's still there . . . so many of the old Langebaan houses have been sold and converted into luxury beach cottages for rich people from Johannesburg—and even from London and America, I've heard."

"Great shame," said Tubs.

Rosa was delighted. She wished she could offer the woman something in appreciation—money perhaps? No, ridiculous. Buy her house? More ridiculous.

She leaned forward over the wall and hugged the woman, whose cheek was coarse against hers. The woman, initially startled, eagerly returned her embrace and told her what a really, really wonderful person she was—and "how good you smell, my dear."

Beyond the car park the beach was wider, more remote. The sand here was more yielding underfoot, harder on the calf muscles. There were fewer people on this part of the beach, mainly strollers and joggers. The teenager with his kite had drifted onto this section of beach; he appeared to be having some difficulty controlling his kite in the air—it cut and banked overhead like a scythe on steroids. Rosa and Tubs eyed it to make sure there was no chance of it swooping down and smashing into them.

They exchanged smiles with the teenager as they passed, the whipping sound of the kite's plastic panels in the wind waxing and waning in their ears.

"We should have stopped for water," said Rosa. This stroll has become a trek." She ran her fingertips across her brow.

"Why don't you rest here on the sand," said Tubs. "Look, it's nice and soft and warm. I'll run back quickly and go'n buy some bottled water—there're quite a few cafés back near the car park."

"Nah, don't be crazy," said Rosa, "I'm sure we're almost there, let's soldier on—but thanks, anyway." She folded her hand into his and gave his fingers a gentle squeeze. His bare arm felt cool and somehow ticklish against hers. For an instant all she was conscious of was his presence. She looked at the sea—the calm, shimmering sea, she said to herself, my Nikki's sea.

"That sea," she said to Tubs. Her voice was barely audible. "If you asked me what eternal looks like, I'd say look at that sea."

"Rosa, you are more incredible than life itself," said Tubs, and she knew he was on the verge of tears. "My dear, dear wife . . ." She put her open mouth up to his and giggled when the walking made their lips jostle.

A narrow footpath twisting between two grassy banks led to a wider starch road that separated the houses from the beach. The grass covering the banks grew in long stalks which wavered rigidly across the footpath, slapping against Rosa's thighs as she passed through. A sudden multiple rustling in the grass made her worry that some scaly low-life would come zipping across her bare feet. "Ouch," she said, quickening her pace. She dashed through the rest of the pathway on tiptoe. Behind her Tubs giggled knowingly. "When I was a boy," he said, "in my village we ate cockroaches and beetles for breakfast." He bent down and scooped something from the path. "Here," he said, holding out his fist to Rosa. "Have a bite."

"You're a disgusting *sweinhund*, she said, grimacing. "Get thee hence!"

She glanced over at the row of houses that came into view beyond the beach. Like those on the other side of the parking area, they had a shabby quaintness that was not her idea of a holiday cottage. These were definitely the working class-fisher family type of housing that she imagined Nikki's family to have occupied in the old days: built like fortresses with heavy brick- and stonework, the typical colonial architecture meant to keep out a hostile world. A number of the houses had iron roofs off which the sun was glancing. "I see no chimney anywhere," said Rosa. "We're on a wild goose chase, for sure."

"Great view of the sea from here, though," said Tubs, looking back across two hundred metres of sea-sand at a sprawling blue-and-white shimmer. "And it's far enough away for these houses to be safe if a tsunami should hit."

She laughed. "Yes, I think I'd rather buy one of *these* places than one over on the other side." She took out her cellphone to photograph the sea and hoped that she would be able to capture a sense of depth in the picture. "But unlike Fish Hoek, it would require quite extensive renovation."

"Get a load of *this*." said Tubs as they began to walk up the starch road. They were nearing a double-story house set in a landscaped garden behind a wrought-iron fence. Its design resembled an eagle with outstretched but lowered wings; its mid-section was propped up by brown marble columns, between which was an elevated patio with braai and swimming pool. In the driveway were parked several luxury vehicles, one of which was an off-road four-by-four with three surfboards tied to its roof rack.

"The inexorable march of gentrification," said Rosa, feeling a tinge of she-knew-not-what. "I'm sure no fewer than two or three of the original cottages had had to be demolished to make way for this . . . this palatiodrome."

"Yep," said Tubs, "probably belongs to a cabinet minister."

"More likely a corporate mogul," said Rosa, thinking of Rob Ferrie. "Cabinet ministers don't earn enough." She wondered if Rob Ferrie owned a place like this. Would she, if she succeeded him, be able to afford a place like this?

The entire sea-facing side of the house—both stories—was glass-fronted. On the upper level adjoining the elevated patio was a shaded balcony on which several people, all in bathing costumes, were milling about. A column of braai smoke was rising from their midst.

"Hey, I'm beginning to feel hungry," said Tubs, patting his stomach. "What's the time?" He looked at his watch. "It's lunch time!"

"Remember, we're looking for a house with a chimney," said Rosa. She quickened her pace.

She tried to picture a young Nikki racing on bare feet down the pathway they'd just come off, down to the beach, her dog Dingus in tow, but could conjure no sense of immediacy. This place did not resemble the image she had in her mind, an image of a small, intimate community living in cramped cottages on the water's edge; rowdy kids swarming all over the beach morning, noon and night; the unbroken sound of children's voices merging with dogs' barking and the squawking of seagulls—a backdrop as constant and natural as the roar of the ocean.

"I wonder if the house we're looking for still exists," she said. "Maybe we're wasting our time."

They passed a house that was partly concealed by two palm trees. A small grey dog emerged at the driveway gate and barked nervously at them. "*Hou jou bek!* Shut up!" said a man who was standing smoking a filter-tipped cigarette in the garden. His head was shaven, and in his right ear he wore a gold ringlet. He had on a vest which exposed tufts of coir-hair protruding from both armpits. A tattoo of the Madonna ran the length of his right forearm; when he raised the cigarette to his mouth, a heavy brass chain slid down from his wrist settling around the Madonna's neck. He smiled at the two passersby, revealing a picket-fence of uneven brown teeth.

Further on, they came on an abandoned fishing boat which lay against a sand dune, its sharply-pointed prow stretching into the air—"like a snout scenting blood" Rosa said of it, smiling. She took out her cellphone to photograph it. "This boat says a lot about Langebaan," she said.

"Decaying or decadent?" asked Tubs.

She hesitated for a moment. "Yeah," she said. "Whatever."

Opposite where the boat lay was a house—"with a chimney!" declared Rosa—the ranch-style garden fence of which was rotted in several places. A drying bottlebrush tree with sagging branches partly obscured their view of the front door, but clearly visible to them from where they stood was a four-panelled bay window facing the road; it was open, and the lace curtain on the inside swayed about gently with the breeze.

"But it's not white," said Tubs. He looked disapprovingly at the peeling green paintwork.

"But maybe it once was," said Rosa.

The chimney sat astride the roof's ridge like a bareback horse rider, its rectangular stack appearing to Rosa as almost coffin-shaped. It had a heavy look—"like any minute it could go crashing down through the roof and into the house," she thought.

Tubs turned to face the sea. He dug his hands into his pockets and straightened his shoulders. "We might as well start walking back," he said. "An ice cold beer would do very nicely right now."

Rosa sat down on the edge of the boat, and although she thought she heard it emit the faintest of squeaks, didn't feel it move under her weight.

"It's for sale," she said, pointing to a small for-sale sign dangling from a wire thread at one end of the fence.

"I wouldn't touch it," said Tubs. "Can you imagine how much work it would take to renovate? Not to mention the cost. You'll have to raze it to the ground and rebuild it from scratch."

Rosa stood up. "I'm going to check," she said. There was a lightness in her step as she crossed the road. "Can't do any harm. Maybe they're giving it away." She laughed in a way that was pleasing to her own ears.

As she passed through the gateway from hard stone road to soft grass she noticed the distinct change in the cadence of her footsteps; she experienced a transition of the heart as she put it to herself—a sudden cleansing intake of air into the lungs—a sense not different from that experienced by the eight-year-old girl at the graveside of her mother as the coffin was being lowered into eternity. Feels like a homecoming she said to herself. And to think, this could be the wrong house, it could all be a ridiculous mistake. I think I'm trying too hard.

She had to bend under a branch of the bottlebrush tree, and as she did so, looked back to see that Tubs had settled himself down on the boat-wreck opposite. Behind him was the radiance of the sea, with the rock island's rough curves against the skyline. She imagined that if Tubs were a smoker, now would be a time that he'd light up. She hesitated at the door before knocking. It was a wooden door in need of a coat of varnish, swollen, bent, twisted, broken in places—a door that would admit all the wrong things; to knock on it would be to threaten it with violence, and she was tempted to simply turn round and leave. But the doormat said *Welcome*. So she knocked and waited. She ruffled the fingers of her left hand across her cellphone; with her right thumb and forefinger she twisted a shirt button; she used one ankle to scrape the sea sand off the other. Good day, sir—why was she expecting a pot-bellied shaven-headed beer-guzzling wife-beater to open the door?—good day, sir, sorry to trouble you, but I see a for-sale notice on the fence, and I was wondering . . .

The muffled footsteps approaching the door from the other side were a telltale sign of carpeting, or at least some kind of floor-matting. Rosa listened to the footsteps as they approached. When they reached the door, there was a brief scrunching of metal against metal: clearly the doorknob needed oiling—it was a brass doorknob, tarnished across its entire surface. The door opened with an agonized groan, the kind that a voice would likely make when a bandage is ripped off a raw wound. It was a woman who opened the door, a woman with blazing red hair. Her pregnancy showed through the flimsy cotton blouse that was irregularly buttoned revealing a belly button that Rosa had often in a previous life joked looked more like a vulva than a navel. Around her neck the woman wore a bead necklace identical to the one Rosa was wearing, and although her complexion was largely describable as sallow, her cheeks matched her hair for redness. In her left arm she held a black-and-white cat which was idly licking her fingers. At the sight of Rosa, the woman's eyeballs froze in their sockets and the plush redness of her cheeks spread into the whole of her face. Her arm fell to her side and the cat dropped nimbly to the floor. She dragged the back of her hand across her forehead, and began a smile. She coughed up the word "Rosa," almost choking on it, and stumbled forward to embrace Rosa.

They stood locked in the embrace, unable to speak, both breathing heavily and struggling to contain tears or laughter. The cat slid about between their legs, leaning itself first against Rosa's shins then against Nikki's. Rosa became aware of Tubs's footsteps on the pathway behind her. She tugged back and looked Nikki in the eyes. "My god," she shrieked. "You're alive! I've finally found you!" then flung herself back into the embrace.

When Tubs came onto the stoep, she took his hand and Nikki's, and thrust them together, shouting, "Tubs! Nikki! Now you must embrace!"

"I must be dreaming," said Nikki. "What a surprise. Rosa, Tubs, I don't believe it." She laughed and crouched down to pick up the cat. "Please do come inside," she said, leading the way across the threshold.

"This is cause for celebration," said Rosa, trying hard to curb the delirium that was threatening to overpower her. "Tubs, we need wine," she shouted. "Wine and food. How about you do us the honour—"

"—of nipping up to the shops and buying some lunch?" he said.

"Yes, and some wine, too."

Rosa flopped down in a grey easy chair; she grinned broadly, keeping her eyes focused on Nikki, trusting that there was sufficient brightness in her smile to hide that her brain was actively registering how shabby the room was, that her teeth were not too exposed in the smile to expose that her attention was divided between delight at seeing Nikki and despair at seeing Nikki's circumstances.

Nikki had sat down on a wooden chair at a rough-hewn table over which was draped a thin yellow cloth. She kept her eyes on her fingers as they re-buttoned her blouse.

Rosa welcomed it when Nikki said, with downcast eyes, "I'm so embarrassed that you found me before I could tidy the place," as it gave her the opportunity to rejoin in a way that would put Nikki at ease, so that Nikki could experience her sudden arrival as cause for celebration rather than alarm. Nikki's trembling embrace on the stoep a minute ago suggested that the sight of Rosa offered less of a threat than the prospect of rescue, and this—rescue—was what Rosa, uneasy about the gentle shifting her weight induced in the springs of the easy chair, then-and-there determined was her mission. Maintaining the brightness of her smile, she rose from the chair, aware that some stickiness tugged lightly at her jeans, and crossed the carpet to where Nikki sat. "I have to hug you again," she said, and was reassured to note how avidly

Nikki responded, rising to meet her, and hugging back with the same trembling hopefulness Rosa had discerned on the stoep.

She put a hand on Nikki's belly and said, "I suppose by now there's plenty of kicking and tapping?"

"Oh yes!" said Nikki. "There's a demanding little character in there. He leaves me in no doubt when he wants anything. He kicks in one way when he wants me to eat, and another when he wants me to play music. I'm amazed how music relaxes him."

"So you've found out he's a he?" said Rosa, her eyes, without moving from Nikki's face nor losing their cordiality, were detecting multiple stains of various sizes and shapes on the surface of the carpet.

"Oh, no! I just keep thinking of him as a he. I actually don't want to know in advance, so I've been picking neutral colours—mainly whites and pastels!" She spoke rapidly and smiled as she spoke, but her eyes continuously shifted about.

They sat again.

On the wall behind Nikki was a framed portrait of a woman that looked to be from the era of the Voortrekkers. Rosa tried to see if the face resembled Nikki's, but her mind was too preoccupied with the suspicion that Nikki, tremulous smile and all, was stone broke as she sat there stroking her belly and her hair by turns. Broke, desperate, destitute, even starving, maybe. Then what about the baby inside her? One question will confirm my fears: are you staying alone, Nikki? Rosa framed it with the same casual politeness unbroken since her arrival. So Nikki! Are you staying alone? Is someone here with you? Who's staying with you?

An unbroken string of words, presaging fearfulness in Rosa of the answer, fearfulness because the answer she had no doubt would precipitate sea-change in their lives. In the interval between the question and its answer, Rosa became aware of the sound of the sea, and thought suddenly of Tubs walking along the surf's edge; no doubt more questions than answers were assailing him right now, but there'd be time to explain.

A dullness came to Nikki's eyes, but the cheeriness remained in her voice. "Oh, I'm alone, but—"

Rosa did a rapid mental appraisal. You're alone, broke, starving and soon to give birth; the house is collapsing around you and your neighbours are rich and snooty and probably don't even know you exist; have you actually come back here to your childhood home to die? Do you really believe you're unloved?

"—there's Plato to keep me company." At the sound of his name, the cat trotted out from under a table and hopped onto Nikki's lap; it settled there in a black-and-white heap staring at Rosa, while Nikki gently stroked its neck.

"When were you going to call, Nikki? My phone's been on morning, noon and night."

"Being alone was good, I think . . ." She pushed the cat off her lap and sat forward, laying her elbows and forearms on the table, and clutching her right hand firmly in her left; she said that being alone gave her a chance to think. To reflect. She kept her eyes intensely on the cross her thumbs made, and said that her cross was her own to bear.

Rosa kept her eyes intensely on Nikki's eyes, waiting for them to rise to meet hers. She wondered how many creatures shared this house with Nikki. There was the cat, so most likely no vermin, but certainly ants, mosquitoes, cockroaches, flies. Maybe termites, bedbugs, spiders, fleas. Pigeons in the rafters, moles in the yard?

Their eyes met.

"It's my child, too," said Rosa, barely audible to herself. She saw a brief flicker in Nikki's eyes, saw the moisture swell up there, copiously run down her cheeks. For a while, neither of them spoke, but retained a softened, unblinking eye-contact.

"Ooh, *snot en trane!*" cried Rosa. "Where're the tissues?"

Nikki laughed. "Oh, I'm sorry, I get so sentimental." She wiped her cheeks with the heels of her hands.

Nikki stood up, hesitated, then went and sat on the couch. "My poor bummy can't sit on a wooden chair for long."

Rosa chuckled. "How long have you been staying here," she asked. "Did you come here straightaway?" She tried to soften her tone. "Why did you need to run away?"

"A fresh start—for the baby's sake," said Nikki, the fingers of her right hand splayed across her belly. "That's what I kept telling myself: a fresh start *for the baby's sake.*" Her eyes were on her belly, and to Rosa, it seemed as if her words, too, were directed at her belly.

The cat, Plato, bounded up and curled itself against Nikki's thigh. She stroked its neck with her left hand. "'Can it work?' I asked myself," said Nikki, looking at the cat, and pausing, as if waiting for it to reply. "Can a fresh start that begins in misery . . . denial . . . abrogation . . . be *fresh*? I had enough sense to know it was a laughable notion, but I just needed to get away, I suppose, and any excuse was a good excuse."

"The first few days were great," said Nikki. Her eyes lit up. "Solitude . . . the constant smell of salt in the air . . . and seeing the sea every morning when I opened the curtains, and constantly hearing its roar . . . I would walk along the beach, along the water's edge, and relish the iciness of the water splashing between my toes. And then come back to this creaky but beloved house—so full of all my Addo spooks!

"I spent hours talking to Plato, here, just as I used to do to Dingus, all those years ago," she said, and gave the cat's neck a gentle squeeze. "It was the most natural thing under the sun to have a conversation with my cat . . . and of course, with the baby, too."

Nikki laughed, and Rosa laughed in unison.

"I told them about you and me." She was silent for a moment, keeping her eyes away from Rosa's.

Rosa felt a sudden itch in several places, and stirred in her seat.

"I told them that I would try to love them as I'd been loved by . . ." her voice trailed away . . . "You."

Rosa rose from her seat. She did not try to restrain the tears that noiselessly flooded up and overflowed. She joined Nikki on the couch, with Plato between them. They fell into each other's arms and sobbed on each other's shoulders without finding it necessary to speak.

When Tubs returned, several decisions had already been made. Nikki would be returning with him and Rosa to Cape Town today; she would be staying with them in their house in Pinelands at least till the baby was born; Rosa would immediately arrange for a gynaecologist and a hospital for the birth, and sometime soon, they would need to think about buying or selling Nikki's place here in Langebaan.

"He'll have no problem with it," is what Rosa had said when Nikki, wide-eyed, enquired. He will go along with the idea. Just watch him jump into action." And she was right, Tubs beamed at Nikki while Rosa was putting it to him. He nodded his head non-stop as Rosa spoke, and appeared to her to be wracking his brain with questions of how he could be an important part of making this work well.

"Once the child is born . . ." said Rosa. "That's the most important thing right now."

"Of course," said Tubs. "There's enough boot space for all your stuff, Nikki. But if we can't manage to pack everything in first time round, I'll be happy to make a return trip to fetch the rest."

The cat, thought Rosa. I hate cats, but I guess it'll have to come along, too. She hoped it had no fleas or tics.

Tubs was going out of his way to assure a tearful thankful Nikki that it would be a pleasure for him for her to come stay at his place in Pinelands.

Rosa allowed her fingers to get all sticky from the highly spiced fried chicken Tubs had brought for lunch, and got fatty prints all over her wineglass. Chicken, wine, coleslaw and bread in her mouth all at the same time, she was enjoying it, enjoying the turn of events. She was the kind of mindless-happy where you suddenly took off your shirt and bra and danced around the room with bare titties shaking. She stifled a giggle, and chewed more furiously. "God, but this chicken's delicious," she said. "Tubs, please refill my glass—it's OK if I get shloshed, I'm not driving."

After lunch, they went for a stroll on the beach. Me and my two spouses, said Rosa to herself. She noted that Nikki was strong on her feet and cheerful; it meant, despite the boniness of her shoulders, she was healthy, which in turn meant no cause for alarm, no likelihood of needing emergency measures in place. Tubs was cheerful, too. As she'd expected, he'd not made a big deal of the gesture for Nikki to come stay with them in Pinelands. No bullshit about the spirit of Ubuntu or dumb remarks like, "Our house is your house." She was pleased about how immediately he had changed attention away from Nikki's endless declarations of gratitude to the practicalities in hand—to questions of packing, of securing up the house for her absence, of letting the neighbours know she'd be moving. She liked the way he had immediately fell in with the idea. In the same way that she knew she'd do the same for him, she had never doubted that he would. Her father would be all quizzical and uneasy, and would hate the cat! Rosa could laugh about it under cover of the general gaiety among the three of them strolling there on the beach. They had taken the direction away from the crowded beach near the car park, and were walking along a section where the sea was less hospitable to swimmers, the beach to picnickers. They had to pick their way among scattered rocks, sharp bits of seashell, washed-up seaweed, dogshit drying in the sun, and had to be wary of the surf slapping up hard against their calf-muscles. The sun had shifted slightly beyond overhead and was closer to the island behind which in a few hours it would settle for the night. Rosa was active with her cellphone camera; all the pictures she took showed them laughing. She took a selfie of the three of them. "Brilliant," she said, "brilliant" when she called it up onto her screen; she and Nikki were on either side of Tubs, teeth and eyes glinting, and the sky behind them in the picture was a pure golden blue.

Tubs will be my sex partner and Nikki my emotional one. I will spend each night in bed in his hot embraces while Nikki, in the bedroom downstairs, will sit up reading a book till drowsiness overtakes her. And we'll all live happily ever after.

In the few minutes it took Nikki to pack, Rosa went about the house securing doors and windows and drawing curtains. Tubs gathered up the meal things and went to find a bin along one of the streets. Rosa couldn't find dishwashing liquid, so rinsed the glasses under the tap and left them on the draining board to dry. Cracks in the walls of every room, blotches on all the ceilings, watermarks on the carpets . . . the telltale signs of a leaking roof. If the place couldn't be sold, was Nikki planning to spend winter here with the baby? Apart from the picture of the Voortrekker-*tannie* in the lounge, there were no other photos on display in any of the rooms Rosa entered, so no chance of seeing what a young Nikki or her *mense*—her parents, her brothers—looked like.

Everything that Nikki wished to bring along she had fitted into a battered suitcase which Tubs had no difficulty hefting into the boot. Without looking directly at Nikki's eyes, Rosa checked for any sign of sorrow, but couldn't tell. Nikki, as ever, was chatty and cheerful, and didn't look back.

Rosa hoped that at the last minute the cat would disappear somewhere over the rooftops or refuse to get into the car, but no such luck. She was acutely aware of the cat's presence in the car as they took the road back to Cape Town, and hoped that he would sit still and not climb over the seats. It occurred to her that Nikki would not have been able to employ the services of a vet, which means the cat could be diseased. His name was Plato—Rosa had not expected anything less grandiose, but had thought Nikki might have opted for humour in a name instead, something like *Pattercake*, or *Bunface*. On the way out of the village, they stopped at a supermarket to buy bottled water and cat-food. The sun was low on their right as they gathered speed on the open road, settling on a day that Rosa was sure she would remember for the rest of her life.

In bed that night, Rosa said, "I'm amused how hyper-active we are!" and wrapped herself more tightly round a pliant Tubs. Tonight she was the aggressor, the breaking wave; tonight, as seldom otherwise, she was the one that took their love-making to the brink of assault. His flesh was clammy to her fingernails, salty to her teeth. More than once, her knee caught him somewhere soft and vulnerable, evoking from his throat pain and ecstasy in one breath. "It's a dogfight," she thought, and giggled.

Afterwards, he went and drew the curtains back for them to look out at the stars. She sat huddled and naked in his arms and wondered what night looked like over Langebaan Lagoon. They sat in silence, smiling, watching the sky, panting faintly, knowing that before long they would be having crackers and beer. What was Nikki doing? Was she in dreamland or was she lying awake, attentive to the newness of her surroundings? Or was she sitting up, cat in the lap, sobbing into her hands?

Rosa stifled an impulse to talk about her, needing to wait till the moment was right. She was glad when Tubs raised the subject. He said he was touched by Nikki's childlike joy, especially when they were settling her in her room earlier that evening.

"Such absolute delight on her face," he said. "And that hair," he said. "So wild, and so unnaturally red!" He chuckled. "But so beautiful, too."

They switched on the lights and both laughed at the state of the bedding. "Crumpled and wet," said Tubs. "Like my um-diddly-dum."

"You tidy the bed, Tubs," said Rosa. "I'll go down and prepare the snacks. Are you having cheese on yours?"

She pulled on a gown and headed for the door. "Put on something decent," she said over her shoulder. "I'm going to invite Nikki up if she's awake." She was out the room without waiting for his response.

Downstairs, a little thrill ran through her when she saw light under Nikki's bedroom door. She hesitated a moment before gently knocking and whispering out, "Yo, Nikko? Are you awake, Honeybunch?" She let herself into the room, and was momentarily transfixed by the glittering beauty of Nikki seated upright in bed, vivid in the light of the bedside lamp, a book in her lap, Flaubert's *Madame Bovary*. Her impulse was to rush up and embrace her, and she had no doubt she would be eagerly received; in that moment she knew, and could see in Nikki's eyes that she knew too, that Nikki's extended absence had done nothing to douse the fire of their mutual passion, that Nikki's arrival under Rosa's roof had created the perfect opportunity for a re-ignition of what they suddenly realised was a living if dormant, passion. Rosa drew a deep, slow breath. She knew that resistance was the only option if disaster was to be forestalled.

"You're awake," she said, staying at the doorway. "Come up to our room. We're going to have a snack." She dashed off, to avoid hearing Nikki's remonstrations. "Crackers and cheese," she shouted as she headed for the kitchen. "Or would you prefer anchovies?" She went back to Nikki's room and peered in the door. Nikki hadn't moved, but her eyes had widened. "You can't have a beer, so will it be apple juice?"

"It's two a.m.," said Nikki with a weak smile. "Maybe it's better that I sleep." She stroked her belly with both hands.

"It'll just be for a few minutes, Nikki," said Rosa, turning away from the door. "Will it be cheese or anchovies?" She tried to keep her voice as light as possible, worried that Nikki might feel obligated not to refuse anything.

"Let me help you up," said Tubs to Nikki when she came into the room. He held out his hand for her to grasp as she anchored herself on the edge of the bed then swung her legs up. "Thanks," she said, a little breathless. "This pregnancy makes me feel really unbalanced. I keep thinking I'm going to fall forward. It sometime feels like I'm carrying a big wrecking-ball inside me!"

Rosa put the tray of snacks and drinks in the middle of the bed, and hopped in alongside Tubs. She hoped that the smell of the anchovies would not bring the cat Plato up to the room, but then remembered that Nikki had closed the door on him downstairs. It pleased her that Nikki displayed no hint of discomfort at finding herself squatting in the middle of the night with Tubs and Rosa on their marital bed, sharing cheese and anchovy snacks. It was a relief to her that Tubs did not treat Nikki's presence as an intrusion, that on the contrary, he seemed delighted at this unusual twist to what for him and Rosa was a most intimate private ritual. In a bantering tone, she told anecdotes about the characters at Lumina—Yon-Issie Yacoob—dry as a bean, Mickey Swanepoel with his coat of itchy dog-hair, Clyde Petersen whose shoulders were permanently on Viagra, and Leigh Irving-Fucking-Moore—Ms shabby ex-glamour goddess, eliciting loud continuous laughter from both Nikki and Tubs.

Nikki's eyes had thickened noticeably. "You must be exhausted," said Rosa. "Thanks for coming up—tomorrow's Sunday, we can all sleep late."

She insisted on walking Nikki down the stairs, partly for fear that Nikki might trip and fall, and partly just to steal a moment's privacy with her.

They reached Nikki's bedroom door in silence, only the rustling of their bedclothes audible in the semi-darkness. Nikki put her hand on the doorknob and hesitated, stiffening as she felt the fine silken press of Rosa's breast against her back. Her heart beat faster with Rosa's warm breath on her neck and Rosa's arms enfolding her waist. She turned round slowly, her breathing more audible as she met Rosa's full glistening eyes.

"Thanks," said Rosa in an emotion-hoarsened voice, and bent forward for their moist lips to lock.

Behind the closed door, Plato mewed softly.

They giggled and separated, and Rosa dashed off to her room, leaving Nikki smiling, confused and almost collapsing with sleepiness.

Chapter Ten

Rosa parted the kitchen window blinds, and morning light came flooding in. She smiled to herself. Heaven in Cape Town today, yippee. She saw that the cypress in her back garden stood motionless, no wind. Yippee. She was about to turn away from the window, when her eye caught some movement in the flowerbed which skirted the yard's perimeter wall: a quick flurry among the dianthus, then a black and white dash onto the lawn—Plato.

. . . Which means . . . Rosa's eyes shot to the door. Unlocked. Can she be up already? *Should* she be up already—what time did she go back to her room last night?

Maybe she just got up to let the cat out, thought Rosa. Maybe she's back in bed sound asleep. Rosa smiled as her mind's eye pictured Nikki all balled-up in sleep. It was how she was expecting to find her when she, Rosa, was to arrive at her door with a tray-load of breakfast this morning. To surprise her with breakfast-in-bed was the reason Rosa was up so early, the reason she was crazy enough to have forsaken the extra quality-time against Tubs's back. She giggled when she recalled his sleepy remonstration as she'd peeled herself off him and dashed out the room.

She turned the door handle and stepped out into the yard where, outside, the air was like velvet against her arms. Head aslant, Plato fixed his eyes on her as she walked on bare feet across the tiled paving in the direction of the lawn and swimming pool. What to make of cats, she wondered, knowing it would be important for her to win Plato's affection, however irksome the effort might be. *Love him and he will love you in return* was maybe the right dictum, but easier said than done.

"Yo, Ro'!" she heard. It was musical in her ears. "Come and join me, the water's divine!"

Full of smiles, she went round to the shallow side of the pool, where Nikki was in the water up to her neck. I hope she's got something on, thought Rosa, her eyes flashing over to the low-roofed cottage set back against the garden wall. The curtains there were drawn, which meant, even if her father was awake, he was not able to see out onto the yard and pool where Nikki might well be bathing starkers!

At the poolside, the tiles were warm underfoot—more confirmation of what a great day it's going to be, thought Rosa. She sat down at the edge of the pool and dangled her feet in the water, absorbing the initial sensation of cold as a boxer would a first sparring punch to the ribs.

"I've been getting approving nudges from the little babba all the time I've been in here," said Nikki, her teeth vivid against the flushed frame of her face. "I'm sure he's going to go ballistic when I get out." She was sitting back against the water's hold and allowing her feet and hands to float in its pull-and-push. Her open mouth dipped below the surface of the water then bobbed up and spewed out a thin curving stream.

"Must be his Langebaan genes," said Rosa. She could see that Nikki was wearing a whitish two-piece, but couldn't tell whether it was a bikini or bra-'n-panty combo—hopefully the former, she thought with a giggle, again thinking of her father and looking over in the direction of his cottage.

"Today's the first day of the rest of our lives," she said, immediately wondering what made her make such a dumb-sounding remark. "Let's promise ourselves brilliant lives," she added quickly, trying to keep her tone playful. "Starting with breakfast. I'm making it. What'll you be having—fried eggs? Fruit? Cereal? Coffee? Toast? All of the above?"

"Ah, Rosa," said Nikki, whose eyes became reflective. "Things have moved so quickly. One moment I'm languishing in Langebaan, the next—"

"—You'll never believe how happy I am that you agreed to come back with us," said Rosa, forcing a smile, determined to be cheerful. She could tell that Nikki was struggling to find an appropriate response, and went on quickly, "Please don't worry about anything. Every base is covered."

Nikki's body became motionless.

"From day one," she said, looking Rosa in the eye, not blinking. "This has been the world's most unequal relationship—*by far.*" Rosa wanted to speak, possibly to remonstrate, but Nikki gave her no chance, and continued, maintaining unblinking eye contact. "And that's my problem, Rosa. Much as I want to be in a relationship with you, it can't be *such* a relationship." She seemed relieved for having said it, and renewed her arm and leg movements.

"Behold the sky," said Rosa, throwing her arms up to the sky. "Gonna be a gobsmackingly beautiful day in Cape Town today." She smiled full-toothed and hoped Nikki would follow suit, but no. "Come on, Honybunch, don't fret, you know it makes me sad," she said, continuing to smile as broadly as she could. "Shall we postpone the heavy-talk for another time?" Her tone was mock-pleading. "Please?"

Plato came up alongside her and pressed himself against her hip. "He loves you," declared Nikki with a smile. "And I'm sure he's as grateful as I am—"

"—He's a lovely creature," said Rosa, tentatively placing her fingers along his spine. The fur was soft and warm, and she wondered with a brief shudder what living things might be nesting in there. "Such expressive eyes," she said, running the palm of her hand along his back, reassured by its smoothness. She felt the gentle scratch of his whiskers against her flesh as he tried to lick her wrist, but was not discomforted by it. "Such an aristocratic look," she said, beginning to feel what she hoped might be the beginnings of affection for him, but at the same time wishing he'd go away, bugger-off.

"Move over, darling," she said to Nikki, then lunged forward into the pool, causing her negligee to blossom outwards on the surface of the water. She rose at Nikki's side and spewed a stream of water into her face. They laughed out hard and loud.

Tubs appeared in the kitchen doorway wearing only his sleeper shorts. A quizzical grin appeared on his face when he saw the two women in the swimming pool.

"Make way for me, I'm coming in," he shouted, and dashed off the threshold, sprinted across the tiles and dived into the pool. Plato charged away towards the dianthus border. Rosa and Nikki whooped as he came sailing through the air and braced their shoulders against the splash. He swam with rapid strokes towards the opposite end of the pool, kicking up a noisy trail of surf as he went. Rosa's impulse was to wrestle off her negligee and follow him, but images of her father's disapproving look deterred her. Instead, she groped about in the roiling water to try to gather in the floating bits of her fragile garment. She felt maddened by delirium and for an instant thought she might black out. *Polyamory!* She whispered to Nikki, and both of them laughed.

Later, up in her bathroom, she turned the shower on full blast and although she had to shield her eyes from the prickling sensation of it, was comforted by the sheer deluge that engulfed her. She squeezed large dollops of shower gel into her hands to create a rich white lather that she messaged into hair and skin, and watched it rapidly dissipate under the force of the water. Her thoughts were running wild, and she applied the lather more vigorously in hopes of calming them. She was aware that she'd been smiling non-stop for the past hour but wasn't sure how to stop it or if she even wanted to.

She knew that down in the guest bathroom, Nikki was showering too. If cellphones were waterproof, we'd be texting each other right now, she thought, restraining an impulse to laugh out loud. She wrapped her fingers round her necklace and gave the beads a brief squeeze, convinced that Nikki was doing the same to hers right now, and that she was "thinking of me!" while doing so.

The world's most unequal relationship—by far.

"I can't be in such a relationship," Nikki had said. "But"—it occurs to me I should have retorted, thought Rosa—"but we live by the dictum *from each according to her means.*"

Equality-inequality should not be a criterion by which to evaluate a relationship Rosa told herself with conviction. She turned off the shower and was momentarily disoriented by the immediate silence around her. She stepped out and grabbed a towel. What's *unequal* got to do with anything? My craze for her is unequal to hers for me—so what? Shouldn't that means we're all-square?

I would rather die than be responsible for wrecking your marriage.

Ah. That famous line from that famous email.

We didn't get that far, thought Rosa, in our conversation by the poolside. What would I have said to that?

She scoured herself hard with the towel, so that the shower gel fragrance in her pores was released into the damp bathroom air.

She pulled on a jeans and sweater and hurried downstairs.

Out on the back-stoep, the smell of bacon and sausage reached their nostrils, and without thinking why, all of them felt the subtlest relaxation of tension in their minds and bones.

"Be sure to fry enough for Plato, too," Rosa called out over her shoulder towards the kitchen.

"Roger that," came Tubs's reply.

Bill was wearing sunglasses, but it was possible for Rosa to see his eyes through the shaded lenses and know that his cheerfulness was genuine.

"You might not believe this," he said to Nikki, smiling broadly, "but I was a victim of so-called male morning sickness when my late wife was pregnant with Rosa."

"Really?" said Nikki, leaning forward in her chair. "Did you suffer all the usual symptoms?"

"Most of them, I think. The doctor said it was psychosomatic and treated me for anxiety."

"And did it work?"

"After a while, yes. The symptoms disappeared but not the anxiety." He looked at Rosa, beaming. "She still causes me the same amount of anxiety today," he said and laughed—maybe with just a little too much force, thought Rosa, pleased nevertheless.

In the trees outside the garden wall, several birds squawked in unison, as if joining Bill in his laughter.

The sun was at its ten o'clock height. In the distance could be heard the faint pealing of a church bell. The sky was so blue it could have been painted on by an amateur artist. Between Rosa's elbows on the plastic garden table stood the simmering mug of coffee that Tubs had prepared for her. All around her, Sunday unfolded like a carefully-crafted symphony.

"How many months to go?" Bill asked, and Rosa noticed that his voice was gentle and polite.

Nikki smiled and looked down at her belly. She laughed suddenly. "Ooh, he just kicked," she said. "As if to say, 'come on, answer the nice gentleman's enquiry.'"

The steam from the coffee cup rose to Rosa's lips moistening them, reminding her of Nikki's lips last night.

Her heartbeat accelerated.

They were seated on the patio outside the kitchen door under a fiberglass canopy that protected them from the direct rays of the sun and gave a bluish tinge to everything, even Plato's coat. The cat was lapping from a bowl of milk that Tubs had set out for him on the edge of the patio. It struck Rosa how healthy-looking he was—nowhere near as starved-looking as Nikki.

Her father continued to banter and make small talk with Nikki— no doubt highly intrigued by how this pregnant white redhead and her cat just happen to be there when he wakes up on a random Sunday morning, and behaving as natural as—how did Hemingway put it, Rosa asked herself with an amused frown?—*as dust on a butterfly's wings*! Rosa stifled a giggle. He was bound to question her to death in the car when she took him to Langa tomorrow morning—let him stew till then!

Rosa noticed that Nikki's eyes widened involuntarily at the sight of the laden breakfast trolley that Tubs wheeled in from the kitchen. He was wearing only a linen apron over his bathing trunks, and it seemed *positively decadent* to Rosa how much his shoulder and arm muscles were accentuated for being so starkly naked. She wasn't sure if it was Tubs's Fabulous-Man physique or the sheer opulence of the breakfast or both that evoked the eye-widening response in Nikki, but both were worthy of awe and wonder. In that instant she became convinced that in a polyamoric relationship, Nikki and Tubs would *definitely* go physical. Holding her cellphone below the table, she dashed off a message to Nikki: *Hands-off, bitch – he's mine!* ☺

Nikki's phone rang almost immediately, a tinny lilt of *The Entertainer* hardly audible above the chatter round the table, and Nikki's eyes instinctively shot towards Rosa, who couldn't conceal a mischievous grin. "Come folks, help yourselves. Don't let it get cold," Tubs was saying. At the same time, Plato, who had sidled up alongside his legs, bounded into Nikki's lap and was keeping his eyes intently on the food that Tub was transferring from trolley to table. The message back from Nikki said: *What happened to, To each according to her needs?* ☺

Incredible, thought Rosa. There is such a thing as ESP after all.

"A feast of gemstones!" said Bill of his plate of breakfast. "Tubs, you're an *artiste suprême*." He took off his sunglasses and pulled his chair closer. His breathing had sped up and his face was a picture of glee. "Let the games begin!" he said. "One, two, three—go!"

"Delectable's a word that storms the mind," said Nikki. She dished egg, sausage and mushrooms onto her plate. "Cuisine's among your multitude of talents, isn't it Tubs?"

"He's more than just a pretty face," said Rosa, and pictured Tubs in bed. A little groan escaped her throat, and she concealed it with laughter. "The African male's come a long way since shedding his loincloth."

She could hardly have hoped for a better start. Such cordiality all round! She's a hit with them, they're a hit with her, said Rosa to herself, all the time remaining tuned into and avidly participating in the bantering talk around the table. And they love the cat, too—and he loves them. *And we'll all live happily ever after*, she felt like texting to Nikki, but no, this would definitely break the spell: it wouldn't do to draw attention to what's coming so naturally, she thought. Boy, this sausage is good. "Tubs, where did you learn to grill sausage this well?" she said. Her beaming eyes met his beaming eyes. "A past, present and future master of the art,"

I should actually be feeling guilty as hell for the way I'm deceiving these two most precious men-in-my-life, thought Rosa. It's because they trust me so implicitly that they've fallen for this low deception of mine, she thought. They're loving Nikki so much—and her dumb cat, Plato, too—as an act of generosity to me. This is their way of saying to me, *Dear, dear Rosa, nothing pleases us as much as pleasing you.* An elusive itch played around the nape of her neck.

Nikki offered to wash the dishes, and Tubs said to her not to worry, "it all goes into the dishwasher." He stood up and started packing the dishes onto the serving trolley. "Let me prepare you something to drink," he said. Coffee for Rosa and Bill, apple juice for Nikki, and some fresh milk for Plato.

The secret has to be not to be *sexually* committed to each other, Rosa said to herself. It's as simple as that. She smiled and sent a text message to Nikki's cellphone: *Everything's fine. Nothing must be different. Except no sex.*

Within thirty seconds, the following message came back: *yawellnofine.* Out the corner of her eye, Rosa could discern with what exaggerated attention Nikki was listening to Bill as he explained something to her, and how sleepily Plato lay in her lap—a docile blend of black and white. She suppressed a guffaw.

"She's the sister I never had," said Rosa.

And despite himself, Bill had to laugh—a pure spontaneous musical laughter, thrust out into the morning air. "If I knew you'd wanted a sister, he said, "I'd have arranged it with your mother." His laughter continued, in cascading peals. "But she wouldn't have been a redheaded Aryan."

The sun, like a redheaded Aryan, rose behind the trees of Pinelands.

Rosa searched for a quick rejoinder. "No," she heard herself say. "More likely a red-bereted communist—truer to your hearts than I could ever have been." Oops. She held her breath in the sudden silence which ensued.

"Now what's that all about?"

His voice to Rosa's ear was a mix of pain and puzzlement, and she felt the briefest tinge of self-loathing.

"Sorry, Dad," she said, trying to keep her voice light, and avoiding his eyes. She gave the button in her hand a hard press, and kept her eyes on the driveway gate as it lumbered open. "Didn't mean to be bitchy, Dad, sorry!" She tried to keep her smile going.

She pressed another button in her hand, and the garage door slid down. She pressed a third button and the car doors unlocked with a pop. They got in, and the immediate sense of intimacy induced by the car's interior made her feel a pang of endearment towards her father.

Rosa started the engine, and said, no longer needing to try to keep her voice light, "the inside of this car is like a mother's warm embrace." She hoped he would smile, would sense she was truce-seeking, and would allow the journey to be at least not unpleasant.

"And what would you know about a mother's warm embrace?" he said, his eyes fixed on her profile. "Weren't you abandoned at birth?"

Out the corner of her eye she could see he was smiling, and this made her smile too. She tried to think of something appropriate to say, but all that she could utter was, "I wish she hadn't died when she did."

Rosa allowed the vehicle to roll off the driveway paving, and waited for its familiar slide onto the road surface before accelerating in the direction of Forest Drive. As always, it seemed as if the car was driving itself.

"So, she worked with you?" Bill said.

"That's right," said Rosa. We've had this conversation before, she thought, and smiled—he knows we have, but he's circling me; clearly his curiosity about her is overpowering him.

"Your secretary or assistant or something?"

"No . . . not secretary . . . business analyst. There's no such thing as secretaries anymore, Dad."

"But, if there were, she would have been your secretary?"

Rosa smiled. "Next you're going to tell me how good it feels that the tables have turned so decisively in this new South Africa of ours, right?"

"Not so long ago," he said, "we were a sub-species. Today they seek our charity."

Rosa's cheeks enflamed. Her fingers tightened on the steering wheel. She felt a slight reeling in her brain. Blackbirds flitted in amongst the treetops along Forest Drive. She couldn't hear their tweeting, the car windows were sealed. Her father, who had put on his sunglasses, seemed all of a sudden so close to her she felt smothered. She rolled her window down a sliver for some cool morning air to cut in.

"She seems a very nice person," he said, "what's she expecting, a boy?"

Rosa remained silent.

After a moment, Bill said, "for some reason, most people want a boy, but I was overjoyed to have a daughter."

"And your wife?" said Rosa, hardly opening her mouth. "Was *she* happy to have a daughter?"

"Oh, yes—"

"Well, you could have fooled me."

The traffic lights at the corner of Ringwood Road were turning amber as they approached. Rosa put her foot down and sped through as the lights changed to red.

"If she was so happy to have a daughter, why did she neglect her all her life?"

"Now, whoa!"

"Yes, I know—you're going to say a girl's favourite bogeyman's their mother."

They turned out of Forest Drive, and as always, it felt to Rosa as if they were emerging from a tube of trees. On their left, beyond a stretch of open grassfield, the sun rose over the railway line. Rosa kept the speedometer close to a hundred. She wanted this trip to end.

"When's she due?"

Rosa turned on the radio.

"I wonder what the forecast is for today," she said. "Feels like it's going to be cool despite the sun." She glanced briefly over towards her left, where her father sat immobile behind his sunglasses.

"Due?" she said. "In a couple of months, I think." She started singing along to the tune on the radio.

Today they seek our charity . . . The line played over and over in Rosa's head. Why did she find it so hurtful? Was it because of the complete absence of malice—the worst insults are those not intended to be—or was it the usual irritation one felt with most older people's prejudices? Her father thought he was so enlightened, yet he was incapable of seeing anything in terms other than black versus white.

The traffic was slow this morning, even at this early hour, slow and thick. There was no opportunity for switching to a faster lane, the mood was such that no-one would allow you in, you just had to sit tight, you just had to wait and hope that it would thin out, would speed up sooner rather than later. Trapped with just your inane radio and your more inane thoughts.

Rosa's impulse was to check her phone for messages, but although she knew she'd be able to do it, she resisted—the way today has started for me, it could easily get worse. The rear window of the car ahead of hers displayed two stickers. One read, *Smile: Jesus Loves You* and the other, *If you can read this, you're too close.* She smiled. She wished Nikki were in the car with her right now. She wished they were on the coastal road right now, speeding off to Fish Hoek.

She noticed that the car ahead had suddenly sped up, that she could no longer read its window stickers. Yes! She checked her wing mirror, swung her car into the fast lane and set off at speed up Hospital Bend.

At the office, she filled her coffee-mug, settled into her chair, turned on her computer and said to herself, let me text Tubs.

Just wanted to double-check: you're OK with Nikki staying?

Of course
You're not just saying so to please me?
Course not
My father thinks she's a basket-case
??
Can't understand she's a FRIEND

We could have arranged hotel accomm instead
I'm fine with her staying with us
You're one in a mill
You're my sexy wife

Luv U2

If he knew the truth, would he feel betrayed, she wondered. There's a version of this story that should make complete sense. "If only my mother were around," Rosa said to herself. "She would understand completely."

She text-messaged Tubs again.
Can we meet for lunch today?
Sounds good—Waterfront?
Waterfront

She got to the sea-facing restaurant before Tubs did, and noticed with delight how his eyes lit up at the sight of her. She had chosen a table out on the balcony which commanded a view of the Atlantic, the harbour-basin and the mountain. She rose to her feet as he neared the table, and thrilled to the fragrance he exuded and the touch of his lips against her lips.

"You are the living proof that God loves me," Tubs said, as he sat down in the chair on her left.

Their table was positioned alongside an ornate wrought-iron railing, beyond which, at one level down, stretched a curving row of beach umbrellas—*rondavel*-shaped—shielding the patrons of the restaurant below from the bright overhead sun.

Their table, too, was shielded from the sun, but by an extended slanting rooftop, on top of which could occasionally be heard the cooing and scratchings of—what?—seagulls, no doubt.

A waitress approached with menus. She wore her hair in zigzag cornrows, with braids like a bead curtain flailing round her ears and shoulders. Most noticeable to Rosa were her breasts, their fine symmetrical curvature under the corporate T-shirt. And no make-up—no *need* of make-up, an African beauty bequeathed by nature itself. She spoke to them in English, a clipped private-school English which somehow to Rosa, enhanced her beauty.

Rosa scanned the menu, wondering if she'd be jealous if it happened that Tubs was having an affair with a girl like this. Or with any girl, for that matter. Or any guy.

The idea of Tubs having an affair with a *guy* seemed so absurd that for a moment Rosa's head spun. She looked up into the waitress's face, and was greeted by a respectful smile.

She returned the smile, saying to herself, just dare, bitch, just dare—but it was good-humoured, and the smile was one of genuine friendliness.

There was the usual mid-day bustle about the Waterfront, with streams of people, mainly tourists, crisscrossing in all directions on all pathways, including the boardwalk past their table. Out in the harbour below, watercraft were jostling in the cluttered space of the bay, stirring the greasy water, evoking a dull lapping sound that was audible to Rosa when she listened for it.

"So you *don't* have a problem with Nikki staying?" She needed him to repeat it one more time, more for him to convince himself than to convince her.

"No, not at all. She's great, and I like her cat, too—old Plate-O'milk."

"I know it's *terribly* unfair of me . . ." Easy-now, easy-now, she said to herself: that doesn't sound too genuine.

"Please say no more. It's fine, it really is. I'm hoping we can host her all the way through her pregnancy, and beyond if need be."

He leaned towards Rosa, lightly tapping his shoulder against hers. "Oh, to be in bed with you right now," he said, barely whispering.

Rosa giggled.

"She's going to have to be with us at least till the time of her confinement," she said. "And I'm not sure what happens afterwards."

"Don't worry about it. She can stay as long as you want. I don't have a problem with it."

"That's really great of you. I owe you one."

"One what?" He laughed. "I'll remind you in bed tonight!"

A multi-level cruise boat was leaving the harbour. No doubt taking tourists to see Robben Island, thought Rosa. She pictured herself, Tubs, Nikki with the baby bundled in her arms, and Plato at their ankles, all on this cruise boat together, smiling in the wind, on their way to visit Robben Island together, one big happy family.

"I'll be Uncle Tubs to the baby, and the cat will be his Cousin Plato," Tubs said.

"Nikki will be thrilled," said Rosa. "It'd be a great weight off her mind. She'll be able to think through the longer-term at her leisure, without the pressure of having to find immediate alternative lodgings."

I think I can tick that box, thought Rosa, feeling joyous. "Let's drink a toast."

"First thing, the cat will need to be taken to a vet," she said.

"He looks fine to me," Tubs said.

"But I'll only relax when I know for sure that he's healthy."

The waitress brought their lunch, a low-carbo protein pasta dish for Rosa and prawn stir-fry for Tubs.

"Imagine he's carrying something that could wipe us all out," Rosa said, laughing suddenly.

"This looks delicious," said Tubs, drawing his plate of stir-fry closer. He seemed to notice the waitress for the first time. Glancing up at her with a smile, he said, "I hope you've got reserves of this left in your freezer—I might need seconds."

They spoke about Nikki, about the need for a GP, a gynaecologist—and a midwife?—a private hospital and later, for the baby, a paediatrician. They wondered whether Nikki was on medical aid, but doubted it. They wondered if she had any money, but doubted it—maybe a few coins in her purse (did she even own a purse?). Rosa remembered that Nikki had not claimed her severance pay from Lumina when she left. And then, of course, there was the house at Langebaan that was currently up for sale.

"I'm pretty sure she's flat broke," said Rosa. "And the proceeds from selling the house—*if* she sells the house—when will she see that?"

"Damn, but this food's good," said Tubs. He scooped a forkful into his mouth, and crunched away, bright-eyed.

"Your dad seems to like her," he said.

"Yes, seems to," she said, feeling a sudden surge of anger.

The Atlantic looked threadbare to her. "Like a worn carpet," she said to herself. "Pathetic. Condemned to perpetual motion by forces beyond your control, yet beautiful for all that."

Chapter Eleven

I t was unmistakable, she was hearing the tune of *Baa, baa, black sheep*. She snatched up her cellphone—yes!

For a moment, she remained propped up on her elbows, cellphone cupped in her left hand, trying to restrain outright laughter, wanting not to disturb Tubs who lay unmoving in the dark alongside her, snoring just-audibly. She stared at the lit-up screen and said to herself, "we're going to have a baby!" Then she swung her legs out of the bed, and, trying to make no noise, dashed downstairs to Nikki's room.

A shadow passed across the sliver of light under Nikki's door—Plato? Or was it Nikki already out of bed? Rosa tapped lightly on the door, took a deep breath, and opened it quickly.

"It's a joke, right?" she said, smiling and breathless.

"Ooh, I wish!" said Nikki, whose belly was a dome-shape under the blankets. From the side of the bed, Plato peered round at Rosa with head askance and eyes rounded, before jumping up and settling himself at the foot end.

"But it's premature, surely?" said Rosa, coming into the room, trying to keep her voice down. She closed the door with shaky hands.

"Seven months," said Nikki, who chuckled suddenly. "My goodness, Rosa. Have you seen your face? You're beaming. You look as if you've just won the lottery."

Rosa laughed. "I'm so excited, she said. "Did you say 'seven months?' We'd better get moving, then."

She had her cellphone with her. She speed-dialled the gynaecologist's number. While it rang, she went and perched herself on the edge of the bed alongside Plato, stroking his back with her free hand, and ruffling the fur in his neck. The number rang. She waited.

"Are you nervous?" she said to Nikki, who had pulled the blankets up to her neck, and whose face seemed more pallid than usual.

"Maybe. A little, I think."

Rosa stroked and stroked the cat's fur.

When Doctor Morrissey answered, he wanted to know what the intervals were between the contractions. He wanted to speak to Nikki for confirmation. Yes, it sounded like labour. She would need to come in to the hospital straight away. He would meet her there.

A thin mist was visible among the branches of the pine trees beyond the garden wall. There was no moon in the sky tonight, but dull starlight and streetlight reflected in patches off the car's bonnet as a sleepy Tubs reversed out of the garage. He allowed the motor to idle, knowing that the girls would soon be out. He saw the light go on in the old man's cottage, and knew that his father-in-law—vigilant as ever—would be coming to ask, "what on earth's going on?"

"To the hospital?" Bill said to Tubs when he came out, dressed only in a knee-length cotton shorts. They can't travel alone. It's three a.m. This is Cape Town." His whiskers glistened in the pale light. "Tell them to wait," he said, turning around sharply, and headed back to his flat. "I'll ride along with them."

Rosa was impatient. "I wish he would hurry. What if she gives birth in the car? We don't need his protection—this is Cape Town, not war-torn Cambodia." Tubs laughed when he heard Nikki giggling inside the dark cab alongside Rosa. He stood at the side of the car, a fidgety Plato in his arms. "Here he comes," he said, when he saw Bill emerging from the flat. "All the best, Nikki!"

A uniformed attendant, in tie and blazer, was standing at the doorway. He smiled at them as they came in, and with a half-bow, pointed the way to the reception desk.

Our oddness doesn't seem to register with him, thought Bill. No doubt, in a place like this he sees oddness all the time. "How well lit up this place is," he said when they walked into the reception hall. With one sweep of the eye, he took in the plush leather settees in the waiting area, the themed prints of African rural life in their matching aluminium frames on the walls, the blue, flat-weave carpeting that swept through the place like an underfoot skyway, and, instinctively, suspicions were aroused within him—why he couldn't say. "This place looks so—commercialised," he said, hoping that Rosa would hear the disapproval in his voice, but she appeared too preoccupied with Nikki, around whose back her arm was encircled, and to whom in bantering tones, she was offering non-stop words of encouragement.

Bill went over to the seats in the waiting area, where there was a low table with a glass top on which were two stacks of magazines and a vase of fresh-cut flowers. A woman with a boy on her lap seemed to recoil ever-so-slightly as Bill neared and took up a seat close to them. She smiled when Bill said to the boy, "Hi, there, little fella, how's it going!"

An orderly in green uniform pushed a stretcher through a set of double-doors into the reception area, and continued straight on through another set, out of the reception area. Bill was just able to see the patient on the stretcher before they disappeared. That's the only thing so far, he thought, that tells me this place is a hospital.

He noticed that the woman with the boy on her lap was staring at Rosa and Nikki, who were seated with hands intertwined at the reception clerk's desk. After a while, when the admissions process was completed, and Rosa joined him in the waiting area, he could tell that the woman was intensely aware of their conversation but was trying to appear disinterested.

A wheelchair was brought for Nikki, who chuckled at the notion of having to use it. "I'm a tough aunty," she joked with the orderly. "As soon as the kid's born, I'm going back to the fields to finish my ploughing."

Rosa gave Nikki a prolonged hug, and kissed her several times on the lips. Bill wondered what was going through the minds of the woman with the boy, the reception clerk, and the uniformed man at the door.

"I'm not leaving this place till the baby's born," Rosa said to Nikki. "I wish I could be in there with you."

Nikki disengaged from Rosa, and came up and hugged Bill and kissed him on the mouth. He hoped his whiskers didn't prick her or that his return-hug didn't seem too clumsy or eager.

Before disappearing through the double-doors, Nikki looked back, and with a broad smile, blew them a kiss.

"Not sure why we couldn't be waiting at home," said Bill.

"I'll drive you back, if you like," said Rosa.

"If you're staying, I'm staying."

"Really, it's not a problem, Dad. I'll drive you back."

"I'm sure there's a coffee shop around here, somewhere. Let's go find it."

The waitress in the coffee shop had a pen and notebook. When she wrote, the bracelets on her wrist writhed and jangled.

Rosa ordered espresso—short, with no cream, please. "Something tells me I'm going to need more caffeine than usual today," she said, smiling.

Bill smiled, too. He was struck by his daughter's radiance. Astonishing, he thought, that her sleep was interrupted at 3 a.m. and then, no doubt, she would have had to fall about to bring Nikki here in a rush, but those things have done nothing to blight her freshness. Her teeth are the best part of her, he mused. Just like her mother's!

He turned his eyes away from her face for fear she might detect the emotion he was feeling—a puzzling sense of sadness, of loss. He wished he could have felt less uneasy about her weird affection for this redheaded woman. He found it strange that she should be so crazy about this Nikki—crazy enough for me to be sitting here with her in a hospital coffee shop in the middle of the night waiting to hear if it's a girl or a boy!

"When Nikki said I was her next-of-kin," said Rosa, "you should have seen the look on the face of the admissions clerk. She wasn't sure if Nikki was joking or not." Rosa took out the photocopy of Nikki's admission form and found the place where it said, *Next-of-kin: Mrs Rosa Lethlabe.* There was merriment in her eyes. "It's official. I'm her next-of-kin," she said. "And I'm going to be the baby's aunty and godmother. If it's a her, she will be Nikki-Rose. And if it's a he, Nicky-Ross."

"You sound like this is a game you're playing," said Bill, trying to keep his tone matter-of-fact. "Have you thought of all the implications?"

Her espresso came. She stirred half-a-teaspoon of sugar into it.

Elbows on the table and shoulders hunched, she looked Bill in the eye, and, smiling, said, "Now, Dad, should I respond to the question or to the attitude?"

"That's the kind of answer your mother would have given me," he said. "You don't know how much like her you are."

"I wish I could be in there with her now," said Rosa, suddenly reflective. "But they said I'm not the husband." She sipped her espresso." Were you present at my birth, Dad?"

"Yes, I was." Bill laughed. "It was a circus. The birth took place in our bedroom, with a local midwife and half-a-dozen women from the neighbourhood all lending a hand. I had to go bury the afterbirth in the backyard."

"Was it in some village, or here in Cape Town somewhere?"

"It was in Cape Town, but it was like it was in some village."

They both laughed.

"I'm feeling peckish all of a sudden," said Bill. He sought eye-contact with the waitress to ask for the breakfast menu.

"You looked un-human," he said. "Like a little tadpole."

"Were you disappointed that it wasn't a boy?" It was spoken in a tone that Bill interpreted as bantering. He recalled, as he had many times over the years, that when Rosa was born, Zoliswa had seemed less happy than inconvenienced. But this was not an impression he would ever share with Rosa.

"And then you morphed into this beauty," he said in the tone he used to use for reading to her when she was six.

Rosa sensed an effusiveness behind his words, and could see in his eyes the all-too-familiar clouding that signalled deep emotional stirring. I'm right, of course, she told herself. I've always been right on this point: they would rather have had a boy. She was sure her mother, had she still been alive would have been as disappointed as her father that their daughter became a capitalist businesswoman, not a socialist comrade. The thought was accompanied by a swift stiffening of the temples. She wished she could think of something light-hearted to say, but no words came to her.

Her fingers tightened round her cellphone. "I think I should message Tubs," she said, "and let him know that we're going to be waiting here till the child is born."

Back in the waiting room, they chose to sit opposite the TV set which was mounted on a flexible steel bracket above a line of art prints on the north wall. From where they sat, their eyes could wander from the TV screen to the reception area where the night-duty clerk was busy handing over to a day-shift colleague—a middle-aged woman whose cheeks and lips were heavily made-up, and who spoke incessantly in subdued but urgent tones. The double-doors leading to the operating theatre were also visible to them, and, despite herself, Rosa found her neck stiffening every time someone came through those doors.

The only other person in the waiting area was a thin young man seated just under the TV set, wearing a black woollen beanie low over his brow, the Nike swoosh slightly off-centre. His gaze was fixed on a spot on the floor in front of him, and although he wore a winter jacket, his shoulders were hunched up, as if he were cold. He seemed indifferent to the world around him. Rosa stared hard at him for a minute in hopes of willing him to make eye contact with her, but to no avail. Clearly, he was in a state of anguish—no doubt someone who mattered was in the operating theatre right now.

Rosa looked at her cellphone to check the time: 07:45. They'd been there for close on five hours, and yet no word on Nikki. Twice already, Rosa had enquired from the receptionist about news from the operating theatre, and both times the answer was a polite, "they are still busy, ma'am."

Her father sensed her unease. He recalled that when *she* was born, the whole process had taken a matter of minutes—no sooner had the head shown through than the whole child came sliding out into the world! So why's it taking so long with Nikki?

Rosa texted Tubs, no news yet; worried; hoping no news is good news; will keep you posted. He replied: holding thumbs.

Bill fidgeted in the soft chair, his elbows heavy on the armrests. He was fighting a drowsiness that was invading his bones; he doubted that yet more coffee would postpone the rising compulsion for sleep. The last thing he needed now was to become a burden to Rosa. I *must* subordinate my needs to hers, he thought, glad that he had decided to accompany her here this morning.

Rosa was preparing a message to the office to let them know she'd be late, when the double-doors swung open and a man with a stethoscope around his neck came through. He was wearing a green doctor's jacket with a matching bonnet-style surgical cap, and was clutching a sheaf of papers in his hand. His impulse was to approach the heavily made-up woman at the reception desk, but then his eye caught Rosa's, and it was as if he knew it was she he was coming to talk to.

"Are you . . .?" His eyes flashed from hers to Bill's, then to the papers that twisted audibly in his fingers. "You're here about—"

"—Nikki Addo" Rosa spat out, regretting the harshness of her tone.

"Yes, Nikki Addo," the doctor said. "That's right." His eyes lingered on the papers which continued to rustle in his hand, and she knew to expect the worst.

"I'm afraid I've got bad news for you . . ."

Rosa's outpouring of grief was brief and furious—*a veritable cloudburst* thought Bill, as tears rolled down his cheeks, too. Clearly, she loved this Nikki . . . something that will forever be a matter of wonderment to him . . . He observed how she quietly sobbed into her hands, how convulsively her body shook. He wished he could put an arm around her, but feared she would shake it off. On hearing the news of Nikki's death from the hesitant doctor, she had slumped into a chair in the waiting-room, and gone what he thought of as *stone-cold silent*, before her tears overwhelmed her.

He could only cry along with her, too inadequate for anything else; yet, this is what family should do, he said to himself, grieve together, in a silence louder than words. This sadness and pain at the death of some weird white girl had brought him closer to his daughter than any time since the death of his wife. He knew that it wasn't Nikki's death that was making him cry, but his daughter's uncontrollable mourning of it. Sitting in the chair alongside her, he dared to take her hand into his and squeeze it, elated that his gesture was not rejected.

Opposite them, the images on the TV screen were in rapid, colourful motion, while in the seat below the TV set, the man in the Nike beanie remained unstirred. Bill's ear picked up the smooth voice of the receptionist, who was speaking in Afrikaans to someone on the phone. He couldn't understand what she was saying, but guessed from the tone that she was speaking with affection to a child. Rosa put her head on his shoulder, and he tightened his hold on her hand, careful not to cause her discomfort.

She wished her dad would hold her in his arms, would offer her a consoling shoulder—would *understand* her grief, but he seemed so bewildered, he just sat there in silence, himself seeming to need consoling. *Now's* when I need Tubs, she thought, alarmed at how close she was to blacking out. She knew she was in the grip of something more powerful than herself, and it both scared and exhilarated her. The thought that Nikki was dead was grotesque and maddening. It just couldn't be true!

Rosa felt her father's hand on hers, and was comforted by the warmth of it. She allowed her head to find his shoulder, and was not surprised to feel his stubbly chin brush her forehead, making affection for him surge in her chest. She thought of God the way she had thought of Him when her mother died—as this offended and offensive brute who called in His options entirely on whim, and her raw gut was to defy Him, no matter what. He could do His worst, which was nothing but an abuse of His inestimable power—when all else fails, kill.

But the baby's fine, the doctor had said. It's a boy . . .

A boy, thought Rosa. Nicky-Ross. My Nicky-Ross.

Within half-an-hour, Tubs was there, rushing up to Rosa to embrace her. His heart beat fast—she could feel its rhythmic thump-thump-thump against her chest—and his men's fragrance seemed extra-intense in her nostrils. She was overjoyed to see him.

Ah, thought Bill, he has a revitalizing effect on her. Himself feeling a sudden reinvigoration, he rose swiftly to his feet to embrace his son-in-law.

"Hell, Rosa," said Tubs, squinting, "you must be devastated."

She took a deep breath and closed her eyes for a moment. "The one thing I'm clinging to is the baby," she said. "The baby's fine, we were told, but I must see him immediately." A muscle twitched in her cheek. "If I'm not dreaming all this," she added, "then Nikki is dead and we will have to live with that. But the baby . . . the baby is fine the doctor had said."

"I am the next-of-kin," said Rosa. "You can check on the admission form." The heavily made-up woman had a troubled look. "Yes, no, I understand," she said. "But let me just check on the system." Her eyes glued to her computer screen, she said that it's just that it's unusual for next-of-kin not to be family—"if you know what I mean," she added with a mirthless grin. "I'm just going to call my supervisor to discuss it with you," she said, and picked up her phone.

The supervisor was a big-boned man with thinning blonde hair. In the pocket of his threadbare white shirt, a cellphone and two ballpoint pens protruded. Rosa took an instant dislike to him, knowing that his role in her life was to do God's will, which was to frustrate her. She felt a deep and purple scorn for the politeness he showed her when leading her to his office, for the calmness of his voice which could be nothing other than a trap to lull her, and for the shabby pretentiousness of the exaggerated neatness of his desk—how can you be a serious professional when there's so much order in your work space! The light in his office glinted off his specs, making it difficult for Rosa to discern his eyeballs. His hairy hands lay limp on his desk like two pet animals in repose. As his attention toggled between his computer screen and the papers that lay before him on his desk, she had no doubt that she was creating for this brow-beaten-looking supervisor a new, unwelcome challenge. No doubt, he would also have to refer her to *his* supervisor.

"Mrs Lethlabe," he said, in a kindly voice, correctly pronouncing the name. "There is no problem. You will certainly be able to see the baby."

Hell, and here I thought he'd make me jump through hoops! Rosa was unable to suppress a smile of relief. The supervisor smiled too, and said that he understood how she felt, how difficult the news of Miss Addo's unfortunate passing must be for her, but that he was happy that he could say, thanks to the mercy of The Lord, the child was OK.

Maybe I was wrong about him, thought Rosa. Maybe he's also one of God's disposable playthings—a hapless mouse scampering around between the paws of a cat, stupidly thinking he had a hope in Hell.

"We will have to keep the little one on life-support for a while." He said. "He's several weeks premature, so we had to put him on a respirator as soon as he was born."

Life support's something I could use right now, thought Rosa. How tired I suddenly feel! She sat there in front of the supervisor sighing repeatedly, and unable to prevent her shoulders from drooping. She was in the grip of a yawning fit that threatened to dislocate her jaws. She knew that if she allowed her eyelids to linger on *close*, they'd lock fast and she'd collapse there in a heap of sleep! Her mind was a jumbled, out-of-control tableau of images—of Nikki, Tubs, her dad, the baby, God, everything. She hoped that her hair was in place, that her eyes still sparkled, that her teeth continued to be the best part of her—that her voice remained all-melody . . . that the image this supervisor had of her was the one that she wanted him to have of her.

"I was hoping I'd be able to see Nikki's gynaecologist," she said.

"Yes. I know he hasn't left the hospital yet. I'll make sure he sees you before he leaves."

The supervisor asked her whether Tubs and her dad would wish to accompany her to see the baby, but she said no, just she—there will be plenty of time for them to see the baby later. The supervisor said that that would be fine, she should just follow him, and he would take her over to Intensive Care. "Once again, Miss Lethlabe," he said, half-bowing and with bended knees. "I am deeply sorry about your loss."

At first Rosa had some trouble seeing the baby amid the jumble of tubes and gauges, but told herself I'm just overwrought—then it morphed into view, and a weak smile came to her face, at the same time lines of tears rolling down her cheeks onto her breast.

She stared at the baby, rapt. It was no taller than an A4 page, and might in fact have been an animal—a being in some pre-human shape, which of course, was not necessarily unnatural. She thought about tadpoles—they were pre-frogs, and her eyes sought out the telltale signs that he was human: two arms, two legs, five toes on each foot: one, two, three, four, five, yes! And five fingers on each hand—those tiny fingers, they'd each be able to pass through the eye of a needle!

It wasn't possible for her to get a good glimpse of his face, as it was covered by an oxygen mask, but she guessed from the paleness of his skin, and knew that if she wished hard enough, he was going to be a redhead like his mother.

A glass wall separated her from him—viewer from viewed. She was not the only viewer on her side of the wall. Both to the left and right of her were young men and women with cellphone cameras, looking in at babies who, like Nicky-Ross were also attached to complex-looking machinery. These people, who were obviously the babies' closest relatives, chatted excitedly under their breath, clearly thrilled and anxious at the same time.

On Nicky-Ross's side of the glass, uniformed nurses moved between the many incubation units, each equipped with its own computerized and medical gizmos. Like most things, medical science these days was a matter of mastering machinery. There was something other-worldly about the scene beyond the glass barrier, a place that Nicky-Ross would have to be rescued from, but yet the only place right now which guaranteed him (and her) any hope of any kind. A nurse came up to Nicky-Ross's unit, moving in the same robotic way that characterized the movements of all the other nurses who were engaged in similar routines at other incubators. She lifted the lid, and Nicky-Ross's fragile breathing seemed to speed up—and Rosa realized that her own breathing had suddenly sped up. The nurse smiled briefly at Rosa through the glass panel, then turned immediately to the apparatus that connected the baby's navel to a sac on a pole, and began adjusting it in a clearly-practiced way. Before moving on to the next unit, she also adjusted various dials on various devices, and noted down on the baby's record chart, the readings visible on the monitors that were attached to his wrists via long looping cables.

Standing there staring at the delicate scrap-of-a-person that was Nicky-Ross, barely two hours old and destined, she was sure, to make his impact on the world in only a few years from now, Rosa felt hugely energized. Her calmness and sense of self-control were restored, and she knew that on her own—without working up a sweat!—she could beat the entire world if need be. The child would survive, thanks to the wonders of modern medical care, and would grow and thrive, thanks to the wonders of a mother's love—and she would be the one who would be dispensing that mother's love.

You, Nicky-Ross, will be the reason I survive your mother's death. You, Nicky-Ross, will be the reason your mother—for me—will survive her own death.

PART THREE

Chapter Twelve

When Rosa and her dad stepped out the doors of the hospital, the mid-morning sun was high, and the birds in the trees were melodious. Cape Town was well into its day, with the city's traffic sounds echoing off the mountain-face to create a background blur in the ear. As if emerging from some overnight sleep, Rosa's cellphone came alive with flashes and buzzings; multiple screen icons simultaneously lit up as stored messages and apps—seemingly in a wild flight from captivity—began to rapidly auto-upload. Without changing her stride, Rosa took the phone into her palm, and deftly began tapping responses into the keypad with her thumb.

Bill shuffled along at his daughter's side, barely awake and struggling to keep pace. He noted how adroitly she operated that little whizz-kid-of-a-machine, but it only brought him a sense of gloom. It's her competence in all things that has landed her in this unreal situation, he thought with a pang. A birth and a death. Good God. Was he dreaming? Thank God she had Tubs to see this through with her.

With her free hand, Rosa found the car keys and activated the unlock mechanism, never slowing down her operation of the cellphone. She's extraordinary, thought Bill, all fatherly bias aside. She seems to take everything in her stride, while here I am busy falling off my barstool.

In the car, she thanked him for having accompanied her to the hospital, and he recalled the moment when she collapsed onto his shoulder, overcome with grief. He knew then that that would be one of the big moments of his life.

At home she showered under a ferocious torrent of water, solid as ice, hot as lava.

Plato's mew sounded plaintive in her ear, and she knew he knew. She took him onto her lap and rhythmically stroked his neck while she quietly wept in the silent house. For a long time she just sat in her gown at the dining-room table, stroking the cat in her lap, watching the sun's rays slanting into the room, and thinking of Nikki. Her father had no doubt by now fallen into a deep restorative sleep; bless his soul, she thought, giving to a renewed outburst of tears which, try as she may, she could not stem. She realized she was feeling a grief that as a child she should have experienced when her mother died but was unable to. Death can be so . . . disempowering, she thought, and knew that she should not fight her reaction to it. She took another shower, and it felt invigorating. She messaged Ferrie, and told him she'd be coming in—"I should be there within the hour," she said, and forced herself to think of work.

In Ferrie's office, Rosa spoke in slow, clipped tones. "I'm OK," she said, and found herself having to hold back her tears. She smiled. "I'll probably need some time away to attend to the funeral arrangements and to make sure the baby's future is taken care of."

"Yep. He'll need to be placed in foster-care. Do you know if there's any next-of-kin?"

"Well, apart from me," said Rosa, and noted how Ferrie's left eyebrow twitched, "there's a brother in Australia—Perth, I think. But Nikki's had no contact with him for years. He might even be dead already. So, I'm her only family, as it were." She tried to smile.

A troubled look came to Ferrie's eyes, and Rosa wished she could think of something light to say. She became aware of the smell of decaying vegetation in the air, and guessed it was from the floral arrangement sitting on a low coffee table in a corner of the office, fading away there like a shabby, aging diva.

Back in her office, Rosa's heart jumped when she saw on her desk the printout of Victor Addo's profile page, which her analyst had downloaded from one or other social networking site. Attached to the printout was a stick-it note that said, *Perth 6 hrs ahead of CT.* Rosa took the printout in both hands and studied the photo of Nikki's brother that was on it. His chin was raised, accentuating the corded neck muscles on either side of his throat. The chin was broad, clean-shaven, flat, matching the forehead for stoniness. It wasn't possible for Rosa to get a good look at his eyes in this picture, they were too narrow. There was a moustache; it resembled the eyelashes—little blond triplets in the picture. And he was smiling, despite the fact that his lips were closed, it showed clearly in the curves of his cheeks. Alongside the photo she read, *Victor Addo, civil engineer.* It was hard to say from the photo if his hair colour was red or just plain blonde.

Would Nikki have wanted me to notify him? If the difference is six hours, then it will be early evening in Perth right now. He will have had his supper, and will probably be sitting watching TV—or maybe be in a drunken stupor? No, not likely. From his photo, he didn't look the type.

Rosa dialled and held her breath.

"Hullo."

"Hullo. Is that the Addo residence?"

"That's right. Who's speaking?"

"Hi, my name is Rosa. I'm phoning from South Africa. From Cape Town. Is Mr Addo in?"

"What's that?"

"It's about his sister, Nikki. Can I speak to him please?"

"Nikki?"

"That's right, ma'am. Are you Mrs Addo?"

"Hold on."

"Hullo. This is Victor Addo speaking."

"Mr Addo, hullo. My name is Rosa. I'm a friend of your sister, Nikki."

"Nikki?"

"That's right, your sister Nikki."

"What is this about?"

"I'm afraid I've got bad news for you, Mr Addo."

"Yes?"

"Nikki passed away today."

At supper that evening, Rosa told how there was this huge silence on the other end. "He just went totally quiet."

Her father and Tubs listened in silence.

"When he spoke again, his voice was broken. I couldn't restrain my own tears. He spoke with a South African accent, but certain words he pronounced like an Aussie, for example, I *cunt* believe it."

Bill and Tubs smiled. "Says he wants to come to the funeral," she added.

"Did you tell him about the child?" Tubs wanted to know.

"Yes. That's why he's keen to come."

Before leaving the office, Rosa had phoned the paediatrician to find out what time he'd be at the hospital this evening, and if she could see him then. She timed her departure from the office accordingly.

The paediatrician, Mel Cochrane, had for Rosa, an artificial look, as if he'd been custom-built in a factory. A single quick glance enabled Rosa to conclude that he was a stylish dresser, with a taste for expensive accoutrements—his prominent Gucci watch alone was a giveaway. But there was no fragrance in the air about him, which surprised Rosa. He spoke in gentle, measured tones as he explained Nicky-Ross's condition to Rosa. They were both standing at the glass panel looking in at the baby in his incubator.

"It'll be touch-and-go for the first forty-eight hours," he said to Rosa. "The main aim is to stabilize him—his breathing, his feeding, and to make sure he catches no infection."

With the exactness of an audio textbook for beginners, he described to Rosa what the treatment regime would be for Nicky-Ross in coming days, what the different indicators being monitored meant, why she would not be allowed into the baby's ward for at least the next forty-eight hours, and which websites would be helpful if she wished to know more about pre-terms in general.

"He's not out the woods, yet, I'm afraid. I checked him over for any obvious abnormalities, but so far so good—you know, ten fingers, ten toes, two ears, one nose, that sort of thing. We've conducted all the standard tests. The results will start flowing in from tomorrow onwards, then we'll have a better idea."

In his state of the art incubator, Nicky-Ross lay motionless, except for the rhythm of his chest. Rosa looked at him with adoration; the beating of her heart sped up. He was just a small part of the elaborate system of life-support technology across which his one wee life was distributed—the hardware, software, middleware, malware, spyware, shareware, lights, cameras, action. Although he's the subject, he's also the least important part of this intricate machinery, this man-made universe. Was his mind already working? Was he capable of independent thought? If so, he could be forgiven for thinking that that high tech bath tub he's in is the whole cosmos. Just as we who know better assume the known cosmos is the entire cosmos . . .

. . . and for thinking Mel Cochrane is God Almighty.

She let Mel Cochrane know that Nikki had not been on medical aid but that she, Rosa, would be taking care of the bills; she would phone his office tomorrow to provide details. She thanked him with a profuseness bordering on hero-worship, which she immediately regretted as unbecoming.

Do newborns feel pain? There's an awful lot of plastic tubing fitted to all parts of the little guy's body, thought Rosa. She pictured the padding pasted down over his left nipple and wondered which would prove to hurt more—the application of the padding or its removal, later. And all the needle pricks. If he suffered pain, he'd actually see Mel Cochrane as the devil.

Maybe our ideas of God were formed in the cradle . . . or incubator.

Chapter Thirteen

After supper, she shared with Tubs her intention to adopt Nicky-Ross.

"You're joking, right?"

"You'll never know how close Nikki was to me."

"Oh, I know, I know."

"What do you mean by that?"

"What do you mean what do I mean? You rescued her from virtual destitution, didn't you? Which I had no problem with, as you know. So, how close she was to you is no issue. This is completely different. You can't be serious about wanting to adopt her child."

"I've never been more serious in my life, Tubs. But what's the big deal?"

"What's the big deal? Where do I even begin! In the first place, what about me? What about us? How can we have a child of our own if you're going to adopt this white kid?"

"So it's his whiteness that's the issue?"

"Well, of course! But that's not the whole issue."

"This is the new South Africa, Tubs. Race is no longer an issue. What they're calling transracial adoption has become a norm."

"But, Rosa. We're talking black parents-white child, here. How many of those have you seen? Do you even think they'll agree to this?"

"Who's they?"

"The authorities responsible for approving adoption applications, of course, who else?"

"I'd like to see them cite race as an issue. I'll drag their pitiful arses through every court in the land."

"Ok, so the authorities in their infinite progressiveness agree. What about me? Do I not have to agree, too?"

"Of course you do. But how can you refuse? Look, I know this is pretty darned radical, and that maybe we haven't spent enough time talking about our own plans for children, but how does this stop us from having our own kids?"

"Whether or not we have our own kids, how do we raise a white kid? And he'll then be the eldest! He'll stick out like a sore thumb! It wouldn't be fair to him, how can it be? He'll grow up with a mountainload of complexes."

"You're picturing him at the supper table with all our black faces surrounding him?"

"Yep, and he'll have to call us Mom and Pop. We'll be wiping his bum for him for years before he can do it himself. I'll have to read fairy tales to him at night, and when he's naughty, I'll have to beat that same white bum. No Rosa, I just can't see it."

"But, at work, don't you have white people reporting to you?"

"That's different—they're not family. There's nowhere near family-type intimacy."

"We'll all get used to it, Tubs. We need to think of the child as a child, a person, a human being."

"Of course I see him as a child and as a human being. But I don't know if I'm ready to be the first black man on earth to adopt a white kid. In any case, as I said, I don't see the authorities agreeing. As new as the new South Africa might be, I can't see it being ready for this . . . in any case, what about so-called public opinion? Have you thought that wherever you go you'll be gawked at, and no doubt in many cases with hostility? And not only from white people but also from other black people?"

"Of course I've thought about that, but why should that put us off? Anything new will attract attention. But if we're the first, we might actually set off a trend, and before you know it, it will be a norm."

"And the brother? What about the brother? What if he wants to adopt the child?"

"That's what worries me."

In bed, Tubs's arm across her hip was like a concrete beam; the hairs on his arm were abrasive to her fingers; his crotch against her rump was causing pins and needles. How easily Nicky-Ross must have slipped out! No bigger than a ten cent coin. Was Nikki still alive when he was born? Did she get to hold him against her breast, hear his first cries in the open world? How were they able to save *him* but not her? Tubs's forearm against her stomach was a dead weight arousing her nausea. She'd end up doing it right there on her pillow . . . her whole left side would get covered in the mess. She pictured the mess that must've come pouring out of Nikki . . . not unlike a projectile-vomit, with Nicky-Ross in the middle of the flood, clinging to his umbilical cord, holding on for dear life. Was his first cry a cry of joy? Of pain? Of anger? Was Nikki able to bear the pain of birth and death? What hurt more, what hurt most? And Nicky-Ross? Surely he must have sensed the death there present at his birth? What for him was more painful, the birth or the death? It shouldn't have worked out this way, her mental image of herself said to her mental image of Nikki. I know, is all that Nikki could say in reply, with a typically-wry Nikki-smile. Rosa's chest slowly heaved, and tears began to flow from her eyes and nose. A protracted whimper escaped from her lips, but it did not disturb Tubs's smooth purring at the nape of her neck.

She worked her way free of Tubs and the blankets, and sat up, staying still in the dark till her head, her heart and her breathing calmed. She placed her feet on the carpet, and with the sleeve of her nightie wiped her face. She left the room and made her way down the stairs

169

to Nikki's room. She switched on the light, and as expected, there was Plato perched in the middle of the bed; he moved aside for her to get onto the bed, and settled himself in her lap, where he lay in apparent indifference as she just sobbed and sobbed.

When Rosa left home in the early morning dark, the south-easter was in an aroused state. It made rapid whipping sounds in the trees, and drove masses of blue-grey fog across the highway; it buffeted the car like a prodding finger, forcing Rosa to grip the steering wheel more tightly. Her throat had a strained feeling, as if she'd been talking too much. She wished she had had a second cup of coffee before her departure from home, and that she'd shown Tubs—and Plato—a bit more cordiality, but attempting to fake it would have been too exhausting.

She caught sight of her face in the rearview mirror, and clicked her tongue in annoyance. Her eyes were puffy, her lips were pouty and her complexion was the look of oak bark. The interior of the car, which at other times induced such a pleasant sense of intimacy, this morning made her presence feel like an intrusive stranger. She had the wild impulse to nonsense-text Nikki, and experienced a flash of joy at the thought, but it was instantly extinguished.

With a rough hand, she turned on the radio full-blast, flooding the cab with sound so violent it set off a thumping in her eardrums. She turned the volume down, and sensed a faint smile form within her, then slowly die.

Tubs had not responded in the way she had hoped. Of course, she'd not been so naïve as to expect him simply to accept the idea (though she would not have been surprised if he had!). What bugged her was his tone, it was so . . . discourteous.

"Raging winds," said the radio host, "throughout the Peninsula and Boland today."

Tubs had never before been discourteous towards her.

The car was on Hospital Bend, and, as always, seemed to self-navigate round the extended curvature of the road. Because of the weather conditions, Rosa made sure to keep her speed within manageable limits.

If Tubs refused to budge, that would be the end of their marriage.

As the car reached the top of the bend, a sprawling Groote Schuur Hospital receded on Rosa's right, barely visible in the encircling fog. She wondered how many babies within those walls were on life-support. She pictured Nicky-Ross, little more than an amoeba, engulfed by his apparatus; she pictured the day she would bring him home, the joy on Tubs's face . . . on her Dad's, on Plato's. One big happy family . . . destined to live happily ever after.

The sea and harbour were not visible in the fog, and only glimpses of the mountainface showed through as Rosa took the descending road to the City Centre and Foreshore.

When I bring him home, thought Rosa, he will still be small enough to fit into a shoebox. He'd be delicate as a chicken, and traces of red fuzz would be beginning on his tiny head; his hands would be curled into minute fists which he'd hold below his chin like a boxer. And Tubs and Dad and Plato would crowd around excitedly. And then he'd grow into this big clumsy oaf! I'd scold him for never shaving, for wearing his jeans too low over his bum, for the ugly tattoo which he would've had done without my permission, and for spending too much time on his smartphone.

Rosa laughed out loud. Cars passed her on her right, and curious motorists, catching sight of the laughing woman, just smiled to themselves.

And he'd be proud of me, she told herself, proud that I'd been his birth mother's best and only friend, proud that I would've sacrificed my marriage for him, proud that I could rise above the pettiness of white-and-black.

When she arrived at the office, the first thing Rosa did was make herself a mug of coffee. She felt as though she'd had an hour or two too little sleep, and hoped that the coffee would fix it; she sipped from her mug with relish, but her throat remained dry.

Nobody else had yet arrived at the office, and she felt as alone as she had in her car driving in to work. She took out her cellphone, keyed in Nikki's number, and pressed the green button. At the prompt, she spoke in clear and measured tones, listening to herself say, Hi, Nikki. It's me. Just to let you know Nicky-Ross and I are doing fine. Missing you stacks. She hesitated before terminating the call, half-certain of Nikki's presence on the other end.

She was sure Tubs would budge—because he had really liked Nikki, and he loves her cat, and he wouldn't want to break up with me. He'll get used to the idea of black parents-white kid. And I'll repay him by bearing him his own flesh-and-blood child. Tubs's image appeared to her so vividly that she could discern his individual eyelashes and, on his cheeks, the wide-spaced pores like scattered seeds.

Leigh Irving-Moore was demonstrating something to Ferrie on her computer tablet. Their eyes were fixed on the tablet screen; he seemed engrossed. All the time, Leigh was explaining something, but in a whisper, so no-one else could hear. It looked important.

At the sight of Leigh Irving-Moore's low-cut blouse, a short burst of fury inflamed Rosa's cheeks; she hated Leigh, hated the pretentiousness of her double-barrelled surname, the tiny gold cross that dangled in the bitch's curvature, the hair that was always styled to look not-styled. But above all she hated the way she would always cozy up to Ferrie, always find some way to hog his attention.

Clyde Petersen came and chose a chair alongside Rosa, settling noisily into it. He didn't notice that his coffee spilled when he clunked the mug down in front of him. "Yoo! The wind is berserk this morning,"

172

he said. "Did you see, it blew over a truck on the M5? There's the mother of all traffic jams into Town—I'm amazed I made it here by eight." He glanced at his wristwatch, saw that he had spilled his coffee, and proceeded to wipe it up with the edge of his hand.

Issie Jacoob's eyes met Rosa's, and seemed to glint in knowing sympathy. She looked away quickly, not wishing for any complicity in her as-yet incomprehensible rage.

Ferrie called the meeting to order at eight fifteen, even though Swanepoel was not there yet—caught in traffic on the M5, no doubt. "I was summoned," said Ferrie, "to a conference-call with the Jintao management yesterday morning." He paused, and Rosa could see in Leigh's eyes that he had shared this information with her beforehand. "They followed up the call with an email," Ferrie continued, "essentially putting the deal with us on hold."

Ferrie read the email, and added, "So you see, there's something they're not telling us, and my guess is they're thinking of taking us back to the negotiating table."

"You think maybe they've got a Plan B in the pipeline?" said Leigh.

On cue, thought Rosa.

"I do indeed," said Ferrie. "For that reason, we need to re-visit our feasibility doc and go over it with a fine-tooth comb. We need to re-test every part of it. Each one of you must please go update your section of the document and circulate to all of us. Then it's back here tomorrow at eight for however long it takes for us to subject it to the mother of all scrutinies."

He repeated the same message in different ways until all appeared to understand. "What we need to establish," he said in closing the meeting, "is how much room we have for manoeuvre."

She was ten minutes late for a ten o'clock progress-report meeting with her project teams, but even as she was apologizing for being late, she began to see in their body language that the reports they would be presenting would be negative. In the meeting, her phone was on silent, but her screen showed the many calls coming through. While she listened and responded to her teams' reports, she was able to send off text messages to her callers. In one case, it was necessary for her briefly to leave the meeting to talk to a customer whose call couldn't be deferred. It infuriated her that her teams were falling behind on so many of their deliverables; it would get her into trouble with her boss and undermine her reputation with her peers; she struggled to keep the pitch of her voice restrained while trying to communicate the seriousness of the lapses; the team members seemed impotent as well as indifferent, and this infuriated her more. She resorted to threats. The failing projects couldn't continue to sustain the kind of losses and inefficiencies that had become emblematic. There would be a stage-gate meeting in three weeks' time, and doubtlessly, the Project Sponsorship Board would call for aborting the worst-performing ones—unless . . .

The meeting overran its scheduled time by some twenty minutes. When she got back to her office, Rosa found a message on her desk which had been left by Swanepoel. "I need to interrogate some of your numbers, Rosa." Hardly had she sat down to return several of the deferred calls than in stepped Swanepoel with a large file of papers under his arm. "These variance reports can't wait," he explained. He needed to have his summary-report to Ferrie ready first thing tomorrow morning. It irked her that she needed to spend so much of her valuable time coaching Swanepoel through his own responsibilities. If he had any brains he'd have been able to figure out eighty percent of the so-called queries that surfaced in his variance reports. He would definitely be offered a termination package under her regime.

A 100g chocolate bar from her desk drawer, along with a mug of coffee, would serve as lunch. If she were spared interruptions, she'd be able to get through a particular document that demanded her priority-attention, since it was the subject of a consulting assignment for one of her more important clients. She had closed her door but this did not prevent people from sticking in their heads, apologizing profusely, then stating why it was necessary for them to interrupt. In addition, the phone rang continuously, and while she was able to deal pretty smartly with the various issues raised, she was finding it impossible to sustain the right level of attention to finish work on her consulting document.

Several times she tried to get through to the hospital admin manager to arrange a meeting. Eventually she heard his voice on the other end, and immediately recalled the phone and pens in his shirt pocket. She was phoning, she said, because of the birth and the death; she needed to arrange a funeral and arrange an adoption. Where does she start? Right, said the manager. He was taking care of the details on his end. When would she be able to come through for a meeting? He would set it up and let her know.

She wondered if Nikki would have survived the birth had she, Rosa, been more purposeful in trying to track her down. Maybe the birth would not then have been premature. She wished she had romped around in the sea at Fish Hoek with Nikki instead of worrying about getting her hair wet. Would Nicky-Ross be a sea-lover like his mother? She would need to get him a dog as soon as he got home, so that he grew up with his own Dingus from the word go.

Almost thirteen hours had sped by, and she was once again alone in the office. She noticed that her breathing was at a heightened level, and that a rhythmic buzzing that had started in her temples had spread to her cranium. She resisted the impulse to drink more coffee, and decided instead to run through a tried-and-tested relaxation routine involving measured breathing exercises that she was confident would see her freshness restored.

When Tubs phoned, she was pleased to detect a gentleness in his tone that clearly indicated contrition. He'd like to prepare sole for supper, he said. How did that sound? "Delightful!" was her reply. "I'm just stopping at the hospital, then I'll be home. Should be within the hour."

The wind tore into her car on the highway, forcing her to concentrate to hold a steady line. She saw that there was no fog over the sea, but that all colour had been reduced to shades of grey. The lower slopes of the mountain were visible but had a dampened-wood look. In her mind, she and Nikki were busy preparing supper in the cottage at Fish Hoek; it was warm and bright; beer was flowing freely—and so much laughter! All they did was laugh and smoke cigarettes, and always their flesh touched in that deliciously confined kitchen space. She was not sure how much of what she was imagining was recall or invention. All she knew was she would not be able to anticipate how she was going to cope with Nikki no longer there.

At the hospital there was no oxygen mask over Nicky-Ross's face, just a thin plastic lead with a pair of prongs going into his nose. His head was uncovered, but because the light was so dim it was difficult for her to know if the cap of dark around his head was red or not. She was once again looking in at Nicky-Ross through the clear glass panel, and was again struck by the number of gauges, monitors, cables attached to him.

"He's had a good day," said the nursing sister in a kindly voice. She was standing alongside Rosa, holding open and paging through a large Manilla folder marked with Nicky-Ross's name. Just above the left breast of her navy-blue uniform was pinned a purple name tag with her name inscribed in gold; it refracted the light with each movement of her hands.

"Are all those attachments really necessary?" Rosa asked, not so much for a yes-no reply, but to signal her concern that they must surely be traumatizing the baby.

"We were able to take him off the ventilator," said the sister. "But his medication and nutrition have to be administered via infusion-drip.

Also, we need to take blood from time to time, and to monitor things like his heart rate, blood pressure, and—"

"—I understand," said Rosa, tears suddenly filling her eyes.

"I understand how you're feeling," said the nursing sister, closing her folder, and staring intently into Rosa's eyes. "I know that the little fellow lost his mother, and that you're now the only person in the world for him." She drew closer and briefly hugged Rosa. "I wish you strength, my dear."

The sister left, and Rosa stayed on, staring through the panel at Nicky-Ross in his incubator. Except for the rapid rise-and-fall of his chest, his body lay limp and motionless. He's more a part of the machinery than of the human race, thought Rosa. Look at all those dials and monitors! A green wave pattern coursed steadily across a computer screen mounted above the incubator. To the side, two small aluminium devices displayed coloured numbers incomprehensible to Rosa. The devices were linked to each of Nicky-Ross's hands by flat braided straps. With her forehead against the glass, Rosa tried to speak to Nicky-Ross, but no words would come.

On the way to her car, she allowed the wind to tear into her, and felt a strange delight in being battered that way.

On the table, roses—twelve red, in a one-of-a-kind sculpted Zimbabwean stone vase; strongly scented droplets on petals and leaves evoked in Rosa's mind thoughts of death and the sea. From the kitchen came sounds of dishes and cookware as Tubs prepared the sole. On the carpet in the dining room Plato, with plaintive eyes, was perched in the strike position. He loped the space that separated him from Rosa, and sprang into her lap; he crawled his front paws upward on the front of her dress, holding his mouth towards hers as if to receive a kiss.

She smiled at the cat, but his eyes stirred heavy emotions within her. She lifted him to her shoulder, where he brushed her neck and necklace with his fur before sliding down her back to the floor.

Sauvignon Blanc was the choice of wine—5-year old Bordeaux, taken from the cellar by Tubs for this special occasion of his wife's grief. He uncorked the dusty bottle, for its fragrance to curl out and integrate with the smell of roses and sole.

"She had such a zest for life," said Rosa, staring into her wine. "I wish I had more pictures of her."

Tubs and Plato listened in silence.

"Nicky-Ross is going to make it," she said. She raised her glass to her lips and inhaled before drinking. "Where's Dad this evening?"

"He wanted to retire early this evening," said Tubs. "Still trying to catch up on lost sleep."

The sole was prepared with parsley and coarse white salt. Rosa's appetite was voracious. She finished her two fillets and two glasses of wine, and was glad to hear there'd be dessert to have as well. "My thoughtful caring husband," she said.

Plato had settled in a corner of the room.

"Do you think he knows?" Rosa asked Tubs. The cat's eyes widened, and a tension became visible in his body. "He certainly knows when he's being spoken about."

"Hard to say," said Tubs. They both looked smiling at the cat, who rose and walked over to Tubs and pressed himself against his legs. "Maybe not that she's dead, but certainly that she's gone."

"I think we should download a picture of her," said Rosa. "Print it out, and display it in her room for him."

While she worked at the printer, Tubs went and found an unused photo-frame, into which the picture of Nikki—smiling all teeth and red hair—was fitted. They set it up on the chest of drawers in what was Nikki's room, and eagerly watched Plato's reaction.

"He doesn't seem to have figured this is Nikki," said Tubs, holding the picture in front of the cat's face.

"Perhaps we should put the picture right here on the bed," said Rosa. "He's bound to twig, sooner or later. And this space, here," she added, pointing to the bare top of the cupboard, "this is where the urn will stand."

"The urn?"

"Her ashes."

For a moment, Tubs seemed frozen. "You really loved her, didn't you?"

"She died so suddenly," was all Rosa could say, in a tearful, reed-thin voice. She sank slowly to the bed, and took the cat onto her lap. Tubs joined them, embracing his wife, gently kissing the tears from her cheeks. His breathing had accelerated, and was audible in his wife's ears as little panting staccatos rivalling the gusting wind outside. Tears had come to his eyes, too, and he was able to hold them in check by repeating banal comforting phrases over and over into his wife's ear. He urged her to let it all out—it's OK to cry; you need to cry. He created a concavity with his chest for her to sink against and cling to.

She realized that they had fallen asleep right there on Nikki's bed, shoes 'n all, when she felt an impulse to check the time. Tubs was lying against her, his lips against her eyelash. When she stirred, she felt a gentle tremor in his arm which lay across her belly, but his even breathing continued without interruption. At the foot of the bed Plato lay curled up, dozing, his body partly covering the framed picture of Nikki. We should stay here like this, thought Rosa. A vigil. Perhaps we should light candles, burn incense, say a prayer. The thought induced an instinct to cry, but she suppressed it. *Nikki's ashes—her life reduced to dust. No, impossible!* Enough mourning, she told herself. Enough with sombre-thinking. Things need doing—including collecting the ashes and maybe scattering them in the Langebaan Lagoon. Rosa rose to a sitting position, checked that Tubs was not disturbed, then placed her feet on the floor. Before standing up, she caressed the cat, and winked at him and smiled. Then she noiselessly left the room and went to go'n have a shower.

Chapter Fourteen

The hospital's admin supervisor called Rosa the next morning to ask if two o'clock would be OK for a meeting with the director of hospital services. "Oh yes!" she said, and immediately set about re-arranging her diary.

The room to which she was shown was not the office of the director, but a sparsely furnished cell, more like an interrogation-than-meeting-room, with pictureless white walls and a single window set high above eye-level. The single light bulb was not so bright that Rosa couldn't stare directly at it. Her eyes scanned the room for cameras—*it wouldn't surprise me if I were under surveillance, here.* Her instinct was to protest: this was a private hospital, and *I'm a client who's paying top-dollar.* But she knew she wouldn't protest, or act in any way that might jeopardise her chances with the adoption.

She chose not to sit—there were three steel-framed chairs in the room—but to stay on her feet, and to drift around in the confined space, which was almost wholly-taken up by the chairs and a round imitation-wood table.

Tubs had phoned her at work this morning to wish her well with this meeting, and to offer to take care of the funeral arrangements. This was a plus in a morning of minuses caused mainly by sudden unexpected hassles with the China project. Ferrie was becoming more and more demanding as his fear of losing the deal increased, and she found herself continually having to sit through tension-filled meetings with him and her colleagues, as well as having to produce numerous time-wasting reports to settle the spooks in his mind. He was not pleased that she had had to break away for this visit to the hospital—*the eyes showed it,* she said to herself as she pictured his bulging eyes and frazzled brow. Too bad.

The director of hospital services was five minutes late, but this did not bother Rosa—kinda at my tolerance borderline, so no big-deal, Rosa said to herself with an internal smile. She was surprised at the youthfulness of the director, who looked no more than a slender virgin fresh out of high school.

"My apologies for being late," she said, revealing a set of teeth bright as braai embers. "Please sit down—I'm sorry about this venue. Unfortunately my office is being renovated."

She carried two Manilla folders under her right arm and a ring-bound notebook and ballpoint pen in her left hand. Each time she leaned forward, her hair slid around like water in a swinging bucket, and she would unconsciously tuck strands of it back behind her ears.

She opened one of the folders, and took a moment to scroll through the documents in it, before looking up at Rosa who had sat down in the chair opposite her.

"We are ready to release the body," she said, scratching the side of her head. "But there is no *obvious* next-of-kin."

"Her next-of-kin is *me*," said Rosa, who sat with legs crossed and arms folded. "Even though it's not *obvious*."

The director narrowed her eyes and smiled. "Technically," she said, "one's next-of-kin would be a close *blood* relative. Or one's husband. "

"Technically there *is* a blood relative," said Rosa, also smiling. "But he's far from close."

She told the director of Victor Addo's existence, that he'd emigrated to Australia in the year dot, and that there had literally been no contact between him and his sister since. The estrangement had been so absolute, she added, that it would surely erase any claims a blood relative might have.

"We will have to try to contact him," said the director, taking up her pen, and writing something in the file in front of her. "That's how it goes."

"As it happens, I managed to find a phone number for him," said Rosa.

The director paused in her writing, and looked up expectantly.

"I phoned him to notify him of his sister's death, and he said he'd like to attend the funeral." Rosa unfolded her arms. "But I doubt that he'd want to be responsible for arranging it." She chuckled to herself. *G'day, Mr Addo. We have a corpse for you, special delivery, mate.*

The director began writing again, and as she leaned forward, her hair swept down in two symmetrical waves on either side of her face and converged over her cheeks and eyes. With practiced motions of her left hand she swept the tufts back behind her ears, not pausing in her writing.

"If we could get his consent, we could release the body to *you*, and you could then take care of the funeral arrangements. We'll need to get an affidavit from him."

"Sounds fine," said Rosa. "I've no doubt he'll sign one."

The director wrote some more. "Let us have his phone number then, and we'll arrange to get the affidavit."

She closed the folder and opened the other one. "About the baby," she said and hesitated, her eyes taking on a reflective look. "Here, too, we would have to have an indication from the brother—"

"The baby's father was never known. His mother had various relationships. It is my intention to adopt the baby," said Rosa, sounding more emphatic than she intended. "Whether or not the brother approves," She folded her arms again.

The director appeared unfazed. "That will be up to the courts to decide," she said. "As a hospital, we are obliged to discharge the baby into the care of a specialized institution. We have ties with a number of children's welfare organisations." With a toss of her head, she flicked her hair back.

"If I wished to foster the child until the adoption process is sorted out, would you be able to discharge him into *my* care?"

"No, that would not be possible. There are strict legal guidelines, and a clearly defined process to be followed. As a hospital, our role effectively ends once we have discharged the baby, which, as I just mentioned, would have to be into the care of a specialized institution. It would be up to them to decide who will foster the child if there is a delay with the adoption process."

"It would make sense, would it not, for them to appoint the likely adoptive parents as the foster parents? This would make for the perfect transition."

"You could check with them, but in your particular case, I doubt it. In the first place, you're not the closest living blood relative. Secondly, what if there are others also interested in adopting the child? Besides, the child might require the kind of specialised care facilities which an ordinary person could not provide. Another question would be: how experienced are you at parenting—what if the child got sick while in your foster care, what if he died?"

Rosa made no reply. In her opinion, these were subjective questions, all—the kind resolved by precedent or by some decision-maker's discretion, which were essentially the same thing. Short of outright bribery, the only question that mattered was, how does one exert influence in the matter?

Back at work, she was bombarded with urgent, hostile appeals by several of her project teams, including the China project team, to approve emergency funding for the mitigation of various contingencies. In each case, the amounts were substantial, and although budgetary provision was in place, the effect would be draining of Lumina's cash resources. Yet, despite her best efforts, she could find no alternative but to sign on the dotted line. In several instances, she was tempted to either escalate the decision, which meant *refer-to-Ferrie* . . . or simply to postpone it. But that was not her style. In every case where she could not find sufficient reason to reject a request, she signed. It left a scar on her mood; something was not right. Ferrie would not be happy with any explanation she provided, no matter how much sense it made—just as *she* wasn't. It's a matter of principle. So many requests for contingency funding. There was an unmistakable pattern, here: the idea that she, as project sponsor was not doing her job, nagged at her mind.

There was a long list of return-calls waiting, mostly from irate clients; in several instances, she was requested to pay them at their offices a personal visit, which would have meant dropping everything and flying out to Durban and East London to resolve problem-issues on the spot. She resisted each one—why not a video- or tele-conference, instead, she insisted? Or, when there was no other option, she offered to check whether one of her colleagues could stand in for her, a thought which irked her: however, for her to leave Cape Town for even a day at this point was simply out of the question.

She was able to make some dent in her reading backlog, ensuring that the priority-reports got her best attention. Damn. In too many instances did she uncover anomalies that called for further investigation. She spent a substantial amount of her time that afternoon firing off terse, irate emails to her people, demanding explanations.

"The secret of my success," said Rosa to herself, "is that I've always been 80 percent proactive, twenty percent reactive. That balance has been upset. Right now, I'm a headless chicken, and it's showing in my results."

Before leaving the office, she browsed through a document she had referred to Ferrie for review, and was dismayed to see the huge number of edits he was proposing, just about every one of them trivial. Damn. Nitpicking with a vengeance. "I don't have time for shit!" she said out loud. If I upped and suddenly left, this place would be so seriously fucked.

The wind howled in from the south-east, bringing with it a shattered rain that stabbed like dust particles at the windscreen. When Rosa switched on her headlamps, the fine crystalline shimmer that was illuminated by the light blinded her for a moment; she steered carefully, glad that she was leaving the office after the rush hour was over.

At the hospital, she got a parking bay close to the entrance doors, and dashed across the parking area as best she could on her high heels, to avoid the worst of the wind. She was greeted by the wide-smiling faces of the security man at the door, and of the night-duty receptionist, who informed her that Dr Cochrane had left a message, he would like to see her when she arrived.

She was struck by the beauty of Mel Cochrane's shirt, blue gingham slim fit. Saville Row for sure—she knew, she had gotten one of those for Tubs last time she was in London. The paediatrician's chest hair edged up over his open collar, creating a soft bed for the Kruger Rand pendant that dangled there. Although she could pick up no fragrance about his person, he oozed hygiene. Fresh as a mountain stream, she thought, as he approached her, extending his hand in greeting.

"Today you get to hold the baby," he said, and smiled when he saw the sudden rush of stars in her eyes.

To get to the neonatal ward, they had to follow a wide, busy corridor, with numbered doorways on both sides of it, through which could be glimpsed patients in their beds. Rosa was close to swooning, so unreal was the prospect of actually holding Nicky-Ross in her arms. She did her best to keep pace with Cochrane, who seemed oblivious of her at his side. Their feet on the linoleum floor made soft padding sounds which were far too distinct in her mind—how on earth can I be focusing on my footsteps at such a time in my life? A stretcher with squeaky wheels was pushed past them by an attendant who looked like a cartoon wharf rat she'd seen somewhere. She stole a glance at the patient in the stretcher—a balding old man with plastic leads attached to his body. He winked and smiled slyly at her. She winked back.

It did not surprise her to see that the neonatal ward resembled a meticulously-crafted laboratory—a controlled environment, probably not unlike God's workshop—where the Master Builder prepped His creatures for the natural world. Was Cochrane a latter-day version of the Word-Made-Flesh? So much white!—the ceiling, the walls the floor; the hand of the interior designer was to be seen in the contrasting effect of the pastel blue of the curtains and the darker blue of the upholstered chairs. Even the alcohol sanitizing gel that they used on their hands, in its blue-and-white plastic dispenser-bottle, fitted into the overall scheme.

Nicky-Ross's incubator was the fourth in a row of five. The moment Cochrane lifted the lid, the baby stirred—"looka the little armies 'n leggies," thought Rosa, struggling to restrain the whoosh of ecstasy that almost bowled her over. Cochrane carefully detached some of the leads attaching Nicky-Ross to his life-support apparatus, and lifted him off the bedding.

"Here we go," he said, passing the baby into the nest that Rosa made with her breast and arms. The baby flailed about, and let out a brief squeal. With a shock of terror and delight, Rosa felt his living weight transfer to herself, and felt a sweat breaking out all over. My heart, she said to herself. That's what he is, my precious throbbing heart.

"You may hold him for a few minutes," said Cochrane, whose face showed his delight at Rosa's delight. "His body's still quite delicate, so he'll feel discomfort if he's held for too long."

Cochrane went over to the nurses' station to use the phone, and Rosa knew she'd be able to hold the baby for at least as long as he was gone. She sat down slowly, trying to minimize any jerkiness in her movements. She looked intently at the baby's face, and it seemed to her he sensed he was in the arms of someone who loved him. She was sure it was not her imagination that he was relaxing if not luxuriating, in her arms—and his smell? Is it him I'm smelling or just the lotion they use to wash the babies with? There was a tiny indentation in his chin just below the bottom lip, which gave his mouth a pouted look. Rosa searched for Nikki's likeness, but the only resemblance lay in the pallor of the cheeks and forehead, and in the reddening scalp. Maybe when he's able to open his eyes, she thought, then I'll see Nikki more clearly.

She wasn't sure if it was Cochrane or she who suggested coffee, but there they were, the two of them, trotting off along the wide busy corridor to the coffee shop, their feet again making soft padding sounds on the linoleum floor.

The air became less rarified as they entered the coffee shop. They were greeted by the smell of coffee and wood polish, as well as surreptitious stares by one or two of the few customers there. They were shown a table by the wall, and Rosa suddenly thought, I'm starving. But even as the slim-trim waitress readied to take their orders, she knew she would not submit—pastries were not her thing.

From the way the waitress greeted him, Rosa could tell Cochrane was a regular here. She took Rosa's order, then looked shyly at Cochrane and asked if he would be having a latté as usual.

"As usual," was his reply. "And, of course, with hot milk, please."

"Of course."

Rosa settled back in her chair, and felt she was relaxing for the first time today. There was something serene about this place right now, with its dim pastel shades, muted sounds and absence of hustle-and-bustle. Before her was the radiant face of Mel Cochrane, brightened by the lamp above their table. It occurred to her that he would be seeing her face with equal clarity; she hoped her eyes betrayed no stress.

He was curious about her relationship with the mother, he said.

Rosa was uncertain how to reply; she heard herself say, "We were best friends," and wondered how much anybody could glean from such a bland nothing-statement.

"She had no known relatives," she continued. "Other than a brother, who's been living in Australia for years. So, me and my husband, we will be taking care of the funeral arrangements. We're also planning to adopt the baby."

"You're picking up all the bills, too," said Cochrane, smiling.

Rosa smiled, too.

From behind the counter came the whirr of coffee beans being ground. Rosa sensed she was being stared at, and looked around. A sixty-something woman at a table close by was eyeing her with a friendly smile. Rosa smiled back.

"What if the brother also wants to adopt the baby?" Cochrane's right eye narrowed.

"Then we'll have a contest on our hands," said Rosa, trying to project a calmness that she did not feel.

"It could take months to resolve," said Cochrane, seeming to lose interest in further discussion.

Their orders arrived, filter coffee for her, latté for him.

He stirred in his sugar. "Meanwhile," he said, his eyes on the spoon, "the baby will be in foster care." He looked up at Rosa as if he had issued a challenge.

"Yes, I know. But I will try to get them to place him in *my* foster care." She sipped and winced, the coffee was unexpectedly hot.

"Good luck," he said. "Right now, bonding with a mother-figure is critical for the little one's all-round health. In the absence of any other option, it seems like you're the best bet for this role—at least while he's here in hospital."

"You'll not know how much it means to me, hearing that from you, the baby's paediatrician," said Rosa, close to tears. "I'll be doing whatever it takes to become Nicky-Ross's foster mother and then his adoptive mother. Whatever it takes."

She took another sip of the scalding coffee, and winced again. "It's difficult to explain," she said. "Nikki and I were best friends. From the moment she fell pregnant, she and I were going to co-parent the baby. You'll see on her admission form, she put me down as her next-of-kin. We were closer than mere family could ever be."

Cochrane nodded as she spoke. "We need to steer him through this vulnerable pre-term period," he said. "It'll be several weeks before he's out of the woods. It'll require total commitment—from me, you, the hospital, everyone."

They ordered more coffee and latté, and he explained that Nicky-Ross's most important need right now was to hear her voice. "If you were close to his mother," said Cochrane, "he will have heard your voice while in the womb, and he will recognize it if he hears it now."

In response to Rosa's quizzical smile, he added, "Oh yes, one's hearing develops in the womb. He'd have heard the beating of his mother's heart, her blood-flow, the rattle of her lungs when she coughed. And while in there, he'd have picked up external sounds, too—your voices, the barking of dogs, cats mewing, the microwave beeping. And music, singing, laughter, as well—he needs a lot of that now."

In bed that night, she was passionate in her love-making with Tubs, but her mind was on Cochrane and Nicky-Ross. He'll need to hear my voice, she told herself. He'll wonder why he no longer hears his mother's voice. My voice will have to become his mother's voice.

Next day she got the saleslady at an electronics store in the Waterfront to help her select "the best" audio recording device on the market—one which reduced sound distortion and background noise to an absolute minimum, and that had "the longest" battery life. Then she stopped off at the bookstore and came away with a book of nursery rhymes and eight titles chosen from the category, *baby—2 years old*. She stopped off at the music store and picked up an assortment of CD's that included children's songs, chamber music and lullabies. Before heading back to the office, she bought some cuddly toys—a teddy bear, a koala bear, a rabbit, a rag doll, a lion and a tiger.

In the afternoon, she Googled bird songs and children's laughter, and saved these to her flash drive.

Chapter Fifteen

Rosa shifted into reverse gear, then allowed the car to roll down the driveway into the street. She glanced eastward and saw that the trees and rooftops of Pinelands were still dark against the early-morning sky. There were no clouds and no south-easter; it was going to be a good day, hooray.

Bill got in, and they set off—it was her turn to drop him off at Langa this morning. He yawned and sat back against his seat, and allowed the drone of the motor to lull him into a doze. He heard her say, "Dad, I'm going to be adopting the baby." He thought he was dreaming; he jolted so hard his seatbelt locked.

"Right. Tell me I'm dreaming, Rosa," he said, turning sharply towards her.

"No, you're not, Dad." She was smiling. "He's the cutest thing in the world!"

"But, you see the irony, here, don't you?" He paused till she shifted her eyes in his direction. "Where in the world do black women adopt white babies?"

She looked rapidly back at the road, and he concluded with satisfaction that his words had produced the desired effect. He tried to chuckle but his throat just made a scraping noise. "You'll become a laughing-stock, Rosa. This kind of thing doesn't happen in the real world."

She remained silent, suddenly aloof.

"People will gawk," he said. "You'll be all over the social media." Again he tried to chuckle, and again his throat just produced a dry scraping sound. "Your mother would not have approved," he said. "She'll turn in her grave if this goes ahead."

The sun was rising, and shafts of light came angling acutely into the vehicle. Her face was caught in a first glow, which accentuated the petal-softness of her cheeks. He asked himself how it was possible that he had had a part in producing this finest of beauties.

"I see the irony, Dad," she said, her voice calm as steel. "You talk of black women and white babies, and I ask myself if my ears deceive me. You, who brought me up to believe that race is a fiction invented by the—"

"—Nice try, Rosa," he said, this time able to muster a chuckle. "You know this is not about race."

"Then why talk of black women and white babies?" she said, her tone rising. "This is not the apartheid era," she added rapidly. "And even if it were, do you think I would have buckled under *their* laws?"

It's astounding how much she reminds me of her mother, thought Bill, momentarily lost for words. Again he wondered how he had played a role in producing this fine creature, and sighed as a strong surge of pride gushed through him.

"That kid'll not forgive you for being his mother," he heard himself say, and noticed how instantly her eyes blazed. "His buddies at school will mock him for having a black mother, and he'll feel ashamed of you, Rosa."

"So! Finally it's revealed. There's a black nationalist lurking under that socialist skin of yours after all. How'd you manage to conceal it for so long, Dad?"

Her calm self-assurance irritated him. She was turning this into a sparring session to avoid confronting reality, but he felt sure his truths were hitting home. "Don't be flippant about this, Rosa," he said, trying to match her calmness. "Sadly, the world's not ready for something like this. If you really cared about the child's future—and I don't doubt you do—then why not set up a bequest for him, or something? Why adopt him? Why want to *own* him?"

They turned out of Forest Drive onto an open Jan Smuts. The car sped up as if of its own accord.

"Dad, when you and your wife decided to raise your newborn daughter as a leftist and an atheist—"

He laughed. "Touché, Rosa. Do you regret it?"

"Sometimes—often—I'm this driven, bitchy, westernized, capitalist monster who hardly speaks a word of isiXhosa. Yet, I'd rather be nothing else. No, I don't regret it, and Nicky-Ross will not regret it, either."

In no time, they were at the turn-off to the N2.

"Having a white kid for a grandson is going to take some getting used to," he said. "Make sure he calls me *Tata.*"

At the hospital, an ambulance, with motor still running, was blocking the entranceway. Two attendants in navy blue uniforms and with stethoscopes round their necks were hastily unloading a stretcher. Their faces were troubled. Rosa stole a glance at the patient—a woman, lying on her left side, with right hip bulging under the blanket. Her eyes were wide open, defiant, unseeing. *My* look, thought Rosa. The expression I'd be wearing if God dealt me a low blow.

She entered the hospital thinking, nothing could be worse, nothing, than if he were to grow up ashamed of me.

Her cellphone beeped. A text message. It was Ferrie: *See me before meeting this morning.* Oh, fuck off.

She strolled through the corridor leading to the neonatal ward, looking askance into several doorways that she passed, and was amused at the number of butts, penises, tits on view—patients have no inhibitions at this hour of the day!

Nicky-Ross was a mass of tubes and wiring; he was surrounded by devices that beeped, flashed, whooshed, throbbed, binged, pinged and clicked. In a multitude of colours, electronic screens displayed numbers, waves, degrees, percentages, charts, graphs and tables. He was completely naked, except for the oversized nametag on his left wrist. He lay with arms and legs splayed, exposing bright pink genitals. Light brown liquid substances were going into him, and dark yellow liquid—pee, no doubt!—going out.

Rosa felt her neck muscles tighten. She was certain that his amount of life-support had been increased overnight. She tried to catch the eye of one of the ward nurses, but no luck. I must be calm she told herself, calm, calm, calm.

She thought she saw a twitch run through the baby's left hand, but couldn't be sure, it didn't seem to register on any of the monitors. She looked closely to see if the hand would twitch again, but couldn't keep her eyes from blinking. Her hand inserted itself through a porthole . . . wondrously, for she had no conscious part in that. She watched as her hand inched itself towards Nicky-Ross's inert cluster of fingers . . . touch it. The contact caused explosions to ripple through her temples, as the baby-fingers immediately groped for and tried to encircle her forefinger. She spoke in hoarse, pleading whispers, certain that he could hear her, certain that he would *know* her.

She became aware of a nurse's presence at her side, of the nurse saying to her: "He was a bit restless during the night."

"All this extra machinery," said Rosa, feeling angry but not understanding why. "Surely it must be very traumatic for him. All the pricking and prodding. His delicate flesh. The pain. He must be having a really rough time."

"There was some vomiting, during the night, not too much. Dr Cochrane examined him this morning – "

"Dr Cochrane was here already?"

"That's right, ma'am. He's doing his other ward rounds now. He'll be back at about nine, again."

Rosa prepared a text message for Ferrie. *Stuck at the hospital. Baby not doing too well. Waiting to see paediatrician. Will contact you asap.*

She put her hands through the portholes, took Nicky-Ross's hands in hers, felt their minute tickle against her flesh. "So precious," she said. "So delicate." The baby's head jerked; his eyes opened then closed immediately. "So cute," she said. "So delicate, nothing but a newborn chick." She held her palms facing up so that his fingers lay against them. His fingers scratched, hesitated, scratched, hesitated. She spoke, using his name repeatedly, watching, feeling for his reaction. She hoped her presence, her warmth, her fragrance, her smile would take his mind off the needles, the tubes, the beepers, the effort entailed in securing life. She said to him that she'd be getting him a little doggie-woggie, that she would take him to the beach—*often*—that she would be his utter servant and slave. She told him that he need never worry about being loved, that that would be the one thing he could be sure of in his life. When there was any movement in his body, her heart beat faster, and she tried to relate the movement to what she was saying.

After half an hour, she left the neonatal ward, and went to the waiting room. There she checked her phone, and listened to the message from Ferrie, *Hi, Rosa, I understand. We'll go ahead with the meeting re China this morning. I've asked Leigh to chair. See you later.*

She went back to Nicky-Ross's ward, sanitized her hands, and returned to him at his incubator. She told him the story of the elves and the shoemaker, sang to him—*Three Blind Mice, Nkosi Sikelel', iAfrica, Once in Royal David's City.* She told him how much he was going to love Tubs and Plato and his Tata, Bill. She promised to make a recording of their voices and come play it to him.

When next she went to the waiting room, she spoke to Tubs on her phone—gave him an update on Nicky-Ross and told him she was waiting to see Dr Cochrane.

"I've already started on the funeral arrangements," Tubs told her. He said he'd text her throughout the day to keep her posted.

Should she tell Nicky-Ross all about Nikki Addo? She wished she could pick him up, but there were just too many attachments! She stroked his hands—flesh to flesh—and spoke and spoke. Hang in there, li'l babba. Stay strong. Life's good, you'll see, it's worth fighting for. Bob Marley came to her mind, and she smiled.

Don't worry about a thing,
'Cause every little thing gonna be all right.

Cochrane arrived shortly after nine.

"Anything earlier than thirty-seven weeks," he said, "is premature. The little guy arrived at under thirty, which ramps up his mortality risk considerably. You can understand why we have this big focus on so many details, no matter how small. Dozens of things can go wrong, and each could be a threat, if not to his life then to his *quality* of life."

Rosa struggled to concentrate. They were standing at the side of Nicky-Ross's incubator. Her eyes kept straying to the baby in the incubator. She had so many questions to ask. Cochrane was answering the questions she wished to ask, but not in the right order.

"Quite simply," continued Cochrane, "with all this hi-tech, we are trying to mimic the world of the uterus, trying to simulate the ideal habitat for him, but no matter how greatly modern technology has advanced, it's still a poor and crude substitute for nature."

Was he talking to me? wondered Rosa, or swatting for a paediatrics exam?

The paediatrician's eyes were on her as he spoke, and they emitted what seemed to be a sympathetic glow.

"We're keeping a close eye on his breathing," said Cochrane. His eyes shifted to the baby. He bent over and adjusted a line to the baby's leg. "We're happy with the way his lungs are developing," he said, looking back at Rosa. "But his breathing still needs to be assisted."

He reached for the bunch of papers on a clipboard hanging on the side of the incubator. Scrolling through the papers, he said, "Right now, his feeding requirements are presenting us with our biggest challenge. He's not ready for breast milk yet, so we're having to go the intravenous route—we're feeding him a whole cocktail of stuff . . . the package includes a specially formulated combo of salts, carbohydrates, fats, proteins. Vitamins as well. With feeding, it's the big picture that matters. Apart from ensuring that he gets the right nutrition, we have to administer his feed in just the right way. It's easy to overfeed and to underfeed. We're trying to stabilize his fluid balance, as we call it. He's passing too much of his feed out via the urine. This means we're having to administer glucose, to prevent hypoglycemia. For all that, his weight gain's been OK, so far."

The energy suddenly gone out of her, Rosa simply nodded her head without speaking.

"So far, we've been able to keep him free of infection," said the paediatrician, hanging the papers back on the side of the incubator. "Because he's preterm, his vulnerability is heightened, as his immune system's not fully developed. As it happens, we have to be doing so many blood tests and attaching all those lines and tubes to his little body—they're necessary of course, but they add to the risk of infection."

"Is there anything you're not telling me, Doctor?"

For an instant, Cochrane's eyes took on the huh?-look. Then he said, "He was born two months premature and he's got no mother. No amount of sophisticated state-of-the-art neonatal hi-tech can substitute for a mother. No amount of paediatric know-how or modern medicine can fill that gap. It's a massive gaping hole, Mrs Lethlabe."

Rosa went to the coffee shop. The table that she and Cochrane had sat at last night was vacant. She chose it and ordered espresso.

There were not many people in the coffee shop, but the matching brown table-and-chair sets gave the place a feel of tranquil crowdedness.

No use rushing to the office, she told herself. By now the China meeting will be over. She moved the condiments tray on her table to one side so that she could open her laptop. The coffee shop's Wi-Fi enabled her to connect to Lumina's network. There were several e-mails waiting to be read, mostly rubbish, but she was interested to see that Leigh had already posted minutes of this morning's China meeting.

Her espresso arrived, seductive in its small white porcelain cup.

"I think I'm going to need another one in five minutes," she said to the smiling waitress.

It was hard to glean from Leigh's minutes whether there were any new material concerns needing to be addressed. Using her cellphone, she sent Ferrie a text message. *Will be in soon. Little one OK.*

She dialled Tubs's number.

He said, "How does Saturday at ten sound? The Maitland Crematorium? They've got a venue that we can use if we want to conduct a service. There's apparently even a priest for hire, if needed."

"Tubs, I'm still at the hospital."

There was a brief silence. "Are you OK? Is the baby OK?"

"Yes, I think so," she said in a tired voice. "It's just I think Nikki's death is maybe hitting me harder than I thought it would . . ."

"Yes, I can understand that."

"But it's the baby we've got to worry about, Tubs. He's got no mother and no father. He's got nothing. He's only got you and me."

Back at the office, Ferrie couldn't see her immediately, and suggested she come back at two. She went back to her office and dialled Perth, Australia.

Victor Addo sounded pleased to hear her voice. He thanked her again for "being there" for Nikki. He couldn't thank her and her good husband enough for taking care of the funeral arrangements, and, Saturday morning? Yes, he was sure his travel agent could have him in Cape Town in time for the funeral.

"I won't have a problem with accommodation," he said to Rosa. "But, would you be able to collect me at the airport?"

"Of course," said Rosa.

They spoke about Nicky-Ross—"he's not out of the woods, yet," said Rosa. "And it's distressing, the sheer number of pipes and tubes connected to his little body. Poor thing."

"It's good to hear he's got no infections," said Victor, when Rosa was done updating him. "And that there's been no need for surgery, so far—touch wood."

"I'm thinking of adopting him," said Rosa, shocked that it came out without any premeditation.

"Really?" Victor's voice seemed to take on a sharpness. "We were talking about it, my wife and I, and we were thinking that as Nikki's only family, maybe it's our responsibility."

"Nikki and I were extremely close," said Rosa. "We were like family," she added, and tried to chuckle. "So it would be appropriate—"

"—Well, maybe that's something we could look at when I get there. I want to thank you and your husband again. Looking forward to meeting you in the flesh."

Leigh's flesh had a uniform pallor from the neck down to her cleavage. A tiny spattering of moss-green capillaries was visible on each breast just at the juncture of their parting. Rosa guessed there'd be more of that green web-work as you closed in on the nipples.

Like rotting seaweed, thought Rosa, staring briefly at the decaying floral arrangement on the coffee table behind Leigh, who was dressed in her trademark white low-cut two-piece ultra-mini. As she sat there in Ferrie's office, her left thigh—crossed over her right—was the most prominent part of her. Without looking directly, Rosa traced the amount of green that threaded randomly across that expanse of flesh, and noted how raw—how freshly-shaven?—the pores looked. Monstrous, thought Rosa. Nothing's more grotesque than an aging beauty. Her instinct was to rush off a text to Nikki's phone number.

Ferrie's brow was furrowed. He asked Rosa to tell him how the baby was doing.

To Rosa it seemed a mandatory question, lacking sincerity. "Not too good," she said, thinking to herself, This is a fucking conspiracy—what is she doing here? She added, "He's not out the woods, yet."

"Sorry to hear that," said Ferrie, turning immediately to a pile of documents on his desk. "And the funeral?" he asked, rifling through the documents.

"Saturday morning," said Rosa. "At ten at the Maitland Crematorium."

"Really sad," said Leigh.

Rosa felt a searing heat run through her temples. She ignored Leigh.

"I remember her," Leigh continued. "Always cheerful. Such beautiful red hair."

Ferrie cleared his throat. "Rosa, I've asked Leigh to join us," His eyes darted from the paper rustling in his fingers to Rosa's eyes, to Leigh's. "You've been under so much pressure, lately."

Ah, so it *is* a conspiracy, thought Rosa, a blinding fury rocking her senses. The only thing that matters, she told herself, is that I stay cool—I can't let her think it's a big deal. She turned to Leigh. Their eyes met. They smiled.

"Damn Chinese," said Ferrie. He clicked his tongue. "Giving us all these hassles."

Inconceivable that Victor Addo will walk away with Nicky-Ross, Rosa said to herself while at the same time anticipating that Ferrie was going to relieve her of the responsibility of managing the Chinese project.

"We've got one more thing to do," said Ferrie. "And that's to build a Johannesburg scenario."

"A Johannesburg scenario?" asked Rosa, hoping her tone conveyed curiosity rather than naivety.

"Lumina's a Cape-based firm," said Ferrie, speaking with less unease. "What if the Chinese are looking to invest in mining? What if they're looking to partner with a firm located in the heart of South Africa's business capital rather than on the periphery, as we are? If you think about it, Cape Town's nothing but a tiny seaside town."

"And if they're looking at South Africa as a platform into the rest of Africa," said Leigh, leaning forward towards Rosa. "Then—"

"—Yep, I get it," said Rosa. "It would make sense for us to develop a business plan for such a contingency."

"Exactly," said Ferrie, tightening his grip on the document before him. "This is a first-draft of such a business plan; it was prepared by Leigh, who, as you know, is our Jo'burg exec."

He fixed his eyes on Rosa's.

If Victor Arsehole Addo wins adoption rights, it means Nicky-Ross relocates to Perth—unthinkable.

Rosa shifted in her seat; the effort to keep her face neutral was causing a stiffening in her back. She wished this meeting would end so that she could go address her real priorities.

"For this reason," said Ferrie . . .

Here it comes, thought Rosa, once again turning to Leigh with a smile.

"For this reason—and to free you up to enable you to focus on the tragedy that's befallen you with your friend's sudden death, and the baby and what-not, it would make sense for Leigh to take over the management of the China project."

"That's very thoughtful of you," said Rosa in the sweetest voice she could muster, aware that some mild remonstrating would be in order. "But, really—"

"—Don't worry about it," said Ferrie. "Leigh has kindly agreed. I've asked her to get cracking straight away, so please don't worry. If you need to take any time off . . ."

No more than forty five minutes were needed for the details to be hammered out. Leigh would "run with" the China project going forward; Rosa would be a key resource supporting Leigh, and—naturally—would work closely with her to ensure the ultimate success of this critical project. Leigh would forward a copy of her first draft of the Jo'burg scenario, and Rosa would provide feedback. It was to be hoped, said Ferrie, that this relief would enable Rosa to focus her main attention on her personal issues as well as her other projects, several of which seem to have run into some stormy weather.

Back in her office, Rosa phoned the neonatal ward and was relieved when she heard that Nicky-Ross "was fine," that he was holding his feed, and that his sleep pattern was satisfactory.

She sent an e-notice to the Lumina staff:

Many of you will remember Nikki Addo who worked here as a business analyst not so long ago. I regret to inform you that she passed away suddenly. If you wish to attend the funeral, it will be held at the Maitland Crematorium on Saturday at 10h00.

Almost immediately the inundation started: Oh yes, I remember Nikki—bright, cheerful redhead. What? Passed away? How sad! What was wrong, was it an accident? Shame! Did she have any family? Saturday should be fine for me. Oh, I'm so sorry, she was such a nice person. What a shock it must have been to you, Rosa—I know you two got on very well, she had a very high regard for you; we were all so shocked when she suddenly resigned and just left without even serving her notice period.

Rosa phoned Tubs. "I'll be stopping off at the hospital as usual," she said, adding that Ferrie had "very kindly" encouraged her to take off as much time as she needed to attend to affairs relating to Nikki and Nicky-Ross.

"I'm also going to try to see a lawyer," she said. "A friend of Nikki's. About the adoption process. I think we're going to need legal help."

"After work?" Tubs asked. "Who's the friend?"

"Yes, after work. A lawyer-friend of Nikki's that I met briefly a while back when Nikki took me for drinks to a little bar which she used to frequent. *Monsters*, it's called. I'll let you know."

She had scheduled daily late-afternoon meetings with each of her project managers, sessions intended to last no more than thirty minutes each, for them to report progress. She had authorized the additional funds that they had demanded, but the unexpected cost to them—the *quid pro quo*—was that she would micro-manage their operations; they would have to suffer the indignity of frequent, regular report-backs on small details—and at day's end, too, when they would usually be winding down. She had not needed to say it—it was clearly understood—any future deviation from project plan would be *their* fault, and there would be consequences.

Ferrie looked in on his way home. She was struck by the haggardness of his appearance. He should have retired years ago, she thought. She had no doubt that his decision to replace her with Leigh on the China project had exhausted him.

"Thanks for taking it so well," he said, sitting down.

So. I took it well? You're relieved I didn't throw a cadenza?

"The more I think about it, the more I'm convinced the China deal is going to stand or fall on Johannesburg."

He's incapable of seeing any other alternative, thought Rosa. If China demands we become a Johannesburg-based company, then it means we have to relocate our offices. And it would mean Leigh becomes the next CEO.

"You're a brilliant exec, Rosa," he said. "I'm relying on you to give Leigh as much support as you can."

At this point I should up and resign, thought Rosa.

"Don't worry," she said, producing a smile that Ferrie's eyes told her came across as bright. "We've got it in hand. Leigh's already mailed me a copy of her Jo'burg draft. I'm looking forward to reading it."

In her car on the way to the hospital, Rosa told herself that she was sure she would find multiple holes in Leigh's report, and that Leigh would say, "It's just a first draft." The important thing was not whether it was a good or a bad draft. The important thing was: is Johannesburg feasible? Is it possible for us to create a *feasible* business case based on Johannesburg? Why do I feel so negative about this?

She turned on the radio and selected the isiXhosa channel.

I hardly understand a word of isiXhosa, she said to herself, trying to understand the fast-speaking DJ. I've become totally alienated from my birth culture. She tried to smile.

She turned the radio off.

In principle, we probably shouldn't be getting into bed with China. Yet, if Ferrie's right, we're dead without them. Scary.

At Nicky-Ross's side, she quietly sang the words of *Nkosi Sikelel', iAfrica, Amapondo*, and *Pata Pata*, muting the click-sounds. What other songs did my dad sing to me when I was little?

"Shall I show you how to change his nappy?" asked the nurse on duty. "Ha. Look how your face lights up!"

Rosa took a deep breath. "Do I need gloves?" she asked, trying to control her voice. Nikki's image was crowding her consciousness, and a sweeping sensation, like a wind across the Foreshore, was stifling her breathing.

"You've sterilized your hands," said the nurse. "That's fine. You stand round that side, and I'll stand this side." She put her gloved hands through the portholes, and undid the tube connected to Nicky-Ross's navel. "Here," she said to Rosa, pointing to the strips that held the nappy in place." You simply need to detach these—easy peasy lemon squeezy."

The moment Rosa touched the nappy, the baby squirmed. Rosa stepped back in some alarm. The nurse chuckled. "Ooh," she said, "Look how embarrassed we are! Don't we want Mommy to see our little willy, then?"

Rosa recalled the first time that, as a child, she tried to hold a hen in her hands—how she couldn't, because it kept flapping its wings so wildly. How her dad had laughed and laughed.

The nurse laughed as Nicky-Ross's wriggling obstructed Rosa as she worked at getting the nappy off; how clumsily Rosa was wiping his bottom with a soft pad, how Rosa struggled to get the new nappy on. How Rosa sighed when it was all over.

"That was great," said the nurse. "Don't worry, it gets easier each time."

"I'm sweating," Rosa said. "That was seriously scary, I kept worrying I'd hurt him."

"It would be OK for you to pick him up and hold him against your chest," said the nurse. "Just for a short while, though; his body's still quite tender. Shall I help you?"

Rosa settled back in the soft chair, holding Nicky-Ross against her chest, which the nurse had suggested she bare, to enable "skin-to-skin" contact.

At first it felt like he was a parcel coming undone, and she kept worrying bits of him would detach and fall to the floor. She worried that the rigid movements of his shoulders indicated pain, discomfort; that the soft moans coming from deep within him indicated distress. She worried that her touch would infect his skin, cause bruising, itching, inflammation. Tears came to her eyes as she felt the prickly touch of his finger-tips on her chest, as she felt their shared warmth on her body and in her nostrils.

"Did you hear, Nicky-Ross?" she whispered into his ear. "The nurse said I'm your mommy. That's right, little babba, I'm your mommy."

The nurse came back and helped Rosa settle him in his incubator. Rosa tucked in the teddy bear alongside him, and found spaces all around for the other soft toys—the koala bear, the rabbit, the rag doll, the lion and the tiger.

She hugged the nurse—perhaps a tad too long, too tight? She felt obliged to apologise, and did so with a silly laugh.

"Tomorrow it's a poo nappy," said the nurse.

Back in her car, she found it impossible to drive off before her breath had calmed. She sent Tubs a text message, saying, *You'll never believe! I just changed the baby's nappy*, and reminding him that she would be stopping off at *Monster's* en route home to see if she could locate Nikki's lawyer-friend.

Monster's was pretty much as she'd recalled—maybe dingier. From where she sat, she had a good view of the whole room, including the entrance-way. The place was filling up gradually, mostly with young people in denim jeans, and carrying cellphones, but nobody she recognized, till—that had to be her, the lawyer! Rosa's heart sped up when she saw her come through the door, a pensive-looking brunette in a jeans which accentuated her buttocks. She wore a thin white blouse through which her bra was plainly visible, and in her left hand clutched a cellphone and a pack of cigarettes.

Rosa watched her go up to the counter, choose a high-stool, joke with the barman, and order beer in a green bottle.

The lawyer raised the bottle to her mouth, and simultaneously, with her other hand, tapped the keys of her phone. When she put the bottle down, it was half-empty. She squeezed her lips between thumb and forefinger, and adjusted her bum on the barstool. Rosa noticed she was tapping her foot, and realized it was in time to the house-music, which, up to that point Rosa was oblivious of.

Well, here goes, thought Rosa, rising from her seat and strolling over to the lawyer's side.

"Hi, there. Mind if I join you?"

The lawyer shot her a startled glance which changed instantly to a gleaming full-toothed smile. "Rosa! My goodness. How good to see you."

They wrapped their arms around each other.

"Grab a stool. What are you having, whiskey? Just as I thought, same as what Nikki would have ordered. Where is the witch, anyway? She just disappeared into thin air—how many months since we last saw her or heard from her? You're looking fabulous."

Rosa lowered her eyes. "Nikki's dead," she said in a flat voice. "She died suddenly, in childbirth. A beautiful baby. Premature. The funeral's—"An alien groan rising in her throat stifled further speech.

"My god," said the lawyer, hopping off her barstool and taking Rosa into her arms. "My god."

Rosa clung hard, wishing to prolong the embrace, sucking in the sheer warm-heartedness that she felt come flooding over to her. There was a pleasant mangle of bar-noises in her ear—clinking glass, chatter, laughter, music, feet and chairs scraping, and yes, the invisible sounds, too, of fans whirring and fridges humming. This was a place where people came to be happy.

"It's so terribly, terribly sad," said the lawyer, wringing her hands, and glancing round at her pack of cigarettes on the counter, but refraining from smoking.

"The funeral's on Saturday morning at ten," said Rosa. "At the Maitland Crematorium. I came here to spread the word among Nikki's *Monster*-friends."

"I can certainly help with that. I'll let everyone know."

"There's something else that I think I'm going to need your help with," said Rosa. "I know you're a lawyer, and I would have phoned you, but didn't know what name you'd be listed under in the telephone directory or on Google."

"Angelina van der Poel," said the lawyer. "Angie."

"It's about adopting the baby, said Rosa. "Nikki has a brother, an ex-South African living in Australia . . ."

"She recognized me immediately," Rosa said to Tubs. "She was shocked to hear of Nikki's death."

Plato nestled in Rosa's lap. "I wonder if he can smell Nicky-Ross on me," said Rosa, stroking the cat between the ears. "She's very keen to help us with the adoption process, especially after I told her about Victor Addo."

"I've taken off from work tomorrow morning," said Tubs. "To go with you to the hospital. I figure if I'm going to be the baby's father, I need to be a more physical presence. I'll also then be able to go with you to visit the lawyer—Angie van der Poel, you say?"

The supper Tubs had thoughtfully prepared for her was a pan-fry of salted fish with rice and beans, and with a strong garlic aroma. She cooed at the sight of the smouldering heap it made on her plate, and ate it with an enjoyment that brought pleasure to the eyes of both her husband and the cat.

When she was done eating, they went to the lounge, where she set the new audio device to record selections from the CDs which she'd bought that morning.

"We also need to record our voices," she said, "including Plato's. What does one do to get a cat to mew on cue?"

"The programme for Nikki's memorial should be a souvenir," said Rosa. "A tribute in its own right. We should not spare cost or effort in producing one that will become a treasured keepsake over time. As Nicky-Ross grows up, every time he looks at it, his eyes should shine in wonderment."

"We'll need a picture for the front cover," said Tubs.

"Let me see what I've got." She opened the *Pictures* folder on her cellphone, and clicked the folder labelled "Nikki." "Come, Plato. Help me select one." The cat seemed to understand. He had jumped onto the couch, and had snuggled up against her hip. His eyes widened, and he sniffed about when the album of Nikki's photos appeared on the cellphone screen.

Rosa scrolled then stopped abruptly, reverse-scrolled and paused. Her face lit up.

"Yep, *this* one. It has to be this one. Look at her hair bursting out in all directions." Rosa laughed. "Classic Nikki."

Rosa's heart constricted as she recalled the taking of this selfie. It was on Fish Hoek beach, when Nikki had just come storming out of the water, and without saying anything, had simply grabbed her cellphone and snapped herself. The photo was in brilliant colour, showing Nikki's wild exploding hair in several shades of red—a mass of knotted tendrils, wet, buoyant, riotous. And the lips! Rosa's eyes lingered on those lips which were parted just enough for the tips of the teeth to protrude. Lips like berries. So ripe, so edible.

"Yes. This is the one to go on the programme," said Rosa, forwarding the picture via Wi-Fi to the printing machine. "We should also blow it up as large as possible, and frame it to put on the coffin."

"Her hair pretty much defined her, wouldn't you say?" said Tubs, holding the printout of Nikki's selfie in both hands.

"I agree," said Rosa. "When you speak to the undertakers, be sure to let them know to fluff it out, so that it rises all round her face through the viewing panel." She smiled as she pictured the corpse of Nikki in her coffin—"looking like The Sleeping Beauty."

Three of the bookshelves were tightly packed with leather-bound volumes of South African Law Reports dating from 1994. Other shelves contained numbered rows of lever arch files and ring binders, along with legal and business textbooks and stacks of regulations and government gazettes.

Angie's footsteps were like drumbeats on the wooden floor as she brushed past Rosa and Tubs, and went and squeezed through the space between her desk and a rectangular table loaded with paper files. She sank into her chair, causing the wheels, joints and springs to wail.

"I inherited the practice from my father," she said, finding space on the crowded desk-top for her portable computer. She pointed to a framed photograph of an old man and a young, curly-haired boy. "That's him, with my son, Jason."

The smell of degrading paper was thick in the air. A fire-hazard if ever there was one, thought Rosa, casting her eye about the dingy office and taking in the forest of wood and paper that surrounded them. She could sense that Tubs would not be able to tolerate this airless, dimly-lit capsule—this twilight zone—for too long.

"Nicky-Ross, you say? Is that the name his mother decided on?" Angie's eyes shifted to the coffee filter machine on her desk. "Can I offer you some coffee?" She arranged mugs, spoons, sugar and milk on a wooden tray, which she balanced on a stack of files on her desk.

"It's a plus in your favour," she explained, "A plus that Nikki had confided such an important detail to you and to no-one else."

"If the brother does indeed decide he wants to adopt Nicky-Ross," said Rosa, "and it's virtually certain he will, it means we will have to go head-to-head against him in court, right? Or is there any other way of settling it?"

"Looks like it's going to end up in court," said Angie. "And he'll have the inside lane, being family."

"But surely the mere fact of family shouldn't be decisive in its own right," said Tubs, briefly raising his hands. "Throughout his entire life in Australia the dude's never once in any way acknowledged his sister existence."

"The courts are *vrek*-conservative," said Angie. "They'll need a lot of persuading to rule against family." She placed the tray of steaming coffee in front of Rosa and Tubs. "Sugar? Milk?"

"I—me and Tubs—we've got some compelling facts in our favour, though," said Rosa. "Nikki stayed with us under our roof rent-free, fed and feted for several months before her childbirth. On her hospital admission form she named me her next-of-kin, and it's known that Tubs and I are picking up all her bills." Rosa paused to sip from her mug; the coffee was bitter and papery. "On her discharge she would have returned to our place in Pinelands, where she and Nicky-Ross would have resided as family with all their needs—material and emotional— taken care of by us, cost-free. And, if I may add, Tubs and I would have been appointed godparents of Nicky-Ross. We were all Nikki had in the whole wide world." Tears had come to Rosa's eyes. "Also, we've fallen in love with Nikki's cat, Plato—he's one of the family, now."

With the aid of a rubber-tipped stylus, Angie made notes on an electronic device which she clutched in her fist. "A key factor," she said, "is how the court interprets what's in the best interests of the child," She sat with her right ankle resting on the opposite knee. She had finished her coffee in one gulp.

"Are you referring to the whole race-and-culture question?" Rosa asked.

"Yep. We will have to remind the court that so-called cross-cultural adoptions have become a norm in South Africa, and that the same criteria which were used to approve previous cases need to be applied in this one. Anything else will be naked racism—everyone's terrified of being called a racist, so we should milk this angle."

Tubs chuckled. "I suppose we're going to have to falsify our race and religion on the application forms," he said. "We usually say "human" and "none," but this time round we're going to have to say "Xhosa" and "Christian," I guess."

Angie smiled. "Yep, a small price to pay."

"What happens in the meantime?" asked Rosa. "You know, between now and the actual adoption?"

"Foster care," said Angie. "That is, if he doesn't need to stay hospitalized all that time."

In response to Tubs's request for her to open the window, Angie stretched across to the sealed venetian blind covering the window behind her and put her hand through the slats. They knew the window was opened when they heard sounds of street traffic and felt a gust of fresh air in the room.

"The paediatrician, Dr Mel Cochrane, has arranged for me and Tubs to fill this vacuum while Nicky-Ross is still in hospital," said Rosa. "I'm sure he'll support a recommendation that we be appointed foster parents pending the adoption-ruling."

"In addition," said Angie, "we should arrange for a social worker from the Department of Social Development to interview you and also provide a recommendation."

"What if it backfires," said Tubs.

"You mean if she recommends *against* you?"

"Yes."

"It won't happen."

Angie offered them more coffee, but both declined. Rosa had no doubt that the same dry bitter taste on her palate was on Tubs's, too.

Their eyes were on the rapid movements of the stylus in Angie's hand.

"It would help," said Angie, before looking up from her notes, "if the biological father recommended in your favour." She looked at them with a smile. "It's a long-shot, but who knows what's needed to clinch it?"

"I'm guessing that the likely father was one of three habitués in our circle at *Monster's*," she said. If she could persuade them to do a paternity test and then to sign an affidavit recommending yourselves . . .

"But it's a long shot," she repeated. "And for starters, they'd have to admit to having slept with Nikki in the first place. This is something they can't be forced to do, not even by court order."

CHAPTER SIXTEEN

Through the massive glass wall on their right, arriving and departing planes were clearly visible from where they stood in the crowd gathering round the arrivals door. Young kids were crowded around the window, eagerly watching, their hands up against the glass, and raising their voices above the ceaseless announcements coming over the public address systems.

Bored with the wait, Rosa's eye was idly fixed on the big screen that continuously recycled the same half-dozen ads. Over and over and over. "Everything in this place is larger than life," she said to Tubs, who smiled.

"Like every other airport in the world," he said. "I'm sure it won't be long now."

The announcement that Victor's flight had landed had been heard more than an hour ago, and all the arrivals boards confirmed this. "What could be taking him so long?" Her impulse was to want to go over to the coffee shop, but just then she sensed a stiffening in Tubs's body.

"That's got to be him," said Tubs. A tall, shaven-headed man wearing a mahogany leather jacket and scurvy-looking jeans had just come through the sliding doors into the Arrivals Hall.

Rosa looked anxiously for any resemblance to Nikki in the craggy tanned face, but could see none, and entertained some doubt whether he really could be Victor Addo.

Let's check," said Tubs, and strode away from the waiting crowd in the direction of the new arrival who seemed puzzled as Tubs approached.

Rosa saw them exchange words then shake hands, and knew that he must indeed be Victor Addo.

She joined them and, smiling nervously, introduced herself. His voice was the same as on the phone—at a kind of halfway-house between Afrikaans-South African and *Austraailian*.

"So you're Rosa?" he said, a clearly incredulous look in his eyes.

Now she was glad she hadn't disclosed she was black—the look in his eyes was precious! She whipped out her cellphone camera and snapped his picture before he knew what was happening.

"Welcome to sunny South Africa," said Tubs, whose teeth shone like the sun. "Or should that be "welcome *back* to sunny South Africa?" Tubs forced a laugh. "Still the best country on God's earth."

Victor's baggage trolley was loaded with two bulging suitcases as well as a portable computer in its black cowhide casing, and an open plastic carrier bag. Over his shoulder, he had a heavy-looking polyester carry-bag, most likely containing his onboard stuff.

Looks like he's planning a lengthy stay, thought Rosa.

"That's fine, thanks," he politely but resolutely declined Tubs's offer to push his trolley.

Methinks the age of baasskap was already over by the time he left the country, Rosa said to herself, suppressing a grin. Maybe the very reason he left South Africa.

They slowly made their way through the airport throngs to the parking garage. Tubs was talking non-stop, engaging Victor in bantering talk about South Africa, Cape Town, and whether things looked very different to Victor, who seemed overwhelmed and might have wished he could be on his own to assess his position.

"I definitely don't remember all these shanties," he said once they were out of the airport and on the N2.

"Yep," they stretch for many kilometres," said Tubs, "They're an indictment of our government."

From the passenger seat, Rosa positioned herself so that she could make eye contact with Victor in the backseat. She had decided that she would be on her friendly, charming best, and behave as if she assumed that her being black was for Victor the most natural thing in the world.

"I guess you're feeling pretty exhausted after your long flight?" she said.

"Yes, rather," he said. "Table Mountain hasn't changed."

They laughed.

On their right as they drove in the direction of the City and Victor's hotel, there was evidence of new housing development, and Rosa noted that Victor's eye lingered on the building-site as they passed it.

"You might remember," she said. "That's Langa where those new houses are going up." She smiled. "Although we're so far into the new South Africa, a place like Langa is still an urban ghetto for black people."

He looked at her with uncertainty, and hesitated before replying, "I guess it takes time eradicating poverty." After a moment's silence, he said, "Where do you live?"

"Pinelands," said Rosa. "A great place to live." She had no doubt he'd know that it used to be an all-white upper middle class suburb in the old days.

He enquired about what work they did, and nodded knowingly when she said Tubs worked for the state and she was with an investment firm called Lumina. No doubt, she thought, he'd Google *Lumina* once in his hotel-room, and marvel at her profile.

The tall buildings of Cape Town's city centre came into view as their car glided over the freeway to the Foreshore.

"The baby," said Victor, then hesitated, his brow furrowed. "How's the baby? Who's the father? Who's caring for the baby?"

"Nikki never ever spoke about the father," said Rosa, keeping her voice neutral. "The baby—Nicky-Ross—was born two months premature. He's still in hospital, in the neonatal intensive care unit.

He's expected to be there for several more weeks, but he's doing fine so far."

"I need to make a plan to go see him." Victor seemed to be talking to himself.

"That's fine," said Rosa. "We can take you."

"No, no." He seemed to regret that it came out so vehemently. "I don't want to inconvenience you." He smiled at Rosa, a look of supplication in his eyes. "I'll make my own arrangements. But thanks very much."

"We've been keeping close touch with the baby and the hospital. As I mentioned to you on the phone, we'd like to adopt him."

She was as surprised as he to hear herself say that.

He shifted in his seat—so abruptly that the safety belt locked.

For an instant an electrifying quiet came to the car. Only the gentle hum of the motor and the distant sound of the wind outside were audible. *The bullet's through the church*, came to Rosa's mind, together with the image of Nikki explaining the saying to her. She held her smile and kept her eyes fixed on Victor's.

"Yes," he said, a hardness having come to his eyes as he focused them on hers. "I know you said so." He shifted his gaze to the side window, and watched the sea flow by on his right. "But it's—just—out of the question."

He had booked into a five-star hotel in the Waterfront, with imposing views of the ocean. A bell-boy who, like Rosa and Tubs, was black and spoke perfect English in a private school accent came to the car and unpacked his baggage, while he cast his gaze about, his eyes reflecting approval of his surroundings.

Both Rosa and Tubs had gotten out of the car to say cheerio to him. He said to Tubs, "You've got a beautiful car," and thanked him profusely for meeting him at the airport; they shook hands, and, bowing to Rosa, he said, "looking forward to catching up with you soon, ma'am."

"Oh yes," said Rosa with enthusiasm. "As soon as you're settled in, we must get together. There's so much to talk about."

"So, what do you think?"

"Ha. I think our black faces were a really rude awakening."

"I'm more than ever convinced he's going to want to take Nicky-Ross back to Australia with him."

"Yep. That much seems clear."

On Wednesday morning at sunrise, Rosa and Tubs were at Nicky-Ross's side. For Rosa, the baby seemed to sense their presence—recognize it—his eyes opened briefly and seemed to stare at the ceiling, as if he were trying to say, Mom? Pop? Is that you? She handled him with assurance, much to Tubs's admiration. She was able to assist the nurse in undoing some of the attachments and in lifting him to her bosom, chatting to him in constant, smiling cadences. Tubs marvelled as the baby's movements noticeably settled, as his arms and legs seemed to feel towards Rosa. She held him against her chest, then in the cradle of her arms, then to her chest again.

"Now it's your turn, Daddy," she said to Tubs.

She glowed as he nervously took the baby into his arms; she joked with him about how he sat, ill-at-ease, anxiety in his eyes for the entire five minutes that he held the baby.

She changed the bedding in the incubator and rearranged the soft toys—today it was Tiger's turn to lie next to Nicky-Ross.

Lastly, before they left, she changed the baby's nappy, and said to Tubs, "Watch closely. This is going to be *your* job."

At work, Ferrie told her he thought she was being a bit picky in her review of Leigh's draft. "Over-critical, I would say," he said, and tried to soften his words by grinning. "But thanks. I said to Leigh she should check carefully through your points and incorporate the relevant ones."

The relevant ones? They're all relevant, idiot. She smiled at Ferrie. "It's a good draft," she said. "I think it will work as the perfect scenario if we go that particular route with the Chinese."

In the course of the morning she dialled Victor's number, but was prompted by his network service to leave a message.

"Victor, hi, it's Rosa, here. I trust you're well. Just calling about the funeral arrangements—the tributes, pall-bearers, hymns, that sort of thing. I'll try calling you later."

Within a minute she got a call back.

"Hi, Rosa. Yeah. About the pall-bearers. I managed to contact an old family friend—Uncle Robbie. He'll be at the funeral on Saturday. I think we should let him be a pall-bearer, if possible."

"Uncle Robbie? Sure, not a problem."

"And, about hymns. I've got few I could recommend. I'll e-mail them through to you."

"Wonderful. Oh, and something else. Nikki stayed with you, right? So her personal and other stuff will be with you. We need to discuss . . . perhaps after the funeral?"

"Certainly."

Late in the afternoon, Rosa got a call from Angie.

"Hi, Rosa. Good news. I put the word out among the *Monster's* crowd, and spoke to each of my 'suspects' personally. There are three guys on my list of possible fathers. I've arranged to speak to each one privately. I'll keep you posted."

"Great."

"Something else. If Victor Addo's going to make a bid for Nicky-Ross, the hearing is certain to be sprung on us at short-notice, unless he's going to be able to stay in the country indefinitely—which is highly unlikely. So we need to ready ourselves."

"We spoke on the phone earlier today about the funeral arrangements. He wants to see me after the funeral about her 'stuff'—

personal and whatever else. I am aware of a property in Langebaan, the old family home."

"Don't part with anything. Nothing belongs to him. Everything belongs to Nicky-Ross."

"We'll put a flower in the coffin from you, Nicky-Ross," said Rosa, feeling a fist clench then unclench within her chest. She made an effort to smile but felt it only as a tightening of her cheeks and temples. She held the child against her heart, and shared its beat with him. She was sure she sensed his blood-flow—awkward, curious, irregular—seeking alignment with hers. Tubs lightly rested his elbow on her shoulder. He touched the child with his fingers, breathed on him, gazed at his delicateness. His gaze shifted to his wife's face; he saw the largeness of her emotion there, and noticed how it made his breathing speed up.

She lay the child on his back, chatting with him while she worked his nappy loose. The soft poo that she wiped away with a square cotton pad was mainly-yellow, touched in its substance with hints of blue. Or maybe it was the light. Everything in this ward was artificial. She reattached the plugs that linked Nicky-Ross to his life-support system, allowing her touch to linger there for a moment. For perhaps the first time she was picking up the resemblance between the baby and his late mother—something that flitted between the paleness of his skin, the redness of his scalp, the fluttering of his eyelashes. But perhaps her determined mind was simply making her see what she wanted to see.

The single rose she had picked out—the one that she would be placing in the coffin for Nicky-Ross—had the tight redness of a newborn's pinched face. She had scattered drops of water over its calyx and thorns, and stored it overnight in a wineglass, hoping to arrest its youth and beauty till the fire—the intention was that it would burn with Nikki, ashes to ashes.

She emerged from the hospital with Tubs, hand-in-hand, into the sudden morning light. In two hours, there would be the funeral. And then, the beginning of the rest of her life. Tubs at her side was tall, comforting. She thought she would recognize the sound of his steps no matter where. And his smell. She tightened her grip on his hand. Would there be time for a quickie before the funeral?

The wrought-iron gates stood open, and Rosa was able to drive through into the crematorium grounds, disturbing a flock of pigeons on the asphalt roadway. She slowed the car, allowing it to drift the length of the short drive past a thick grove patch. The stone chapel was on her left, casting its shadow westward in front of itself, and her impulse was to drive up to the wooden doors before she caught sight of the *parking* sign directing her the opposite way.

She checked her watch, and saw that there was still an hour to go— *before show time*! Ideal. She would have a reasonable spell alone with Nikki. Alongside her on the car seat lay the rose that she would be placing in the coffin *for Nicky-Ross*. She had shaved off all the thorns and sprayed water over it before leaving home, and noted with joy that its petals seemed somehow to have roused themselves. She was aware of its sweet smell, which she hoped would cling to the car's upholstery and to her fingers.

She got out of the car and walked slowly towards the chapel, carrying the rose in an upright position, like a ceremonial flame.

It pleased her to see that the undertakers had already arrived. Their hearse was backed up to the chapel's doors, and an attendant in a black knee-length coat was shutting the tailgate.

"I've just unloaded it, ma'am," said the attendant with a bow. "The flowers, the framed picture—they're there, as requested."

He led her into the chapel, which had a sombre air about it, despite the glow of three ornate chandeliers. Natural light came in through high windows, but only sections of the pew stalls were illuminated. Where the coffin stood, on the right inside the doorway, the light was at its faintest.

"Thank you," Rosa said to the attendant. "I'd like to stay alone with her till the mourners start arriving."

Nikki appeared to be sleeping. They always appear to be sleeping, Rosa said to herself, recalling her mother's corpse. Something to do with undertakers' sleight-of-hand. And they got her hair right, fluffed out like we asked. Check. And the flowers are beautiful—Tubs, take a bow. Roses, chrysanthemums, lilies—all white—interspersed with purple verbena were thickly stacked on a bed of green buds and leaves, the whole made to look like natural, flowing triumphalism.

Rosa looked from the framed portrait to the corpse and back again, trying to assess which looked more genuine. She smiled. Beautiful in life, beautiful in death. She slid the red rose in so that its head lay alongside Nikki's cheek, and allowed her fingers to linger against the icy skin. Her impulse was to photograph Nikki in her coffin, but some vague tremor pulling through her shoulders made her think better of it. She laid her hand on Nikki's shoulder, and articulated in her mind: Nikki, you died so that my marriage might live. Yours was not an unfortunate death in childbirth. You willed your own death. You died to ensure that there'd be no risk of my leaving Tubs. You bequeathed us a child so that we might strengthen our marriage, so that I would not have cause for distraction. You loved me more than you loved yourself. And you gave me your one begotten son. Would I have sacrificed my life for you? I don't know. But I do know I wouldn't hesitate to sacrifice my life for Nicky-Ross. If I listen attentively, I can actually hear the waves at Langebaan. I can certainly see the wild red girl and her clumsy dog cavorting on the sand. I can see seagulls wheeling overhead where they run—running for running's sake, she and the dog with the ridiculous name. What drove her brother to suicide? What drove the other to

Perth? Is there an unhappy shared gene lurking inside Nicky-Ross? The house at Langebaan. We will visit it even before you think your first conscious thought, my Nicky-Ross. It will become part of your DNA. And Tubs! If she lived we would have formed a polyamorous marriage, I know it. Me, you, she, Nicky-Ross and Plato. One big happy family.

The organist was first to arrive. Mr Kolbe, he said his name was. All ten fingertips were upturned from a lifetime at the keyboards. His specs were so thick that his eyes seemed to float behind them, and his perfectly-shaped teeth were stained with nicotine. Yes, Mrs Lethlabe, he said. He had gotten the list of titles from her husband, and would start playing immediately. "I'm familiar with the organ, here," he said, his eyeballs all fidgety. "I've played it several times. It's got a beautiful tone."

Within a minute or two, the tune of *The Holy City* began to insinuate itself into Rosa's consciousness. It seems to be coming from the woodwork, she thought, her eyes turning upwards to the rafters. She allowed the music to seduce her senses, bring tears to her eyes, shudders to her soul. The multiple scents from the flower-spray on the coffin were beginning to suffocate her, and she breathed deeper in the hope that that would prevent her passing out. The music was like a wall of water, a dream.

Victor Addo appeared at her side. He was wearing a double-breasted suit and a wide black tie with a gold clip. He bent forward to whisper to her that he'd like to introduce her to Uncle Robbie. She saw alongside Victor a dried-out octogenarian no taller than a strylitzia bush, who carried about him a mild urine-odour, and seemed not to know who he was, where he was or what he was doing there.

Victor's eyes narrowed at the sight of Nikki; he stood unblinking at the side of the coffin, head bowed, hands clasped. It seemed to Rosa that he wished to speak but was too overcome by emotion. She gently put her arm through his, and whispered, "She was too young."

She felt his hand close round hers, but still he did not speak. Tears had come to his eyes, as well as a puffiness. He disengaged from her arm, and, turning to Uncle Robbie, escorted the old man to a seat inside the chapel.

He returned, and stood with Rosa at the side of the coffin to greet the mourners as they filed through.

"What you've done," he said to Rosa. "It's incredible—arranging this funeral . . . look at this glossy hymn sheet . . . the organist . . . the priest . . . the flowers." He cast a rapid glance at the corpse. "The cremation . . . it must have cost you and your good husband a fortune . . ."

The organ had not stopped playing for a moment. A part of Rosa's mind was rapt, following the rises and falls of the melodies, her heart responding to their mood-flows. She was sure that had Nikki been alive and present at this event, they'd have been exchanging glances and giggles, and texting each other non-stop.

Tubs arrived with Bill; Tubs and Victor greeted each other like old friends; Victor praised and thanked him for the funeral arrangements, and said he'd never be able to repay him.

Angie van der Poel arrived, dressed in denim jeans. Her necklace shone in the dim light of the chapel. She smiled at Rosa and briefly hugged her.

"Pleased to meet you," she said, when introduced to Victor, but seemed to leave much unsaid, as her eyes lingered on him a fraction.

The priest wore a black cassock and white clerical collar. He clutched a large leather-bound prayer book from which protruded several page markers. He spent a moment with Tubs going over details for the service, before requesting that the pall-bearers be assembled. With his eyes he communicated to the organist to wind down the tune he was playing, and to get ready for the one that would signal the start of formalities.

The funeral attendant in his knee-length coat appeared and attached the lid to the coffin, ensuring that all Nikki's hair as well as the rose from Nick-Ross were sealed in. He marshalled the pallbearers to take their places on each side of the coffin, then signalled to the priest that all was fine.

Rosa did a quick count, and was pleased to conclude that a good plus-minus twenty people had pitched, mostly employees from Lumina, two of whom had agreed to be pall-bearers. They smiled at Rosa as they took up their places.

"Please stand," said the priest in a voice that to Rosa was surprisingly imperious.

The organ struck up—*All People that on Earth do Dwell*—and the retinue, led by the priest, commenced up the aisle.

Trailing behind, Rosa recalled that at her mother's funeral, her dominant feelings were anger and defiance against God, and impatience for the whole show to end. She remembered that her father and his comrades had turned the funeral into a noisy political rally, where all the speeches were shrieked, and where they all massively exaggerated her mother's virtues.

Today, she said to herself, as she took in the restrained nature of the event, it's a dignified affair . . . but a kind of desolation is beginning to creep into me, now.

The service started with a hymn. The congregation, small as it was, rose full-bore to the strain. *Oh, Lord my God, When I in awesome wonder.* Rosa sang along uncertainly, trusting the universality of the melody to guide her through as she followed the words printed in the hymn-sheet. *Consider all the works Thy hands have made.* Her nose was sharp. No incense was visible, yet she was sure she was detecting its deadwood pungency, stronger than the smell of the flowers on Nikki's coffin—or even of Tubs's men's fragrance. She caught sight of Mr Kolbe, swaying at the organ, singing along with lusty teeth. Could it be coming from the nicotine on those mossy teeth of his? She stifled a giggle. The priest was carrying the incense smell on his cassock, she decided. Or maybe it was an embedded smell—in the woodwork, the smell of accumulated death, maybe deep-seeped into the walls of this old, spooky chapel. No, she would have picked it up sooner.

The rostrum was a waist-high mahogany box equipped with microphone and reading light. A quiet fell on the congregation when Victor plodded up to it to deliver his tribute. The sound of his fidgeting was magnified by the microphone, as he flattened the folds from his notes and fumbled for his reading glasses. He cleared his throat.

"I must start off by thanking Nikki's friends," he said, then repeated it when he realized he had not spoken into the mike. "Nikki's friends, Rosa and Tubs . . . for their great kindness, not only in caring for Nikki in her final days, but also for arranging this wonderful ceremony here today, for us to pay our last respects. As Nikki's only living relative, I am touched and deeply grateful to you, Rosa and Tubs. You have shown us what true love means." His fingers tightened on the handrail where he stood.

"It is a matter of deep regret to me and my wife and kids in Australia that Nikki passed away so suddenly, that we were not able to communicate with her before her tragic death." His voice trailed off, and it was clear he was battling to hold back the tears. He paused for a long moment and grimaced.

"Although I've been living in Australia for a number of years," he continued, "and it was difficult to maintain close contact with my dear sister here in South Africa, our love for each other remained undiminished across time and space. This is the power of love. This is what it means to be family."

Looking at his notes, he continued, "I have so many treasured memories of when we were little kids growing up in Langebaan, how much she loved the beach, the sea, and being able to run around on the white sands with her dog whose name was *Dingus*."

At this, a smile not so much arose from the congregation as rifled among it, something like the sound of paper crinkling.

Rosa listened enthralled, as Victor recounted what he called "tales from Nikki's childhood." He related numerous anecdotes intended to touch and amuse; always Nikki appeared in a positive light—she was this bright, cheerful, adorable kid "for whom," Victor emphasized, "God had so much in store."

"He cut her life short," he said, peering over the heads of the congregation. "He took her away from us all too soon," he said, a sudden hoarseness in his throat. "But He left in her place a beautiful baby boy."

There were tears in his eyes, brightened by the chandelier-lights reflecting off his glasses. "Many of you will be familiar with the Biblical quote:

But Jesus said, Suffer little children, and forbid them not, to come unto me: for of such is the kingdom of heaven.

"The news is out, God loves children. Now we know why He gave us this little baby. Maybe that is also why He took Nikki away from us in the prime of her youth. She was really just a child."

He fumbled in his pants pockets and produced an off-white, folded handkerchief. "Excuse me," he said while he methodically unfolded it, panel by panel. He clasped it round his nose with the fingers of both hands, then blasted into it—once, twice, thrice, four times. While the congregation looked on, he rapidly refolded it—in reverse order, panel by panel, then thrust it back into his pocket and continued.

"Let me end off by appealing to you to pray for the little child who lost his mother giving birth to him, and who is still being cared for in hospital. Let us ask the good Lord in his gracious mercy to speed the little one's recovery. I thank you, ladies and gentlemen."

Tubs had engaged a soloist with a guitar to perform *I'll be missing you*—a teenage girl with vine-creeper tattoos covering both arms. She hung over her guitar and appeared to be singing to it. Her voice was steady and piercing. Rosa found herself gritting her teeth as the soloist plucked at her guitar and sang.

Every step I take, every move I make
Every single day, every time I pray
I'll be missing you

"The good news is, she lives in God," said the priest, but without apparent conviction. He read from his prayer book that Christ had died and risen from the dead. "And so," he added, "In Christ shall all be made alive."

Rosa took the rostrum and felt a brief sweep of panic, a kind of cold wind on her forehead—chilling, not cooling. An expectant silence had quickly settled over the congregation. All eyes were on her. She fixed her gaze on the clock that was suspended over the entrance-door, and kept it there throughout her speech.

"The sea, the sea. The freshness of the sea. Every time I think of Nikki I feel the wind in my hair, there are seagulls overhead—clouds, blue sky . . . an endlessness. There's a roaring in my ears, my cheeks feel a kind of yearning. And that blue green turquoise lapping and rolling. Waves, water, salt. My heart, something in my heart, struggles to be free, to be able to run wild. Exhilaration . . . maddened by joy. That's what one feels, experiences, every time one thinks of Nikki.

"She was generous with her soul. She shared it freely. Her family, her friends, her pets—the dog named Dingus and the cat named Plato—all tasted its nourishing sweetness. The essence of Nikki . . . what made her such a precious human being, was a humble, fragile, loving, selfless, fun-seeking, witty, enchanting spirit that made you feel bigger and better than yourself.

"Even if you knew her only slightly, you will know what I mean when I say she was like the day-break, a new dawn. Something that cleanses. With her you always had that sense of anticipation, something to look forward to—things are gonna get better! *Everything's Gonna Be Alright*!

"She always startled you. She was amazing in every way. She had this blazing mop of red hair that defined her look. The way she walked the way she spoke the way she chewed the way she breathed the way she tipped her glass the way she blew smoke the way she laughed the way she . . . She made you want to be like her, change your hair, change the way you walked, talked, chewed, laughed . . .

"Nikki's cat, Plato, knew she was dead. When she didn't return from the hospital, Plato knew that it was not just a prolonged absence. He knew that she would never be coming back. He knew that she would not be able to come back. He knew that she had died.

"Cats are like human beings. They can love without understanding. They are capable of knowing love, just as they are capable of knowing death. The way he expressed his grief was in a sudden change in his normal behaviour. His eating and sleeping patterns changed. He became restless, and his movements became clumsy, erratic. He would moan strangely, and just lie in Nikki's room staring endlessly at her photo.

"He drew closer to me and Tubs and my dad. All of us, in the days since Nikki's death, often just sat around doing nothing, saying nothing, just drawing strength from the presence of one another. That's what the death of a loved one does, I suppose—draws people closer. It makes you think about how fragile your life is, how ultimately, it is meaningless without the person or persons who by their love for you, define you.

"For us, this was not just the death of a loved one. This was the *sudden* death of a loved one. And when you look for an explanation, when you try to make sense of it, all you see is a vast unfeeling universe. You look up into the night sky, and you're transfixed by the beauty of the moon, the stars, the clouds, but you're also terror-struck by its unfeeling endlessness. You are dramatically confronted with the truth of your meaninglessness. It's frightening. You realize that all you have is the love of another meaningless person, that without it, you truly have nothing, are nothing in the most devastating sense of the word. It has to define the way you live your life going forward. You begin to understand the need for human solidarity. "You are all I have, I am all you have." And you begin to understand that this is what makes rational living possible.

"Nikki's son, Nicky-Ross has been born into this vast, unfeeling world, where all he can hope to have is the love of others. We, who benefited from the generous love of his mother, will now have the glorious obligation of returning the favour. We owe it to Nicky-Ross to ensure that he is made dizzy by our love, that he drowns in the excess of it. Buckets of love, oceans of love. Love as deep as the Langebaan sea. We must make sure Nicky-Ross can count his wealth in million-dollar love-bills.

"So, we have a death and we have a life—a welcome and an au revoir. And we must hope to—dare to—intervene in nature's relentless cycle and leave our stamp on both the death and the life. Long after we are gone, when beings from another world enter our earth-space, they must see the evidence of our human existence, like rock paintings in caves—beautiful, enigmatic, permanent."

A mood of lightness arose among the mourners as they filed through to the hall adjoining the chapel. They were greeted at the entranceway by three smiling teenage girls dressed in black T-shirts and jeans, with white aprons tied round their waists. Fading away in the background was Mr Kolbe's rousing rendition of *To God be the glory, great things He hath done*, soon completely drowned out by the gay chattering that had started up in the hall.

Rosa was one of the last to enter the hall from the chapel. She smiled as she considered that crossing the threshold from chapel to hall was like passing from the Valley of the Shadow of Death—you were instantly transformed from mourner to guest, from sombre to cheerful.

A table laden with gourmet snack platters had been set up in the centre of the hall, and guests were milling round to help themselves. In one corner of the hall was a separate table with tea and coffee and an urn. Rosa spotted lawyer Angie van der Poel making her way to it, and joined her there.

"It'll be one of those three, I'm sure," the lawyer said while pouring herself a cup of coffee. She might have been speaking to herself—her voice was low, her eyes were on the pouring—but Rosa, whose gaze had settled on the group of three men chatting near the exit doorway, turned her eyes swiftly away from them, as if she had been accused of something shameful

"They look so yummy," said Rosa. "I don't blame her."

Angie chuckled. "As yummy-looking as these snacks you've laid on." She turned and headed to the snacks table. "Breakfast, here I come," she said with gusto, and began to fill a plate—prawn-and-avocado tartlets, smoked salmon wedges, cheese wedges, assorted cracker biscuits and croissants, strawberries, chicken wraps, sliced kiwi fruit, tempura mushrooms . . .

Rosa was pleased to see that most of the mourners had stayed for snacks, and how energetically Tubs was moving among them—the perfect host. She was sure Nikki would have been pleased, too.

He looks at home, she said to herself when she caught sight of Victor Addo. He had unbuttoned his jacket and his shirt collar, and held a large glass of fruit juice in one hand and a platter of snacks in the other. He was speaking to the priest, who appeared to be listening intently to what he was saying. Close by, Uncle Robbie was seated with his plate of snacks on his lap, chewing away like a happy dog. On the chair beside him stood his drink, which Rosa expected he would probably spill over himself sooner or later.

"But I've been wondering if we shouldn't let sleeping dogs lie," said Angie, coming up to Rosa and nudging her towards some chairs away from the other guests. They sat down.

"When I think about it," said Angie, "Maybe it's not such a good idea to try to trace the biological father." She bit into a croissant, and a flake of pastry got stuck to her upper lip; she flicked her tongue, and it was gone.

Rosa grinned. She watched as one of the caterer's attendants approached the three men at the exit doorway to offer them snacks from her tray, and noticed how animated they became, joking with the attendant, no doubt flirting with her.

Doubtlessly, thought Rosa, they'd all like to get her into bed, the scum. Like they did Nikki. A mild spark of rage ignited within her. She thought of Nicky-Ross in his incubator, snarled up in his welter of cords and plugs.

Angie chewed and spoke. "A few scenarios have popped into my head," she said, keeping her voice low. "For instance, we establish paternity, and the father decides *he* wants custody of the child—to hell with you or Victor Addo."

"Yeah . . ." Rosa smiled, twisting her mouth. "Or he decides he doesn't like the idea of black people raising his flesh-and-blood."

"But let's say he agrees, and signs for you and Tubs to adopt the child. It's not out of the question that he could become a nuisance in your lives. In other words, instead of just signing and disappearing into the sunset, he could end up thinking he has a say—a veto—over how you raise *his* kid and forever be poking his nose into decisions you make concerning the child."

"I'd set the dogs on him," said Rosa. She raised her cup to her mouth and slurped.

"On the other hand, discovering he's the father of a child he can't acknowledge could destroy him psychologically—that is, if he has a conscience."

"I suppose another psychological negative for him could be having to live with the knowledge that at any time word could reach his wife that during their marriage, he had fathered an illegitimate child."

Angie finished her coffee. "In the unlikely event we did manage to get them to do a paternity test, and in the unlikely event we did establish who the father was, and in the unlikely event he did recommend you and Tubs—"

"—The courts might nevertheless rule in favour of Uncle Vic Addo?"

"Bingo."

There was a shattering of glass. Uncle Robbie had spilt his drink.

Chapter Seventeen

Their case was to be heard in one of the smaller courtrooms, situated on the cold side of the building, where the blazing overhead lamps provided little warmth or light, and if anything, seemed to be sucking the living air out of the place. Rosa drew a deep breath. She shifted closer to Tubs, who gave her hand a reassuring clasp. From where she sat, despite the dusty greyness of the air, she could easily discern the pores on the magistrate's plump cheeks—a youthful-looking magistrate, who wore her spectacles close to the tip of her nose, and who seemed uncomfortable in her baggy robes.

She's young, thought Rosa. Maybe too young. What does she know about death and motherhood?

Rosa was seated between Tubs and Angie van der Poel. She wished both would embrace her. At the adjoining table sat Victor Addo and a man whose upper lip was concealed by a bushy brown moustache. His attorney, no doubt, thought Rosa, casting a disdainful look in their direction. The enemy. Why do we have to settle this in court? If we did it the traditional way, out behind the boys' lavatory or deep in the woods at dawn, Tubs would whip both their arses, and that would be that—a beaming me would walk off with the baby! Instead, we have this adolescent, pock-faced magistrate decide who wins.

"Well, here's where the rubber hits the road," said Angie, who was seated on Rosa's right. Or the shit hits the fan, thought Rosa. Angie smiled briefly, but the shudder that ran through her pupils did not go unnoticed by Rosa.

The magistrate had sleek cola-coloured hair that was lively as quicksilver, energized, it seemed to Rosa, by an independent power-source, the way it moved about as if of its own volition; once, twice when the magistrate tried to slap it back with her hand, she almost dislodged her spectacles. She took a sip of water from the glass on her desk, tucked her bell-shaped sleeves behind her elbows, coughed once, twice behind her right fist, then enquired whether everyone had had an opportunity to read the social worker's report. She declared that the hearing had been urgently called to consider the Lethlabes' application to adopt the baby, Nicky-Ross, and his uncle Victor Addo's counter-application. She read through the preliminary protocols, satisfying herself that all was in order, before turning to the social worker's report, a bulky document which lay on the desk before her.

"Let me start by thanking the social worker for a very comprehensive and meticulously-drafted report in such a short space of time."

She offered a clipped smile in the direction of the social worker who was seated in a row behind Rosa's.

"I have carefully noted the social worker's recommendation," said the magistrate, leaning forward in her chair. "In a nutshell, she has only praise for the Lethlabes, and is quite sure that they would make excellent adoptive parents for the baby Nicky-Ross. However, she says—let me quote . . ."

The magistrate picked up the document from her desk, and began to read. "She says—and I quote—'It is unusual anywhere in the world for cross-racial adoptions to occur in the direction 'white-child-to-black-parents.' Unquote."

Peering over the top of her spectacles, she focused her gaze on Rosa. "I must emphasise that I have no preconceived notions in this case. We will listen to both sides, and attempt to make a decision that is in the best interests of the child."

The social worker—a Mrs Arendze—had the sleek look of a gull in a windstorm. Her nose was beaked, and her hair—each strand of it—was tied back into a plastic clasp the size of a beer mug. In the witness box she sat unmoving as dried concrete, waiting for Angie van der Poel, who was noisily flipping through a sheaf of papers, to cross-exam her.

"So, Mrs Arendze," said Angie, walking over to within two or three metres of the witness box. "By what criterion do you sort children for adoption—is it by this thing called race? Do you decide, 'Oh this is a white child, so we must find white parents?'"

"It's not about race, *per se*," said Mrs Arendze in an assured voice. "It's about placing the child in an environment that's best for him or her. If it happens that he or she ends up being a white child in a white family, well then that is just incidental."

"Why is it," said Angie, "that from time to time we see a child from an indigenous African background being adopted by parents of European descent, but never the other way round? Surely that's a case of double standards?"

"Very few white children come up for adoption," said Mrs Arendze, addressing the magistrate who appeared rapt. "And so, we have very little difficulty finding homes for them. Black children, by contrast, are always in oversupply, and consequently, we are always struggling to find adoptive homes for them. There is never a waiting list for a black child there is always a surplus of black children. It's not their fault, it's not our fault, it's just the nature of things. This is the main reason why we would be willing to consider approving the request of any suitable white family to adopt a black child."

She turned her eyes to Angie. "It's not a matter of back-to-front logic—or double standards. It's a matter of stark reality. We have to solve problems in the real world. We are not living in Cloud Cuckoo Land." The flesh around her eyes tightened.

"So, Mrs Arendze," said Angie. "In your recommendation you have declared the Lethlabes suitable, but have thrown in the 'but' of race. The honourable magistrate here has, not without reason, praised the thoroughness of your report. In it, the Lethlabes tick all the boxes necessary to be considered suitable adoptive parents for the child Nicky-Ross. In terms of your findings, their credentials are impeccable. However, but for the accident of race, there would have been no *but* in your report. Is that correct, Mrs Arendze?"

"We have seen," said Mrs Arendze, "that even in the most advanced societies—here I'm talking about the US and the UK—inter-racial mixing and adoption across colour lines are way, way in the minority. It's something that will always be an exception—a social anomaly. It's no different in South Africa. To willfully make this poor child the subject of a cross-racial adoption, especially in the direction 'white-child-to-black-parents' would be to expose him to the risk of permanent psychological damage. Do we want that kind of blood on our hands? I should think not." The flesh around her mouth tightened.

"Do my ears deceive me?" Angie's cheeks turned scarlet. "Mrs Arendze, I seriously beg to differ!" She raised her voice: "To place this child in a home which is truly non-racial would be to provide him with a rare and valuable gift! With the Lethlabes he will be brought up in a climate free from the scourge of racial prejudice and the devastating impact it has had on our lives and relations throughout the history of this country. His adoptive parents—if they were to be Mr and Mrs Lethlabe—would teach him how to value and respect people for themselves not for their race or other arbitrary feature. We need more of this kind of adoption, not less, don't you think?"

Mrs Arendze made no reply. She sat motionless in the witness box as if on a nest of eggs. Faintly, the sound of the City's noon gun penetrated into the room. Rosa looked at her watch; the magistrate's eyes turned to the clock on the wall. Angie turned away from the witness box, muttering. "No further questions."

Victor Addo's attorney, Faffie Swart, was bent over his notepad, writing, and looked up with a start when the magistrate invited him to come forward, if he wished, to cross-examine the social worker.

He hurriedly slotted his pen in alongside the three others which were clipped in a row in his jacket pocket, cleared his throat and ambled up to the witness box where Mrs Arendze waited, hunched.

Faffie Swart's upper lip was concealed by a brown brush-moustache; when he smiled, his lower lip curved like a schoolchild's drawing of a boat, to reveal a row of seven uneven teeth, each one a colour different from the others. Standing within hugging-distance of Mrs Arendze, he clasped his hands behind his back, gazed over his protruding belly at the floor in front of him, and spoke in a soft, clear voice:

"May I take this opportunity, Mrs Arendze," he said, "to also praise and thank you for producing such an excellent report in so short a space of time. It has really helped us to understand the complexities we are dealing with in this case."

His remark produced a fleeting smile on the face of Mrs Arendze, who seemed to be sinking into herself in the witness box—her neck was no longer visible between chin and shoulders, and her nose was level with the handrail.

"If I may pose a purely hypothetical question, Mrs Arendze," said Swart. "Counsel for the Lethlabes has left us in no doubt that Mrs Lethlabe and her husband are a very westernized, middle-class couple, who, if the racial aspect were not a consideration, would no doubt be able to provide Nicky-Ross with a very comfortable home, at least in material terms. But let's say—God forbid—they should lose their lives in a tragedy. What happens to Nicky-Ross then? Who takes over the parental role? Does this mean that Nicky-Ross will then be raised by the next-of-kin of Mr or Mrs Lethlabe? If so, it surely means the child will be Africanized, if I can use such a term—he will have to go live in a township like Langa or Khayelitsha. Surely that would be unthinkable?"

Why doesn't Angie raise an objection, wondered Rosa?

"We cannot be so naïve," said Mrs Arendze, "as to think that just because the laws on our statute books have changed there is no racial

239

prejudice in this country." She clucked her tongue. "We will be doing this poor child serious harm if we let him—as a white child—grow up with black parents. Through no fault of his, he will be stigmatized in society. This is not something of our making. We all wish it would be otherwise." She turned her eyes on Rosa. "It's a fact for all with eyes to see and ears to hear that a black child growing up as the adoptive child of a white family faces no such problem. It's a wretched truth, but a truth nonetheless."

"Thank you, Mrs Arendze, I have no further questions," said Swart, openly exchanging grins with Victor Addo as he made his way back to his seat.

"Mr Addo, can you please explain to the court what you understand by the term *race*?" asked Angie van der Poel, raising her eyes from the wad of papers in her hand. She went and stood within touching distance of Victor, and fixed her eyes on his.

"I'm not sure if that is a catch-question," said Victor, his buttocks shifting audibly on the wooden seat of the witness box. "We all know what is meant by race," he said. "You have the white race and you have the black race. The Chinese—they are a race." His eyes narrowed as he held Angie's gaze.

Ah, die drol is in die drinkwater, thought Rosa, wishing she could relay this by text-message to Nikki. Do they have Wi-Fi in Heaven?

Angie smiled. "What would you say, Mr Addo, If I told you that there is no such thing as race, that it's been scientifically proven to be a myth?"

"Well, you can call it what you will, but it's undeniable. People are different. You and I, we are white. Mrs Lethlabe, there, she is black. I have the utmost respect for—"

"—So, how is Mrs Lethlabe *different*, Mr Addo?"

240

"As I was going to say, I have the utmost respect for Mrs Lethlabe. She is a wonderful person—"

"—How is Mrs Lethlabe *different*, Mr Addo?"

"Mrs Lethlabe is a black person. My nephew is a white person. I am sure there is nowhere in the world where a black family has adopted and—"

"—How is Mrs Lethlabe *different*, Mr Addo?"

"She is black and my nephew is white! What more do you want me to say?"

The magistrate's hair flashed.

"I want you to explain to the court how being black (whatever that means) disqualifies you from adopting and raising a child who is considered white (whatever that means)."

Tubs's grip tightened on Rosa's hand.

"It's a question of westernization, that's what it comes down to," said Victor, crossing and uncrossing his thighs in the cramped space of the witness box.

"Westernization?" Angie affected a bemused grin.

"Yes—look, I'm not able to provide a dictionary definition of the term, but it's all about descent. Nicky-Ross is *descended* from Europe, whereas Mrs Lethlabe is an African person."

"And that makes her unfit to raise him?"

"Our cultures are different."

"Culture? Let's check that. Does Mrs Lethlabe speak English?"

"Yes, but—"

"—No 'buts,' Mr Addo. You said 'yes,' to the question. I'm sure you'll agree she speaks *perfect* English—maybe even more perfect than you or I. And last time I checked, English was a European language. Do you know what she does for a living, Mr Addo?"

"No, but I'm sure—"

"—You don't know? Well I'll tell you, Mr Addo. She's a top executive in a top global investment consulting firm. She makes multi-million dollar decisions every day. She has a large number of people of all backgrounds reporting to her. Your late sister, Mr Addo, whom you say is descended from Europe, *reported* to this African person, Mr Addo—Mrs Lethlabe was her boss. Have you seen the car Mrs Lethlabe drives? It's one of the finest cars in the world, and it was manufactured in a European country called Germany—a car that you and I (whom you categorise as 'white') can only dream of driving. And have you seen her passport—are you aware that in her young life she has visited almost every country in Europe, the centre of your Western world, something that I'm sure *you* have not done? She resides in a place called Pinelands, Mr Addo, an upmarket suburb in Cape Town that you will surely recall was reserved exclusively for persons of European descent in the days when you were still living in South Africa. Do you get my drift, Mr Addo? If 'westernization' is your criterion, then nobody is more qualified to raise your nephew than Mrs Lethlabe."

Rosa's heartbeat picked up speed. She flashed a glance at Victor's attorney at the next table, wondering why he had not attempted to interrupt Angie's tirade; He was hunched over his papers, writing away at such a pace that his shoulders shuddered.

Victor's eyes betrayed the look of an unjustly victimized donkey. Seeming to speak to himself, he uttered in a monotone that Angie was exploiting the racial aspect of things, that she was overlooking the most obvious reason for him to be granted the adoption right, namely, that he and the child were *family*.

Angie's cheeks reddened. "Surely, a person's humanity is all that should matter, Mr Addo—no?" She swiftly ran a hand through her hair. "You will be aware that Nicky-Ross's mother, Mr Addo—your sister—identified Mrs Lethlabe—not you—as her next-of-kin. So, if 'family' is a compelling ground for deciding the adoption option for Nicky-Ross, then surely Mrs Lethlabe should be regarded as *family* in this instance? And if so, you should step aside and allow her to adopt him?"

"She is not *real* family," snarled Victor.

"Mr Addo," said Angie. "You insist that it is "better" for a child to be reared by what you call his "real" or biological family rather than by strangers, which means you believe that blood will naturally care more. Yet, you—as the child's mother's blood brother—turned your back on your sister when you left South Africa. There is not a shred of evidence that in all the years of your absence you communicated with her in any way. How, then, does family 'naturally' care more?"

"Nicky-Ross is my family," said Victor. "I am the closest person to him on God's earth. When I set eyes on him for the first time, something incredible happened to my heart." Victor blinked. He raised a hand to his left breast, then withdrew it abruptly. He continued in a subdued tone: "Yes, I might not have been the best brother to Nikki." He flashed a side-long glance at Angie. "But nor was she the best sister to me. Communication is a two-way street. What effort did she make to contact me? Family relationships should not be over-simplified, because then they'll be misunderstood." His voice gathered volume. "The fiercest and bitterest fighting happens inside families, but this doesn't mean there's any less love inside families. I loved my sister!"

His eyes had moistened, and he rubbed at them with his thumbs.

Angie crossed the floor and positioned herself to the left of the magistrate.

"Your Honour," she said. "Who best to be guided by than the baby's mother, herself? We know that she considered Mrs Lethlabe to be her next-of-kin, despite the fact that she had a natural brother alive-and-well and living in Australia. She exercised her preference. We know that in the months preceding her confinement, she lived under the roof of the Lethlabes in Pinelands—she and her pet cat, Plato. It was a healthy loving, caring relationship—that, despite the obvious differences in what we've come to call race and culture. Those differences were totally irrelevant to Miss Addo. Only small-minded bigots would have seen any problem in her choice. Here was human nature at its finest. This is what Nikki Addo would have wanted for her child—a warm, caring, loving environment in which he could thrive and flourish. This certainly would have been in his best interests. How can we reason that just because one party is black and the other white this constitutes sufficient reason to deny an adoption? What has black and white got to do with anything? To invoke race or colour is nothing but to revert to old-style apartheid-thinking. Nikki has proven that it is possible—that it is correct and desirable—that we uphold differences without demanding separation, in short, that her son be raised in terms of the finest and most precious of human values. She paused for breath. "As for the question of family, we can see that in this case that is nothing but an irrelevant technicality."

She turned her gaze to Victor. "The Lethlabes," she continued, "want to adopt Nicky-Ross out of love; you, Mr Addo out of duty. They would raise him in a richly diverse South Africa, you in a sterile whites-only Perth. Here Nicky-Ross would take his place equipped for life in a vibrant twenty-first century, there for existence in a social and cultural backwater. Nicky-Ross is a South African, born into a country with a unique cultural history. This country's diversity is its strength, it is Nicky-Ross's heritage. To take him to Australia would be to violate his claim to this heritage. It would be totally against his interests. It would be nothing short of scandalous. We would be sacrificing his national identity to secure some spurious biological identity. As far as we know, his mother had no intention of taking him out of the country to be raised in a foreign land. If he is taken to Australia, this will be a denial of his rights. He is a weeks-old baby. He can't defend his rights. We have to do it for him. We have to question your agenda, Mr Addo—is it to ensure the child's welfare, or simply to prevent the Lethlabes from adopting him?"

Rosa tensed all the muscles in her body to restrain herself rising to her feet and cheering. She stole a glance over her shoulder and picked out Bill's eye—he was seated close to the back of the room—and exchanged winks with him.

"Mr Addo," began Faffie Swart, running a finger across his moustache so roughly it seemed he would dislodge it. Although he spoke with emphasis, neither of his lips was visible behind the bushy moustache. "Tell this court, what can your nephew look forward to in Australia?"

Before Victor could answer, Swart continued: "Will he really be stuck in some cultural backwater? Will he be brought up in a sterile, loveless home? Explain to this court how the child's best interests will be served by moving him to Australia and by keeping him within his biological family."

Victor rose to his feet. Before speaking he tugged at his tie and lapels, then placed both hands on the witness box rail. "May I stand, your honour?"

The magistrate nodded.

"Of course it is crazy to suggest that Perth is a whites-only cultural back-water. It is also crazy to suggest that moving the child from South Africa will somehow be to deny him his so-called South African heritage. What South African heritage? Nicky-Ross is descended from Europe. By moving him to Australia I will in fact be bringing him closer to his *real* heritage."

"What kind of family life can the child look forward to, Mr Addo?" Faffie Swart smiled, cupping his palms over his belly in the shape of Dürer's Praying Hands.

"It is a great pity my sister went and had a child out of wedlock," said Victor. "Despite how she might have turned out in later life, Nikki was not raised that way. We come from a fairly traditional family background. Our parents were God-fearing Christians, and part of a stable country-town community. We were taught values that perhaps Nikki, for whatever reason—who's to know what influences she came under?—values that, unfortunately, she appears to have flouted. As her older brother and only living relative, I must take some of the blame for that. As I stand here now I deeply regret that I did not maintain contact with her here in this country."

His eyes moved from Swart's to the magistrate's. "I have no doubt that if I did, she would not have gone off the rails and had an illegitimate child. We don't even know who the father is. I can and would like to make up for it by adopting her son, and bringing him up according to the same values my parents taught us."

A tear glistened in his left eye. "Nicky-Ross will become my child. He will be brought up in a loving, safe, Christian home-environment. My wife and my children will love him and be concerned only about his welfare. By growing up in Perth, he will have access to the finest opportunities—the best schooling and education. He will be safe, he will be free. He will be among his own people. And if someday he wished to visit South Africa, he could then pop in at the Lethlabes and thank them personally for what they've done for his mother."

Smiling so that their teeth showed, both he and Swart turned and nodded to the Lethlabes before resuming their seats.

"In closing our case, your honour, I don't have much to say. Counsel for the Lethlabes has tried to discount the importance of race and culture in what I can only conclude is a desperate attempt to serve the selfish interests of the Lethlabes. If they really cared so much for the late Miss Addo as they claim, they would not try to expose her newborn orphan-son to the risks entailed in their adopting him—they would instead go out of their way to support all moves to have him placed within a family structure that will reinforce his—not their—needs: in short, with Mr Addo and his family.

"Counsel for the Lethlabes is confusing racial integration with racial mixing, Your Honour. Integration happens at the level of society. Thus, there is no reason why Nicky-Ross, if adopted by white parents, could not be perfectly integrated in a multi-racial society. It's happening all around us. White children born in South Africa are fitting perfectly into South Africa's multi-racial society. Racial integration happens in the schools, in the churches, when one goes to the supermarket or uses public transport. But racial-mixing, on the other hand, is something altogether different. It is something that happens at the interpersonal level. We fool ourselves if we think only white people are opposed to the mixing of the races. Racial-mixing is something opposed by the majority of black people themselves. There is a general aversion to the idea of inter-marriage and all that it entails.

"In South Africa we have an over-abundance of black children waiting—hoping—for adoption into a family like the Lethlabe family. Why don't Mr and Mrs Lethlabe seek to dip into this crowded pool? Why do they need a white child? We have heard that Mrs Lethlabe is a super-woman, that she holds this incredibly senior position in this incredibly global consultancy firm. She has this brilliant car, this wonderful home in Pinelands. Truly, she walks on water. The only trophy she doesn't have in her fabulous cabinet of trophies is a white child. Makes you think, doesn't it?

"In conclusion, I must once again emphasise the importance of looking at the factors which will promote nurturing, and for this reason we should not underestimate the importance of biology in strengthening the child's natural sense of belonging, and how this in turn will influence the child's psychological well-being, particularly in his formative years. We dare not wittingly place Nicky-Ross in a situation where he'll grow up confused about who he is and where he belongs. Like Mrs Arendze, who produced such an instructive report, I say, 'do we want this kind of blood on our hands? I thank you, Your Honour."

"Your Honour, counsel for Mr Addo seems less concerned about whether Mr Addo is granted adoption rights to the baby Nicky-Ross than that the Lethlabes—on the basis of their so-called race—should be denied the opportunity.

"The absurdity of Mr Addo's case can easily be illustrated if we looked at one or two hypothetical scenarios. For instance, what if it were discovered that Nicky-Ross's father is not (by Mr Addo's criteria) *white*? What if he were—horrors—by Mr Addo's criteria, *black*? In an instant, all Mr Addo's concerns would be up in smoke, and he would probably rush to catch the next flight back to Perth.

"I have no doubt that to one who perceives the world through racist glasses, a few teaspoons of black blood in Nicky-Ross's veins would—sadly—make all the difference.

"But while we lament such backward-thinking, we must also acknowledge which way the world is headed, and thus, what at the end of the day, is best for a child growing up in this world. Things have changed a good deal since Mr Addo was last living in this country, Far from wishing to retain strict segregationist policies among different groups of people, we South Africans now wish to do just the opposite. Since Mr Addo's departure all those years ago, a process of enlightenment has been under way. The new normal is for people to integrate—in all spheres of social life we are attempting to break down artificial barriers of whatever kind. With the Lethlabes, Nicky-Ross would be raised in a modern family environment that will equip him for a future world in which people are people, not blacks or whites.

"In conclusion, I just want to deal with the bogus-argument that Nicky-Ross will not discover his sense of identity if he grew up as a child of black adoptive parents. Without drawing attention to the fact that such an argument has not prevented so-called black children from being adopted by so-called white parents, I want to refute the very notion. With the Lethlabes Nicky-Ross's similarities and differences will be equally celebrated; neither his similarities nor his differences will present any obstacle that their love for him would not surmount.

"At the end of the day, it's going to be love that counts. The report of the social worker makes it clear that they have demonstrated their love for Nicky-Ross, his late mother, Nikki, and even her cat, Plato—in super-abundance. Mr Addo, for his part, has maintained a hostile estrangement ever since leaving the country so many years ago. It would not be wrong to say he *abandoned* his sister—who was his family, his blood. How can such a person be entrusted to raise her son—and then in a foreign country to boot?"

"No, don't make love to me, Tubs – fuck me. Brutalise me. Harder . . . faster. More. Yes. Fuck. Fuck. Fuck. Oh . . ." "Are you OK? You're crying!" "I'm OK – don't stop. Yes. More. Hurt me, beat me, flog me. Ah, yes! Rough, rough, rougher . . . Blood. Draw blood."

Her fingernails dug into his soft, wincing flesh, they raked across his back, seeking blood, drawing anguish from his throat; she tightened her thighs around his waist and squeezed till the pain of squeezing made her shriek.

"Rosa . . ."

"No talking, please no talking."

Her body slackened. He fell off her. She sobbed and sobbed.

"That's my blood-flow speeding up," she said, laughing out loud. "You're tickling me, but don't stop."

It was Plato. He had hopped onto the bed, and was licking at her bare shoulder, sending small strips of tickle through her neck. She had fallen asleep onto her forearms, which were numb and creased from her hair. She rose to a sitting position, and took the cat into her lap. "You and Nicky-Ross are the dearest creatures to me on earth," she said. Images of Tubs and her father flashed to her mind. "In her lifetime I should have taken a selfie with all of us on it, including you, Plato. But who would have thought she'd go die on us?"

Tubs appeared in the doorway, hands in the pockets of his nightgown.

"Little fella was scratching at the door," he said. "So I let him in. He must've gotten worried when he heard you screaming . . . Are you OK? I put on the kettle . . . Maybe you'd like some—"

"—Brandy, please, Tubs . . . no, I'm not joking. I would like a tot of brandy, please." She placed her hands gently round the cat's belly, and raised him to the level of her eyes. "Sometimes," she said, "when I look into your eyes, I see Nikki."

"Rosa . . ." A pained expression came to Tubs's face.

"I'm OK, Tubs, really. I'm sorry. Don't worry, I'm OK. Mix in a little water with the brandy, please." She embraced the cat, nuzzling her face into his smooth fur.

The magistrate was fidgety this morning. Her hair like a live, furry cat covering her skull, was in continuous motion, flouncing around her ears and neck, getting into her eyes, refusing to be stilled. Her specs seemed hell-bent on sliding to the tip of her nose; no sooner would she thrust them hard back up against her eyebrows than they would commence their inexorable downward slide. Her hands, her fingers were busily sifting and shuffling and rearranging piles of paper on her desk. She kept losing her pen among the piles, and twice within a minute, nearly knocked over the glass of water at her right forearm; twice too, she could be heard to say *shit* under her breath.

"We're not dealing in absolutes here," she said. "How can we be certain of anything in the future? We have to look at probabilities. It is *probable* that the child will enjoy a better future growing up with his natural family. We must avoid taking risks with a child's long-term future. It is safer to place the child within a structure and a set-up where more of the circumstances and conditions are natural to him rather than unnatural."

She paused in her reading to take a sip of water. Her lips, which left an imprint on the glass, gleamed. She swept a rapid glance over her spectacles at the assembled courtroom, tucked her hair back behind her ears, and her sleeves back behind her elbows, then continued to read. "The child's welfare is paramount." Her voice sounded moist. "This is a deeply embedded principle in all civilized law. It absolutely must be the overriding consideration that guides us as we seek to discharge our duty towards this child."

Rosa's impulse was to rise from her seat and depart the courtroom, and simply to keep on walking. Of course, she'd known there was a more than fifty percent chance this acne'd magistrate would rule in favour of Victor Addo—that the safe option would always be the preferred option. There was a sense of pins-and-needles in Rosa's hands, her feet, her heart. She had stopped listening to the magistrate, and was attempting by an act of will to staunch the rage that was bursting up within. Her thoughts turned to her mother—what would Zoliswa have done in these circumstances, Zoliswa who had preferred to sacrifice everything rather than make an accommodation with apartheid? Is this *my* apartheid?

Angie passed her a paper on which was written, *We must take this to the high court.*

Just because you're dead, Rosa said in her mind to Nikki, these people think they can arrogate to themselves the right to dispose of your child according to *their* whims and criteria, as if he's some kind of thing—a rug or a sofa! They think that by dying you have surrendered your right of choice—death, the great nullifier! But worry not, Honeybunch, I will never allow that to happen.

"According to her report," said the magistrate as she adjusted her specs on her nose, "Mrs Arendze had consulted the baby's medical specialist, a Doctor Mel Cochrane." The magistrate's hair slid over her shoulders, and swung like laden thuribles on either side of her ears. Without stopping in her reading, she flicked it back with a lightning-fast twist of her neck. "Doctor Cochrane's advice," she read, "is that the child will not be ready to travel for at least another six months." She looked up from her papers. "In the interim, he will require specified medical attention, which will include continued hospitalization for at least another three-to-four weeks."

As soon as the magistrate declared proceedings closed, Rosa strode over to her and shook her hand. "Thank-you," she said. "It couldn't have been easy to come to a decision in this case. Although I'm disappointed that you didn't award for me, I respect your judgement."

"Ah, I'm so glad you understand," said the magistrate, brushing her hair back. "One has to be brutally objective in these matters." She squeezed Rosa's hand. "May I compliment you on what a fine person you are—you and your husband."

Tubs, witnessing the cordiality between his wife and the magistrate came over, and also shook the hand of the magistrate, and thanked her, though he wasn't sure for what.

Summoning her brightest smile, Rosa crossed the floor to where Victor and his attorney were standing.

She offered her hand to Victor, but he opened his arms to embrace her. "Thank-you for being such an incredible friend to my sister," he said into her ear, and she could feel the emotion in his voice. Instinctively, her arms tightened around his shoulders.

"It's been difficult," she said, "but I'm glad we've crossed this hurdle." She kept smiling. "I accept the judgement," she said. "I'm not going to appeal. I realise that to prolong or extend the process would be as traumatic for you as for me."

"That's very gracious of you," he said. "I have only praise for you and your wonderful husband."

"Before you return home to Australia," she said, "we should meet to discuss the interim arrangements. As little Nicky-Ross's aunty, I would like to pick up all the bills—there will be medical expenses, and, of course, when he's discharged from the hospital, he will need to be placed with a private baby-care facility. There are some fine ones here in Cape Town. There's also the airfare to Perth—"

"—You are an amazing person," said Victor, struggling to hold back his tears.

"Don't worry about a thing," she said. And in her mind she added, Cause every little thing gonna be alright.

Next morning she was in office an hour before sunrise. By the time Ferrie put his head in to say good morning, she had completed a detailed analysis of her personal financial position—happy that her wealth had silently grown itself by the confluent magic of compound interest and congenial market forces to a level where forthcoming decision-making would be relatively easier—and drafted a provisional budget anticipating likely expenses related to Nicky-Ross in the next six months. She had also looked over the most recent reports on her ailing Lumina projects, and pencilled in options for corrective action to be discussed with the respective project managers in the course of the day. The thirty-two emails that awaited her when she arrived at office grew to forty-seven before she could commence with reading them, and stood at sixty-six when she replied to the first one read.

Ferrie's conversation was mostly light and inconsequential, but as she expected, he mixed in a fleeting reference to Leigh, clearly in the hope that Rosa might say something reassuring. She didn't, and he left with a perturbed look in his eyes.

By eight-thirty she'd had her third mug of coffee, but there was no reduction in the strange elation she'd been feeling all morning. Between eight-thirty and nine-thirty she presided over three meetings during which she approved spend-requests in excess of a million rand.

She called Angie van der Poel on the phone. "I'm leaving for the hospital, now," she said. "Can I call round at your office at about eleven-thirty or twelve?"

Another week had elapsed, but for all the hi-tech support he was getting, Nicky Ross in his incubator continued to look more dead than alive. Rosa's eyes filmed over at the sight of his wretched excuse-for-a-body, still small enough to be concealable in a shoe-box, still more foetus than birthed human being. As always, his breathing was regular but laboured—frenzied!—as if he'd just completed a hundred-metre dash. Tiny—and for Rosa, itchy-looking—red blotches had appeared across his forehead. *They were definitely not there last night!* His flesh was clammy and unresponsive to her fingers, and she wondered, as she caressed and caressed his body, whether her touch was not an additional source of torment for him. She scrutinized every millimetre of his body. A large, continent-shaped bruise encircled the intravenous needle attached to the back of his hand. Rosa tried to recall if the bruise was there last night, or if it was *that* big. She noticed that his urine bag was swollen, and that it would soon need replacing. Its contents were an opaque sepia colour, and there were minute dots floating in it. The mass of tubes that connected him to his life-support apparatus continued to be the unmovable sword in her heart—the one thing that could destroy her composure, her self-possession, and transform her into a snivelling wreck.

"Don't look so glum, mum," said the friendly-looking nurse—Nurse Bushula, according to her name tag—who came over and stood by Rosa's side. "The little *inkwenkwe's* doing fine."

"It certainly doesn't look that way," said Rosa, trying to smile. "When I look at him lying there in that brutal entanglement of wires, all I see is trauma." She came close to begging Nurse Bushula to hug her.

"I know what you mean, said the nurse. "He's not out of the woods yet, as we're always saying, but he's on the right track." She set about replacing the urine bag.

The baby started crying, a fragile whimper that seemed to require an effort to produce.

"Dr Cochrane was here this morning, and expressed satisfaction with his progress. Have a look at the graphs, and you'll see they're all moving in the right direction."

Rosa's eyes shifted to the overhead monitor and sought out the top green line which was rhythmically, endlessly recreating itself, and alongside which a numeral, accompanied by a constant beeping of the machine, was fluctuating between 177 and 191.

The baby's crying seemed to intensify.

"I've no doubt his crying and restlessness is bothering you," said Nurse Bushula. "Ah, little one! Our little gift from Heaven! What ails thee so, why so cranky this morning? But don't worry, Mrs Lethlabe. He will settle down soon enough. Dr Cochrane this morning prescribed something for us to give him to calm him down."

"I'd like to stay with him for a little while," said Rosa. "And hold him in my arms."

"That would be really good for him," said Nurse Bushula. "I'm sure it'll help him to settle down. I'll look in on you a little later." She pulled the curtain round to enclose the area, while Rosa undid the clips to Nicky-Ross's apparatus.

In the privacy created by the curtain, Rosa unbuttoned her shirt and slipped it off, and with her finger nails unhooked her bra and peeled it off, too. The baby's flesh against her flesh sent shock-waves through both their bodies. His fingers groped along her neck, her chin. She tickled the fingers with her tongue, and smiled as they reacted by trying to pinch her lips. She had draped the baby's blanket over his naked back to seal in the warmth, which was gradually building to a shared presence between their entwined bodies, a presence that Rosa knowingly fantasized as a corporeal Nikki come to join them.

Why so tearful, little babba? What are you lamenting? Your mommy's death? Well, then, cry little baby, cry, and I will cry with you. As she spoke, the baby's crying became more hesitant. His eyes flickered and seemed to Rosa to be searching for her face. Gradually, all the jerking and quivering came to be superseded by a rapid, barely-audible breathing. Rosa felt her own muscles relax. My hand still covers eighty-percent of your whole body surface—you've so much growing still to do! Just a little kitten, just a little chick.

Within the area cordoned off by the curtain, the noises of the machinery were familiar and comforting to the ear; from beyond the curtain came gentle intrusions of what had also to Rosa's ear become normal, familiar NICU sounds. All, along with Nicky-Ross's breathing against her neck, had a lulling effect, and Rosa willingly succumbed, drifting into a deep, delicious slumber.

She knew, when she awoke, that she had been sleeping a blissful sleep. She had no recollection of any dreaming, and savoured the immediate sense of freshness that she felt. Mentally sanitizing! Nicky-Ross's body started to move very gently shortly after Rosa opened her eyes. She knew he was waking up, too, and hoped that his sleep was as therapeutic as her own. She continued to lie back in the big leather chair with Nicky-Ross, covered in his blanket, secure against her breast, hoping to prolong the peacefulness of the moment. Her thoughts turned to the setback she'd suffered in court, and she asked herself a question that she had been asking herself repeatedly since the pock-faced magistrate had issued her verdict: *Should I contest the judgement?* Her instinct told her it would be a waste of time and money, and that unless she was able to mount some significant additional factors in her favour, another court would probably come to the same decision.

Returning the sleeping child to his bed in the incubator was like placing an egg back in its nest. She re-tied the connections to his feeding line and lung monitor. Instantly, the screens lit up with a jumble of colours that merged into a smooth flow of low green bars. Just barely within her hearing range, Rosa was able to discern a metallic, rhythmic ticking—Nicky-Ross's heartbeat, or the machine's.

While Rosa was putting on her shirt, Nurse Bushula's head appeared round the curtain. The nurse smiled broadly. "I looked in a couple of times, and loved how soundly you were sleeping. It was a beautiful sight!"

Before she left, Rosa changed Nicky-Ross's nappy. She rearranged the toys surrounding the child, placing the teddy bear at his side so that it lay against his arm. She set the play button on the recorder, and set the volume so that in her judgement, the sound would be just within the child's audio range. She wanted him to pick up the voices, the sounds, the music as a subliminal experience, as an infusion, as nourishment.

On her way out, Rosa texted Angie van der Poel – *On my way, be there in about 20 mins, OK?* She'd arranged to meet Angie at a restaurant in Sea Point—anywhere rather than the lawyer's suffocating workspace.

"Vic Addo has not once objected that you're paying for everything," said Angie. "If anything, he's been damned grateful for it."

"I was hoping it would count for something," said Rosa, "But he's ended up winning the baby."

"It might yet count for something," said Angie, feeling in her bag for her cigarettes. ". . . If you're hoping for free access to the baby when Addo returns to Australia."

From where they sat on the twelfth-floor balcony of the Sea Point restaurant, the shimmering Atlantic was bluer than Rosa'd ever seen before.

Angie lit up, and blew a stream of smoke vertically into the air. The scent of the burning tobacco stimulated Rosa's appetite, but she refrained from ordering food. Instead, she asked the waiter for coffee.

"Yep," said Rosa, "I've given up the idea of trying to win foster-care rights. My main concern now is that Nicky-Ross be placed in the best private care facility when he's discharged from the hospital—also, that Dr Cochrane continues to be his paediatrician. I'm prepared to pay whatever it's going to cost."

"I can't see Addo objecting to that," said Angie. "The *quid pro quo* needs to be that he authorises the foster care home to allow you free and total access to the child at all times, as if you were the natural mother. He needs to let them know that you are his stand-in here in Cape Town while he's back in Australia."

"I'm worried he might demand I hand over Nikki's stuff that's at my place."

"Tell him that it's part of her estate, and there are legalities to be attended to before you can part with anything."

"He might at least wish to see what there is."

"Let him look all he likes, but he's to take nothing. Also, if you can keep quiet about the property at Langebaan till we've confirmed that Nikki was the sole owner . . ."

Before returning to the office, Rosa took a leisurely stroll along the beachfront promenade. It was stone-paved for its entire length, thus presenting no obstacle to her stilettos. Her imagination had Nikki walking alongside her, arm-in-arm, chatting merrily. People are staring, she said to herself, no doubt because of this silly smile on my face.

In the days preceding his flight back to Perth, Victor Addo was thrice invited to dinner at the Lethlabes, and thrice accepted. On the first occasion, he brought wine for Tubs, and flowers for Rosa. The first dinner was a candle-lit affair; Tubs had prepared roast lamb, which Victor referred to repeatedly as "succulent" and "superb." Rosa had arranged the flowers in a vase on the table, and took numerous pictures with her cellphone camera. She described the flowers as "so colourful!" and "so beautiful!" and was able to identify lilies, carnations and chrysanthemums in the mix. Much of the small-talk was around South African wines, about which Victor appeared unusually knowledgeable. For most of the evening, Plato hung around Tubs, refusing even to look at Victor when the ex-South African tried to pat him. Victor seemed embarrassed as well as relieved, and shifted the conversation to "weird Australian animals, such as the wombat," which he said looked like a cross between a bear, a rat and a pig. Even though he knew that Tubs would be driving him back to his hotel, he was careful not to get shloshed, maybe to avoid the risk of blurting something he'd later regret. For most of the evening, there was no talk of Nikki or Nicky-Ross, other than brief remarks about how the little one was recovering. Rosa toyed with the idea of suggesting that she—when the time came—deliver Nicky-Ross to his new parents in Australia, when Victor, speaking in exclamation marks about the beauty of Cape Town, declared that he "couldn't wait to bring his whole family out to see the place, when time came to collect the baby."

Dinner number two followed hard on the heels of the first, and also happened around the Lethlabes' dining-room table. On seeing the spread laid out before him, Victor was moved to call it a feast fit for a king. He was keen to know about a number of the dishes that Tubs had prepared, and begged for the recipes. "This is what I miss most about South Africa," he said. "The food." He was so happy and relieved, he said, that he would be able to sleep in peace at night knowing Rosa and Tubs were here to look out for Nicky-Ross while he, Victor, was all those miles away in Aussie. "I couldn't have hoped for better," he said. "I know the child will want for nothing, and will have all the love he deserves." Again, Rosa was on the verge of suggesting *she* bring the child home to Perth when Victor declared how excited he was at the prospect of showing his family around "this enchanting city."

Third time round was on the Saturday preceding Victor's departure. The Lethlabes had prepared a yellowtail braai, and just the sight of the fish on the grill brought emotion surging to Victor's throat. He got very drunk that afternoon, but did or said nothing to embarrass himself. He wondered why Rosa's father had not attended any of the occasions, but guessed it was because the old man was reclusive. Tubs had thoughtfully put together a collection of old South African classics, including *Hier sit die manne in die Royal Hotel*, and *Paradise Road*. Victor knew most of the words, and sang along joyfully. "I've been so blessed," he said with a slurring tongue. "You are incredible people. When—not if—you come to Perth you will stay with me and my family. Let Nicky-Ross see what a wonderful aunt and uncle he has here in South Africa."

At the airport next morning, he clasped each of them in a tight, prolonged hug. The genuine affection that Rosa saw in his eyes brought her close to tears. He waved exaggeratedly till he was out of sight through the boarding gate.

In the car on the way home, Rosa turned to Tubs and said, "That was hard work, but we probably got the best deal under the circumstances."

"You mean because he agreed to give us unrestricted access to Nicky-Ross while the child's in foster care?"

"Exactly right," she said.

They went and had breakfast at a waterfront restaurant, choosing a table close to the water's edge—"so that we can smell the salt," said Rosa. She set her camera to video-function and panned over the sea in the hope of capturing the scalloping effect that the water made as it rolled into the bay.

"What a beautiful city Cape Town is," she said. "You've got to be crazy to voluntarily give it up."

Tubs took this as a reference to Victor. "We should have urged him to move back to Cape Town with his family," he said, "and raise Nicky-Ross here."

"He seemed pretty eager to catch his plane back to Perth," said Rosa. "The next six months are going to fly by. It's all the time we have left to spend with Nicky-Ross, before he gets snatched away from us forever."

After breakfast, she got Tubs to drop her off at the hospital, where she stayed at Nicky-Ross's side till Tubs collected her after eleven that night. Next morning she was back at six, before the night shift was done.

According to the framed certificates on the wall behind him, Mel Cochrane had obtained his medical degree from the University of Cape Town, and seven years later, his master's in paediatrics from King's College, London. He sat behind a highly-polished antique mahogany desk which, in response to Rosa's enquiry, he said was inherited from his father. This made her think of Angie van der Poel—*I inherited the practice from my father* she had said. The magic of generational wealth.

Through the window of his office, Table Mountain was vivid in the morning sun, and seemed so close it might have been in the very garden outside.

"The air in your office feels as sanitized as an NICU," said Rosa. "Just sitting here makes me feel like all my sins are forgiven."

He chuckled. "That's the way I feel after bungee jumping."

In his left hand he held a shiny grey stainless steel device no bigger than a postcard, and with his thumb he instructed it to project an image of Nicky-Ross's medical report onto an overhead screen.

"You'll be pleased," he said, "very pleased, to see that there's been a huge improvement in the little guy's overall condition." He looked up with glowing eyes and teeth, and Rosa's heart jumped.

"You'll see," he said, gesturing towards the screen, "All his vitals are looking good. Our first task was to ensure that his development outside the uterus would parallel what would have been expected had he gone his full term inside it."

Scrolling through the report, he murmured some of the more significant findings—"respiratory muscles developing well, chest wall stable, breathing rate, heart rate, bone development, muscle tone . . . all well . . . no infections, urine clear, gastric capacity OK . . . check, check, check . . . weight not there yet but catching up fast. Yep, all his readings have gone either from bad to good, or from good to great."

"Music to my ears," said Rosa.

"It won't be long before we'll be able to take him off all his feeds and monitors, and then we'll be able to shift him out of NICU and shortly thereafter, to his foster home."

"When do you expect to be able to confirm his readiness to travel to Australia?"

"Still too early to say for sure, but I'm sticking to my initial forecast of six months."

CHAPTER EIGHTEEN

She dropped Bill off the comrades' place in Langa, and turned back towards Washington Avenue. She didn't take the left turn back to the highway, but continued on in the direction of the police station where she took a left into Mdidi Street. She followed its twists and turns through the old township, past the newly-erected shack settlement known as *Fidel Castro*, taking care to avoid the increasing number of potholes in the road. She almost hit a fowl, which went squawking away, flapping wildly. Her full trust was in her GPS, but she knew it wasn't foolproof or even necessarily the best way to get to your destination in a place like Langa. Despite the brightness of the morning, this part of the Langa Township had a dank, dark look-and-feel. So many people about—mostly bedraggled young men on street corners whose eyes stayed ominously on her till she was completely out of their range. Clearly, in her shining luxury vehicle she was a huge anomaly in this part of the world. Perhaps many who gawked thought a film star or other celeb had strayed into their space—or that maybe they were simply hallucinating.

Everything about this part of town was depressing. Washing on so many lines, threadbare items of clothing out to dry in the morning sun, but which because of their squalidness looked unwashed. The houses were small and close-packed, sub-economic units built by the municipality in the nineteen-fifties. Everywhere along every road, so many shanties! Tiny children, mere babes, playing without any adult in sight, outside so many of the houses and shanties. Rosa's mind turned to Nicky-Ross: unthinkable that he could end up like this. Is this what Vic Addo's attorney had in mind when he said it would make more sense for me to adopt one of these kids? She tried to relax, to slow her breathing, but could feel the longer it was taking to find the place—*I hope I can find my way out of here, again!*—the more agitated she was becoming.

Despite her GPS she shot past her turn-off, and only just managed to see the name board through the corner of her eye as she sped by. She backed up, and steered the car into Amandla Street. None of the houses was numbered. Outside one of them, a ramshackle building, sat a barefooted old man on an up-turned oil drum, taking in the sun. His sad eyes followed her, and seemed to be saying I can see you're lost—I am too, but in a different way. She wanted to stop and check her bearings with him, but was worried she might need to speak in isi-Xhosa. Besides, there was a mangy-looking dog prowling around, and she wasn't going to take any chances. She might have given up, but out of the blue, her GPS suddenly declared that she had arrived at her destination. Her heart skipped a beat. She slowed the car, trying to divine which of the number of close-packed bungalows could be the one she was looking for.

Her cellphone had been going non-stop. She worried that Ferrie or Leigh might urgently be needing to speak to her. She checked. Mercifully, of all the missed calls, only one was from Ferrie, and, since he hadn't follow it up with a repeat call or left a message, it was clearly something which could wait. There'd been a call from Tubs as well, but she'd call him back from the office. She didn't want to be sitting in a car in a strange neighbourhood mucking with her cellphone—it would attract the wrong kind of attention. As it was, she had little doubt that a thousand secret eyes like sniper guns were trained on her from every window in sight.

The place to her immediate left was built of cement blocks with a rusting corrugated iron roof. The walls were unpainted, and cracked in several places. Round the front of the house was a low, uneven fence of dry wooden stakes, a number of which were either broken or tottering, with several simply missing. She switched off the motor and took a deep breath. What if she were at the wrong place? What if she goes in and is never seen alive again? The place was dimly-lit, like a computer-screen image seen against a low backlight. A woman with a quizzical, suspicious eye came to the door. She looked past Rosa at the gleaming car parked in front of the house. Then turned to Rosa with a look of hostility. She bared her teeth, and addressing Rosa in isi-Xhosa demanded to know why a princess in a big flashy car would want to be visiting her humble abode. All Rosa said was, "Kubheka," in a barely-audible voice, for the woman's expression to change completely to one of subservience. *So! I'm at the right place—the Lord's name be praised!!*

The woman invited her into the dimly-lit front-room which was airless and dusty, filled with a large couch-and-chair set that she wondered how they had managed to get in through the doorway. Rosa realised she was sweating when she smelled her own fragrance, suddenly prominent in her nostrils. She remained standing while the woman disappeared through a doorway into a darkened backroom. In the front room where she stood, a TV set was on, playing what was clearly an American soapie.

Kubheka was a short, stout man, wearing a tattered Che Guevara T-shirt. His head was shaven and polished. In the darkness of the room, it shone with a dull glow, his face looking like a wax candle, with his pate the flame. His cheeks and eyes and the tip of his nose were equally shiny. There were large gaps in the scraggly salt-and-pepper beard which dotted the sea of his face like loosely-connected islands. He was clearly over sixty, and was probably older than her father, Bill. He did not appear to be surprised or quizzical. He approached her with a mild, polite countenance, and uttered a low, "Molo, Sisi," to which her reply was an equally low, "Good morning, Mr K."

He motioned for her to follow him, and led her through a cluttered kitchen into a narrow backyard. She was surprised to see how well-tended the yard was, with several rows of potted plants. Against the concrete wall opposite the kitchen door was a row of flowers in bloom, and scattered about the rest of the yard were what looked to Rosa like herbs of many different sorts. She was sure that a small green tree in the shade of the house was cannabis, and her impulse was to ask, but she restrained herself. The sun was bright on the yard. Rosa felt herself relaxing, feeling a sense of relief.

"If you're here for the kind of reason I think," said Kubheka in English, "then it is safer for us to talk outside." He spoke with a pronounced Xhosa accent. "I grew up in the apartheid era, so I'm always on my guard. As a result of a conversation inside someone's house that was bugged, I ended up doing time on Robben Island. I don't trust this new South Africa of ours. I certainly don't want to be doing time again."

She smiled, uncertain how to respond, but wishing to show empathy. "I completely understand, Mr K," she said. "My parents, too, were activists in the anti-apartheid struggle." Her impulse was to explain that that was what had led to her mother's untimely death, but she didn't want to seem too anxious to establish her credentials.

The woman that had admitted her to the house brought two kitchen chairs and placed them in the shade of the house. She returned with a faded wooden coffee table, and positioned it between the chairs.

Kubheka went and sat down, and Rosa followed him.

"My father told me about you," she said, not naming her father. "I am hoping you would be able to help me as you helped him." She paused for breath. "I need to leave—the country—clandestinely."

Kubheka's eyes were impassive. He crossed his legs, and waited for her to continue.

"With a baby," she said. It sounded untrue in her ears, but finally it was out. Her heart pounded; she wished for a cigarette. "I'm thinking I'll need to be driven—in a car, I suppose—to the Lobatse border post in Botswana, maybe." *Surely I'm dreaming?*

The woman appeared with a tray with tea and ceramic-looking biscuits. First Rosa then Kubheka poured sugar and stirred; each took a biscuit.

"It's a beautiful day," said Kubheka. "I've never left this country, he added, seemingly with a note of regret in his tone. "But nor would I wish to, it's so beautiful." He bit off a piece of his biscuit; it sounded like a distant rifle shot.

"What you will want me to do will doubtlessly be illegal," he said, seeming to address one of his potted plants. "You realise that you—and I—could end up in jail—literally, right?" You need to be very clear on your requirements, as we will have only one single chance to get it right. I can assure you, we *will* get it right. Whoever referred you to us—your father?—will know we've been doing this since the nineteen-sixties, and we're experts at it." There was no hint of arrogance; clearly, he was interested only in reassuring her.

"Let's talk about what you need," he said. He took from his trouser pocket a ballpoint pen and a small bent notepad.

"I will need papers. Me and the baby. He's not mine, but the papers will have to show that he is." She was out of breath. She bit into her biscuit, and it felt as if a load of dry cement had been poured into her mouth.

"So you need false identities, then?" Kubheka wished to know.

"I'm not sure," said Rosa. She hesitated. "You see," she said, "within hours of my departure from Cape Town, the police are likely to issue a nationwide APB on me and the baby."

She slurped at her tea, which was weak and cold.

"You'll definitely need false ID's," said Kubheka, writing in his notepad.

"Since I'll never be coming back," said Rosa, suddenly alarmed, as if the reality were striking her for the first time. "I'll need to be able to access everything from Botswana, from abroad. I'm referring mainly to my bank accounts."

She was suddenly exhausted. Her thoughts shifted momentarily to Nicky-Ross. She pictured him in his incubator, on his back, weighed down by his life-support apparatus. Something like a silent wail rent her heart.

"Yep," said Kubheka, continuing his writing. "We're talking dual IDs."

"It's not my baby," she said. "But the papers need to show that he is."

"Yes, you said so," said Kubheka. He put his pen and notepad down on the table, and took up his cup of tea. His eyes shifted to the mountain. He appeared to Rosa as if he had assumed the meeting was over.

"It's a white baby," said Rosa, and felt that in saying so she had just violated every principle which had hitherto underpinned her life.

Kubheka appeared unmoved, as if this mighty revelation had little significance.

With a single sip, he filled his mouth, and Rosa watched his throat expand and contract, before he said in a matter-of-fact tone that that was an important detail, and that to get across the border, she would need to be in the company of a white husband.

"It's going to cost you a lot of money," he said. "And as you can see," he added, waving an arm in the direction of the house, "little of it will end up in my pocket."

He walked over to the middle of the grass patch, and she followed. "There are a number of—shall we call them 'agents?'—along the way," he said. "They take enormous risks, each one of them. This is why you'll end up forking out probably more than you're expecting to."

She steeled herself for an impossible sum, but was relieved to hear that—high as the amount was—it was not beyond the range of her expectations.

"That's a ball-park figure," he said. "We will obviously need to harden it up once we know what services, exactly, you'll be requiring."

He looked into her eyes and smiled. "I have to repeat," he said, "we are about to embark on something that in every single country on earth would be illegal."

All she could say was, "I understand, Mr K."

Kubheka saw her to her car. "When you come again, come in a less flashy car—this one attracts too much attention. Also, come at night, when there's less chance of being noticed."

She drove off, her heart beating wildly. She laughed out loud. "Nikki! Nikki! Can you hear me there in Heaven? The bullet's through the church, Nikki! The bullet's through the church!"

Chapter Nineteen

Ferrie's office had a glass wall on the west side, providing what his visitors would often refer to as a "stunning view of the mountain."

This morning the view was covered in low-hanging cloud, and his visitor—Rosa—instinctively turned her attention away from the view, and settled her gaze on him, and wondered if or when Leigh would be joining them.

"My wife's nagging me," he said. "*When are you going to retire?* She wants to go back to England. *Our grandchildren are growing up without us.*"

He spoke a bit about his grandchildren—a boy and a girl, both under ten. "They video-call us all the time; not a day goes by without them sending us pictures of themselves via social media. And they keep asking when we're coming home—to England, to them." He smiled, and it seemed an effort. "They're plucking at my wife's heartstrings."

A hardness came into his eyes. He swivelled his chair, to enable him to plant his elbows on the desk. Rosa noticed his wrinkles had deepened. Is this it, she wondered. Is he going to fire me, now?

"We're going to have to jettison some of the projects you've been working on," he said. "Not because they're failing, although a couple of them are—but because circumstances have changed, and they're no longer feasible."

Bullshit, she thought.

"Because the Chinese have pulled out?" Her voice was calm; it was less a question than a statement.

"Correct," said Ferrie. He sat back in his chair. "We're haemorrhaging money," he said. "The Chinese deal would have been a hedge. We no longer have something to fall back on if your projects fail. We can't take that risk."

"But we launched my projects before there was any prospect of a deal with the Chinese."

I should just get up and walk out, she thought. Now he's going to give me the yes-but line.

"Yes," Ferrie said, "but I've recently reviewed the company financials, and must say I was alarmed at just how much cash is flowing out— we're pinning too much of our hopes on a rosy future."

So! Now that you're leaving for Merry England, fuck Lumina's future. As long as there's liquid cash to fund your retirement. And she felt as if she were sitting through a turning point in her life. She crossed her arms, and folded her right leg over her left. The question is, who will be leaving Lumina sooner, you or I?

"You don't think we should do a formal risk assessment, Rob?" She attempted to sound unperturbed. "To test your gut feel—because, that surely is what it is?"

His eyes flashed, the veins in his neck bulged. He sat forward in his chair, and spoke in a low tone. "What you're referring to so disparagingly as my gut feel—"

"—Apologies. I didn't mean to be disparaging—"

"—What you refer to so disparagingly as my gut feel is the same sound judgement that built this company up from scratch, when you were still a pikaninnie."

Rosa's eyes narrowed. "A pikaninnie?" Her heart thumped in her chest. "You're obviously too stupid to realise just how insulting that was."

"How dare you call me stupid, I could fire you for that."

She rose from her chair, and with a magisterial flourish of her left hand swept up her cellphone which she had placed in front of her on his desk. "And I could have you arrested for referring to me as a pikaninnie."

She headed for the door as he just sat speechless, teeth bared, breathing hard.

"You might be interested to know," she said, holding aloft her cellphone, "I recorded every word."

Back in her office, she flopped into her chair, and said out loud, "well, now we have a good old fucking how-do-you-do." She started up her computer, and checked her desk phone for voicemail. Could I have conducted myself better? Was I wrong to use the term *gut feel*? No! It was a case of the-truth-hurt. Was my reaction to pikaninnie an overreaction? No! He's lucky he wasn't dealing with Zoliswa, she'd have laid him waste! Rosa laughed a short, punchy laugh. And my parting shot—that I'd recorded everything. He looked like he would have a heart attack then and there. That was cruel. Maybe I should tell him I was lying, but no! Let him stew.

She assembled her project management team—five cheerful young people, all so-called domain-experts, self-consciously excellent performers, who glorified in their own success, but whom the mere hint of negative feedback always devastated.

They were not fazed to hear that their projects might be summarily terminated—aborted!—if it could not be shown conclusively that their projects were feasible.

"There's a concern," said Rosa, "that we're (she raised her hands and wiggled her fingers in the sign of scare quotes) *haemorrhaging* cash," she said. "I need you to spend the rest of this week dotting every single i and crossing every single t on your projects. Next week I'm getting the auditors in to run those projects through a fine-tooth comb."

It was late in the afternoon, as she was preparing to leave, that Ferrie came into her office—"to apologise," he said, "for his unprofessional conduct."

Your 'unprofessional conduct?' You're a pathetic pile of shit, Ferrie.

"I owe you an apology, too, Rob," she said, without making eye contact. "I got carried away, I'm sorry."

"Let's meet tomorrow, again," said Ferrie, turning to leave. "And see if we can find agreement on the way forward."

"I took the liberty of calling in the auditors," she said. "They're going to check for any irregularities, before we close down any of my projects."

"It's not about irregularities, Rosa, it's about feasibility."

"Yes, I understand that. But I need to be sure, for the record."

"OK," said Ferrie, barely audibly. "We can talk again tomorrow."

Chapter Twenty

"Congratulations, Mom," said Cochrane, eyes beaming. "Little fella's four months old today."

"Yep," said Rosa, excitement in her voice. "If my Google sources are correct, we should adjust backwards by one or two months for pre-term, right?"

"Right. And I'm pleased to say he's progressing pretty well."

"But not out of the woods, yet, right?"

"Right."

As if anticipating her next question, Cochrane said that it would soon be winter, and that no matter how much progress Nicky-Ross makes, the earliest he'd be able to travel would be September or October. "We can't risk exposing him to the elements before spring sets in."

At the sight of Cochrane, the word *resplendent* came to her mind—it's that sexy, body-hugging sweater, she thought. Blue cashmere, nothing between it and his hairy chest.

After Easter, autumn changed abruptly to winter. The winds in Cape Town grew stronger and colder; now the sun rose later and set earlier. Most nights were moonless and starless. The racket made by the wind in the pines was incessant and scary; Rosa kept her bedside lamp on overnight, terrified of what utter darkness could look like. She hated the unexpected sounds which would disturb her sleep—was that the sound of a makeshift home being ripped apart? Or a car being dismantled by the wind? Maybe a gravestone clattering along the street, end over end over end? One evening in merciless wind and rain there was the unmistakable sound of a vehicle crashing into something. Tubs and Bill were both awakened, and went to go check. Rosa got up, put on a thick gown and went to make coffee. While they were gone, she phoned the hospital to ask about Nicky Ross. He was fine, *but what weather we're having*, said the nurse. Tubs and Bill returned, soaked; a car had crashed into a tree on Forest Drive, fortunately the driver was OK; despite the horribly twisted fender, he could drive off, much relieved and plenty thankful for their concern. Tubs hot-showered, and Rosa phoned the hospital again. "He's a bit restless, suddenly," said the nurse. "Vomited, but we're busy stabilizing him now." When Tubs got out of the shower, Rosa was dressed—thick jersey; jeans; windbreaker. "We have to go to the hospital, Tubs. Little guy's not OK." But when they got there, he was OK, asleep, his breathing an even purr.

You worry too much, said Tubs, and she was angry at him for a full week.

She always timed her morning visits to the hospital so that they coincided with Cochrane's rounds. He was always pleased to see her, and always updated her in his textbook fashion on how Nicky Ross was doing. Picking up the little guy and cuddling him flesh-to-flesh had become an obsession with her. His body was always so soft and warm! And it was unmistakable, yes, he had begun to recognise her! You could see it in his eyes! In the way his fingers plucked at her cheeks! In the way he folded himself into her embrace. The nursing staff loved her. They were intrigued by her dedication to this little *umntwana*, and amused at her poor isiXhosa—he and I will learn it together, she joked with them.

His hair had started to thicken, but not redden; his poo was usually hay-coloured, and when it was darker she would discuss this with Dr Cochrane, anxious for assurance that there was nothing to worry about. "His lungs," said Cochrane, "they're not the only priority, but they're the main priority." How long will he still have to stay in NICU, Rosa wished to know.

"As long as it takes," said Cochrane, and smiled. "The sixty four million dollar question. With the progress he's making, I'd say three or four more weeks, but don't hold me to it."

"And then to the general ward?"

"That's right. Best case scenario is he stays there for no longer than a week, and will then be ready to transfer to his foster home."

And so, a month later . . .

. . . Just a few short minutes on the Upper Freeway, and they were on the narrow winding road which would take them to *Serenity*. She had done her homework; as soon as Cochrane had mentioned the name, she was into Google to check it out.

Serenity Children's Haven. Let me guess – Christian, how can it not be?

Set in the lush forests of the Constantiaberg foothills; protected from the raging Cape south-easter by ancient pine and eucalyptus trees in all their stately elegance and splendour, Serenity aims to be a taste of Heaven-on-Earth for our youthful guests, our temporary sojourners—so that they may take away, embedded deep within their souls, a replica of God's Eden.

Wow.

The car in which they were travelling seemed to relish this upward-twisting road, like a tiger freed into the wild. It sped through the bends, hardly registering the potholes or the roots of giant oaks in the tarred road.

Tubs in the driver's seat beamed. He flashed around once, twice, to see if his passengers were enjoying the ride as much as he was. His impulse was to test the limits of this machine, but even as the thought occurred to him, the calm, admonishing voice of Rosa from the backseat, "No, Tubs, not so fast—the baby's in the car" demanded restraint.

Securely strapped into his car seat alongside Rosa, Nicky-Ross blinked as shade-and-light rushed over him through the car window, making of his scalp a kaleidoscope of red and grey. Rosa wished to stroke his head, to feel the short soft bristles of his emerging hair against her palm. When his eyes caught hers, they paused, brightened—he smiled, cooed and waved his arms and legs. She gently laughed, and his attention was caught again by the passing images outside the window.

According to the *Serenity* website, the establishment was owned and managed by a retired couple, Earle and Liza Brentwood—former missionaries who, through their work in children's hospitals in various parts of Africa had spent their entire adult lives caring for the "weakest and most vulnerable in society."

From their pictures, both were probably in their sixties; he: specs, balding, cauliflower ears, lines on his forehead resembling Sanskrit, Charlie Chaplin moustache. She—curly brown hair, thickish eyelids, double-chin, and a smile to end a war.

The converging rockface of Constantiaberg loomed above the treetops, and Angie, alongside Tubs in the front, admired it over her specs. She said, "I need to relocate to here. This place is awesome." Her computer was open on her lap. She tried to concentrate on the document she was editing, but the views kept distracting her.

Rosa had eyes only for Nicky-Ross; she sighed repeatedly, and hoped Tubs did not notice through his rear view mirror. She had no doubt she was living through another great turning-point in her life. She was impatient for the arrangements with *Serenity* to be over and done-with, so that the next phase of the rest of her life could commence. By her calculations, the place couldn't be more than a few more minutes away.

The car smoothly glided through a tunnel made by overhead trellises of leaves and branches. Whoosh. On either side of the road, steep gravel banks overgrown with wild grasses, which sway in crevices among jagged rocks, supported the gladeless forests. At intervals, pathways lead off to secluded estates invisible behind high security walls.

They arrived. At the gate, two smiling guards in uniform greeted them, had Tubs sign a book. While they wait, Rosa noticed the high walls and the electric fencing, and was both pleased and saddened. The gates opened, and they entered on a sprawling wooded estate. A short drive along a tree-lined asphalt pathway brought them to the manor-house; it was a double-storey building with walls of shimmering white. It was rectangular, with identical facades sweeping away to left and right of the entrance portal over which rose an ornate gable.

"Just like its picture," said Rosa, suddenly elated.

An ode to beauty, she thought, fit for my prince of hearts. Her blood raced; she so wished Nikki was present.

They emerged from the temperature-controlled capsule that was their car into pine-scented sunlight and a brisk mountain breeze. There were sharp bird sounds in the air—crows, doves, sparrows, but no bokmakierie—no pirriwit-pirriwit, no bok-bok-bok. Rosa held Nicky-Ross against her breast, and said into his ear, soon-soon we will visit Fish Hoek. (And her imagination conjured a brief picture of Nikki's cavorting in the sea.)

The house was foregrounded by moist vivid lawn; it was backgrounded by forest, mountain and sky. It stood in the shade of a giant oak. Under a bent, protruding bough was parked Cochrane's two-door luxury sedan.

She was pleased to see that Cochrane had already arrived. She had no doubt he would, as always, look the part of the suave fashion-conscious medic, and impress one-and-all with his trademark textbook-eloquence.

Their footsteps produced a melodious crunching on the gravel clearing as they slowly converged on the house.

Her eyes flashed a glance at Angie van der Poel. The lawyer's hair bobbed in the wind; it glistened from a recent shampooing. Her specs had darkened in the sunlight; she wore a blue tartan jacket with lapels, and a tight-fitting blue jeans. She carried her laptop against her left hip. Her cellphone was visible in her top pocket. Ah, great, said Rosa to herself. The modern, savvy legal advisor.

No need not check on Tubs's appearance—that had already been done at home this morning.

Your African shirt, Tubs—the one you bought in Malawi, the one which shows off your muscles!

The loose-fitting ethnic shirt, Tubs, the one that's more art than fashion. It would highlight the beautiful sculpted sinews of your neck, and leave your forearms free—to display your Rolex. How yummy you will look. Nikki would definitely approve.

And me? How do I want to appear to these people? *I will choose understated elegance.* The first impression of the proxy-mother of their foster child has to be: *sophistication.*

Everything she saw when she looked in the mirror this morning pleased her. Her diamond earrings flashed with the vibrancy of two mischievous kids; they contrasted perfectly with her staid Kruger-gold pendant. The dress she'd chosen was of a light silken fabric—matte blue—neither too flaunty nor too introverted, not African ethnic but close enough to suggest the possibility of royal lineage, of old money.

What could possibly go wrong?

Cochrane appeared in the doorway to greet them. He wore a cream-white shirt; it was thin, and in places seemed insubstantial, like an encircling mist—as he moved, it now displayed his nipples, then concealed them. His teeth gleamed. He was delighted that Nicky-Ross recognised him. He took the baby from Rosa's arms. He joked with him. Nicky-Ross laughed, revealing the slightest hint of a dimple on his left cheek—a feature of the bio father's face?

There was hand-shaking, embracing, chatter.

A squirrel in the oak tree scampered and dislodged an acorn, which clatters onto Cochrane's car.

They laughed.

Cochrane led them into a brightly-lit foyer. There was a touch of disinfectant in the air. It reminded Rosa of the hospital from which they had just come. She noticed that the walls were not decked with dusty fading portraits of ancestors, as one might have expected, but with enormous colour prints of storybook and comic characters— Paddington Bear, Mickey Mouse, Mr Toad of Toad Hall. It figured, this was a home for children. But the crucifix? Directly opposite the entranceway hung a brass statue of Christ on the cross. Rosa approved the look of it—Christ appeared as victor rather than victim, with arms outstretched and chest inflated, this Christ appeared to be rising from the cross, exultant in victory, an athlete winning the World Cup.

They followed Cochrane past an alcove with a coffee table and a set of chairs arranged around a fireplace. He opened a door marked OFFICE, and they came into the presence of Earle and Liza Brentwood.

In the flesh, Earle Brentwood looked a younger version of his website picture, perhaps because he'd shaven off his moustache. His cheeks were a light ochre, and dry as a pile of dead oak leaves. But his smile was warm and welcoming.

Liza was stylish in her jeans with a narrow black leather belt through the loops. Across the front of her T-shirt was a picture of the Beatles crossing Abbey Road. She extended her arms towards Nicky-Ross, and addressed him in sparkling tones, *who's a pretty babba, then?*

For several minutes, the child was the total focus of their attention. Liza had taken him from Rosa into her cradling arms. Earle had come to stand huddled alongside her. They chatted effusively to Nicky-Ross.

The baby's face had lit up; he chuckled as he moved his eyes from her to him, him to her. He reached out a hand to touch Liza's face. She let his fingertips find her lips; she was delighted by his delight.

It was all captured by Tubs on his cellphone camera.

Rosa exchanged smiles with Tubs, with Cochrane, with Angie. Her eyes did a quick scan of the surroundings. The office was a single room that took up the entire west wing of the building, and on its own probably occupied an area larger than Rosa's whole Fish Hoek cottage. Light streamed in through the large unshuttered window panes, and with it, the sound of the breeze inflected by occasional birdsong. *The air in this room feels thin—absent.* Rosa found herself testing for it by inhaling through parted lips. Her blood-flow was suddenly enlivened, her pulse quickened; she felt the glands in her body start to ooze, to erupt, overflow. She sensed the same was happening to Tubs and Angie, she could see it in their eyes and in the small rapid twitches in their body movements.

Three small birds flashed past the window.

What would Bob Marley have said? Don't worry about a thing, 'cause every little thing gonna be alright? Rosa felt a fleeting tension in her throat.

I must not fool myself, I must be alert. God is a god of ironies.

Manette could be no more than eighteen. She had pouty red lips and what Rosa thought were intelligent eyes. She wore a plain blue nurse's uniform and flat shoes. She had arrived without having been summoned; she was introduced by Liza as "one of our charming young carers." Rosa could not stop herself from greeting Manette with an embrace. She detected a fine fragrance on the young carer's person. She approved, and *just knew* "we're going to get on famously."

"Manette will take care of the little one while we sort out the paperwork," said Liza. A look of glee came to the baby's face when

Manette took him and chatted to him in a musical voice. He cooed and gurgled, and bustled around in her arms.

They left the room.

In a corner of the room was a teak boardroom table with matching chairs. Its surface gleamed in the morning sun. Liza invited all to sit down, and Earle chose the chair at the head of the table. Coffee was brought in. Rosa said to herself she would not be surprised if prayers were proposed.

Angie unfolded her laptop-computer, and immediately multi-coloured images whirled onto the screen. She provided each person with a thin pile of papers, and said, "Most of what's in these documents are standard stuff." She adjusted her spectacles, and referred the group to a document which she said was Victor Addo's signed request addressed to to-whom-it-may-concern to regard the Lethlabes as Nicky-Ross's adoptive parents while the child was in foster-care in South Africa, since he, as the legal guardian, is resident in Australia.

What Rosa took for mild remonstration appears in the eyes of Earle, but she noticed with relief how his eyes softened, how avidly he nodded along as Dr Cochrane clarified the importance of retaining unbroken this chain of devotion which had accompanied the little guy throughout the tempestuous weeks of his young life, so far. Clearly, the Brentwoods trusted Dr Cochrane, and both he and she declared their delight to permit the Lethlabes any liberties that they might choose. However, Angie pressed gently for the signing of the papers.

In her mind's eye, Rosa saw Nikki in bikini on Fish Hoek beach pumping her fists into the sky, yes, yes, yes!

Chapter Twenty-One

"In all my years of doing this," said Kubheka, "I've never had a case like yours." He looked directly into Rosa's eyes, with what seemed to her to be a mix of admiration and disbelief.

An itchiness flared up all over her scalp. She tried to smile, to find an adequate response, to say something that would make sense of her plan—to him and to her.

As if detecting her uneasiness, he chuckled. "Mostly, it's been fugitives on their own, sometimes with wife and kids, but mostly single individual guys—usually with desperate, bulging eyes." He laughed out loud, and she expected him to relate an anecdote from his no doubt vast experience, but he continued, "I see you've come in that same big fancy car of yours."

"It's the only one I've got," she said, and would have added that to borrow or hire a more modest one would have attracted the wrong kind of attention.

"Well, you've come under cover of night," he said. "And don't worry about your car. It's safe out there in the street. You're visiting me, so nobody will touch it."

They were seated in Kubheka's lounge, a cramped, musty-smelling room dimly-lit by a single corner-lamp. The ceiling was low and stained in places, with the section above Rosa's head sagging mildly. Rosa had no doubt that when she left she'd be carrying out the odour from the couch on which she was sitting; it would be trapped in her clothing and carried into her car, and possibly into her house, where Tubs might detect it—where Plato certainly would. (Should she take Plato along to Botswana? No, a compounding of the madness.)

"The passports and the name changes were the easy part," said Kubheka, lowering his voice to the same loudness of the TV set; he had raised the volume as a precaution—"in case the place is being bugged,"

"We're still weighing the options," he said. "One option is for you to be driven from Cape Town to Botswana, but it's a fifteen-to-twenty-hour trip, and would have to be done in one shot, with no overnight stop."

"Agreed," said Rosa. "We'd have to get out of the country before we're missed. And anyway, a road trip would be very arduous for the little one."

"And you'd want to avoid people seeing you, since you'd be something of a peculiarity—white baby, white father, black mother. People would remember seeing that."

"White father?"

"That's part of the first option. You're a mixed-race family travelling back home to Botswana."

Now would be a good time to pull the plug on this crazy scheme, thought Rosa. No matter how much success Kubheka had had over the years sneaking people out of South Africa, how could her attempt at fleeing with the baby possibly work? The likelihood of getting caught was super enormous.

"Option two," said Kubheka, "would be to fly out. You could still be a mixed-race family, but we've got a young white woman who could accompany you on the flight—she'd pose as the mother, and you as a friend or colleague who happened to be on the same flight as she. We'd make it a direct flight at night to Gaberone City in Botswana, and you'd be there in just a couple of hours. But, of course, that has a downside, too. Just think of all those surveillance cameras, and being in close-quarters with so many people in a public airport."

What about a private, chartered flight? was a thought that flashed through her mind, but she remained silent, Kubheka would have thought of that.

"Option three," said Kubheka, "would be to charter a flight."

Rosa smiled.

"A small, private aircraft," said Kubheka. "Take off in the morning, land at a small airport outside Gaborone City in the early afternoon hours, get picked up by our Botswana contact, then be driven to a safe house in a village in the Kalahari Desert." He smiled. "What could be simpler?"

The woman—was she Kubheka's wife?—came into the room with a tray on which were a half-full bottle of cola, two tall glasses, and a paper plate with the same starchy biscuits as she had served last time.

Although there were fatty finger-prints all over the glasses, Rosa had no qualms about sipping from her one directly. She chose a biscuit and listened for the crunch when she bit into it.

"As a precaution," said Kubheka, "we would still have to have a white man or woman accompany you. We don't expect any problems when you land in Botswana, but you never know."

CHAPTER TWENTY-TWO

"Well, I guess if Dr Cochrane says it's OK, then it's OK."

"But we'll have to get agreement from the uncle in Australia as well."

From their office inside the manor house, the Brentwoods had a clear view of the front lawn where Rosa and the uniformed nurse, Manette, were playing with Nicky Ross.

"He's a lively little one," said Earle. "Look at him flounce around out there. He's really taken to her."

"So have I," said Liza. "Such a high quality person. So sophisticated."

"Yep. Have you seen the car she drives? And her jewellery! Look how her earrings sparkle in the sunlight."

"It'll be afternoon in Perth, now. Let me see if I can get the uncle on his WhatsApp number."

She tapped out Victor's number, and set the phone to speaker, so that Earle could also hear the strident ringtone, like a bugle-call, demanding Victor responds.

"Hullo?"

"Mr Addo? Good afternoon to you, sir. I assume it's afternoon there in Perth. I hope I'm not disturbing you. It's mid-morning here in Cape Town. This is Liza Brentwood, phoning from Cape Town—from the *Serenity Children's Haven*, you know, where you nephew—"

Yes, he knew. How was Nicky-Ross? It was good to hear the little fella was fine and getting on splendidly.

When Liza told him the phone was on speaker, Earle shouted out a hello, and Victor responded with a *trust you're well, mate, and thanks again for all you're doing for the little one.*

She didn't want to waste his time, Liza said, but she needed to just check something with him. Would he have any objection to the wonderful lady, Mrs Rosa Lethlabe taking the little one home to her house in Pinelands from time to time? It's not an unusual request, Liza hastily added. Every now and then we get this kind of request, she said, from would-be adoptive parents, mainly so that the adoptee could begin to acclimatise. Of course, this was a slightly different case, but she knew, she said, how much he trusted Mr and Mrs Lethlabe, and besides, Dr Cochrane had had no hesitation in agreeing—for short spells, he had said, like, maybe just for a few hours at a time during the daytime, perhaps on a Saturday or Sunday.

"And we—myself and Earle are quite comfortable with the idea, Mr Addo, particularly since the little one adores her."

Victor was effusive in his praise of Rosa and Tubs. Of course he would agree to it. His tone was like an approving thump on wood.

"That's great, Mr Addo. I'll email a form to you to sign, to formally grant your permission. As soon as I get it back, I'll let Mrs Lethlabe know the good news. I'm sure she'll be delighted.

Rosa's restrained delight on hearing the news was for both Brentwoods a sign of her special breeding. For Earle, the young woman's handsome smile—how her eyes, teeth, cheeks and jewellery all seemed to light up and sparkle in unison, how her hands came together in such a delicate, elegant clasp, how her head tilted to the left, and how her thank-you was enunciated in The King's English—were all a sure sign she was royalty, maybe a Xhosa princess. It would not be inappropriate, he thought, to genuflect before her. It was such a thrill to be able to please her.

Liza, likewise, had only admiration for this daughter of a previously oppressed race. Dr Cochrane and Victor Addo—their unhesitating endorsement said it all; this Rosa Lethlabe was in a decidedly different class.

Before leaving, Rosa went to the nursery to say goodbye to Nicky-Ross. He was in his cot, propped up against a large pillow, and was reaching up with chubby fingers to the fluffy toys dangling from his cot mobile. When he caught sight of her, he cooed and waggled his arms and legs. She lifted him to her breast, relishing the feel of his warm breath and moist lips against her neck. Her oath to him was to serve him unflinchingly. It would not be in the nature of a sacrifice but as a gift, in the same way that he to her was a gift—it would be a mutual pledging of lives, sanctified by the death of his birth mother, Nikki.

No way was he going to Australia.

She drove out of *Serenity* to the raucous accompaniment of birdsong in the pine trees. At the exit gateway, she and the guard on duty exchanged smiles—"see you later," they both said and chuckled.

"Yep, Nikki," she said out loud in the car. *"Die koeël is deur die kerk!*—the bullet's through the church, once again!" and sped off in the direction of the Kirstenbosch Botanical Gardens a few kilometres away. "Coffee, that's what I need." She was breathless, and wished her heart were calmer and her throat less dry. Things were going her way today. She should be more cheerful, but the brazen audacity of her scheme threatened to make her heart stop. *Mind over matter, mind over matter, mind over*—how else do I get through this? Her mother, Zoliswa, had crossed into exile by simply walking across the Botswana border, it was that easy in those days, but no doubt even the hardened, arrogant revolutionary would have felt a sense of trepidation, but she had made it, she had made it all the way through to London—and back—and undetected. I'll make it, too.

At Kirstenbosch Gardens there were plenty of free parking bays. Rosa chose one in the shade of trees. No tourist bus had yet arrived, which meant the coffee shop would not be crowded. Yes, I'm in luck, she declared to herself, as she strolled into the coffee shop. I get to choose *that* table in the corner there with a view of the mountain.

She had brought her portable computer to the table with her. While it was going through its start-up routine, she composed a thank-you message to Victor—*really kind of you!* Her impulse was to add *God bless*—where do I come on this religious stuff? She checked her cellphone for urgent messages. Within a few minutes she was immersed in work. Each time the waiter came to her table, she looked up at him and smiled and said, "Yes, more of the same, please—and don't forget, with hot milk." There were several cellphone and email messages from Leigh. These she attended to first, copying in Ferrie wherever it seemed appropriate. Next she addressed Ferrie's enquiries, and then those of her various project managers, letting them know she'd be in after two, and that she'd then be able to see some of them directly. She wished she could calm her racing heart. You control the mind, you control the world. She smiled to herself. So this is what my daring reduces me to, meaningless incantations, begging The Gods for help! Psyching myself—what a pitiful worm I've become. She stifled a laugh.

By the time she was able to message Tubs on the phone, a packed tour bus had arrived, and a long noisy queue had formed in the coffee shop.

Great news, Tubs. We'll be able to bring Nicky-Ross home for a couple of hours on Saturday—he'll be able to meet his brother, Plato. I'm in the coffee shop at Kirstenbosch Gardens. The views are stunning. I think I'll take a short walk before going to the office. I'm stopping at *Serenity* again on the way home this evening. Should see you at about seven/seven thirty. Yours in love & lust.

She included a graphic of a beating heart.

Outside, the sky was vast and blue. People in small groups were on the lawns and pathways. There's an other-worldly atmosphere about this place, thought Rosa, as she noted how so many people were engrossed in taking photos. The sun was soothing on her neck and shoulders. It kept her shadow in front of her as she strolled in the broad direction of the mountains. She followed a cracked stone path past a field of fynbos sweeping away to her left. The flowers were in bloom; the field was a tangle of yellow and white; it was dense and majestic, sloping away across higher ground towards a distant forest. Rosa paused to photograph the scene, hoping to capture some of its extravagant lushness, but knowing she'd fail—no camera could do this justice. If that dumb magistrate had ever experienced Kirstenbosch on a spring morning such as this she'd know her narrow-minded decision to force-relocate Nicky-Ross to Perth would forever deprive him of this, his birth right. She continued along the path which by casual degrees changed from stone to gravel; it led into a thinly-wooded forest, meandering past a small clump of wild strylitzias and a thin muddy stream. There was a carved bench in the shade, facing the mountains. Rosa settled onto its hard slats, and WhatsApped the photo of the fynbos field to Tubs, with the caption, *How about this for beauty?* Tubs sent back a picture of applauding hands.

Rosa smiled.

From where she sat she could see every fine detail of every gorge and crevice on the mountain peaks which vividly bulged against the clear blue sky. They're making some kind of statement, she thought, maybe to do with their permanence, their immortality versus our—my—fragility.

Ag, nonsense!

She made a conscious effort to relax her body and mind—all too soon I will have to up and leave this magnificent Garden of Eden. She felt herself drifting into sleep, and welcomed the feeling.

So, does the end justify the means? Is the end a worthy end? How heinous are the means? Would Nikki approve? In my situation, what would Zoliswa have done? Kubheka's indifference didn't help. I wonder if he's tied up in drug smuggling or gun running or something—why does the notion of kidnapping not shock him? If this whole thing backfires, he and his entire network will surely go down with me.

Have you thought about your father, Rosa? A timid question in a timid voice. Just as after death Jesus was recognised by the holes in his hands, so after Nikki's death it was possible to know the speaker was she by the rush of red hair surrounding the face Rosa's mind conjured. Of course I've thought of my father, Nikki. He has a pension, he's on medical aid, he lives in a fully-furnished-fully-serviced-flat at the house in Pinelands. He has Tubs, he has the Township comrades. He should be worried about me, not me about him.

Rosa sighed and opened her eyes. The bench was hard, and the cellphone, although on silent mode, was a disturbance as it continually vibrated in her hand. Impossible to relax completely. She looked at the mountain, and got the distinct impression it looked back at her—with an accusatory gaze: No matter your motives, its gaze seemed to say, you're a common criminal.

A brightly-coloured bird flew past her, and settled on a slender branch nearby. Rosa's mind went back to the bokmakierie up at Fish Hoek when she and Nikki for the first time … ah. And now there's no more Nikki … but, OK, now there's Nicky-Ross.

On her way back to the car, Rosa asked herself—not for the first time—how the ill-considered judgement of a small-time magistrate could so irrevocably change the trajectory of 'the whole of the rest of my life!' Had she decided in my favour how fundamentally different my future would be! In a democracy, even a shitty one like ours, magistrates have more power than the mountains.

The parking area was crowded with cars and buses, people—tourists, mainly, milling everywhere. Rosa found her car, and set off for the office. On her way she kept repeating to herself that Nicky-Ross would not be parted from her. If all her elaborate plans added up to Sin-capital-S, well then, so be it. Yet, unexpectedly, at odd times the enormity—the madness—of what she was planning struck her with disconcerting force. At such times she would try to conjure the image of Nikki, would try to feel her there as a living, approving presence. *Nikki on my right shoulder, Zoliswa on my left.*

She had used it once before, and it had worked well, perfectly mimicking her own natural fluid—Tubs had been none-the-wiser. Now, standing naked in her bathroom, she carefully applied the odourless gel, trusting it would do its work again. Fooling Tubs was the least of her worries, but was nevertheless important … poor devil was in for the mightiest of shocks soon-soon. So, despite her frayed nerves, which kept her on the brink of distraction, Rosa felt obliged to indulge his every need, large or small—his freshest memories must be strong and positive, enough to carry him through the hard times ahead.

Tonight a special fragrance named *Hanoi* would be her perfume of choice over the lavender, jasmine and cinnamon. *Make him go mad!* She took the slender bottle in the palm of her hand, and tried to visualise the giggling Nikki in her office all those months ago when they'd unwrapped it. *Produced in the jungles of Vietnam*, Nikki had said, *and brought home by a US vet.* Rosa smiled silently, noting how her image in the bathroom mirror exaggerated the whiteness of her teeth. She closed her fingers around the delicate bottle, and drew her clasped hand to her cheek; for no reason she could fathom, this gesture aroused a sense of sadness in her. *Must remember to use this stuff sparingly*, she said to herself. She unscrewed the cap, and lightly touched the Hanoi to key parts of her body. *This stuff makes me feel like a beast on heat.* The flimsy, gossamer robe which she slipped over her head and arms slid down over her body like a gentle caress. Right, she was ready.

As always, she was the one who controlled—who orchestrated the moves; tonight she needed to extend the amount of foreplay to ensure the fake wetness aroused no puzzlement in Tubs. By the time his fingers found the G-spot, the gel had begun to ooze onto her inner thighs. She was patient and compliant, and could tell that her man was in another zone of ecstasy. "As always," she thought, "we score an A."

When Tubs eventually fell back onto his side of the bed, and she lay with her cheek against his neck, she reflected on how easily she had fooled him. It brought her no joy, just relief—and maybe some calm. When I leave, she thought, something's going to die in him. Tears welled up in her eyes. She stretched for the tissue box on the pedestal at her bedside, trying not to disturb him. His sleep was total. She dabbed at her eyes, and wondered how he would respond when reality struck. It would be the suddenness of her departure, she thought, that would create an initial sense of unreality. And that would quickly be followed by inconsolability. Or am I fooling myself? My dad would be the strong one, the one to console him and Plato. *Hope*—that has to be my trump card with Tubs. Offer him hope. A carefully worded letter for him to find when I'm safely away, offering him the prospect of joining me in my exile. Would it work?

Are you insane? It was less a question than a reprimand, conveying by its tone contempt and affection in equal measure. Her eyelids fluttered rapidly as she spoke. *So, do I get it? You're going to kidnap this sickly white orphan baby and literally disappear with him off the face of the earth?* It was Zoliswa, imperious as ever, with glowering eyes and balled fists.

Rosa thought for a moment, then responded with *What's white got to do with it?*

A muscle in her cheek twitched—or maybe it was a muscle in Tubs's neck against which her cheek continued to nestle. Rosa realised she'd been dreaming, that Zoliswa had appeared to her in a dream, and had had the impertinence—even in death—*to intrude into my life*! As she lay there, Rosa speculated on what turn such a conversation might have taken in real life. Not unlikely that Zoliswa might have played the colonial card—the kid's a descendant of colonial settlers. They stole our land!

Rosa separated her body from Tubs's. Even in death, she presumes that her opinions matter. What arrogance. Rosa smiled and tried to fix her mother's face in her mind, but the image refused to stabilize. She'd be an old crow now, had she lived. I'd scold her right back.

It's going to be one of those kinds of nights, thought Rosa, when I struggle to sleep or to think straight; when my temples won't stop throbbing, when I enter rational debates with spooks. But my plans are taking shape, I should be overjoyed, instead I'm overwrought. She made an effort to visualise the sea at Fish Hoek, to see in her mind's eye the vivid mountains of Kirstenbosch, to feel in her heart the tenderness of Nikki's flesh. She could visualise Nicky-Ross in the bright sunlight at *Serenity*, but not clearly. As she lay in the gloom alongside Tubs's gently snoring body, she struggled to keep her own body from jerking, twitching, tossing and turning. At times her mind was uncontrollable; random images of Zoliswa, Bill, Leigh, Nikki would swirl about. Eventually, the persistent throbbing in her temples turned to a pounding in the whole of her head, and she forced herself up, and felt around in the dark for her gown. She tip-toed out of the room, silently closed the door behind her, and dragged herself downstairs to the kitchen.

Because of her disdain for medication, she was not going to take any pills to soothe her headache away. Instead, she poured herself a glass of milk, and sat down at the kitchen table to wait for the throbbing to pass. I need to get over these emotional episodes, she told herself in an upbraiding inner voice. I need to apply my mind to the practical things, large and small. The bullet's through the church. All that matters now is a flawless plan—A chartered flight, a no-brainer.

Plato appeared in the doorway, and Rosa felt her spirits rise. "Plato!" she exclaimed. "Do come in! How about some good fresh milk, then?" She found a porcelain bowl which she half-filled with milk and placed on the table close to her glass. Fastening her fingers around the cat's body, she hoisted him onto the table, where he crouched down in front of the milk and eagerly lapped at it.

I'm going to miss you, Plato—maybe more than I'm going to miss Tubs and Dad. There's just no way I can take you along. But don't worry, Tubs will still be there for you.

There was a faint tapping at the back door which startled her, but then she heard her father's voice.

"Rosa? It's me, here. Is everything OK?"

She opened the door.

"What are you still doing up, Dad? It's way past midnight."

"I saw your kitchen light go on, and I wondered ..."

"Well, come inside. I'm just having some milk—me and Plato."

"Get that cat off the table."

Bill was dressed in a T-shirt and a light cotton shorts. Rosa noticed his arms and legs were lean and hard. Yep, he's healthy, she thought. Doesn't look like someone who'll be needing frail care any time soon.

And then Tubs appeared in the doorway. "Is everything OK?" He saw that their smiles were relaxed and welcoming. He found a glass and poured himself some milk, and joined them at the table.

"Happy families," said Bill. "What did Tolstoy say? 'They're all alike, but unhappy families are unhappy in their own way?'" He laughed briefly.

"So, what are we Dad?" said Rosa. "Are we a happy family?"

Bill was silent for a moment. He leaned forward with elbows on the table, and arms folded. His eyes were on the glass of milk in front of him. "Maybe," he said in a reflective tone. "But that could change soon."

He became silent again.

"You mean because we'll be losing Nicky-Ross, Dad?" said Tubs. "We'll not actually be losing him, it's just going to be a hard separation, but we'll be able to maintain contact, and perhaps even visit him from time to time." His eyes turned to Rosa, to check for her reaction. "It's like with us, Dad," he continued. "We all have family in different parts of the country, whom we hardly get to see. I think of my parents, who are living in faraway Mdantsane."

"No, Tubs, it's not the same," said Rosa, feeling the pounding starting up in her temples, again. "Nicky-Ross is being forcibly snatched away from his mother. I am his mother. Legal means have been used to kidnap my baby."

There was suddenly a sense of gloom in the kitchen. Everyone became silent, and kept their eyes stiffly on their milk in front of them. Rosa had taken Plato into her lap, and was stroking the back of his head and neck. The faint roar of a passing car on Forest Drive broke the silence.

"But you're right, Tubs," said Rosa, trying to keep her tone light. "The future's not cast in concrete. There's no such thing as living happily—or unhappily—ever after. We have to constantly be making our own happiness, or unmaking our own unhappiness."

Bill finished his milk, and returned to his flat.

Rosa and Tubs were soon back in their bed, and Tubs was soon fast asleep. Rosa lay unsleeping against his back. When she became aware of the first tinges of dawn against the bedroom curtains she promptly rose and went and showered.

He'll be here on Saturday!

A cot and bedding. Diapers—disposable. What toys? Medication—prescribed and for general disorders: upset tummy, nappy rash, pain, sore throat, cuts, bruises, depression, other, other, other. Food. Drink. Books. A pram. Clothes—underwear, overwear. A baby bath, a mat, bibs, bottles, thermometer. Brush, comb. Special detergent. Wardrobe, chest-of-drawers. And a bather! And sunscreen! And a sunhat!

Oh, and a high chair, one that folds. And crockery and cutlery. A scissors for clipping finger nails and toenails?—yes, no, maybe.

Her jeans gave her bum an impeccability found only in colour brochures; it was soundless when she bent her knees to sit or when she squatted down on her haunches to get eye to eye with Plato or, as now, with Nicky-Ross on the nursery floor at *Serenity*— it was a darker blue than the sky but equal in evenness, chosen by her for its casual yet formal look. And the blouse: she had searched long and hard for it; she knew she needed a blouse, and she knew she'd know the one when she saw it, something resembling a surrealistic work of art in blue and white, one-of-a-kind, fit for a goddess.

Today she wore no make-up, so that the Brentwoods could see how her cheeks glowed of their own natural health. This would strengthen their conviction that they were right to grant her liberties beyond what were initially agreed by them and approved by Dr Cochrane. She knew on this first day when she arrived to collect the baby that today it would be three hours, and the next time, maybe four, and so on, until it was an entire weekend. She knew that for them—especially Earle—it just seemed the right thing to do to pander to her wishes, she was so … what would you say? Fabulous?

But they had decided, before she arrived, that the young carer, Manette, would on this first day accompany the baby. "Just as a precaution," Liza Brentwood said in an apologetic tone. "I'm sure everything will be fine, but just in case … Manette is specially trained to deal with anything unexpected. And she won't intrude or get in the way; she'll just be there in case."

Rosa's instinct was to blurt out, "in case *what*?" but today she would humour these Brentwoods. She smiled, and her teeth drew the admiring eyes of both of them. She knew that she stood up well to their scrutiny, that in fact, they really wanted her to. Always hovering within a couple of metres of her, Tubs could be depended on to play his part as the perfect tails side of the coin that was them. He had chosen a tight-fitting T-shirt for the occasion, sparse but stunning. On his face he wore an unwavering smile, and was clearly as excited as his wife to be having the baby for a few hours today.

Back home, she flung the lounge doors open, and let in the rich green smells of the garden.

In her mind she said to Nikki: scrub as you might, but you'll not be able to erase the smile from my face. He's here, he's here, and Plato loves him!!! The look in their eyes when they first beheld each other—I've captured it on video—the equivalence of a big embrace. My father came over, and seemed shy in his presence. All he could say was what a cute little guy. And Manette sits on the tip of the couch, looking awkward and overawed. Tubs offered her something to drink, and she declined in a tiny voice. I must not put a foot wrong in her presence, who knows what she'll report back to those Brentwoods.

My camera's been busy. I've taken shots of Nicky-Ross on his own, with Tubs, with Plato, Manette, my dad, and of course, plenty with me. I've taken some group shots, too—with all of us together, one big happy family. In the lounge, in the garden, near the swimming pool, on the grass, under the trees. And one I've managed to get with a squirrel in the background. Always smiling, all of us, always joyful. He seems so at home here. I've been WhatsApping the pics as I've taken them—to the Brentwoods, to Cochrane, and to his Uncle Vic. I'm sure they'll all see he belongs here—with me.

At one point he broke into tears! But not mournful, more like, *back-off guys, you're fussing me too much*. Manette was up on her feet, but I got to him first, and consoled him in my arms.

"Perhaps he needs a nappy-change," says I, the all-knowing mom. "I'll take him to the room and change him."

Manette sat down, a bit further into the couch's embrace, and accepted Tubs's second offer of something to drink.

Plato followed me and Nicky-Ross to your room, Nikki. There was your colour-picture up on the wall, a big framed blow-up showing your mop of red hair being scattered by the wind, and that smile you share with our son, the one where your eyes narrow and brighten like a fresh new dawn—I so wish you could see his smile, how so like yours!

I laid him on his back, and Plato settled alongside him on the bed to observe the whole show. He smiled at Plato, and I know that Plato smiled back. He smiled at me, too, and gurgled in a way that made me giddy. I spoke to him in a whisper, I said you are mine, precious one, and we are not going to be parted. His face took on a curious expression. I'm sure he understood, Nikki. I'm sure he understood.

Winter was coming to an end!

She knew it, she willed it; the mountain face ahead of her in the dark of early morning, when she drove to work, looked less today like a van Gogh than it did yesterday. Of course there were still blustery rains at odd intervals, vying with warm and sky-blue days; *the old was struggling to die and the new to be born.* The time had come for serious concentration; nothing could be overlooked, mistimed, gotten wrong. Fear and elation mixed in her soul, stretching her temples, bringing sweat to her brow; ripples kept coursing through her body—*soon, soon the limits of my ingenuity will be tested.*

As she expected, the Brentwoods readily agreed that she could have the little guy every weekend; and sure, for the full day, too—let's say, nine to four. And, what about Sundays? Yep, nine to four again. We'd rather he didn't sleep over, though, Liza had said, apologetically, and had added, "But no need for Manette to accompany him, you are such wonderful people."

On warm days, they chose for him his cotton bodysuit, left his head uncovered and his feet bare, and thrilled when he raised his nose to breathe the wind. Tubs took photos of him on Rosa's lap out on the back lawn, with Plato in the foreground and the pool in the background. The little fella appeared curious about the grass, and clearly wished to touch it, but no, said Rosa—germs. If a breeze came up, she asked herself if he needed a woollen cap or to be taken indoors.

My little orchid!

They wished to take him to Fish Hoek, to the cottage, to the beach—to see the sea! But no, thought Rosa, better not to be seen in public too much. Instead, she dreamed in great pictorial cinema-scope of herself and Nikki walking on an imaginary beach, leaving a winding trail in the wet sand, passing the baby back and forth between them. In these dreams, the sky was always red streaked with blue. And always trailing in their wake, a dog called Dingus. Sometimes these dreams went wrong, like when the decomposed body of Chris washed up on the shore, and when Dingus went over to smell it and whimper over it. Damn! At such times Rosa breathed deeply from her navel up, and reminded herself that there was no such thing as purity, even in dreams, just as with sin, evil could only be suppressed, never killed . . . Which means, the best laid plans of mice and men . . . but I will go ahead, and I will win . . . a pyrrhic victory, maybe . . . but I'll take it.

Lumina audits done—tick. No issues found—says so in the report, so there could be no suspicions or maligning of her name after she disappears. Very likely, it would dawn in hindsight on all the usual suspects—Ferrie, Leigh, Swanepoel, Clyde, Yon Issie—that this had been the whole point of her insistence to audit.

All that remained was to ensure the right timing for her notice letter to pop up in Ferrie's email account.

Her financial matters? Pretty much sorted. It surprised her how easy the Internet made it to learn how to move moneys about across the globe from any location to any other location, and how to shift funds between accounts, real and fictitious, without leaving any tracks or trails. Kubheka had offered to put her in touch with a financial expert, but no-thanks, no need! Whatever was within her control was the easy part. Financial matters, sorted: tick.

The notes to Ferrie, Tubs, Dad, Angie, Victor, The Brentwoods, Cochrane . . . all had to surface simultaneously, and when she was beyond reach. A flawless remote virtual electronic activation switch was needed. She would have to create and test one to ensure no possibility of failure. Did she have enough programming savvy? What a pity Nikki wasn't around to do it for her!

But the biggest problem was timing! There'd be only one fractional window, the big-bang would unalterably commence on a Saturday or Sunday morning: at nine or ten o'clock her usual smiling self would collect Nicky-Ross from *Serenity*; the Brentwoods would be their usual fawning selves; her car's boot would be ready-packed—two travel-light bulging bags, one for her stuff, the other for Nicky-Ross's, including his medication. Tubs would, conveniently, have to be away, maybe doing clean-up or maintenance work at the Fish Hoek cottage; weather conditions all the way from Cape Town to Botswana would have to be favourable, at least throughout the morning hours; Kubheka would have a minute's notice to activate his network, every link in the chain would need to work, and flawlessly. What were the chances? Success or death the only options! Would I be in Botswana in time for lunch? That's when I release the email stream!

Her love of coffee had become an addiction; nowadays, there was seldom an empty mug at her side. Anyone sitting close to her could feel the sharp aroma on her breath. She could not think without coffee.

As always, her waking thoughts ran on multiple planes, but nowadays they were driven by an intensity bordering on panic; thanks to the heightened levels of caffeine in her bloodstream she was able to project an outer calm that belied her inner turmoil. Every now and then a slip in her demeanour would create puzzlement in others, like when Tubs detected a rare lassitude in her body at the moment of climax, or when her project team stared at her less in fear than in wonderment at her outbreak of rage for what would normally have been a trivial slide in their performance metrics. And her lapses in concentration when in meetings with Ferrie and Leigh! Rosa berated herself for allowing her mind to wonder at such critical times, thereby drawing the wrong kind of attention to herself. *She was acting strange,* Leigh would say to the investigating officer. *Like her mind was all over the place.* "No wonder," Ferrie would add. "Who would have thought she'd be capable of such diabolical behaviour!"

It occurred to Rosa that she might—perhaps should?—tweak the emerging narrative. Instead of *Black woman steals and flees with white baby,* maybe the headlines should say, *Woman and baby kidnapped!* Wow, kidnapped. There would have to be a ransom note. Her car would have to be found abandoned somewhere—with incriminating fingerprints? There would be a high-profile police investigation . . . sooner or later something would have to surface . . . clues . . . dead bodies? No, wouldn't work.

But even if it would work, Rosa told herself that in principle, she wanted no false narratives: I want the world to know that I chose to fulfill my oath to Nikki, and that I did it the only way I could.

The time for weighing ethics was over; she was not going to allow herself to be overwhelmed by moral implications, by the severity of the judgements and pain of others which would follow when the news broke; only the child's best interests mattered. Joseph and Mary on a donkey to Egypt to escape the wrath of Herod. Me and my fake husband on a plane to Botswana to escape Vic Addo. It would certainly make headline news. Tubs will be inconsolable, at least initially. Her father would feel it as a bullet through his heart, and would blame himself. Cochrane? Angie? The Brentwoods? Maybe sheerest disbelief—maybe a sense of betrayal leavened with empathy? As for the Lumina crowd, probably all, with the possible exception of Yon Issie, would rejoice at the shaming of the arrogant black bitch, good riddance. *How does she possibly expect to get away with it!*

Chapter Twenty-Three

It was not lost on the Brentwoods that their African Princess was arriving at *Serenity* a little earlier each Saturday and Sunday morning, and returning with her baby a little later each time. They had no doubt that before long they'd have to consider a request for the child to be allowed to sleep over in Pinelands.

It was also not lost on them that she absolutely doted on her little Nicky-Ross—something they found mildly disquieting. *She's going to miss him like crazy when the time comes*, had become a refrain in their conversations. *Yep, and he her, they've become so attached. Maybe, too attached.*

"Good to go," said Cochrane. "His flight can be booked."

Chilling words.

She was not going to part with the child.

It was going to be this coming Saturday—in six days' time!

She sat with Kubheka in his lounge, sipping tea and gnawing on the wooden biscuits which his wife had served. The TV volume was turned up, and so Rosa had to speak above a whisper.

"So many things could go wrong," she said, wondering for the umpteenth time if the whole mad scheme shouldn't be called off.

"We're good to go," said Kubheka. "Everything's in place, we just need the word from you."

The lounge was in semi-darkness; it was hard for her to read his eyes, she desperately needed to see confidence there. How certain was he that the plan would actually work?

"We've never failed," he said. "Not once."

"That's what scares me," she said, trying to lighten the remark with a smile.

"It's what scares everyone," said Kubheka. "Often it's the amount of upfront, unguaranteed money which has to be paid, but equally often, the sheer scale of the risk in peoples' minds. When the time comes, they stop believing. "Often, they back out at the last minute, only to expose themselves to greater risk by not going ahead."

"Saturday morning," she said. "There's going to be no going back." She bit fiercely into her biscuit, and it sounded like a gavel being struck.

Chapter Twenty-Four

My dear, dear Nikki!

How are you? Are you well? Are you happy there in Heaven? I know you're not actually in Heaven, because Heaven doesn't actually exist, but you do, albeit in an insubstantial way. I was reading recently of a theory that in other galaxies, time—time's arrow—can move in reverse-gear! I have an equally mad theory: that you are alive in another galaxy, and that you can pick up my thoughts there, and that you will respond to them by guiding my behaviour here on Earth.

So, I'm an atheist with a difference.

Right now, I am walking among the trees at Serenity, with our Nicky-Ross asleep on my shoulder. He weighs no more than a box of breakfast cereal, but fits so perfectly in my arms that I wish this moment would never end. This, Nikki, is Heaven.

We were playing on the grass in front of the manor-house when a squirrel scampered past, startling our little baby, who promptly reached for my arms! Was I too eager to embrace him, to offer him comfort, sanctuary? As his mother, I need to prepare him for the real world where he will encounter monsters bigger than squirrels. You and I, we weren't coddled as kids. I must not coddle this one.

It's a bright day, with a delicious breeze stirring the firs and their shadows. The mountain looms vivid through the trees; there are clouds swarming all around its peaks. Despite the birdsong all around me I can hear Nicky-Ross's breathing, clear, rhythmic, distinctly his. I feel his hair against my cheek, and resist the impulse to nuzzle my nose into it. It's a thick mop, but not yet as red as it will become in time. His body is soft in my arms, he oozes a fragrance that I breathe deeply into my own bloodstream. Nikki, I will die for this child.

But right now the only priority is to live and to execute our flight plans, and flawlessly. Just imagine, in less than a week we start our new life, together and inseparable!

Nikki, are you there? It's the middle of the night, and I'm lying against Tubs's warm back, with my fingers fiddling his navel. I should stop, to avoid re-arousing him—he'll again be all over me with his bulging member! I can't sleep, I'm overwrought. I'm over-thinking things! I worry that I'm overlooking some small detail and that it's going to trip me up! Horrors! I can't get over the worry that I'm too dependent on Kubheka. What do I make of his studied aloofness? Is that the secret of his success? How can he never have failed? So, on Saturday morning it happens. Tubs will be up at the Fish Hoek cottage doing some maintenance repair work; I'll be collecting Nicky-Ross at Serenity, and driving through in my car to the private airport near Stellenbosch. There'll be someone waiting to change the plates on my car. It'll stay at the airport, and only when my pilot signals that I'm safely out of the country, and that I'm ready to release my messages to Tubs and everyone else, will the car be driven to a location which Kubheka has chosen where Tubs will be able to collect it. I worry that I'll forget my luggage in the boot of the car with all Nicky-Ross's stuff, including his medication. And what if I forget our new identity documents at home? The thought of some dumb slip-up drives me insane.

Shit, there I've done it, I've woken the beast. I can feel the hair on his thigh start to bristle, slight but unmistakable. Soon, soon, he will commence the ritual. But you'll be pleased my marriage is intact, and—with your help—will remain so. You need to help me craft the farewell letter to Tubs, one that gives hope, that dispels despair, one that will win him over to the long-term plan. There, he's turned onto his back. His face is close to mine. We smile in the dark. He embraces me. I welcome it. I'm going to miss this.

CHAPTER TWENTY-FIVE

The sky above Pinelands is starless this early evening. The edges of the moon look ragged; the moon looks like it is made of the same substance as the grey streaks of cloud covering the western part of the sky. In the depths of her ears Rosa discerns a gentle roar, which she knows is coming from inside of her—maybe the surge of the blood in her veins. The coal fire which Tubs had started in the mobile grill begins to flare, sending a rich aroma into Rosa's nostrils, throat and lungs. She draws deeply, hoping the smell would lodge in her long-term memory. There is so much her memory needs to store—after all, her exile might end up being forever.

She gazes out over the brightly-lit backyard—at its centre-piece, the swimming pool, where the water sways about like a body on a dance-floor. Her father is sitting on the edge at the shallow end; she watches the water splash around his calves, and can see the shimmying reflection of his feet in it. From where she sits, she can clearly make out the scraggly beard which roams round his chin from ear to ear. He sits there, absorbed in himself. Did he have some kind of premonition? A foreboding? Or is he just preoccupied with his own old man's hopes and dreams?

So—the first night of the rest of my life! Rosa tries to restrain the sudden drumbeat in her temples which the thought evokes. She is sure she has behaved normally all day, nobody would afterwards be able to say, *there was something strange about her that day . . .*

She feels Bill's gaze on her, and wishes she could think of something light to say. They simply exchange a silent smile. Her heart beats harder.

Close to where she sits under the back-stoep canopy Tubs is stoking the fire. He wears nothing but a skimpy bather. His penis is a mound inside it. If she reaches out, she'd be able to touch it, clutch it. She chuckles briefly, and both Tubs and Bill look expectantly at her.

"Sorry, Dad," she says. "Not the kind of joke a nice girl shares with her father."

Bill's elbows are on his knees. It occurs to him that life for him might not get better than this. He reflects that he is happy because she is happy. He worries that as the day for the baby's departure for Perth draws nearer, she will begin to crack up. Tubs should really talk to her about bearing her own kid. How I wish she'd any day now say, *Dad, I'm pregnant.*

She had checked the weather in Botswana for the weekend ahead, and found it would be much the same as Cape Town's, just a few degrees cooler, and with a mild breeze. They would have to dress warmly. Her mind had played with options—a beanie for Nicky-Ross, and his snug brown jacket and thick socks. For herself? Maybe the same lilac pullover she is wearing now.

She would collect the little guy tomorrow morning; she would try to look her best to vindicate the Brentwoods' admiration of her; she would say a special "bye, bye" to Manette and to the guard at the gate. She would savour the baby-smell of Nicky-Ross as she ties him into his car seat, and would wrinkle her face at him if, as he liked to do, he makes a tug at her nose. She would drive off to the private airport, singing "You are my sunshine."

It is going to be a yellowtail braai tonight. Tubs had brought home a specimen the size of a small shark, pre-filletted, smelling of Fish Hoek. Laid out on its sheet of foil it resembles a skinned rabbit. With clear delight in his eyes, Tubs sets about slicing lemons, tomatoes, onions. He is liberal with the salt and pepper. He is two-minded about sprinkling on some crushed garlic—"To be or not to be," he says, smiling at Rosa. "Yes, yes," is her reply. "Don't wrap it till I've taken a photo."

In her haste she trips over Plato, and would have slammed face-first into the seething coal fire but for Tubs's alertness—instinctively, he'd dashed forward and created a shield with his arms for her to fall against.

"Talk about saving face," she says in disbelief. "Can you imagine if you weren't there, Tubs, oh!"

She sinks back into her seat, her pulse racing. "What a close call," she says. "What a close call. But I'm OK, thanks, Tubs, thanks, you saved my life, I need a drink, please refill my glass." Her pulse-rate refuses to slow, and despite her best efforts, she's unable to summon laughter—not even a giggle, about an incident which a few seconds ago would decisively have scuppered all her carefully-made plans.

An omen, it was an omen. Should I call the whole thing off? All it would take is for me to signal Kubheka.

"Damn cat," she says, pretending sternness. "Is that guilt I'm seeing in your eyes? Come here, you bad kitty, come say you're sorry." She stretches out her arms, and the cat deftly springs onto her lap. She strokes the length of his spine, feeling her gentle action soothe her own frazzled nerves.

Tubs is relieved that a disaster had been averted. Just imagine, just imagine, he says to himself. He finishes garnishing the yellowtail for the braai, and wraps it in its foil sheath. "I think this beauty is ready," he says, pleased to note that Rosa appears to have regained her relaxed air. "Twenty minutes on the grill," he says. "And then we dine, hallelujah."

Rosa rises from her seat, and pats over on bare feet to go sit alongside her father at the pool's edge. She puts her arm around his shoulders, and mutters softly that she would so miss him when ultimately the time comes for them to part.

"Huh?" is his response. "Why do you talk of parting?"

"Oh, maybe I'm just feeling sentimental she says. "How on earth did you manage to bring me up all on your own, Dad?"

He hesitates before answering. "I sometimes ask myself the same question, "especially when I see what a fine job I've done." He expects her to chuckle, but, instead, she gently lays her head on his shoulder. "It's difficult to find the right words," she says in a whisper. "You mean so much to me."

He feels her tears on his shoulder, and holds his breath in the hope of restraining his own.

There's a rustling in the flowerbed. Two squirrels appear, sniff the air, then charge back into the thicket.

"If those two are girl and boy," says Rosa, "then soon there'll be three of them—a nice little family."

"It's a sensitive issue, Rosa, I know, but you and Tubs, you're in the prime of your lives. All too soon you'll reach your peak . . ."

"I know what you're saying, Dad . . . that the best time for bearing a child is now."

"Of course, it's your choice. Yours and Tubs's. Soon, Nicky-Ross is gone, Rosa. Now would be the ideal time for you to . . ."

"I know, Dad, I know. My body clock is ticking." She smiles, and says to herself, it's not too late to pull the plug.

They are well into their meal, when Tubs's phone rings. It is Victor, video-calling from his home in Perth. Visible on the small screen are he and his wife. Their images are bright and clear; without trying, Rosa can discern the reddish stubble on Victor's chin, as well as the slender gap in his wife's front teeth. There is an exchange of pleasantries. Tubs scans his phone in slow-motion over the length of the table, and Victor coos at the sight. "Delicious-looking," he says. "Wish I was there."

"Sorry to interrupt your meal, folks," he says. "But I was tied up with emergency work most of the day, and got back home after midnight, here. Just had a shower, and thought I'd call before going to bed. I knew it'd be just early evening there, so I thought we'd call." He looks at his wife. Smiling, he asks her whether she'd like to do the talking, or should he just continue.

"Go ahead," she says. "You're doing fine." She smiles, and as her lips widen, it seems to Rosa that the gap in her teeth widens, too.

Victor puts his arm around her shoulder. "The reason we're calling, he says, is because we went to see our lawyer earlier today, before my work swallowed me up, otherwise I'd have called much sooner. We're calling to say that we went to see our lawyer to discuss adopting Nikki's boy. We explained to him how we've been thinking about the adoption non-stop since the court ruling in our favour. Mandy, here, and I have spent hours discussing the points made by your attorney, and the more we thought about and discussed those points, the more we became convinced that the judge had erred. She should not have awarded in our favour. We went to our lawyer to sign the necessary papers rescinding our right to adopt Nicky-Ross, and declared our wish that you—Tubs and Rosa—be granted parenthood of the baby, Nicky-Ross."

Epilogue

She satisfies herself that Tubs is asleep, then tiptoes down to the lounge. She has her cellphone and laptop with her. Plato settles himself alongside her on the sofa. For a moment she thinks of running her Nikki photo-set on the TV, but realises that she will be needing to use her cellphone.

She is relieved that she is calm. She will need to be, to ensure a flawless roll-back. Firstly, a note to Kubheka:

ABORT, ABORT, ABORT.

He'll probably think, *I'm not surprised.*

Now she is glad she is so methodical. She has no trouble undoing everything that needs undoing. Tomorrow will be the first day of the rest of my life. It has to mesh seamlessly with today, except for the elation of Vic's news.

Before deleting them forever without a trace, she re-reads the missives which would have popped up on the devices of their intended recipients.

My dearest Tubs: First of all, I love you very much. I want our marriage to survive, and I want to bear you a child. I have surrendered to something bigger than myself, something which I hardly understand. What I have done will be treated as a heinous crime, and I will face vilification on an unprecedented scale. Doubtlessly, you will suffer the same, by association. I cannot apologise enough for bringing this on you. DON'T WORRY ABOUT ME. In coming days you will get a sense of how meticulously I've planned this whole thing. Trust me, the future will be as meticulously planned. We will be re-united. We will be able to take up our lives again.

We will find—if not happiness—then fulfilment of our lives. What is happening feels unreal but "was meant to be." Please take care of my Dad and Plato. Once again, I love you dearly, and apologise for doing this to you. I've addressed the practical issues. The house is fully paid. I've paid up the rates and taxes on it for a full year in advance. You'll see I've purchased large amounts of prepaid electricity and water. The fridge and grocery cupboards are stacked. There are no outstanding bills. At the same time I release this note to you, Ferrie and Lumina will be receiving my letter of resignation. I've also prepared notes to Dr Cochrane, Vic, Angie vd Poel and the Brentwoods at Serenity. And to my father. I worry that he has now lost both "his women" abruptly, unexpectedly, painfully. He is an old man. I worry that the effect might be more than he can handle. I need you, Tubs. Please be there for him. And keep the faith. NB: I love you very much. I want our marriage to survive, and I want to bear your child. DON'T WORRY ABOUT ME. Nicky-Ross and I are fine. We will miss you, but hopefully the separation won't be for long. Bye, but only for now.

Dad, I'm not sure how you'll take the news. My disappearance with baby Nicky-Ross will create shockwaves everywhere. You and Tubs will be hardest hit, which is my biggest regret. You will no doubt ponder long and hard on how I could have yielded to such an extreme measure, and might be tempted to compare my commitment to keeping the child, with my mother's commitment to fighting apartheid. But don't, even though both of us were driven by uncontrollable inner-forces, hers was nobly executed. She died for her Cause, I will most decidedly be living for mine. I feel wretchedness and elation. I am quite sure I will not be traced, and that I will be able to raise this precious child according to what his late mother would have wished. Perhaps once I've accomplished my mission, I will be ready to return and to hand myself over to The Law, who knows? What hurts me already, is picturing you and Tubs night after night sobbing silently in pain and mystification, refusing to believe what I've done. I will be weeping, too.

314

But I will be untraceable. Thanks to the wonders of modern technology, though, I will be able to communicate with you without fear of detection. And so, all I want to do in this short note is to say farewell and that I'll be in touch. Who knows what the future holds? If we believe hard enough, we can shape it according to our wishes. I am wishing that soon-soon we will all be reunited as one big happy family. With all my love. I am so going to miss you! Wish me well, thank you. My father, my dad.

Vic, you won, but lost; I lost but won. I'm not proud of myself. I did what I had to do. No court on earth should have had to adjudicate on this matter. I will be vilified, maybe by you more than by anybody else. I will understand. Will you understand? Your claim is based on blood, mine on love. Who's to say who's right and who's wrong? I thought I did the right thing by phoning you to notify you of your estranged sister, Nikki's death—but was it the right thing to have done? I have often thought that had I left you in blissful ignorance there in Perth, things might not have ultimately come down to win-lose, lose-win. But, I must look forward, not backward. As Nikki's chosen next-of-kin, I have a task to fulfil, and it's going to demand my total attention. Vilify me all you must, but at the same time, wish me well, if only for the little one's sake.

www.ingramcontent.com/pod-product-compliance
Lightning Source LLC
Chambersburg PA
CBHW071106250626
47159CB00002B/624